Lap Baby

Lap Baby

AMY Q. BARKER

Lap Baby

Copyright © 2022 by Amy Q. Barker
Unionville, Indiana
All rights reserved.

No portion of this book may be reproduced, stored in a retrieval system, or transmitted in any form by any means—electronic, mechanical, photocopy, recording, scanning, or other—except for brief quotations in critical reviews or articles, without the prior written permission of the author.

This novel is a work of fiction. Names, characters, places, and incidents are either products of the author's imagination or used fictitiously. All characters are fictional, and any similarity to people living or dead is purely coincidental.

Editing and layout by Kira Freed
Cover design by Charlie Alolkoy

www.amyqbarker.com

ISBN: 978-1-7353581-4-7
Library of Congress Control Number: 2022916059

Printed in the United States of America

Also by Amy Q. Barker

Rue

Punk

Bibliointuitive

Maplewood

For Jan

I've never met you

but I really heard *you*

❧ Prologue ❧

ONCE YOU HEAR MY STORY, you'll never fly on a plane again without thinking about me. You might even try to catch a quick glance. At first you'll think, how cute, how cuddly, how soft and warm, cooing in my mother's arms, and then in the next instant, you'll remember, and you'll think, *oh my heavens.*

I must say up front, I'm sorry. Now you'll have to change your routine. Sure, I know how it is—normally you amble down the aisle, keeping your bag and purse out of the way of the armrests and pointy, intrusive elbows. Then you figure out the numbering system—is 12D the window, aisle, or middle seat? Then you hope the overhead bin isn't full so you can keep your bag and coat right above your seat. It'll be so much easier to reach when it's time to deplane. The quicker you're off the plane, the more likely you'll be first in line at the car rental agency, and you know how long that process takes. One person ahead of you adds twenty minutes to your timeline. And that's twenty minutes taken away from your get-together with friends, or your hug from Grandma, or your makeup sex with your husband, or the baseball game at the new stadium with your dad, or the free-food-and-booze reception the night before your work conference.

Anyway, so you're thinking about a lot of things while you're walking down the aisle of the plane. And, of course, you're also thinking, who will I be seated next to? A talker, a drinker, a smelly guy, a person who takes up more than their fair share of the space, a messy eater, a loud laptop listener, or—worst-case scenario—an ugly, arrogant guy with bad breath trying to pick you up. I get it. I know all the worries, all the concerns. And that's just if you're on the plane by yourself. Add a spouse, friend, parent, or child, and your worries multiply exponentially: did I remember to pack everything, did we leave anything at home or in the terminal, how will I keep everyone occupied, did I pack enough snacks, what if we have to go to the bathroom in the middle of the flight?

My point is this: when you board a plane, usually you have a lot on your mind, least of all me.

But from this point forward (I'm really sorry), you're going to think of me. And look for me. And wonder about me. And come up with a plan in your mind for me. I'm not talking about the repetitious demonstrations that we're all subjected to by the flight attendant where they hold up the oxygen mask and the inflatable life jacket.

Although, come to think of it, those may come in handy—you never know. You should probably pay attention and listen.

I'm talking about a real plan. Where, in your brave mind's eye, you come for me.

You try to save me.

And maybe you do.

And maybe you don't.

But no matter what, you think of me.

Chapter I

JULIE GEIGER WOKE UP TO THE SAME RECURRING NIGHTMARE, her body tangled in the sheets, sweat covering her forehead. The nightmare that had become like a familiar heavy stone wrapped around her neck these past twenty years. She was used to the feeling of fire and heat, the panic, the reaching for calm amid the chaos, the this-is-what-you-trained-for-so-get-it-together self-talk, the burden of instruction, the need for steady nerves despite the gaping wound and smell of toxic smoke, plastic, metal, and burning flesh. But she wasn't used to this new feeling of anger and injustice. She'd always turned that inward, made herself sick with it, drank it down with a glass of wine, shot of whiskey, or tumbler of gin. This new feeling was outward-facing, a throwing off of the pain, like the first pitch of a baseball game: release it, watch it fly, see if it connects—then you'll know what it means, then you'll know whether it's a strike or a ball or a foul or a home run. Right now, though, it simply felt like a sucker punch to the gut, and she was fighting mad, wanting to lash out and give a slug in return, a left hook to the side of the head of unfairness, nonsensical inertia, ineptitude, lack of progress, the unthinking bureaucrats in their ivory towers, and the way things were and would always be.

She sat up in bed, wiped her sweaty brow with the back of her hand, and checked her phone: three twelve. What day was it? Her foggy brain registered: Tuesday. She was due at the airport at four thirty, so she may as well get up. Her compact suitcase was neatly packed on the upholstered bench at the end of her bed. She quickly showered and did her hair and makeup. It was June and expected to be a scorcher, so definitely a chignon kind of day—she wasn't in the mood to mess with the straightener or curling iron, and she wanted more than anything to feel cool and composed. Over the years, she had perfected the intricate yet refined strategically placed bun at the nape of the neck for the best airflow, containment, and attraction. When she finished, she used her handheld mirror to ensure that every errant strand was neatly tucked, every bobby pin proficiently hidden. After packing her remaining toiletry items, she zipped her wheeled bag, sipping on a travel mug of hot coffee as she glided out the door of her contemporary chic lakefront-view apartment on her way to the airport.

Half an hour later, she was in the crew lounge at her home base, Chicago O'Hare, eating a banana and talking to Cheryl, who was about to head to her gate for a flight to Miami. Julie asked, "When are you back?"

Cheryl grinned and said, "Not for five days. I'm meeting Tony. We're headed to the Bahamas. Nassau. Nice little getaway."

"Oh my," Julie said with a whimsical smile, then sighed. "I'm so jealous. I haven't done anything fun in ages."

"Well, you should. You work too hard."

Julie shrugged, not denying it. "Saving up. Not sure for what. Well, drink a piña colada for me. Or five."

"I will, believe me. I'll text you when I'm back. We can do dinner, okay?"

"Sure, sounds good," Julie said with a cheery wave.

Julie rolled her bag into the bathroom, taking out her toothpaste, toothbrush, and lipstick. As she brushed, she thought about Cheryl. She was at least ten years younger than Julie and somehow never seemed beaten down by the job or by life in general. Always sweet and happy and outgoing. They had met for dinner several times in Chicago and once in Denver when they were stranded during a blizzard. That was when she told Julie about her on-again, off-again relationship with Tony, a handsome pharmaceutical sales rep from Miami. She said she wasn't ready to settle down and that Tony was the perfect fling, always available at a moment's notice. Julie was a little envious. She'd been divorced for years, and even though she dated on occasion, she hadn't had anyone steady or meaningful for so long that she couldn't remember what it felt like. She was independent to a fault. The fault being that her independence often led to loneliness. Maybe that's why she worked so much. Keeping busy always seemed like the solution. But now that she was older, she wondered if work and busyness were truly enough to stave off those needling pangs, those nights alone, those quiet meals by herself.

Julie finished applying her lipstick and making sure her uniform was neat before heading to her gate, thinking, sure, spontaneity and excitement weren't her strong suits, but what she lacked in social skills, she made up for in strict organization, precision, punctuality, attention to detail, consistency, and ability to ensure that things went according to plan. This was her forte, and she was proud of her ability to assess and handle any complicated situation and parse it into manageable chunks that could be analyzed, simplified, and conquered.

It was why she became a flight attendant. Julie grew up in the Chicago suburb of Evanston, and while her sisters preferred to play sports outside, Julie stayed inside and sorted her Barbies' clothes by color and style, displaying each in the proper Barbie dream home, bus, or (of course) airplane. Later, in high school, she applied these same organizing skills to her schoolwork, excelling in every class and eventually becoming valedictorian and the lead actress in the senior play. The teachers loved her, and the students were either in awe of her, envied her, or wanted to be her, or at least be best friends with her. She went on to earn a bachelor's degree in hotel management, working after graduation as an assistant manager for a small Chicago hotel for two years until she had enough experience to apply for (and get) her dream job as a flight attendant for United Airlines.

Sure, she had her wild, partying days back in her twenties—she'd even been married to a bartender for a while—but so much had happened since then—in her life, in her career. She still maintained a tight control on everything, everyone, and every situation in her world because that was what made her feel calm, complete, and whole. Control. Perfection. Neat and tidy, meticulous. Ordered readiness. But sometimes, when she allowed herself to daydream, she wondered what it would be like to be more like Cheryl—carefree, go-with-the-flow, loosey-goosey, up for anything. However, these qualities were like strange aberrations for Julie; she could neither understand them nor assimilate them, no matter how hard she tried. Like these qualities, she had long since given up on her dream of becoming an international flight attendant. Being fluent in two or more languages was a prerequisite, but to her infinite frustration and exasperation, she struggled to deliver linguistic flow into comprehensible sentences. The individual words were there, hovering in her mind like perfect pop-up pieces of fruit, allowing her to pass the vocabulary quizzes with flying colors, but when it came to casual conversation—the give-and-take required to mimic a native speaker—she simply could not get the hang of it and eventually gave up, crying herself to sleep at night for weeks after failing the in-person fluency test.

Oh well, she said to herself, swiping her badge at the gate with a smile and a good morning to the gate attendant and then to the pilot and copilot, she was going to focus on what she could do. Coincidentally, that was a lot, including being the best *U.S.* flight attendant she could be. With this in mind, she began readying the cabin, working alongside two other flight attendants, Carol from Dallas and James from Detroit. This was the part of the job she loved the most, before the throngs of talkative, unpredictable, often demanding passengers arrived. She made sure everything was in place, complete, and ready—the coffee brewing and stowed in its proper cubby, along with the snacks, drinks, ice, napkins, blankets, pillows, magazines, and brochures. Then she strolled down the aisle, fixing the seat belts, windows, overhead bins, seatback pockets, under-seat areas, headrests, armrests, and tray tables. A minute later, she put on her gloves and, using the antibacterial wipes, gave the cabin a swift once-over. Everything in order, she stood at the front and waited to greet the passengers. As Carol was on microphone and safety demonstration duty, and James was stationed in the back, Julie was the welcome brigade as well as the main contact with the cockpit.

A while later, the plane was in the air, passengers properly snug in their seats, the paperwork signed off, the announcements made, and her hands lying casually in her lap as she awaited the signal that they were above the proper altitude to trigger the move-about-the-cabin ding and begin the beverage service. This was always the point in the flight when she took a moment to stop and think. She was strapped in beside Carol, their jump seats facing the cabin. Carol was quietly looking at her nails as Julie scanned the passengers, seeing an elderly couple talking softly to each other, three teenagers in hoodies all dozing, their heads bobbing into their pillows upon their parents' shoulders, and behind them, a young couple, the wife nursing a baby in her lap with a cloth draped over her chest, the husband holding a toy in his hand and looking out the window sleepily.

That was when Julie remembered the dream. The nightmare. She knew why, today of all days. It always made her shudder, the thought of it causing heat to rise up her neck and constrict her throat. It was because she was meeting Paige tonight for dinner. It had been over a year since she last saw her. Julie had been out West, sometimes for a few hours on a layover, sometimes for a night or two, but she had avoided contacting her. Paige knew why. It was because nothing had changed. It had been twenty years of struggle and strife, talking with the powers that be—the FAA, the NTSB, the airlines, the senators, the unions, the safety counsels, the commercial and financial leaders, the mothers' groups, the pediatrician associations—providing ideas, suggestions, collaborations, joint ventures, new inventions. Anything could potentially be a spark leading to a new solution, no matter how innocuous or small. But it was all for naught. Nothing. Nada. Zilch. Zip. Zero.

And she knew why. It all boiled down to money. Didn't it always? No one was going to chip in a cent to make the necessary changes. And no one was going to say yes to losing money that was already in their pockets. Don't be ridiculous! Silly, naive, quixotic Julie. Why would she ever think that an industry would put human lives before the almighty dollar? So it would stay stuck. Indefinitely. Oh sure, they had their rationale, saying that coming up with one solution caused unintended ramifications that were just as bad. Julie understood that—knew about all the ethical gray space—but still, they couldn't come up with a compromise? That's why Julie was fighting mad and, ironically, why she knew it was finally time to give up, throw in the towel, call it a day. And why she woke up to the nightmare that morning; it wasn't just a sleeping dream—it was waking reality. Her hands were tied behind her back, like handcuffs clenched tight around her wrists, and no amount of good intentions could free them, no matter how hard she tried, no matter how much she wanted an answer, no matter how much she worked for it, willed it, gave of herself for the cause.

The weight of giving up was overwhelming and dreadful, but it was also inevitable. She had come to the end of the line, the last straw. Still, she wondered how she would look Paige in the eye, or Marie for that matter (not that Marie had every truly looked at Julie, let alone really saw her), or Terry (if and when Julie ever got a hold of him), when nothing, absolutely nothing, had changed in *twenty* years.

Chapter II

Paige Montgomery woke up with a pit in her stomach. She would be seeing Julie that night. These visits always prompted such mixed feelings. From a logical standpoint, Paige knew the purpose of the rendezvous was to appease Julie's guilt and emotional fragility. And for Julie to give Paige an update on the progress, if any, of her endeavors to fix the issue. But the thing was, Paige never asked for (nor really wanted) an update. In truth, she would rather just forget the whole thing. She had been a baby, after all. Only twenty months old. Not a shred of awareness—not a flicker of a memory or a flash of knowledge or a spark of fright—about the whole incident. So why did Julie keep in touch with her? Why did she feel the need to meet? Twenty years of regular visits. Paige noted that this latest request had been over a year in coming, and Paige had foolishly thought (and wished) they were over. But then she got the text yesterday, written in the same old way, causing the same old feelings of dread, pity, guilt, and helplessness. "Hi Paige. I'll be in town tomorrow. Are you available? Same place. Is 7:00 p.m. okay?"

Oh well, she had thought, so much for my wish. Paige had sighed and texted back, "Of course. That works. See you then."

She had spent the rest of the day trying to stay busy and not think about the dinner. But here she was waking up in her warm bed, listening to the meadowlark outside her bedroom window trilling his cheery song without a care in the world, thinking to herself, do I have to go? She had never cancelled with Julie before, and she knew she shouldn't, but she really, really wanted to. She got up, showered, and threw on some clothes before heading down the stairs. Her pa was at the kitchen table, eating bacon, eggs, and toast, and drinking coffee.

"Morning, Pa."

"Morning," he replied. "I left plenty of bacon for you on the stove."

"Thanks." She put a piece in her mouth, crunching down on the salty goodness while putting two slices of bread in the toaster and pouring herself a cup of coffee. As she faced him and leaned her back against the sink, she thought about the fact that Pa was getting up in years. She worried about him sometimes. He had a roll around his belly that didn't used to be there. He was an active guy, but still…Ma cooked up meals fit for ten people when they were only a small family of three. Ma did it out of love, but Paige worried if she was slowly loving Pa into an early grave with her butter-laden casseroles and thick Crisco-crusted chicken pot pies. Everything was delicious and kept them warm and cozy during the long, cold Montana winters, but Paige would need to remind Ma to try harder to incorporate more vegetables into their repertoire. In the meantime, she suggested, "Maybe we can go for a ride on Sunday. You off?"

"Uh-huh. Sure, let's do that. I haven't been out to the ranch to see Randy in a while." Pa's best buddy owned a cattle ranch down the road, and he would take Pa and Paige out on horseback for leisurely Sunday rides on occasion.

"Great," Paige agreed. Then she asked, "What's your schedule today?"

"Well, I'm at the bar from noon until ten, and your ma's at the front desk until five. What about you?"

"I switched shifts with Kim, so I'm only doing lunch."

He frowned. Paige almost never took time off or switched shifts. In fact, she was usually the one doing double shifts or taking shifts from other waitresses who wanted a day off. He asked, "Why? What do you have going on? Hot date?" he winked, and she winced. Pa was trying to be funny, so Paige shifted to a quick smile, but it was hard to joke about a dating life that was nonexistent.

"No Pa, no hot date. Actually," she turned away so he wouldn't see her face as she slowly spread butter and jelly on her toast. "Julie wrote me. I'm meeting her in Bozeman at seven."

"Oh," he said, suddenly sober. "I—I thought that was over now."

Paige turned around. "So did I." She sat down beside him and sighed. "I guess not. I mean, it's okay, it's fine—I just wish she would let it go, honestly. It's been twenty years, and she's put up a valiant fight. No one could have spent more time or energy on the reforms, but some things just aren't meant to be. Not to mention, my feelings are different—from hers, from everybody's. Julie's driven to keep pursuing this because she remembers every single moment from that day, and well, mostly, I think, because of that *woman* Marie."

Pa stared at Paige's near curse of the word *woman* with a raised eyebrow. He nodded with pursed lips and finally asked with a resigned air, "She's still in the picture, eh?"

Paige cringed. "I hope not. But who knows? I guess I'll find out tonight. She needs to get off her high horse, if you ask me, but she preys on Julie, as if it's all her fault. It's not fair and I hate it. It's partly why I continue to meet Julie. I want her to know that I don't see it that way. In fact, I'm…I'm really thankful."

Pa's eyes softened. "Exactly. I know *I* thank her."

Paige mirrored his expression and said, "Awww, Pa."

He raked her nose lightly with his knuckle and added, "What about Terry? Anything new from him?"

Paige shook her head. "Nope. You know him—he never wanted to keep in touch with any of us, said he just wanted to get on with his life, get back to his family and forget it ever happened. Maybe he has the right idea. I guess it's more than I can say for Julie or Marie."

Pa nodded silently. After a minute, he got up from his seat, rinsed his dishes, put them in the dishwasher, and said, "I'll be out in the barn for a bit. Do you need a ride to work?"

"Nope, thanks. I'm biking."

"Okay, be careful." He came over to her, kissed the top of her head, and said, "It's really kind—what you're doing—meeting her. I'm proud of you, sweetheart."

She smiled up at him before he headed out the door toward the barn.

Then she went up to her room and packed her uniform, makeup, brush, towel, and purse in her backpack. She got her bike out of the garage and started the five-mile trek to Chico Hot Springs Resort. It was a beautiful June day—not too hot, not too cold—the sun beaming down on her half-tan, half-white skin. She loved these summer days in Emigrant, the tiny Montana town where she grew up. It was just a speck on the map, nestled in the middle of the aptly named Paradise Valley along the Yellowstone River, the Absaroka Mountains shining like rocky beacons in the distance. She rode past the Emigrant post office, the Old Saloon, the general store, Emigrant Outpost, farm fields, and cattle ranches into the town of Pray, where the resort's green-and-white wooden buildings were situated at the end of a country lane. The establishment was out of the way but still had a thriving business and was considered a destination venue for tourists, weddings, couples, spa parties, hiking events, fishing groups, and small-business conferences. Over a hundred years old and on the National Register of Historic Places, its versatility, old-world charm, and hospitality kept the place going, along with dedicated locals like her ma and pa, who had both worked there for over thirty years. Paige started as a maid in the hotel when she was in junior high school, then did a short stint in the gift shop, and ended up a waitress in the historic main dining room.

The base pay wasn't huge, but the tips were good, especially during the summer months. She'd been saving her money to buy a fixer-upper ranch house on the outskirts of town with her best friends, Kyle and Abby. The three of them almost had enough for a down payment, but they wanted to wait a year until they had saved enough for renovations. The house had been on the market a year already, but it was "for sale by owner" and hadn't drawn much attention (probably because it needed so much work and was off the beaten path). They kept their fingers crossed that it would stay available until they could afford it. Because Emigrant was a rural area, the few nice, finished houses that came up for sale usually sold for millions of dollars. The cost of a plot of land was even higher, mostly going to wealthy ranchers or corporate executives wanting a rural getaway. A lot of their friends had gone off to college or moved away after high school, looking for opportunity and affordable housing elsewhere. Outside of ranching and the tourism trade, jobs were scarce and the living arrangements even slimmer.

But Paige, Kyle, and Abby had forged a plan together during their junior year—they would bypass college. Who needed a degree out here in the middle of nowhere anyway? They'd stay local, find jobs in Emigrant, Gardiner, Bozeman, or Yellowstone, and save their money to buy a place together. Then they could get out of their respective parents' houses. They envisioned late-night parties with friends, early morning coffees on the deck overlooking the mountains, picnics among the prairie grasses, and early spring bonfires on the banks of the river. Eventually they could tack on an addition to the house or build a cabin on the property—something that could serve as a rental for tourists during the busy season—get some extra cash on the side to help with the mortgage and upkeep.

They had plans.

Speaking of plans, Paige took her phone out of her pocket, dialed Abby on speaker phone, and clicked the phone into the stem attachment on her bike to talk hands-free.

Abby picked up on the first ring, "Hola."

"Hey. Listen, are we still on for Friday night?"

"Yep, Kyle's driving."

"Cool. Who else is going?"

"Just the three of us, but Kyle's cousin'll be there."

"Oh, who's he? Do I know him?"

"Naw, but you might *get* to know him…," she said meaningfully.

"Ugh. Abby. Would you please stop trying to set me up?" Paige hoped Abby could sense her rolling her eyes over the phone. Why was it that when a couple was happy and settled, they constantly felt the need to set up their single friends? None of Abby's endeavors had actually succeeded, and they had led to several uncomfortable (excruciating, in fact) double dates for Paige.

"They're for your own good."

"Whatever," dismissed Paige. "So, what time?"

"Pick you up at five."

"K—later."

"Later."

Kyle and Abby had been dating since high school. They both worked at Sage Lodge, where, they reminded Paige (too often), she could be making "a ton" more money. Compared to Chico, Sage was a much fancier, much richer, much newer hotel and spa down the road. But Paige had been coming to Chico Springs with her parents since she was a baby. It was familiar and homey and felt like a better, slower, more natural fit for her. And because Paige's parents both worked at Chico, they felt more comfortable being able to keep an eye on her. What Paige didn't tell Kyle and Abby was that she didn't want to subject herself to the scrutiny that a job at Sage would certainly elicit. She knew her face always caused an initial double take. She dreaded the thought that the Bozeman elite, rich California fishermen, and other wealthy tourists would judge her, cringe at the sight of her, wonder if she was contagious, diseased, or sickly. At Chico, the clientele was more relaxed and didn't seem to notice or care about her unusual markings. The tourists were mostly there to lie in the hot springs and drink sugary cocktails or cheap beer until their cheeks were red and their bathing suits puckered from steeping in the spring water. Mercifully, they rarely spent more than a flicker of a second noticing her.

When Paige arrived, she stowed her bike in the shed behind the kitchen and went through the back door, saying hi to the chef and a few waitresses prepping for the lunch shift. She changed into her uniform, brushed her hair, and went up front to talk to her ma. She was waiting on a customer, so Paige hung back for a minute until she was done. Her ma was a petite, soft-spoken brunette with brown eyes and the beginnings of gray strands streaking through her hair. Her face was lined with wrinkles, not from the sun but from the perma-smile she wore. She was the epitome of a perfect employee—punctual, quiet, happy, calm, accommodating—she would listen before she talked, and she truly believed in that old adage "The customer is always right." She was one of the main reasons Chico had done so well all these years. Coincidentally, it was also what made her a great mother.

Today Ma was working reception at the hotel front desk, but sometimes she was the special events coordinator or the restaurant manager or the spa service organizer or head of the cleaning staff or the ice-cream shop attendant or whatever job had the greatest need on any given day. She truly was a jack-of-all-trades and was well respected by the owner and staff. She wasn't just Paige's ma—she was also a surrogate mom to all of them. It wasn't unusual for Paige to come to work and find her ma deep in conversation with a waitress, hostess, or maid who was unburdening herself about a breakup, money troubles, or family issues. Ma had one of those faces and personalities that drew people in.

As much as Paige's pa was loved at Chico, he was more reserved and stuck mostly to the bartending, choosing to handle the rambunctious, raucous pool and bar crowd with his strong, stoic, oxlike presence. Paige knew he was just a softy underneath—your typical teddy bear. But on the surface he sometimes kept people in line simply by pointing his ice-blue eyes at any wayward offender. At home, though, he couldn't have been any kinder or sweeter, always thoughtful and considerate, loving on Ma and Paige in his quiet way. He was their consummate protector. When he wasn't working, he spent his time relaxing in his recliner in front of the TV or tinkering in the barn out back.

When Ma was done with the customer, she called Paige over and said, "Hey sweetie, how's it going?"

"Good. Busy today?"

"Um, let me see—not too bad. The reservations are about three-quarters full, but that doesn't mean the pool won't be packed. You working all night?"

"Just lunch. Headed to Bozeman to meet Julie tonight."

Her ma's eyebrows raised, but she only said, "Oh, I see."

Paige shrugged and said "yeah" and left it at that. Then she changed the subject. "Hey, the rodeo's in town this weekend, and Abby wondered if I wanted to go on Friday night."

Her ma ran her fingers through Paige's long, dark hair and smiled, "You girls are so grown up now…sometimes I forget," she laughed a little and added, "until you start talking about going to the rodeo! But I wonder… there are a lot of out-of-towners and roughriders at those shows."

Paige rolled her eyes with a reassuring tilt of her head, "Ma, please—we can take care of ourselves. Plus, Kyle's going, and his cousin too."

She nodded and sighed. "But hey, aren't you working?"

"Nope, not 'til Saturday."

"Okay, well, it sounds like you have it all worked out." A couple walked in the door and came up to the front desk, giving Paige a blatant stare before catching themselves and turning their attention to Ma. Paige slipped away with a frown right as Ma called after her, "Don't be out too late. Tonight or Friday."

Paige said okay over her shoulder. Loosening her clenched jaw with a sigh, she got busy setting up the tables in the dining room.

As she folded silverware into napkins and arranged glasses and plates, she thought that no matter what strangers thought of her, she really couldn't be any luckier. Of all the couples who could have adopted her, somehow she ended up with the nicest, most generous people anyone could have asked for, and she never took that for granted. In return, they were grateful to have a child at all, having tried to get pregnant for years before finally deciding to adopt in their early forties. The fact that Paige had come to them as a fully formed toddler and not a newborn—a walking, talking twenty-month-old—and from Filipino biological parents—had never bothered them. In fact, they seemed to cherish and protect her all the more because of her background.

The way she came to them was sudden and unexpected. Almost a year after they had completed the paperwork, adoption interviews, and home visits, they still had no child. Multiple prior attempts had failed to "match." And then boom, there she was, being led through their door by a social worker holding her hand. She was wearing a shy smile and a yellow dress. Sue and Roger Montgomery cooed to her as their hearts instantly melted. Her first word to them was *gog* as she pointed at their black Lab, Fergus, who walked up and licked her cheek, prompting the most infectious giggle to escape her lips, much to the delight of her rapt audience. Her name was Diwa Abalos, but the Montgomerys decided to rechristen her Paige Bethany Montgomery. They noticed the tiny, nearly healed cut above her left eyebrow, but the social worker had shaken her head ever so slightly to indicate it was not to be discussed. Then Ma and Pa had knelt down in front of the beautiful little girl, eye to eye, and said, "Hello there, Paige. Welcome to your new home."

Years later, when the spots started to appear on Paige's hands, legs, and face, her parents had taken her to the doctor. They all learned a new word: *vitiligo*. Apparently Paige had an autoimmune condition that caused her skin to lose its pigmentation, leaving white patches like lotus flowers against her naturally tan skin. The patches didn't hurt (for which Paige was grateful) and didn't come all at once; they slowly appeared here and there over time (which made her slightly trepidatious, never sure where the next one would pop up). The disease had no cure, no treatment, and no amount of makeup made it fully disappear (Lord knows she'd tried). It was something she would have to live with for the rest of her life and was the reason working at Sage seemed like an impossibility. Vitiligo was, for the most part, not considered hereditary, so it wasn't related to her biology or adoption. It still broke her parents' hearts when Paige was old enough to understand that something about her was different (based on the stares, grimaces, avoidance, and in some cases, rude comments). As a young child, Paige asked her parents more times than they could count, "What's wrong with me?" They always said, "Nothing. Every human on God's great earth is unique and special in their own way. Anyone who doesn't see you for everything wonderful you are, inside and out, isn't worth a stitch of your time or consideration anyway."

The hostess started to seat several of her tables, so Paige snapped out of her reverie, turning on a smile as she had one last fleeting thought: the skin may be the body's largest organ, but it doesn't define me.

That privilege goes to two other remarkable, powerful, and sensitive organs: my brain and my heart.

CHAPTER III

MARIE STANLEY WAS JUST ABOUT TO START COOKING DINNER when Ryan came through the door in a rush, breathing hard and a muddy mess, which made Marie flinch. She had just vacuumed and shampooed the carpet two days ago.

"Don't you dare set foot in this house without taking off those muddy boots, Ryan David Stanley."

He rolled his eyes at her pronouncement of his full name. "Mom, I'm late. I was supposed to be at Rick's half an hour ago."

Raising up every inch of her petite five-foot-one frame, she blocked his entrance. "I don't care if you were supposed to be at the White House. Off."

He reluctantly peeled off one boot, then the other, hopping as he did so while she hovered over his bent form, ensuring that the boots landed on the welcome mat and not the carpet.

Then she stopped him again with her hand on his shoulder. "The jeans too. And the hat. And the T-shirt."

"Jeesh, Mom!" Ryan shook his head, his teeth clenched, but quickly complied, knowing there was no defying his mom when she was like this. Down to his skivvies, he ran up the stairs as fast as he could, did a quick change, and came back down three minutes later, grabbing his backpack from the floor, running out the door, screaming behind him, "See ya." Marie chuckled. Boys. So much easier than girls. You kept them fed, let them burn off energy, and insisted they wash up once in a while, and they were pretty much as happy as clams and as docile as basset hounds.

Marie didn't even bother to respond, knowing he was gone. She picked up his muddy clothes and tossed them in the washer, then took his riding boots outside and rinsed them off with the garden hose, leaving them to dry beside three other sets of boots in various sizes, laid out in a neat row on a rubber mat next to the side door. Wiping her forehead, she glanced up at the summer ball of sun in the sky, then proceeded to make her way back to the horse barn, where she found Darby brushing down Ryan's horse, Alex.

Marie said, "Now why are you doing that? You know that's his job, not yours."

Darby shrugged with a shy smile. Marie knew she loved horses more than humans, but it didn't mean she should allow her brother to shirk his responsibilities. Darby had always been such a pushover when it came to Ryan. And could Marie blame her? He was handsomer than any seventeen-year-old had a right to be, smart as a whip, athletic, popular, the envy of his friends, who all looked up to him, and his little sister Darby's ultimate superhero. What she lacked in looks and an outgoing personality, he made up for in spades. She worshiped the ground he walked on. Then again, what Ryan lacked in tact and in the art of understanding others' moods and emotions, Darby could pick up on from a mile away. She often used these skills to soothe, tame, divert, and crack the hardest nut, whether equine or human. They both were extraordinary in their own right.

Sometimes, though, Marie wondered sadly if Darby's small group of friends were using her to catch a glimpse (or more) of Ryan, especially during those joint sleepovers where Darby would suggest they go for a ride or watch a movie and her friends would insist they stay inside "to play games with the boys." One girl in particular, Marie remembered at the last party, wanted to "see what the boys were doing in the basement." Marie left the lot of them down there alone for thirty minutes (actually setting the timer on her phone) before sending Bridget down to break up a game of spin the bottle. Bridget—her studious, straitlaced, rule-follower middle child—could be counted on for any assignment, big or small, or in this case, essential. Bridget came back upstairs ten minutes later with a nod to her mother, followed closely by Darby and her friends, all pouting and saying, "This party is lame." Marie sent them outside with instructions to build a fire and the fixings for s'mores. They were miraculously happy again.

On this day, out in the barn, Marie refilled Alex's water and food buckets as Darby kept brushing. Marie asked, "Any requests for dinner?" When Darby didn't respond, Marie went on, "It's been so hot all day, I'm thinking hot dogs and hamburgers on the grill with a side of watermelon. How's that sound?"

"Fine, Mom," Darby answered without emotion.

Marie thought, she's so introverted, I wonder what's really going on in that head of hers. There had always been a bit of an unspoken distance between her and her youngest; she wasn't sure why. They never had those deep conversations that Marie had imagined mothers and daughters were supposed to have. Now that Marie was in her forties and her youngest child was already fifteen, she wondered at times if she would ever have a close relationship with any of her kids. They all seemed to be drifting away from her. Ryan was about to start his senior year and was always out with friends or playing sports, barely gracing them with his presence anymore, let alone spending time chatting with his dear ole Mom. Bridget, nearly a junior, always had her nose in a book and, on the off chance that she was in the mood to talk, wanted to discuss books or her classes or something she had learned watching the latest documentary on PBS. She certainly wasn't the cuddly little puss she had been as a toddler, when she would insist Marie lie in bed with her until she fell asleep, afraid of the boogeyman. And then there was Darby, the sophomore fifteen-year-old going on thirty-five, obsessed with horses, spending nearly every weekend with Kent, driving to various venues for show jumping and dressage, with the occasional eventing activity. Marie used to go with them and made Ryan and Bridget go too. Unfortunately, the other kids began to resent Darby and all the time spent on the road. They preferred to stay home and do their own activities. So Marie became the chauffeur and sports mom to the two older kids while Kent stayed on the road with Darby.

And now, as Marie headed back to the house to get the grill started, she wondered if she was losing them all—*and* her husband. She couldn't remember the last time she and Kent had been out to dinner together, or anywhere else together, just the two of them. They barely slept together anymore, and she didn't mean sex. Although they also hadn't done that in, well, she couldn't remember how long. He fell asleep on the couch while she read a book and slept alone in their king-sized canopy bed.

Marie started mushing the ground beef into patties and seasoning them, thinking, how did everything start to slip away? She couldn't put her finger on the exact moment or even narrow it down to a general time frame. She had been such a fierce protector of her family, organizing their lives into daily segments of activities from the very beginning, making sure the kids were enrolled in the best private day cares, preschools, and private elementary, middle, and high schools. She brought in tutors to assist with their studies, cooks to feed them, nannies to watch them, maids to clean up after them, personal assistants to mark and annotate calendars around their schedules, professionals to teach them tennis, golf, horseback riding, rowing, sailing, and skiing. And that was just the stuff she had farmed out. She did much of the day-to-day work around the house and barn herself, and after that she spent an inordinate amount of time instructing the people she hired in how to do their jobs as competently as she would herself (or, as was often the case, until they were fired and replaced with someone who could).

As far as Connecticut housewives were concerned, she not only excelled, but in comparison to everyone else she knew, she was the *best*. She had always treated the job of "mother" as exactly that—a job that must be managed, organized, controlled, and above all else, perfected. She was the envy of her neighbors and acquaintances at the country club, which just meant that she didn't have any actual friends. Most of the time, that didn't bother her. She was too busy anyway. But sometimes, like on this hot summer day, she almost wished for a bosom buddy, a girlfriend she could call at a moment's notice to share a bottle of wine and an unbridled unburdening of her heart.

So instead, like she always did, Marie bucked up, bottled up, and carried on, putting the burgers and hot dogs on the grill, cutting the watermelon, tossing the salad, setting the table out on the patio with a fresh checkered red-and-white linen cloth, a vase of wildflowers, her favorite rose-petal china plates, and crystal water goblets filled with fresh lemonade. When everything was done and pretty as pie, she called Bridget down from her room and Darby in from the barn, and texted Kent in his studio.

Kent was one of Hartford's most renowned architects and had designed several of its modern downtown buildings. He was so well respected and established at this point in his career that he rarely went into his office anymore, preferring to work from a studio he built ten years ago in the back acreage of their property, overlooking a windy, scenic, babbling brook. His best friend and partner, Dominick Granger, who had been his roommate in college, ran the office now and only called Kent in for the occasional board meeting or "big" client.

Of course, Marie loved the convenience of having Kent so close—just a short walk or quick phone call or text away—especially for the sake of the kids, who loved to peek in on him throughout the day, but there were also times when she felt as though he was stepping on her domain. Wouldn't it have been easier on their marriage if she controlled one hundred percent of the domestic responsibilities and he stuck to the business? Why did he feel the need to stay so close? Wasn't it enough that he stole Darby away from her every weekend?

When they were all seated at the table, Darby and Bridget digging in like a couple of hyenas, Marie mostly thought about that thing she didn't like to think about. Had Kent decided to stay home because he didn't trust Marie with the kids? Was he still worried about her? About her ability to keep them safe, turn them into perfect, responsible adults? Didn't he realize that it was the most important thing to Marie? More important than anything else, more important than herself?

Before they were even married, she had told him that she wanted more than anything to be a stay-at-home mom, and he had agreed. He would be the breadwinner. She would be the mistress of everything to do with the kids and the house. In the beginning, it had been exactly like that. He was building his practice in a newly constructed open-concept downtown office building that he had designed, hiring and training a new workforce while Dominick recruited new clientele. They were living in an apartment, but Marie spent her newlywed days looking for the perfect house for their future life, finally settling on a twenty-acre horse farm. Then she spent the next year renovating the entire inside of the five-thousand-square-foot farmhouse, along with the barn, corrals, and paddocks. Finally, with everything in order, she became pregnant. Kent designed the perfect nursery, complete with handcrafted crib, rocking chair, pull-out changing table, sofa bed for late-night feedings, and a wall-to-wall mural that looked like the inside of an old-fashioned train station.

Everything had been so perfect back then—so neat and tidy and *right*. Where had that feeling gone?

Snapping back to their patio table in the backyard, Marie's face must have revealed something odd because Darby said (exasperated, as if repeating it for the third time), "Mom! Earth to Mom. Hey, can you pass the watermelon? By the way, what's for dessert?"

Focusing on Darby's face as she handed her the bowl, Marie tried not to catch Kent's eye to see the acknowledgment there—that her secret thoughts were known to him. Marie forced a fake smile and said, "Your favorite, sweetie: Boston cream pie."

Marie stood, noticing that everyone's plate but her own was nearly empty. She began stacking and lifting the dishes, promising to be back in a minute.

Just as she pulled the screen door open and propped it with her elbow, she glanced up.

Kent's eyes were watching her, filled with a wistful perplexity and an ancient sadness.

The combination she had grown to abhor.

Chapter IV

Julie's flight into Bozeman arrived right on time at five thirty-four. There were only two flight attendants—her and Jeana—on the small plane. So they quickly marched the passengers off and began the cleanup process. As Julie gathered the remaining trash and wiped down the seat-back pockets, Jeana stowed everything in the galley and finished the paperwork. When Julie came back up front, Jeana asked, "You wanna grab a bite to eat? I hear there's a new brewery in town we could try."

This was only the second flight Julie had staffed with Jeana. When Julie was first getting to know new recruits, she tended to remain professional and distant, not wanting to be rude but also not wanting to reveal too much about herself or her struggles. After all, she remembered how excited, exuberant, and enthusiastic she had been about the job when she started. She remembered getting up each day with a feeling of, where will I go today, what will I see, who will I meet, what new thing will I try and experience? The world was her oyster, and she was ready to jump in with both feet. There was no better way to see and experience it than from the sky and the touchdowns in between. Julie still loved that about the job, even if her wide-eyed innocence and naivete had long since waned.

Plus, you never knew who you'd meet or what you'd encounter. On more than one occasion, she had met celebrities—actors, authors, news anchors, chefs. She'd been thrilled and also, oddly, a little sad because as fascinating as it was to shake hands with someone famous, she recognized on their faces the telltale sign that being known the world over wasn't all it was cracked up to be, especially on a plane, where they couldn't hide or relax. The spotlight of scrutiny and judgment always made Julie feel bad for them. In a way, she understood. She'd had her own bout of notoriety over the years, and it was a double-edged sword in more ways than one.

Julie thought about this with new crew members. She would never want to inadvertently (or otherwise) put a damper on the happy "newness" of the job for the young folks coming up in the ranks. She was glad for the excuse to decline Jeana's offer. "Actually, I'm meeting a friend in town."

Jeana said, "Ah, okay, no worries," then asked with a raised eyebrow, "A friend or a *friend*?"

Julie laughed. "No, I'm afraid my days of meetings *friends*," she echoed, "are mostly over."

Instead of laughing with her, Jeana frowned and asked, "Why is that?"

Julie shrugged. "Oh, I don't know. I'm getting older. I'm divorced." She didn't bother to continue, sticking to her rule of anonymity as much as possible. She redirected with "I can't remember, what's your story? Are you married?" Julie studied the face of the young brunette with the rosy cheeks and bright smile.

Jeana answered, "Me? God, no. I'm going to travel the world before I even think about settling down."

Julie nodded with a smile. "Right. Smart." She stowed the remaining wipes and dirty gloves in the trash and assisted Jeana with the final steps.

Jeana said offhandedly, "Yeah, don't get me wrong, I have my own stash of *friends* in certain cities," she said, laughing and winking, and Julie smiled. "But for the most part, I just want to have fun—you know, enjoy life while I'm young."

"Makes sense," Julie responded, remembering her own youth.

They said their goodbyes to the pilots, who were completing their log-books in the cockpit, and headed out to the gate, their bags rolling efficiently and dutifully behind them.

Julie asked, "So, what will you do?"

"Tonight? Probably just eat in the hotel, which is fine, honestly. I've been working for eight days straight and need a breather. Tomorrow I'll be back home in Denver and have five luxurious days off. I can't wait. My friend Dana and I are hiking up one of the peaks in Keystone on Sunday, and I'm going to conserve my energy until then."

Julie, "That sounds amazing. And impressive."

As they got to the exit, Julie flagged down her Uber, and Jeana headed to the hotel shuttle, hollering back with a laugh, "Don't do anything I wouldn't do. I'll see you in the morning."

Julie waved back, thinking about how that expression really didn't apply in her situation. She barely did anything anymore, so Jeana might as well have said, "Just do *something*, please." She chuckled. Ah, to be young and free, Julie thought with a sigh. Sitting in her Uber with a pleasantly quiet older driver, Julie began to think back to that time before her life took a turn.

She was like Jeana once. When she worked in the hotel after college, she went out pretty much every night she wasn't working. She stayed close with some friends from high school and college and had also gained a whole new batch of buddies from the hotel job. They would hit the nightclub scene in downtown Chicago or go see a band play at one of those small, dusky music venues that boom-boomed on almost every street corner. There was no lack of things to do back then, and Julie was quite the partaker. She organized her partying with just as much fervor as her job. She loved all those sickly sweet vodka and rum drinks and became known as the "sex on the beach" girl. But one line she would not cross was drugs. Her friends sometimes snuck outside a club and smoked or popped pills, but Julie always refused. The one time she had tried weed in college, she became paranoid and felt a complete lack of control over her body, mind, and senses. Looking back now, she wondered whether it was laced with something or if her body was just super sensitive. At any rate, she never wanted to feel that way again. Drinking was so much more effective, not to mention legal, cheap, and easy. When she drank, she was pleasantly numbed while still being fully functional and in control—the perfect combination.

One night, they saw the Smashing Pumpkins at the Metro and decided to hit up a local place around the corner after the concert was over. Julie went right up to the bar to grab a drink, feeling sexy in a slinky red number, her thick brown hair falling down her back in soft ringlets, her lip gloss creating the perfect pucker, and there he was. Rob. The bartender. He was tall with black eyes framed by thick eyebrows, his hair long and pulled back in a pony-tail, his Ramones T-shirt tight across his broad chest. As Julie stared openly, clutching her tiny purse to her chest, she shouted at him, "Screwdriver." Just then, two random guys who were having a heated conversation behind her came to blows, and she got shoved so hard against the bar that it knocked the wind out of her. Julie immediately dropped like a rag doll to the sticky floor. Rob sailed over the bar handily, using his weight to wrestle between the fight, effectively tossing one guy toward the door and the other toward the dance floor, and then he was on his knees beside Julie, his hand cradled behind her neck, asking if she was okay.

Unable to breathe, she was holding her chest and willing her lungs to expand. She blinked up into those huge, gorgeous black eyes and felt herself sinking into their cavernous depths and feeling a flutter in her heart that had nothing to do with having been knocked down. In her fuzzy dizziness, she wondered, has this Prince Charming come to rescue me? Just then, she inhaled a ragged gasp. He smiled down at her with relief, causing her to smile back. He helped her up, his steady arm around her waist. She was still rather wobbly on her feet, so she leaned into his shoulder and thought, he has such nice, strong shoulders, like a bull. He helped her to a barstool and asked, "You all right?"

She nodded mutely.

Someone from the other end of the bar was hollering at him, wanting a drink. He held up his hand, then turned back to Julie with "What's your name?"

"Julie."

"I'm Rob. Stay right here, okay? Julie," he repeated her name as if to commit it to memory or to hear the sound of her name on his lips. "I'll be right back."

And he was. She got her screwdriver, and several others, and when her friends finally came to find her, she told them to go along to the next place without her—she was going to stay awhile and chat. She went home with Rob that night. And for most of the nights after that. He was so different from her, and that's what fascinated her the most. He embraced the chaos and spontaneity in his life, thrived on it. Never wanting to plan anything in advance, he lived from one day to the next. He was the perfect bartender because nothing ever got him worked up, angry, or flustered. He loved the seedy side of humanity, and he was a great listener and a heck of a lot of fun. Julie needed him to loosen her up, and he needed her to take care of him when he forgot to eat or pay the rent or shower. It was a symbiotic relationship, one in which each was the better for it. A year later, on a whim, they got married in Vegas at one of those Elvis chapels, and Julie was the happiest she had ever been.

When she got the job with United Airlines, it was as if all her dreams came true. Neither Rob nor she ever wanted kids. It was just fine because both of them worked crazy, erratic hours anyway. They just wanted the comfort of being in each other's presence, spending time lounging and laughing and loving in their boho chic apartment in Lincoln Park. Life was simple and easy and perfect.

But that was all before—

The Uber driver broke into her thoughts, "This is it, ma'am. Let me help you."

He got out and took her bag out of the trunk, placing it on the sidewalk in front of the restaurant. She thanked him with a ten-dollar bill and as he drove away, she turned to face the entrance with a sigh and a bracing of her shoulders, a soldier waiting to go into battle.

Chapter V

Paige saw Julie come through the door and felt the Coke she was sipping fizz up in her throat. She gave a half-smile and wave as Julie headed straight over to the table, her suitcase rolling behind her like an obedient border collie. With her perfectly pressed uniform, her hair in an extreme bun, and her chin held up stiffly on her thin stem of a neck, Paige thought she looked exactly like a member of a military gestapo. She sighed. It was going to be a long meal.

Paige stood up and gave Julie a brief hug. Julie stowed her bag behind their booth and sat down, quickly waving the waitress over and ordering a glass of red wine. Paige waited silently, noting that despite Julie's I'm-all-put-together appearance, her hands were shaking and she had dark circles under her eyes. Paige wondered absently if the shaking was because this was Julie's first drink of the day or because she was nervous to commence the inevitable unloading of revelations that Paige never asked for nor wanted. Either way, it didn't bode well for the tone and tenor of the night, which almost always started out in this same, predictable, frustrating way.

Julie quickly said Paige looked great, asked how she was doing, and inquired after her parents, to which Paige answered that everything and everybody was fine. Paige politely asked, "And you?" knowing full well there would be nothing to illuminate on that front, but having been raised to respect her elders, she asked anyway. Julie's pinched smile and quick "All good" was exactly as Paige expected. Then she sat waiting for the other shoe to drop.

Julie talked about the "fine" weather nervously and then her flight schedule being full and how she was hoping to take some time off in September to visit the fall foliage in New England. She plowed on almost maniacally about her flight crew, the recent places she had been, sports, movies, and a variety of other topics that Paige had no interest in whatsoever. All the while, Julie downed her wine and ordered another. Paige watched her patiently, sipping slowly on her Coke. Eventually they ordered, Paige a house salad and small pizza and Julie a burger with no bun and a side of steamed broccoli. At least her hands had stopped shaking.

When their food arrived, Paige was beginning to wonder if Julie would ever get to the point of their meeting, so Paige prompted, "Julie—er—sorry to interrupt, but what is this about, well, what I mean is, have you talked to Terry or Marie or—?"

Julie's rosy wine cheeks paled briefly as she took a strategy-stalling bite of her burger (cut up and skewered on a fork, which Paige found so bizarre). Then another swig of wine before answering, "Terry? Oh no, not in years. I did text him maybe six months ago, but no response." She grunted a short, derisive laugh and added, "I guess he was the lucky one, the *smart* one—just walked away and didn't look back."

Paige replied firmly without malice, "I suppose so. I hope so."

Julie's eyebrows rose, then she admitted, "Right...me too," with a quick, dismissive flick of her hand in the air. "More power to him." A second later, defensively, as if Paige had challenged her (on this or anything else, for that matter, which always confused Paige because she never had and never would), Julie pressed, "It's not like I *asked* for this, you know? It's not like my life has been easy. It's not like this didn't affect me just as much as everyone else."

Paige regarded her flaring nostrils and flashing eyes and saw all the years of sadness behind the anger. She responded softly, "I know. Julie...I *know*. No one said it did or didn't. No one has ever said anything like that. No one has ever blamed you."

Julie's quick, bold blue eyes sparked as she countered with sarcasm, "Oh no?! Really? Come on! We both know *that's* not true!"

Not taking the bait, watching Julie's chest heave up and down, Paige said evenly, staring her down, "Well, *I* don't, anyway..."

Hearing Paige's soft voice, Julie calmed a little and flagged down the waitress for another wine.

Paige said, "So, I take it you *have* heard from Marie then?"

Julie breathed a long, drawn-out exhale before replying. She took another bite of burger and drank it down with her new glass of wine before saying, "Yes. Well—no, not exactly."

"Huh?" Paige said, wondering if the wine was getting to her. Paige ate her salad and pizza and waited.

Finally, Julie said, "Not for several months. I text her once in a while with a status update, but she either ignores them or writes back something scathing, with no real intent to understand the challenges or intricacies of the politics involved. When I provide details of the efforts and progress I've made, she's dismissive or rude, or both."

"Hmm," Paige said, nodding sympathetically. She asked, "So, nothing new then?" still wondering why Julie requested they meet tonight after a year of being incommunicado.

Julie drank more wine before replying flatly, "Nope. They just simply won't change the rules. That's all. There's absolutely nothing I can do about it."

Paige didn't say a word as she watched Julie's eyes fill with tears. After a minute, Julie dabbed her face with a tissue from her purse. Paige finally said, "Listen, Julie, from my perspective, I don't mind. I get that it's not ideal, not the outcome you wanted, but you should know that I ended up in a good place with good people. Sure, it's maybe not the life that was expected for me, and I think about my biological parents quite often, wondering what dreams they had, but despite that," she paused, seeing the stricken look on Julie's face before going on, "*despite* that, I have a wonderful family now and a great life. I have tons of friends and a great job, and even though the kids in high school called me the spotted elephant from the island of misfit toys," she smiled, making Julie stumble a little in her grief and stare. "I didn't mind because I always thought that I was lucky—I've had *two* sets of parents who have loved me and wanted me, and that's got to count for something."

Julie's tears really started pouring then as she nodded, unable to speak, but the tears were seemingly from her acknowledgment, not from guilt or grief. After she swallowed and blew her nose, she said with a set jaw, "Okay, okay. Thank you for that. Yeah, so I guess—well, I wanted to tell you—I've decided to throw in the towel. I hope you won't be mad at me, but I just can't do it anymore. I can't put in the effort, knowing nothing will change, and I can't wake up every morning with nightmares, knowing no matter how much I try, how much that day altered the course of history for my life, for yours and others', ultimately it doesn't matter because it won't change a thing." She stopped, her watery blue eyes piercing Paige. She added, "And I suppose—well, I was wanting your—I don't know—consent or permission—or *something* before I say with one hundred percent certainty that I'm done." Then she added quickly, "I'm going to talk to Marie too."

Paige raised her eyebrows at that and took another bite of pizza before responding. She said, "Listen, I wouldn't worry about Marie. You know she won't budge. But if you really feel you need to, I guess I'll leave it to your discretion. And like I said before, for me, you have nothing to ask for. I don't care about the stupid rules. They are what they are. There's no changing them and no guarantee that changing them would have made a difference anyway. In cases like ours, there are no perfect outcomes. I know you're trained to prepare for every situation, but that doesn't mean that even with perfect execution and follow-through, more lives would have been saved or will be saved. Life is too arbitrary. That's how I feel about it anyway. So, you have nothing to ask from me."

Julie took in a deep, shaky breath and said, "Thank you. From the bottom of my heart."

Paige nodded and added, "Besides, I want more for you, quite honestly." Julie sat up straighter at this and braced a little in her seat. "This project-slash-obsession, whatever you want to call it, has clearly...," Paige gestured toward the three empty wineglasses, which caused Julie to blush even redder than she already was and look away, "taken a toll. I know I'm like—I don't know—thirty years younger than you, and you probably don't want to hear this from me, but it seems like you're drinking away your frustration—or guilt. Not to mention, from what I can tell, which maybe isn't very much, but looking from the outside in, I would say your life has sort of been stalled for a while, hasn't it?"

Julie's eyes were down, her hands in her lap, her shoulder slumped. She didn't reply, didn't look up. Paige had no idea if she was even listening anymore, but she pressed on anyway, "Yes, you have your job, and I'm glad for that—you're so good at it, and I know it keeps you balanced. But I want more for you. As much as you've told me over the years that you saved me so I could live a long, full, and happy life, I've been doing that, but what about you? What have *you* been doing to make what happened to us worth it for the others who didn't—well, who didn't, you know…"

Julie finally looked up, sniffed, and said very quietly with desolation in her voice, "Yes, I know. I think about it. A lot. I'm gonna try, I swear, I'm going to, but it's just so—so hard…"

"I get that, but hey, listen," Paige pressed, trying to lock on Julie's eyes, "it's what we should do. Like a tribute to them. And if this is the last meeting we're going to have for a while, or ever, then I need to know you'll do that for me, and for them, if not for yourself. Will you?"

Julie broke away from Paige's eyes guiltily, fiddling with the napkin in her lap for a long time before reluctantly replying, "I guess so. I guess I can try."

Paige nodded, thinking how sometimes Paige was the adult and Julie the child in their strange, twisted, unnatural relationship and also thinking how, on a scale of one to ten, the likelihood that Julie would follow through on her promise was probably a two.

CHAPTER VI

IT WAS MID-JUNE. Marie was driving Bridget to the local library for a PSAT prep class when she saw a text from Julie appear on her minivan dashboard screen. She pressed it and heard: "Message from Julie Geiger: We need to talk." Marie swore under her breath, and Bridget looked up from her book curiously as Marie apologized. She wasn't much of a curser, and this was probably the first time Bridget had ever heard *shit* from her mother's lips. When the screen wanted an answer, Marie replied, a little too forcefully, "NO."

As Marie pulled into the library parking lot, Bridget asked shyly before getting out of the car, "You okay, Mom?"

Marie dismissed her with a wave of her hand. "Yes, sweetie, I'm fine."

"Is it about Matthew?"

Marie started. God, why did she have to say his name out loud? Marie cringed with an instant wave of nausea and a pain in her temple. She pursed her lips and answered curtly through clenched teeth, "No, sweetie, I'm sure it's nothing."

Bridget looked away, out the open door for a second, then came back to Marie's face, leaning across the passenger seat. "You know, you can talk about it, Mom, if you want, I mean. I'd really like to know more, but I feel like you and Dad—you think you have to protect us from—from what happened. But we're older now. We can take it. In fact, I think it would help—for us to know the full story."

Marie's hard face softened, a sigh escaping her lips. Her sweet, smart middle child was so thoughtful, so accommodating, always thinking about everyone else. And, Marie had to admit, rather brave—the only one of her children to ask directly. It had been years since anyone had said a word about it. About Matthew. Sometimes Marie wondered if they even remembered this thing that sat like a weighted stone in her gullet every day of her life. Was it like a strange, vague memory to them—a dream or a foggy mist of words they'd heard once that didn't fit with anything else in their current reality? Marie tucked a strand of hair behind Bridget's ear and said, "Thanks, but it's nothing you need to worry about. It happened a long time ago."

Marie gave her a reassuring smile, but Bridget frowned and said, "Um, okay, but seriously, Mom, you can. Think about it."

"I will," Marie lied, looking out the windshield toward the library. "Hey, you better get in there—you'll be late. Be back in an hour to pick you up."

"Okay," Bridget said with a frown before she disappeared into the building with her backpack slung over her shoulder.

Marie put the car in drive and headed to the grocery store, her usual way to kill an hour when the kids had their activities, at least the ones where her presence wasn't required. At first, inside the well-lit sanctuary of the store, she squeezed the avocados and thumped the cantaloupes, effectively blocking Julie's text from her mind, but by the time the butcher was packaging five fillets in parchment paper, the sweat began to form on her upper lip, her stomach churned, and the racing thoughts crept into her mind like chipmunks burrowing under the wire fence of a garden. Just like the varmints, her thoughts were insidious, noxious, parasitic, trying to steal what was rightfully hers—the calm, sweet, precious mental stability she had built and worked so hard to maintain and protect. In an instant, just like those unexpected visitors appearing without warning to pluck her almost ripe, perfect heirloom tomatoes off the vine, shoveling them into their cheeks like gluttonous cows, she was feeling the familiar beginnings of a venomous rage that caused her to leer instead of smile when the butcher handed over the white-wrapped meat with a smile. She quickly turned away, rushing with the cart down the baking aisle to get away.

She tried to focus, tried to remember her purpose in the store, what else she needed. She placed random items in the cart absently, not knowing what she was doing. A bag of sugar, a bottle of vanilla extract, a package of lemon cake mix, a canister of chocolate frosting. Suddenly, she felt the need to fill her cart full. She headed down one aisle, putting several packages of bagels, buns, and loaves of bread into the cart, then zooming down another, lobbing jasmine rice, flour tortillas, ramen noodles, and matzo into the cart like a basketball player practicing hook shots for a game. More in the next aisle and the next until finally she ended up at the register, the cashier scanning her items disinterestedly while Marie watched and focused on the girl's bright pink nails. Marie studied her hands and scowled a bit, still filled with rage but also feeling the slight flutter of something underneath—an urge to feel full. Maybe these bags of food would start making her feel full again. Maybe that was all it took—to feed oneself, to try new things—maybe she would go home and spread some of the chocolate frosting on her matzo and see how that tasted, how that made her feel different from what she was used to, how that made her insides fill up with a new flavor, a new kind of normal, a new Marie. Maybe then she would be full.

Maybe then she would at least not feel the yawning emptiness that encapsulated her heart, mind, and soul.

She put everything in the trunk of her minivan, then checked the time—she still had fifteen minutes before she had to pick up Bridget. She started the car, turned on the air conditioner, and sat back, her eyes closed, not moving. She let the thoughts of that horrible day hit her like a slap across the face. The anger always came first—the lasting feeling had never really gone away but lived under the surface like a boiling, festering wound. When she pulled that layer away, other feelings came—fear, panic, confusion, chaos—and finally the feeling of wretchedness that was brought on by the smells. The overwhelming odor of jet fuel, followed by burning metal and plastic, scorched flesh, her own singed hair and wool coat. She remembered looking down and noticing her boots were shredded, as if someone had taken a weed whacker to them. That was also when she noticed that her feet underneath the torn leather were bleeding, as were her legs, hands, face, and head. Then, percolating up into her fuzzy brain as she surveyed the surreal scene of Armageddon, came the strange feeling that she had forgotten something. Something that should be there but was not. Something was wrong. Something was missing. Something was gone. What was it?

Then, in a rush, her mind slipped back. It was a sunny day in the middle of July, nearly twenty-two years ago. Marie was in a hospital. She had just given birth to an eight-pound, four-ounce baby boy with bright blue eyes and a mop of brown hair. Her heart swelled inside her chest beyond anything she could have imagined. For the next eighteen months, she swaddled, coddled, cuddled, and cowered over their bundle of joy, never wanting to leave him out of her sight. Even Kent wasn't to be trusted alone with him. The few times a week Marie went out to run errands, she brought the baby with her, despite the fact that Kent always offered to watch him. In retrospect, Marie thought, maybe Kent should have pushed more. It was hard to tell, now that it was all a blur of vague, harsh memories to her. One thing she did know was that Kent was a great father—always calm, thoughtful, methodical, sweet, caring, strong, kind—what every child would want in a father. Marie admired him, more than she would ever admit to him. Yet in those early years, she had held her child like a possession who must, at all times, be mostly *hers*.

After all, it was what they had agreed to. That he would go to work, and she would be the one to raise the children. In fact, she had gone back on the pill soon after Matthew was born, wanting to devote all of herself to this one baby before she could even consider having another. They had fought about that a lot in the first year. Kent loved Matthew and wanted seven more. What was stopping them? They had the means and the house and the support, so why not? But Marie had argued that she wanted to savor their firstborn, like a fine wine—drink him in, in all his deliciousness, breathe in his baby smells and hold him to her breast and feel his warm cheek against hers after he woke up from a nap and remember the exact moment when he laughed and walked and talked for the first time. And absorb and revel in the moment he said, "I love you, Mommy" and "I love you, Daddy." Those were moments that might be overtaken by having another child too quickly. Matthew would be lost in the shuffle. She couldn't have that. So she won out, and they waited.

When Matthew was eighteen months and so healthy and hearty that Marie was filled with pride and devotion, she decided that just the two of them would go for a five-day visit to see her parents in Montana. Marie's mother had been asking about them and begging to see the baby, so Marie said she would come. After all, she hadn't been home in years. When she was seventeen and accepted into her first-choice college, the University of Connecticut, she graduated from her tiny high school and fled her cowboy hometown without a second thought. She met Kent a week into her freshman year and promptly went about fully immersing herself in the East Coast lifestyle. She was determined that this new man would be hers. Everything about her bearing, her tastes, her clothes, her conversation, and even her selection of friends went from Montana rough and dirty to Connecticut clean, intellectual, sophisticated, modern, suave, and smart. Kent barely knew what hit him. He saw a girl with tomboy strength, determined, and beautiful who was suddenly transformed into a woman with tempered wit, popularity, and subtle grace. He was a goner.

For this first trip back to her hometown in years, Marie figured it was perfect timing. She had come full circle—hometown girl made good. She wanted to show off her metamorphosis and her new baby. Marie knew that Matthew, who had the sweetest disposition in nearly every situation, would be a complete champ on the flight, even with the layover in Denver. Marie remembered every single thing about the preparations: counting the number of diapers, outfits (every backup plan considered in case of leaks, spit-ups, blowouts), shoes, toys and a million other things that a baby requires. It makes a mother wonder how an infant who is basically the size of a small dog requires so many more bags and accoutrements than an average adult. It made no sense, Marie thought, laughing, not caring, because it was all for her beautiful, chubby, dimpled, delightful boy. She hummed a tune as she packed and then told Kent on the way out the door that there was deli meat in the fridge for lunches, and four perfectly prepared, portioned, and labeled meals ready for the oven, and two bottles of wine on the countertop to keep him happily fed and busy while she was gone. They kissed tenderly, whispering how much they would miss each other, having not been apart a day in over three years. Kent pushed his head into the car seat to nuzzle Matthew and was rewarded with a giggle, scrunchy fingers, and a warm spittle of "dada."

Bam-bam-bam!

Marie nearly jumped out of her skin as her eyes flew open. Where was she? In the car in the grocery store parking lot! Someone was knocking on her driver's side window. She felt the blood drain from her face. Her heart pounding frantically, she tried to put her present-day thoughts back in order, rolling down the window with a tense smile.

It was the bag boy, saying, "Ma'am, you forgot your bread." He smiled. "I'm sure glad I caught you."

Marie took the bag from him and offered a weak "Thank you."

Regarding her face, the boy's smile changed to a look of concern as he asked kindly, "You okay, ma'am?" Marie nodded, rolling the window back up before he could say anything more, his mouth still open, his brow furrowed. He got the hint and walked away but looked back with a frown as she put the car in drive and got the hell out of there.

Focus, Marie, focus.

At the library, Bridget came walking toward the minivan as Marie quickly typed Julie back before she would allow herself to think or feel another thing: "Friday, 5:00, Cranberry Inn."

The instant response: "I'll be there."

Chapter VII

It was just over twenty years ago, a day like any other in the dead of winter, with the usual snow, ice, and wind. A mild blizzard in the Midwest and lots of accumulation over the Rockies. Air traffic control had added extra time to the schedule for deicing. Julie was flying from Denver to Bozeman. It was busy—so many flights taking off and landing, and people milling about in the terminals like swarms of bees, going about their business, rushing to gates, eating in the food courts, arguing about delays and cancellations.

Julie strutted confidently through it all. Everything for her had been running smoothly and on time. Her efficient nature fit like a glove with days like this, and today was especially sweet because she was due home that night in her own bed, sleeping in Rob's arms. She had left five mornings ago with a kiss on his cheek. He unexpectedly woke up for a moment, grabbed her around the waist, and pulled her body down onto his as she protested with a giggle, "Stop! You'll ruin my uniform."

He responded sleepily, "I'll ruin *you*. Get under the sheets, woman!"

She luxuriated in his arms and his lips for a few minutes as his hands roved over her. Eventually she sat up reluctantly, kissing the scruffy side of his jaw, which always had the most alluring smell, the remains of rugged sweat and liquor from his prior night working at the bar. She purred into his ear, "Five days, sweetie. I promise. I'll be back with bells on."

He released her with a groan and replied petulantly, "That's like forever from now."

She smiled and replied, "More like forever and a day, but who's counting? Listen, after that, I'm off for three days, so we can hang out. Maybe I'll come directly to the bar and keep you company for a few hours. We can go to that club after your shift ends…or get a late-night bite to eat. What about that diner over on Lincoln? As I recall, they have the best blueberry pancakes."

His eyes lit up a little at "pancakes," then the lids slowly closed as he said quietly, "All right. Try not to miss me too much."

"I will," Julie said with a grin, leaning over to give him one last peck on the lips. She grabbed her bag and headed out the door.

Julie snapped out of her reverie when the pilot came over the loudspeaker saying they were about to begin their descent into Bozeman. Julie and Toby, her fellow flight attendant, began their final procedural steps—Julie recited the "We're about to land—please turn off your electronic devices" speech as Toby walked down the aisle checking the overhead bins and passengers' seat belts, tray tables, and seat backs. She hung up the microphone and followed behind Toby with a bag, collecting the remaining trash. Once everything in the cabin was in order, they finished readying and securing the galley and executed the pilot's prompting to "arm doors and crosscheck" before strapping themselves into their jump seats. Julie was smiling and content now that everything was set and feeling free and happy knowing her day was more than half over. She began to wonder absently about the food offerings in the Bozeman airport. They were slim, as she recalled. Such a tiny airport. Maybe she would buy something out of a vending machine to tide her over. After all, she only had two hours to kill before her flight back home to Chicago. She asked Toby if he remembered what the options were, and he said meaningfully, "I bought a granola bar back in Denver and shoved it in my bag."

She laughed. "Right."

Toby then regaled her with a story about his new puppy. "We decided to name him Padua because that first night, we were sitting on the couch cuddling with him, watching *10 Things I Hate About You*, Michael's favorite movie, which, I don't know if you've seen it…?" She shook her head. "It's a modern rendition of *The Taming of the Shrew*, and anyway, the kids all go to Padua High School. Anyway, here's the funny part—as soon as the opening credits come up with this song by Barenaked Ladies, the puppy starts wailing. Like really howling, as if he's being stabbed or strangled. Mournful, sad cries. At first, we felt so bad for the little guy—we were just like, 'Awww, he's so sad. Why are you so sad, buddy? We're here with you in your new home.

We bought you food and toys and a bed (a Burberry bed, no less—I mean, show some respect and appreciation!),' but then, two seconds later, the song ends and he gets quiet as a mouse. Completely bizarre and hysterical. After we finished the movie, we played the beginning again, and sure enough, same response. At that point, we couldn't stop laughing. I promptly told Michael that his name *must* be Padua and that we would just have to mute that part of the movie next time because I couldn't take the baby's cries anymore—they were breaking my heart. Of course, Michael protested, saying that was his favorite part, the opening song—"

Out of the blue, the plane lurched and shuddered as if it had been picked up and tossed in the air for a long, terrifying moment. Julie blinked and held onto her shoulder straps as Toby's words were plucked from his mouth. This wasn't the usual turbulence—it felt like an assault. When it ended, Toby gulped and stared at her with wide eyes, exclaiming in a terse whisper, "What the *fuck* was that?!"

Instead of answering, Julie gave a curt shake of her head, knowing inquisitive eyes and ears were upon them. She quickly braced herself tighter as another wave sent the plane down what felt like a thousand-foot drop in a half-second tumble. At that, she snapped her eyes away from Toby at the sound of screaming coming from the cabin. She watched as if in slow motion at the faces plastered with panic and fear. Bags spilled out from under seats. Elbows and arms were bruised on seat rests. Babies screamed. Elderly passengers coughed and moaned. Books, glasses, hats, sweaters were thrown in the air like flying projectiles. Several of the overhead bins had come open, and Julie thought with an incongruously irritated feeling that she or the passengers or Toby hadn't properly secured them. But she didn't have time to let that feeling rise to the level of full consciousness before another spasm hit the plane. This one was a massive drop, then a tilt forward, nose first, picking up irretrievable speed, a bullet craning toward the unforgiving ground below. Julie's stomach was in her throat, her mind a massive whirl, a tornado of jumbled thoughts.

What was happening? What should she do? Was this temporary? Or worse? Why wasn't the pilot coming over the loudspeaker? Should she unstrap and get up and do something?

And then this: Holy mother-of-God, is this *it*? Are we going to *crash*? Oh my God, am I going to *die*? What do I do? This is what I trained for. This is what I should know like the back of my hand, like an old, worn piece of clothing. Shouldn't I *know* what to do?

Her heart was racing, her palms turning white, gripped to the straps, her breath pumping her chest up and down like the bellows used to stoke a fire. She glanced at Toby and regarded the fear awash on his face, a mirror of her own. The plane suddenly righted itself, and as she bent her neck to look out a distant window, she saw that they were traveling through a batch of thick clouds. She exhaled, thinking, okay, maybe it was just the worst case of turbulence she had ever experienced. That happened sometimes when you descended through blizzardy clouds, right? Okay, take a breath—in, out, in, out, in, out.

Then, to her dismay and horror, Julie heard the pilot's chime and his voice over the loudspeaker, not loud, but loud enough, intended only for certain ears: "Easy Victor." She unbuckled quickly with a swift glance at Toby, one of acknowledgment and shock. They knew what this meant. She opened the cockpit door and stepped inside, still holding the door handle as it shook in her hand. She closed it softly behind her. She said above the rattling of the plane, her voice shrill, "Captain? Easy Victor?"

The pilot and copilot did a strange exchange with each other that left Julie cold. Captain Richards replied succinctly with an edge to his voice, "Yes. We have an engine out. There's something wrong. We've radioed the tower. We're going to make an emergency landing. They're clearing all runways. Prepare the cabin. Do you understand?" He turned his head to stare Julie down, wrenching a confirmation from her frozen face.

"Yes," Julie replied mechanically, noticing for the first time their white-knuckled hands on the yokes, gripping as if they were tight clamps, and that the copilot's ears were bright red. She slipped back into the cabin, closing the door behind her right as the plane caught another wave of turbulence. She was slammed against the lavatory door and then ricocheted to the opposite side, against the edge of the galley cabinets. She grabbed her elbow and hand reflexively, feeling stabs of pain radiating up her arm and shoulder. But she didn't have time to process the injury. She had a job to do. Blessedly, she was no longer in a fog of random thoughts, but filled with an overwhelming sense of purpose and focus. Mercifully, her training and instincts finally clicked into gear.

LAP BABY

She got her balance, stood up straight, taking a swift step to Toby, leaning over with a look of significance upon her face and hollered, "Easy Victor! Quickly! We must prepare the cabin. Come on!" She felt Toby's flash of recognition and pinched her mouth together in a straight line, willing strength into him with her eyes.

At that moment, she breathed in deeply and pulled from an inner reservoir of courage and self-awareness she hadn't known she possessed. Not waiting on Toby, she made the announcement in no uncertain terms, "Passengers, the plane is going down. We need you to brace for impact. Put your head between your knees and your arms over your head. Do not, I repeat, do not take time to gather your things or do anything else other than do as I instruct you. Right now!"

She slammed the receiver down, screamed at Toby to secure the galley. She held up her chin, turned to face the cabin, and grabbed hold of the overhead bins as she marched down the aisle, teetering along the way, forcing passengers' heads into position, shoving their bags deeper under the seats in front of them, closing the handful of gaping overhead bins with a forceful slam. She heard the wails of adults and children alike, but she didn't take time to register what those wails meant. She was here to do her job. She heard Toby securing the coffee pot, the food, the bathroom doors, and then directly behind her, echoing her words and actions.

She felt her ears almost explode as the plane fell again. As both she and Toby flew up and then came crashing down against the floor in a tumble, she had the oddest thought—she remembered learning in high school physics class that in the absence of gravity, in a vacuum with no air resistance, a feather and a brick would fall at the same rate. Were they going to fall like a feather or a brick? She knew one thing: her entire body felt as though the weight of a brick had passed in and through it, like a weighted serpent seeping into her veins and snatching the warm blood, replacing it with thick sludge.

She grabbed onto a seat and pulled herself up, pushing the thought from her mind. She had to hold it together, using every ounce of self-control to focus. In the drop, she had seen several passengers' heads whiplash. She couldn't stop to take note of their conditions, but instead pushed their heads back down between their legs. Then turning to find Toby still on the ground, holding a hand to his head, stunned and bleeding, she lifted him as best she could, dragging him back up to the bucket seat and strapping him in.

She said, "It's okay—stay here, I'll finish and be right back."

She swiveled to the cabin again, seeing a woman hysterical, clutching her child to her chest. In a rush of icy blood to her temples, Julie realized there were lap babies on this flight. Babies with no seat of their own because they were under the age of two. How many? Her mind tried to grasp at a memory from the boarding process—three? Or was it four? No, five babies on board. Good Lord, *five* lap babies on this plane! She knew with dreaded certainty what her training said to do, but she couldn't get her mind to force her limbs and mouth to do what had to be done. She paused for a baleful three seconds, all the while feeling as if her body were being pulled in every direction by one of those medieval drawn-and-quartered machines.

She took a deep breath and plucked up her resolve, going directly to the hysterical woman and saying firmly, "Put your baby on the floor between your legs and get your head down." The woman shook her head and looked at Julie like she was crazy. Julie added, "Wrap the baby in blankets or coats or whatever you have—but put the baby on the floor, now!" There was no time to be polite. Julie physically grabbed the baby from the woman's arms, placing the child down. Just then, the plane reared again and the baby fell back, hitting its head on the corner of the seat-back pocket, and uttered a shriek unlike anything Julie had ever heard before. The look from the mother—venomous, livid, accusatory—Julie would never forget it, but she clenched her jaw and simply put a hand on the back of the mother's head to get her back in position.

After that, Julie dragged herself down the aisle, holding onto the overhead bins or whatever else she could grab, to locate the other lap babies, similarly instructing their parents. One couple outright refused, the father and mother clutching their child in their arms between them and speaking to Julie in a foreign tongue. She gave up and went to the next family.

In the midst of this nightmare, which seemed the length of forty days and forty nights but was actually only several bullet-speed minutes long, the plane was cutting through the air like a knife through soft butter. Julie knew she must strap herself in before they crashed, but she was diligently still searching for the last lap baby. Finally, she found the family in the last row and instructed them until they complied with her coached plea. As she raced back to the front of the plane, she screamed as loud as her voice would carry in the vortex of the tornado, "Brace for impact! Brace for impact! Heads down! Arms covering heads! Feet together! Heads down! Do NOT look up!"

She reached the front and saw Toby slumped over in what she hoped was the impact position and not the result of his head injury. Her hand grabbed the shoulder strap of her seat belt, and she was about to swing around into her bucket seat when the plane hit the ground. She felt like a china doll being smashed against concrete. Her entire body flung forward and slammed against the cockpit door, then reeled back against various inanimate objects and sharp corners. The shock and pain excruciating, and so fast, like a lightning bolt, she couldn't process a single second other than the abject realization that she was being murdered, torn limb from limb.

CHAPTER VIII

PAIGE HAD NO MEMORY OF THE CRASH. She was only twenty months old at the time. But sometimes she had a *feeling* about it. Sort of like déjà vu or like the hairs on the back of her neck popping up. It was eerie and she didn't like it. It happened once years ago at the Bozeman airport. Her pa had sent her to pick up a friend of theirs who was in town for the week. Both her ma and pa were working at Chico, so they had sent Paige in their place. She was seventeen and standing on the other side of the security area, waiting for the man, a sort of uncle figure to her, Big Red, who came and stayed with them once or twice a year and filled every space with his big, rowdy red-headed personality. Paige loved him and was happy to serve as his chauffeur.

As the other passengers began to file out, she noticed most were tourists going directly to baggage claim for their fishing poles or hiking gear, pulling out layers of fleece tucked into oversized suitcases. But then she saw a couple with a toddler in their arms cooing to her as the mother said, "We're almost there, baby. Just a short drive to Grandpa's house and you'll be able to pet the horses and ride the wagon and play in Grandpa's barn. It's gonna be so much fun." The toddler smiled and reached for the floor, trying to get down, but the dad held fast as the mom kept up the distracted talk.

They were gone from view in thirty seconds, but Paige had the strangest sensation, as if she were transported back in time to that day. The day that her parents should have walked off a plane cooing to *her* in their arms. It was almost as if she could feel the solid weight of her father's fingers laced underneath her legs and bottom, her mother touching the crook of her elbow, kissing her cheek, and saying, "Paige, we're almost home—you've been such a good girl on the flight, and now we're going to take you to the place where you're meant to be, in the safety of our unconditional love and devotion." She almost felt those arms and that sense of total encapsulating warmth, like being folded into a group of angel's wings. Standing there, in that brightly lit, loud, impersonal airport, surrounded by strangers, she felt *them*.

Heat traveled up her neck and into her face, and she was awash with confusion. The feelings started one way and ended another because these sensations, on the rare occasions when they came to her out of nowhere, always began with warmth, enraptured loving kindness and security, and then quickly dissolved into what followed—a flurried, hopeless helplessness, the world hurling toward an ending for them—a finality—and no way to stop it.

In the midst of these feelings, Paige always wondered, who were these people—her biological parents? They were complete strangers. She knew their names and that they came from the Philippines, but almost nothing else. Why were they flying into Bozeman that day? Did they have family in America? What did they do for a living? How did they get to America? Who were they? She didn't know anything. She didn't know herself in relation to them. Was she their only child? Did they love her? Why did they name her Diwa? Did that name have a special meaning to them—taken from a grand-mother's name or a long-lost aunt's or mother's middle or maiden name? Did she, Diwa, herself—Paige—have special meaning to them?

Julie had told her once that she believed they were holding her between them on the flight as the plane went down. She remembered a couple clutch-ing a baby and speaking in a foreign tongue, but only as a moment's snapshot in time, so she couldn't be sure. But then Paige's adopted ma and pa told Paige she had spoken English that first day, the word *gog* for their dog. Did her bio-logical parents decide to teach their baby girl English instead of their native tongue? If so, was that proof that they were staying in America indefinitely?

What had her biological parents been thinking that day? The plane crash was so close to where Paige was waiting for Big Red. It was just a heartbeat away, across the runway, in that field in the distance. Did the remains of the lost souls linger? Was that why Paige felt them? All the love they must have felt, guessing in that instant what was happening—that they would probably die that day. Did they pray over their little baby Diwa as the plane went down? Is that why Paige lived—because of their prayers, hopes, dreams for her? What did their intentions mean to Paige now? How could she live up to them?

LAP BABY

She would probably never know. Everything was sealed in the adoption records, including a piece of who she was, then and now. And because Paige didn't want to hurt her adoptive parents' feelings, she rarely allowed herself the luxury of thinking about her biological parents or what life might have been like if things had gone differently. Except when she got this sensation. The love. The panic. Coincidentally or ironically, like this day, there was that odd feeling, in the airport where they were lost. Meanwhile, these sensations were like flickers and flames setting her heart afire until suddenly Big Red was there in her space, in her presence. Her unseeing eyes lost in the juxtaposition, the rapid-fire shift in her vision from steady to unstable to solid again. He brought her back into her body, her tiny frame dwarfed by his massive bear hug. She found herself unexpectedly laughing until the horrid, uninvited feeling blessedly burst and disappeared into the ether.

Until the next time.

Chapter IX

Whoosh! It came to Marie like a lightning bolt. The thing that was missing—*her son, Matthew!* Good God! Where *was* he? He had been between her legs crying one moment and just *gone* the next. But then again, *everything* that was there a moment ago was gone. As she stared at the scene in front of her, she had difficulty processing it. There was snow—a lot of it—on the ground, falling from the sky, blowing around her head. There were flashing lights in the distance and the sound of emergency sirens racing toward the far edge of the runway, where she was wobbling unsteadily in the wind. There were the remains of an aircraft, split in two, the front half upside down, crushed nearly flat and burning in front of her astonished eyes and the back half off in a ditch to the side, partially obliterated. Oddly, the two halves were a football field apart from each other.

She couldn't figure out how she came to be here, didn't remember the crash or how she got out of the plane, let alone how she was still alive, staring at the aftermath. It was as if she was removed from herself, watching everything from above, a disembodied spirit trying to analyze a puzzle that could not be solved. Then she had a thought: maybe *I'm* a spirit. Maybe I'm dead. Maybe this is one of those out-of-body experiences that people have when they die before they ascend to...to wherever...the beyond. Am I in the beyond? But wait, she thought, didn't I just smell jet fuel and burning plastic and metal and bodies? Didn't I just notice my own blood, my own broken body parts? Was that real? She pushed a finger into a jagged, red cut on her arm and cried out with a wince. It hurt. She felt that. Okay, did that mean she was alive? Did spirits feel pain?

When she looked up, suddenly there was a woman gripping her shoulders. Her clothes were hanging off her (was that a United Airlines uniform?) and she looked as though she had been to hell and back. She asked a direct, lucid question, causing Marie to validate that she, Marie, must be alive.

"Are you okay? Ma'am, are you okay?"

Marie stared at her vacantly for a second, then finally said, "I—I don't know. I think so."

The woman led her gently toward a snowy field, all the while piping into her ear, "We need to get away from the plane. There's a lot of fire here and even more fuel. I'm worried about explosions. I need you to come to the side and sit until the emergency crews get here. You're going to be okay. I see you, um, have a few injuries—that's okay, it's going to be okay—just lean on me, that's right, this way, put your weight on me. Here we go, sit down here and stay put, you hear? I'll send them your way soon. Don't move. Do you understand?"

Marie nodded as she was gently placed on a bed of snow. She suddenly realized the excruciating pain in her feet and lower legs, and looked down to see swelling and an ugliness forming below her ankles. She started to whimper as the woman turned away, back toward the remains of the plane, but then Marie grabbed her wrist. The woman lost her balance and came down with a yelp on the snowbank beside Marie. That's when Marie noticed the woman's thigh had a huge gash that was open and bleeding as well as innumerable other cuts, bruises, and scrapes. At that moment, though, Marie didn't care because that lightning bolt had pricked her conscience again—this time with full clarity.

Marie looked directly into the woman's blue eyes, her hand still locked around her wrist, and seethed, "*You* told me to put—*my baby*—between my legs. On the floor! Between my legs! My baby! My Matthew! You told me!" Marie paused, seeing the recognition and utter helplessness bubble up in the woman's eyes. Marie felt it and wanted to drill it in and twist. "You remember, don't you? That was what you said to me. To put my precious little Matthew on the floor. But where is my baby now? WHERE? *You go get him!* Go get my Matthew! And don't come back until you have him. Do you hear me?!"

The woman's eyes got wide, and with one swift, curt nod she stood up, releasing herself from Marie's grasp, and replied, "Okay."

Marie's narrowed eyes watched the woman stumble away. Marie sucked the icy air into her lungs, wringing her hands, wondering if the power of will and intention could force something into being. She hoped so because she had never wanted anything so much in her life. That woman had given her instructions that were so asinine, Marie could only suspect they had been developed by a bunch of inept, celibate men who thought they would suffice and never be needed. And yet here was Marie, following the woman's instructions despite her gut instinct that they felt all wrong, despite her *mother's* instincts that there must be a better way, a more logical way, a safer way, despite the fact that the last thing Marie remembered was her Matthew reaching up for her, crying his eyes out, wanting his mommy to pick him up, fold him into her arms, protect him. But she had been instructed to keep him down, and so she had.

Marie's rage-filled heart screamed. She promptly turned to the side and vomited in the snow.

A few moments later, she sat back up again, feeling faint and in shock. Suddenly there was a man sitting in the snowbank beside her. The same woman, the flight attendant, had dragged him from the crash site and left him there and was now heading back to the plane's burning fuselage. Marie looked at the man, who was hunched over, holding his bloody head in his hands, and didn't say a word, rendered speechless by the cataclysmic end-of-the-world feeling permeating her core. She thought absently, were they the only ones? Where were the others? She was one. The woman was two. This man was three. What about Matthew? What about the rest of the passengers? There must have been, what—at least a hundred people on that plane? Maybe more. It was nearly full. She remembered because she had hoped for a whole row to stretch Matthew out beside her, but instead they had been scrunched into a three-seater with an elderly couple. Twenty minutes into the flight, Marie's legs had started to cramp with the weight of Matthew on her lap. A little while later, she had grown exhausted entertaining him with snacks and toys and books, none of which really worked for very long. Plus, his diaper was soon full, and she had spent a dicey fifteen minutes struggling to maneuver and balance his wiggly body in the postage-stamp-sized lavatory for a diaper change.

But, of course, that was all before the plane started shaking like a leaf. And that was before the woman told her to put Matthew on that cold, rumbling, unstable, unforgiving floor! Why had Marie done it? Why hadn't she refused? She knew better than that woman. She was Matthew's mother, for God's sake! She knew what was best for her Matthew. Not this random woman, not this bully who had the gall to touch her baby *and* to push her head down. Who did she think she was?!

All of these thoughts happened in the blink of an eye as Marie sat fuming next to the moaning man with the head injury. She was so incensed that she almost missed two things out of the corner of her eye. One: The fire trucks were there now, dousing the burning remnants of the plane, the snow swirling in near whiteout conditions amid their efforts. Alongside were several other emergency vehicles and swarms of workers milling about. Two: The woman, the flight attendant, was headed back toward them, a bundle in her arms, her face somehow different from a moment before when she had dropped off the man—this time defiant, triumphant, elated.

Once Marie's fuzzy mind registered what she was seeing, she stood up and attempted to go directly to the woman, her arms outstretched, but her knees buckled under her. No amount of adrenaline could sustain the injuries to her legs and feet for the reach. She fell back down in the snow with a thud, the man lifting his head for a moment to glance at her as if he hadn't noticed her until now. Marie didn't have time to take him in, though, and instead screamed at the woman, "Is that—? Is that my baby?! Is that my *Matthew*? Give him to me! Give him here NOW!"

The woman dutifully complied, handing the baby over, the tears streaming down her face. She hollered as best she could, her voice a squeaky, wretched wreck, "I went back and heard a cry inside—it sounded like a baby, so I ducked in as fast as I could, trying not to collapse anything or get burned." As she said this, she began staring at her wrists, hands, and fingers, which were red and swollen. Marie felt a note of sympathy, seeing that she *had* been burned. All the while, the baby, clutched to her breast, wailed in her arms. The woman went on, "The sound—it was faint, like it was muffled in a locked area or something—I tried crawling through the debris to get closer, but at first I couldn't figure out where it was coming from. The plane's all topsy-turvy, upside down," she pointed, and Marie nodded, "so I had to reorient myself. Then I stepped onto something, and it moved. It was one of the overhead bins. The clasp, it had been closed, but suddenly it was open and there he was, looking me right in the eye, none the worse for wear. I snatched him up and brought him here."

She smiled down at them as Marie and the baby cocooned together like in a manger scene in a snow globe, the virgin Mary clutching her Christ child.

Julie added, "It happened so fast...I can't believe it." She looked back at the crash site and said, "I don't think they'll be letting anyone back over there now. This will be it." At those ending words, she sat down beside them in the snow, clearly spent, the energy and determination disappearing from her face, her shoulders slumping forward, her head in her hands, the realization of what she just said sinking in.

Marie was rocking Matthew back and forth in her arms, her hair falling over his head and body in a shield. Her tears fell upon him like a river, mixing in with the snowflakes. She had never felt such gratitude and relief in her entire life. Good Lord Almighty, her prayers and anger and sheer will had brought him back to her! Knowing the devastation, how had she been so lucky? How had *he* been so lucky? Found in an overhead bin! And the latch had sealed him in. Extraordinary! How had he landed there? From the floor to there...crazy. One in a million. She began to wonder if he was hurt. The woman hadn't said, but maybe she hadn't thought to check. Just then, as she was pulling Matthew away from her chest, where he had finally quieted against her, to look him over, a group of emergency workers were upon them, kneeling down with their boxes of medical equipment and accessories.

A man in a paramedic uniform began assessing her injuries, softly questioning her and eventually putting his hand on her leg, causing her to jump in pain. He shouted above the din of the chaos in the background, "Oh, sorry. This here?"

Marie said, "Yes, my lower legs and ankles—there's something wrong with them—I'm not sure what." He peeked closer, beginning to touch her legs gingerly, when Marie shouted, "No—no, you can look at me later. Can you examine my baby first? I'm not—" her voice broke, and she had to clear it, "Not sure if he's hurt or not."

"Of course, hand him over. Let me check."

As she lifted Matthew, he instantly began to cry, which broke her in two, but she gave him to the man anyway. He began touching and testing his limbs and squirmy body, feeling for injuries, gauging the baby's reactions along the way. There was a small cut on the baby's forehead, and for that, the man pulled a piece of gauze out of the box and touched it to the spot. Looking more closely and seemingly finding it negligible, he went back to his examination.

As the man worked slowly, methodically, Marie's patience ran thin. She wanted more than anything to have Matthew back inside the walled fortress of her embrace. It was then that she noticed something strange. Matthew's eyes. They looked different from what she remembered. In fact, she thought his whole face wasn't exactly right, nor the hair.

He had thick, slightly curly light brown hair.

The baby in front of her had straight, wispy dark brown hair.

And black eyes.

Matthew's eyes were the bluest blue, like the color of a robin's egg.

The baby was wearing a footed one-piece pink romper.

It was dirty from the crash, covered in soot and ripped in a few places.

But still pink. Undeniably pink.

She had dressed Matthew that day in a pair of navy jeggings and a red-checkered flannel shirt.

The baby had no shoes, just the attached footies of the fleece pajamas.

Matthew had been wearing a pair of brown Velcro infant sneakers.

Her heart froze in her chest.

No.

No—no—no—no—no—NOOOOOOOOO!!!

It was the snow.

Blinding her.

It was the chaos.

Outside.

And in her mind.

It was the trauma and shock.

It was her injuries.

It was a trick.

Of her mind.

She looked to her left and nearly growled.

A trick.

Of the woman.

It was *her* trick.

Chapter X

It was Friday, and Julie was driving to the Cranberry Inn, thinking back on her visit with Paige and wondering absently what Paige was up to. Probably hanging out with friends. It was weird to think that Julie would never see her again. Julie had used her fight against the lap baby rules as a reason to keep in touch. Now that she had given up and the emergency crash stance for lap babies would remain on what she deemed the nonsensical floor, literally and figuratively, she would have to walk away from that part of her life, including Paige. And yet, being around Paige gave her a sense of comfort, purpose, right-ness with the world, however small. Watching Paige grow from a curious tod-dler to a grammar school sweetheart to a budding teenager and now a mature, smart, beautiful, upstanding young woman, Julie felt an almost maternal pride and an overwhelming feeling of gratitude. Paige was alive and well. Outside of that one critical moment, Julie recognized that she had almost nothing to do with Paige's happiness, but she still wanted to bask in the glow of it.

They were both survivors.

And that meant something.

Sadly, though, it was out with the bad *and* the good. She had to leave behind the struggle that had consumed her for the past twenty years. And she had to leave Paige to strive and thrive and be alive without Julie's well-meaning, touch-base visits—or was it Julie's need-for-validation visits? Julie wasn't sure. She'd been so obsessed with the whole thing for so long that her perspective was skewed. The more Julie thought about it, the more the lines became blurred and unreadable, not to mention untenable.

Regardless, she had lost more than just the fight. She had lost everything. Her marriage. Her friends. Her family. Now Paige.

All for nothing.

She had lost.

White flag.

She *was* lost.

And she was alone.

Now she had to face the woman, Marie, her near arch-nemesis, who would probably relish throwing blood onto that white flag. Julie knew it and dreaded it. Quite the opposite of Paige. But it had to be done. These visits over the years with Marie had always been hard, like drilling holes through granite. There was no give to the woman. And Julie couldn't necessarily blame her. On an intellectual, logical level, she understood. Marie needed a scapegoat—someone to torture, fault, *slay* for what happened that day. And it most certainly couldn't be herself. Or the fates. Or God. Or the airline industry. Or the cruel, inexorable, unexplainable universe of horrible things that happened to good people every day for no reason.

Oh no.

It had to be Julie.

She understood, but could not—*would* not—allow it to absorb into her emotional core. Or at least she tried not to let it. Sometimes it snuck in anyway. This was why she drank. The alcohol helped keep the seeping, seething, accusing guilt from burning up her inner self. It was always so close, knocking on the door, waiting to get in, wanting to crack open the timid, tenuous hold on her defenses with its steely, bitter arrows, bullets, and grenades, but she numbed it all with a fifth of gin, a vat of wine, or a gallon of beer. Really, whatever was handy.

And when she wasn't drunk, she used Marie's accusations as a weapon, an energy source to fuel her fight, to prove to Marie that she could make something good out of something bad. In the beginning, right after the crash, Julie was filled with a fire in her belly so strong, it could have heated an entire nation. She was going to turn the behemoth around. She was going to be David to the industry's Goliath. She was going to come up with a solution, then sell the powers that be on it, and the future would be bright again. The red, festering wound that had been the crash would be healed and sealed with a new balm. Then Marie would have to forgive her, maybe even thank her. Or

LAP BABY

at least acknowledge that yes, Julie hadn't been able to save Matthew, but she was saving countless other babies in the future. And that would be enough.

Right?

Julie gripped the steering wheel of her rental car, shaking her head, thinking back on her foolish, naive bravado back then—everything she had tackled, tried, tested, and eventually *tainted*.

Julie had formed a committee, brought in focus groups, worked with management, created a multi-team, multilayered task force, held marathon brainstorming sessions, presented findings, statistics, analytics, safety data, ideas, and solutions to federal agencies, mothers' groups, pediatrician associations, safety councils, airline representative unions, legislators, Congress, every gathering of leaders and influencers in the industry.

Could the babies sit in a free seat next to a parent, in their own car seat?

This would require seat and seat-belt modifications, and the airlines couldn't possibly accommodate all the different types of car seats. There are already airline-issued car seats that can be purchased for children of a certain weight, but their use requires purchasing a ticket.

Could there be a foldaway baby seat that could be unfolded, expanded, and used in the event of an emergency?

This would require redesigning every aircraft. Where and how would such a seat be stored? Above every seat? On the floor? Up in the galley? How many would be needed? What if we didn't have enough? Who would design them? How would they be tested? How could we ensure they were safer than simply leaving the baby on the floor? Would we have to train the crew in how to use them? Would the passengers have to be trained too? What would be the cost?

Could the parents of a lap baby have a different emergency stance position than the rest of the passengers? Instead of head between the knees and arms overhead, maybe kneel down facing their seat, their head on the seat cushion, their baby cradled in their arms below the seat?

This type of position is not safe for the parent or the child.

How do we know?

We've tested all positions and determined that facing forward, head down is best.

Could the parents and the lap baby be moved to a different part of the plane in the event of an emergency? Maybe several bucket seats could be made available up front or in the back, allowing for redesigned shoulder straps that could fit around both parent and child.

Same response. Would not be safe. Would require testing. Would cost money.

What if we changed the cutoff age (for ticket purchase) from two years old to one? After all, two has always been an arbitrary number, not based on science, research, or data. By changing the cutoff age to one (or younger), we would reduce the number of lap babies and cut the risk in half.

Reducing the number by half means doubling the cost to parents. Parents will vote against this change because of the cost. If they're worried about their child's safety, there is nothing keeping them from buying an extra ticket for their baby now. We don't restrict this option.

What if we simply banned lap babies and said that all *children, no matter their age, must have a purchased ticket and an assigned seat?*

This extra charge to the parents would be cost-prohibitive, leading them to choose other modes of travel, most likely automobile, which has a much higher rate of accident and injury than airline travel—and, of course, would lead to fewer people traveling by air and lead the airline industry to require higher ticket prices for the rest of the traveling public. And what would be the cost of that? To the airline? To the travelers? To the industry? To the parents? To the babies?

The answer (always): Too much.
What is the return on investment? What is one life worth?
No baby has died in an airplane crash in twenty years.
You do the math.

There's no guarantee that a new solution would work any better than what we have now.

Total failure.
The effort was.
She was.
She wasn't David.
She wasn't anybody.

And here was the rub, she realized, from Marie's point of view: Paige *had* lived. Despite the misguided, unhelpful emergency instructions. Despite the odds. *And* Paige would have a full life. Or at least a chance at a full life. Whereas Matthew's life was cut short. And Marie couldn't understand or acknowledge that, because then the whole horrid thing would somehow make sense and *wouldn't* be totally arbitrary.

Which was ridiculous. A plane crash *was* arbitrary. If the engine died, if it was in the middle of a blizzard, if the deicing in Denver didn't work sufficiently, if they could never definitively decide what caused the crash.

Who died. Who lived. It *was* all arbitrary.

But Julie sometimes asked herself, had Paige maybe, just maybe, survived *because* her parents followed the instructions? Or because they *hadn't* followed them? How did Paige end up in the overhead bin unscathed? How had Julie known to go back into the burning wreckage to hear her, to find her, to save her? Could she have done more? Less?

Four babies had died in the crash, as well as one hundred forty-two adults. Julie's mind was sick to death, sick to the core with these insidious, creeping thoughts.

Was it a miracle?

What *was* a miracle, after all?

Something not tied to concrete evidence, not causal, not perfect.

Was it meant to be analyzed?

Dissected, like a formaldehyde frog in biology class?

Torn to pieces to poke at the soft, vulnerable, juicy insides?

What would be left after the dissection?

Julie drew in a jagged, bracing inhale. Right now, as she drove to meet Marie, she would make herself think of something else. Focus, Julie, focus. What was the point in speculating? Circular thoughts led in only one direction—nowhere.

She needed to keep her wits about her or else she'd never get through this night. She had vowed not to drink. Instead, by force of will, she would push those sneaky, useless thoughts and crushing baser desires away, opting for deep breathing and mindfulness exercises. She put the radio on the classical music channel and attempted to suffuse the piano concerto into her throbbing templates and weary, overwrought psyche. Breathe in. Breathe out. Hum. Look out the window at the lovely scenery. This was a cute village, wasn't it? Notice that pretty house right out of the 1800s with the shiny black shutters pinned back with the most adorable shutter dogs. And the flowers! Clearly the work of a great landscaper. Every house in this town looks right out of Bedford Falls. Living in Chicago, it was rare for Julie to be outside the blacktop jungle of city skyscrapers and blocks filled with designer shoe stores. She tried to focus on every single house, every single dog being walked, every single person on the street, every single distracting thing she could cling to, become absorbed in, fling her fear and anxiety onto.

But as she pulled into the parking lot of the Cranberry Inn, her mind was instantly flooded with the memory of a scream: "Go get my Matthew!"

Julie put her face in her hands, turned off the car, and wept.

Chapter XI

ABBY AND KYLE PULLED UP TO PAIGE'S HOUSE. She jumped in the back seat of Kyle's truck with a "Howdy, partners!"

Abby turned around and replied, "Hey, girlfriend! TGIF! You got your boots on? We're going to the RO-dee-o!!!"

"Fri-YAY! Uh-huh. Can't wait! It's been forever. When was the last time we went?"

Kyle answered, "Livingston Roundup last year."

"Fourth of July!" Abby exclaimed.

"That's right," Paige said. "We saw that one guy break his hand, remember?"

"Ew, yes! Why did you remind me?"

Kyle interjected, "Part of the joy of the rodeo."

Abby and Paige cringed.

"I guess it could have been a lot worse," Paige said.

As Kyle drove down the road, Abby chatted about work and their mutual friends and miscellaneous things, holding Kyle's hand in the front seat with both of hers, rubbing and fiddling with his thumb and fingers.

Paige was used to being their third wheel, but still, every once in a while she began to wonder how she'd managed to become a nearly twenty-two-year-old with no sexual experience to her credit. Every year she wondered if this would be the year for the big *shebang*. The big, miraculous, life-altering event, or so she imagined and hoped. Kyle and Abby had been sexually active since high school, but while their dalliances progressed naturally into a full-on exclusive relationship, Paige never had a hint of anything remotely close to a second date with anyone, let alone anything physical beyond three uncomfortable, awkward kisses with two high school boys and one summer busboy at Chico. She dreamed about something more, quite often. She sometimes sat up late at night reading romance novels and fantasizing about what it would be like to have a handsome stranger touch her in places no man had ever touched before. During those times, she touched herself and found comfort in the fact that she knew everything down there was working properly, even if it had never been graced with a man's attention. But she knew this wasn't enough and yearned for more.

She figured she never got beyond a few kisses because she looked so different from everyone else. It was almost as if boys were afraid to see or try anything more with her, as if she were something foreign, like a complex toy from Russia that no one wanted to learn how to operate. Or they were afraid the spots on her skin were contagious, like leprosy. Sometimes she found it frustrating because yes, she was Filipino by ethnicity, and yes, her skin had white patches, but she was also a girl growing up in Emigrant, Montana, wanting to be touched and loved just like anyone else. Her parents always taught her that all that exterior stuff was just that—*exterior*—like the drapes on the windows, the siding on the house, the paint on the walls. Why did any of that mean so much, or anything, after all? It was just the chocolate sauce on top of the ice cream, *not* the ice cream itself. Why did everyone judge the book by the cover? She knew she had so much to offer, that she was deeper and more multifaceted than her skin color or lack thereof. Sometimes she wondered if anyone would see past the surface and get to know the real Paige—the one waiting to be found, unlocked, explored, and cherished.

Years ago, Paige had asked her pa how he met her ma, and he'd said, "At Chico. It was as if I'd been struck by lightning." She wondered what he meant, and he'd said, "Well, sweetie, sometimes people are drawn to other people for inexplicable reasons. Attraction isn't always logical or predictable, but when it hits you, there's no denying it. Sometimes you just have to give in to it and allow yourself to be swept away."

Paige frowned as Abby finished talking and leaned back into her seat, her head turned toward Kyle, her hand still in his, and he made a kissy sound as he turned to stare at her with that loving look, that secret glance they always shared.

Then Abby, maybe sensing that Paige was frowning and feeling out of place, turned to her and said, "You know, Kyle's cousin—the one I mentioned the other day—his name's Mike Kacey. He's amazing."

"Why's he so amazing?"

"He's a bull rider," said Abby significantly, with a widening of her eyes.

"Shit" was Paige's one-word reply. "You mean he's *in* the rodeo?" They were headed to the Gardiner Rodeo (the Upper Yellowstone Roundup), which was a smaller affair than the Livingston Roundup but still pretty intense. She'd never met anyone who performed in a rodeo. So, this was Paige's set-up—good Lord!

"Yeah." Abby went on, "He's something to see, that's for sure. I don't know how he does it night after night."

"Brave," Kyle interjected, "or crazy."

"Both," Abby agreed.

Kyle added, "He's really good. Just you wait. He grew up on a ranch in Wyoming. Been doing this kind of thing his whole life."

Paige asked, "Did you used to do that too, Kyle?"

"Um, hell no. Mike's my dad's sister's kid, and he was always unruly when we were kids, like a wild colt. He would try anything and feared nothing. He's still that way. He always thought I wasn't up to par because I wouldn't do half the shit he did. Told me I was a wuss, but I said being smart doesn't make me a wuss." He shrugged and smirked at Paige in the rearview mirror. "I actually haven't seen him in a while, since Christmas last year, so it'll be good to catch up." He paused for a second and stared conspiratorially at Abby, then said, "I think you'll like him."

Paige narrowed her eyes. Here we go, she thought…

Abby rushed in with "I mean, he's sort of a mini-celebrity, actually, and we thought, while he's in town for the next few days, we could—the four of us—hang out."

A rush of nerves struck Paige. She asked, "Doesn't he hang out with the rest of the riders after the show?"

Kyle answered, "Not always. I told him we were coming, and he offered to take us out for drinks afterward."

"You told him about me?" asked Paige, feeling a tinge of anxiety in her gut.

"No, not exactly—just that we were bringing a friend. That's all," Abby replied innocently enough.

Paige took in a deep breath and sat back for a few minutes, thinking. She was definitely in need of some broader socializing than the usual

Emigrant set, and it was rare that she ever met or hung out with anyone new. Something different, for a change, sounded kind of…nice. Plus, hadn't she just been thinking about finding a man who would see her for who she really was? Maybe, just maybe, *this* could be the man. It didn't hurt that she thought she looked quite pretty that evening, having worn a new red button-down Western shirt that showed her curves, a black cowboy hat, a pair of cut-off jean shorts, and her favorite cowboy boots. Her long black hair tumbled down her back in soft waves, and she had paid particular attention to her eye makeup, her black eyes framed like large windowpanes with a curtain of thick black lashes. A lot of her friends used those fake lashes nowadays, but Paige never had to—she had always been rather proud of her naturally wide black eyes and thick, dark lashes that only required a minimal amount of eyeliner and mascara to make them pop. She had topped the whole ensemble off with juicy red lip gloss.

She said with a little excitement in her voice, "Okay."

The rodeo was in full force when they arrived, dust filling the hot evening air, the stands a sea of cowboy hats, the pens and corrals teeming with calves, steers, broncs, bulls, and riders. Paige took in the spectacle with a grin. Most everyone in Montana grew up around ranch animals, and Paige was the same, but she was also somewhat different in that her family worked in the service industry, so they weren't around that lifestyle every day. From the moment Paige got out of the car, she was enthralled.

They bought their tickets at the gate and proceeded through the entrance to the stands. Some folks were standing around the edge of the main pen to get a better look at the events, but Kyle, Abby, and Paige sat down in the third row of the stands. Some of the riders were already practicing in the center of the ring, skillfully reining their horses and using lassoes as if they had been born on a saddle. Paige took it all in, her eyes focused on every detail.

The rodeo began and proceeded to wow, with each event seemingly more daring and dangerous than the one before, causing the crowd to *ooh* and *aah* at all the right intervals. Paige, Abby, and Kyle were no different, their eyes laser-focused as riders took down calves and steers, rode the broncs and bulls, guided their bodies and horses into feats beyond what was imaginable or even realistically sane. And yet, the riders performed with strong, unflappable hands and amazingly muscled thighs and arms.

A while into the show, Kyle pointed and said, "There's Mike. See him on the side of the stile? He's about to jump on the bull. Don't miss it. He'll only stay on a few seconds."

The announcer was on the loudspeaker with a deep, grainy-gravelly voice that Paige instantly felt reverberate in her core as he said Mike's name. It was a strange feeling—anxiety for this man she had not yet met, but who was her potential "date" for the evening, and he was about to ride a colossal, raging monster of a creature that wanted nothing more than to buck him off and gore him to death.

The three of them sat there frozen, Paige holding her breath as the buzzer sounded and Mike and the bull shot out of the pen like a cannon. Mike bounced up and down like a tornado. He pitched forward, then back, then to the side, all the while his handsome face intent on his task, his bowed legs clutching the sides of the bull like a vise, one hand straight up in the air, the other gripped tightly to the bull's strap. They both writhed around for what seemed like a lifetime, and Paige found her heart beating hard, her breath caught in her throat. Finally, just as casual as a walk in the park, Mike slapped the bull's back and flung himself off, quickly stepping aside to avoid the beast's horned daggers. It was over almost before it began, and the scoreboard stopwatch registered 8.23 seconds, which Kyle said was really good. He said if the judges liked his form, he could win.

After the air came back in Paige's lungs and they were all laughing again, she asked, "What does he win?"

"Not exactly sure, but I think a chunk of cash."

"Whoa, cool."

In a little over eight seconds! The most money Paige had ever made was five hundred twenty-eight dollars over a wedding weekend at Chico where she had been running around so much that her feet had become swollen and blistered. But that much money made her feel as though she had won the lottery, so she didn't care about her feet.

She didn't have to wait long to meet the man. A little over an hour later, the show was over, the prize money given out (Mike won), and the three of them headed over to the area where the riders were congregating, meeting and greeting their fans, signing autographs, taking photos. They stayed back a few feet to let Mike finish. Kyle waved at him, and Mike tipped his hat with a smile and a finger in the air, letting him know he was almost done.

It was around this time, while Kyle and Abby were canoodling next to Paige and she was starting to feel like a third wheel again, that she stepped away a few feet, turning to take in the scene—horses, riders, fans, bulls, steers. Then, out of the corner of her eye, she noticed a guy standing alone, off to the side, just like she was. He was leaning back against a metal corral fence, staring down at his phone, one elbow crooked in the rail behind him, one boot bent into the lower rung of the fence, his head low so that his cowboy hat tilted over his face. He almost looked like one of those metal cut-out cowboy silhouettes that people stand up against the side of a barn. Paige started to smile, thinking how ridiculous it was that she just thought of a directly-in-front-of-her, real-life man as a replica metal cut-out. This man clearly *was* a cowboy, not a fake. And clearly a *man* too. And good-looking at that. He was tall, maybe six-three, with broad shoulders that stretched against his gray T-shirt and black vest, and long-legged, filling out his well-worn jeans in all the right places.

As Paige tried not to be obvious about her ogling, she turned toward the corral just as a steer ambled toward her, breathing loudly, stopping two feet away, the fence between them a barrier. Paige and the steer were in a staring contest, face-to-face. She hoped the cowboy wasn't watching as she pulled her hat off her head, waved it, and hissed at the steer with as much menace as she could muster, "Shoo!" The steer, undaunted, nostrils flaring, stayed put, breathing even harder. She stuck her tongue out, tried to shoo him away again, and then, giving up, began to laugh.

She ventured a glance at the cowboy and saw a little crooked smile peek out from under his hat as he looked up at her—*oh my!* Paige's heart went pitter-patter like it never had before and caught in her throat. She shrugged as if to say, "What can I do? This steer is obsessed with me." Just then, as the cowboy and Paige were locked in a secret inside joke, both outright grinning at each other, Kyle called her over to meet Mike.

She turned away reluctantly, went and shook hands with Mike, and said stupidly, "That was quite a show!" He had a sharp jaw, black eyes, and wiry limbs. He wasn't tall but was strong and sturdy like the branches of a lodgepole pine.

He smiled graciously and said, "Why, thank you."

She could feel him assessing her, maybe wondering what the deal was with the spots on her face or maybe just looking at her the way a man would look at a woman he just met. Being polite, he asked, "You come to the rodeo often?"

"Not so much," she answered honestly, looking away rather sheepishly, and turned to Kyle.

Kyle jumped in and asked Mike, "Hey, will you be able to get away tonight? We could head to the K-Bar or to the Saloon...?"

He grinned and replied, "Actually, I have something better in mind." Then, he turned his head slightly and waved to none other than the cut-out cowboy.

As the cowboy sauntered over (there was no other way to describe his self-assured walk), Paige felt the full force of his ruggedly handsome face and bright mocha-colored eyes that were fixed upon *her* (along with a wicked grin) for just a moment before turning his attention to Mike. They grabbed each other in a rough bear hug that seemed out of place in this testosterone-filled arena. Paige glanced at Kyle, who was staring at them both in confusion—he didn't know who the stranger was either. What was even more flabbergasting was the fact that this man seemed oddly familiar to Paige, and she didn't know why. In her small sphere of friends and acquaintances, she couldn't think of a single person who looked or acted remotely like this guy, but somehow she felt as though she knew him.

She frowned and waited for introductions, which came when the two finally let go of each other, still staring like happy, tail-wagging puppies. Mike proceeded to say, "Ben, this is my cousin Kyle and his girlfriend, Abby. And this is their friend..." Mike turned to Paige with a quick apologetic frown. "Um, I'm so sorry, I've forgotten your name." So much for a set-up—clearly Mike wasn't in on the arrangement, and Paige was suddenly thankful for that.

"Paige," she said, taking the cowboy's hand. A hand that was rough and soft at the same time and brought a strange spark into her core, along with the cowboy's direct stare—the kind of stare that was unabashedly appreciative, the kind of stare that says, "I see you and I want to unearth treasures and mountains and valleys and streams and gold behind those eyes, and I could take a long time doing it and love every second of the excavation." The kind of stare Paige had never experienced before, and it shook her. She gulped and stepped back, dropping his hand as if she'd been shocked. She had a flashback to that conversation with her pa—the laws of attraction were indeed unpredictable!

Her thoughts were suddenly racing—Ben, Ben, Ben…Paige tried to think if she knew any Bens. None off the top of her head. She must be losing her mind. Then she thought, of course she didn't *know* this guy. Wouldn't she have remembered knowing a guy like *this*? Luckily, the cowboy, seeing her distress and confusion, turned his attention to Mike with a prodding grin and said, "What pansy-ass crap was that? You had at least two more seconds in you."

Mike chucked him in the shoulder and answered, amused, "Dude. No. Like you could have done better? All that matters is I *won*."

"Fair enough," Ben agreed. "I think the bull was fat. And tired. And lazy."

"Shut up, you ape," Mike retorted with a laugh. "By the way, I don't necessarily take criticism from a man who's actually, as we speak, wearing *makeup*."

Paige focused her eyes on him and was shocked that, yes, in fact, he was! Just a little bit of cake foundation and eyeliner. *Why on earth…?* Before she could process that, Ben tossed his head back in a long, easy belly laugh that sent a wave of heat up and down her spine like that feeling of sliding into a warm bath after being outside in the dead-cold winter for hours. She melted and stood staring, fascinated.

As if from far away, she heard Mike say to Kyle, "Come on. Ben's got a little place down the way. We're going there tonight."

Abby nearly screamed, "All right!" and Kyle grabbed her hand and led the way toward the parking lot as Mike, Ben, and Paige followed, but not before Abby turned to Paige, her eyes as big as saucers, and mouthed "Holy shit!" while pointing significantly at Ben.

Chapter XII

MARIE PULLED UP TO THE CRANBERRY INN and got out of the car quickly, not allowing herself to take a moment to think or procrastinate. If this conversation had to happen, which Julie apparently thought it did, then Marie was going to face it head-on. No pussyfooting around it. Whatever Julie had to say, Marie could and *would* hear it. She had learned over the years to put her feelings aside—in fact, she was quite the expert at not displaying any emotion over anything, especially not the repetitious drivel Julie had been peddling for as long as she had known her, wanting absolution that Marie would never give. Marie's lack of feelings was one of the many reasons she was the envy of the women at the club, the other mothers at school, the board members of the charities she served, and the neighborhood wives. She was bold, brave, nonplussed, unflappable. She could be counted on to get a job done without drama, yelling, or any superfluous nonsense. She never raised her voice, but when Marie spoke, people listened. If she was behind a project, it got done right, on time, under budget, and in a way that made everyone involved feel as if they had been the masterminds, as if *they* had pulled it off. Of course, in reality, it was Marie who had controlled the strings behind the scenes, not for the glory, but because she was good at it and because at the end of the day, despite her stoic exterior, she measured her worth by these innocuous successes—and by her tightly controlled mothering and household management. Competence and accomplishment ruled her, filled her, made her feel *alive*.

Walking into the 1889 hotel with its quaint, historic vibe and its wrap-around porch with strategically placed rocking chairs and wicker tables, Marie wondered why Julie always wanted to meet here. Their discussions, which had the underlying tone of battery acid, almost seemed an affront to the location or as out of place as a blizzard in summer. But, whatever, thought Marie, at least it was relatively close to her house. Once again, her goal was to get in and out as quickly and efficiently as possible. She bypassed the hotel check-in desk and turned directly to the hostess stand in the brightly lit, ornately decorated restaurant. Seeing Julie off in a corner, Marie nodded, indicating to the hostess where she was headed, and promptly walked over and sat down opposite Julie.

Marie noted that Julie looked well put together, like she always did, her hair and makeup perfect, wearing a black pencil skirt and a white sleeveless blouse, her figure toned and tight, but her blue eyes were slightly swollen, and her cheeks had tiny bursts of red blood vessels that peeked through the makeup in certain spots. Probably as a result of the alcohol, Marie thought. Julie was three years older than Marie, but the years seemed to be showing more on Julie, at least on this day. Julie seemed a little more haggard and frayed around the edges. Attractive but worn. Marie thought, well, it's only fitting. Alcohol did that to you after a while, and it was clearly what she used to assuage her guilty conscience. Marie's next thought was that it was kind of impressive that after all these years, Julie managed to not only be a functioning alcoholic, but a *well*-functioning alcoholic. Marie supposed there was something to be said for that. She wondered how Julie managed it. She must be ultra-organized, pouring herself into her work with a singular focus—probably imposing a strict routine and thorough discipline to manage it—both the work and the drinking. Well, what did Marie care? If that's what got her through the day, more power to her.

Marie saw that Julie was only drinking water and decided she would start with a thorn by ordering a glass of chardonnay. When the waitress brought it over, Marie spent a long minute fondling the wineglass before taking a long sip. Julie licked her lips and looked away.

Finally, when Marie put the glass down, she cut to the chase. "Well?"

Julie took a deep breath and answered, "Yeah, um, thanks for meeting me. You'll be happy to hear that this will be quick, and the last time."

"Oh," Marie said flatly, with little interest and a forced smile. "And why is that?"

"I've made a decision, for your sake and mine. For all our sakes, I suppose."

She paused, and Marie took another slow drink and waited. "I've decided to stop trying to fight the rules."

Marie sat there staring, not saying a word as Julie's upper lip began to sweat.

Julie cleared her throat and continued, "I feel like I've exhausted all possible avenues for change, and I've hit a brick wall. I don't know where else to turn. I've tried my hardest. You *know* the effort I've put in through the years, but—but I just can't seem to—well, they won't change, nothing will change, no matter what I say or do, so I've decided to give up."

Marie nodded, processing. Then Marie's anger flared within her breast. God, just like she did with Matthew, the woman was giving up! Fucking weak bitch! But if Marie had learned one thing these past twenty years, it was that no amount of presenting this woman with the facts made Julie realize the amount of damage caused by her actions that day. Marie assumed this last meeting was Julie's way of wanting resolution, forgiveness, or a reason to walk away scot-free. Well, Marie wasn't going to give her that.

Marie assessed Julie's cowed face with pinched lips and a steely gaze. She offered no emotion as she said, "Julie, there was really no need for you to come all this way to tell me this. I always assumed you'd fail, just like you failed that day. As I've told you before, none of your charades or wrangling with the airline industry were ever going to change a thing, least of all what you did to Matthew, what you enforced that day. I've always known you can't move a boulder with a twig. You and I both know in our hearts," Marie paused for effect and was rewarded with the reddening of Julie's face and two exasperated tears slipping out of her eyes, "that no matter what the rules were back then or what they are now, things should have gone down differently that day. And if you had only just *let me be*, Julie, I would still have Matthew. Wouldn't I?"

Julie was really crying now, shaking her head and mumbling, "No, no, that's not necessarily true—we don't know, we can never know—what—how to handle things in an emergency—what is the right thing to do at the time—we will never really know—it was a plane crash, after all…"

Marie gulped down most of the rest of her wine with a sneer, regarding Julie without sympathy. She said, "Yes, we *can* know, Julie, and we *do*, so let's just let it go at that. Are we done here?"

Julie dabbed her napkin to her face, sobbing into the cloth for a few minutes. She finally said, "But—but what about Paige?"

Marie exhaled angrily. "What *about* Paige? She *got* a life, didn't she? Probably through no fault of your own, I might add, just in case you were going down that road and taking any credit. It may have been *despite* you. Her parents had the wherewithal to ignore you, which is exactly what I should have done—"

Julie cut in with a wobbly voice, "We don't *know* that—"

"Oh, come on, sure we do," replied Marie flippantly. "There is no way that baby ended up in an overhead bin by chance. Her parents *put* her there."

"N—n—no, I don't think so, I really don't think so...when I last saw them, if in fact it *was* them, they were holding her—"

Marie held up an exasperated hand. "Listen, all right, all right, we've been down this rabbit hole about a thousand times, and I really don't have the time or energy to deal with it again. But suffice it to say someone got the short end of the stick. And we both know who." She paused to breathe hard through her nostrils, then added, slightly calmer, "Paige was just a baby and had nothing to do with the way things went down that day. I would suspect, like me, she's probably *over* you at this point. Why does she need to be burdened with your presence, your constant reminders? Why would she need *you* for that? I'm sure she's painfully aware of the fact that she will never know her biological parents—that the entire course of her life was inexorably altered that day, and not for the better. So why don't you just leave her alone?"

Julie whimpered, "I will. I have. I met with her and told her."

"Well, then," Marie said with finality, waving the waitress over for the bill. Julie was still silently cleaning her face with her napkin when Marie threw a twenty down on the check, stood up, and said, "I guess that's it."

Julie grabbed Marie's hand with an utterly wretched look. Marie paused, staring down at her fingers scathingly. Julie said with saturated sadness, "Marie, I *am* sorry. I am *so* sorry."

"Those are just words," Marie replied coolly. "Goodbye, Julie."

Marie wrenched her hand away, tucked her purse under her arm, and stalked out of the restaurant without a second glance.

Chapter XIII

Julie sat there stunned, regarding Marie's retreating form, still feeling the cold imprint of her hand. Twenty years. Three hundred sixty-five times twenty. And then some. The crash had happened in the dead of winter. It was now summer. It had taken Julie these wretched few months to build up the nerve, the resolve, the determination to speak her peace and to prepare for the inevitable ensuing fallout. Living with the pain and guilt and shame, not to mention the weight of an entire plane full of people, all deep in their graves, and not even now, when she had unburdened her soul, swallowed her pride, and apologized, could she be given an ounce of grace. It's not as though Julie was asking for forgiveness or acceptance or an acknowledgment of the hours of hard work and effort she put into the cause for twenty years. She took that in stride, like a calling, her reason for surviving, her purpose for living. But for Marie to say her apology was *just words*?

Julie took a tissue out of her purse and blew her nose. Then she flagged the waitress over and ordered a double scotch and a salad. She leaned forward, resting her beleaguered head in her hands. She rubbed her temples. She thought, just words! Good God! Those are NOT just words. They are the lifeblood that is my battered soul. Most people would have let the guilt swallow them whole. Would have killed themselves. Would have walked away from everything and everyone, never to be heard from again. Not even considering the lap baby rules, surviving a plane crash was a lot to process. The injuries, the PTSD, the nightmares. And God, the guilt for having made it out alive was sufficient to drive anyone mad! The whys and what ifs were overwhelming. In fact, when Julie thought about their fellow survivor, Terry, she totally understood and often envied him—he walked away and went back to his life, seemingly without a second thought. Not to mention, he was utterly out of touch, despite her repeated attempts to keep in contact, and could she blame him?

After what they'd been through, some people simply checked out.

It wasn't as though Julie hadn't considered it over the years.

Those first few weeks of agony, the months and years that followed, it was always in the back of her mind, like a monster nipping at her heels. It was why she still had the nightmares. And why she drank—to push away the memories and pain.

But ultimately she was a woman of action, not one to wallow, not one to avoid, not one to let the monster capture her, consume her. She had gone back to work. Rather quickly. Too soon, possibly, because that work entailed stepping back on a *plane*. Every day. To her, though, it was the only way to face her demons head-on. And she had. Back in her routine. Everything in its rightful order. That was the way. No, she hadn't run away like a cowering, trapped animal. She hadn't turned her back, pretending it hadn't happened. Didn't that count for something?

Then, in addition, as though it was standing in a bright white spotlight, she saw her mission come into focus—she would change the lap baby rules, and that would be her solace, her way to funnel the devastation, loss, grief, and pointlessness into red-hot action—a sort of panacea as well as a way to siphon meaning, purpose, and hope from those lost babies' lives. Julie wanted to use the trauma as a catalyst for positive change. And despite what Marie may or may not think, Julie wasn't solely motivated to seek a solution based on Marie's hatred. It was because it was the right thing to do. Julie saw an injustice—something that didn't make sense and could be changed for the better—so she tried to rectify it.

That was more than anyone else had done.

Why, then, *why*, was it never enough for Marie?

Or for Julie?

Julie fumed silently, chugging her drink and digging into her salad. Oh well. It was done. There. Crying about it didn't help. Spilled milk. Neither did drowning in it. Unless it was with alcohol. Numbing it was best. So, she ordered another drink.

When she finished, she paid her bill, walked over to the hotel receptionist, and asked if there were any available rooms. Julie knew she was too drunk to drive to the airport, so staying over seemed the practical thing to do. She had done it before, although it had been four or five years ago. Despite all the ugliness between her and Marie, she loved the quiet, quaint inn. And then, with a broad grin, she remembered the equally appealing tavern out back.

Screw Marie, Julie thought, her softer feelings dissolving along with her inhibitions—I'm going to make a night of it. She didn't have to be home until Monday for her next shift. And she had brought a suitcase of clothes, just in case. Room key in hand, she went out to her car and brought everything in, taking it up the grand staircase that led to the second floor. The room itself was garishly decorated with green ivy wallpaper and a matching quilt on the bed, but it was cozy and clean, so she proceeded to unpack. She changed out of her skirt and blouse and into a pair of jeans and a white V-neck T-shirt. She touched up her makeup, then brushed her hair until it fell in thick, cascading waves down her back. She grabbed her purse and headed downstairs toward a small sign that said "Cranberry Tavern" with an arrow pointing down a flight of cement stairs.

How adorable is it, she thought in her buzzed mind, that you entered this place from a separate door, like a speakeasy from the '20s. This tavern was the "bar and grill" type, with an actual wooden grill right as you walked in, presumably where the proprietor used to sit and take your two bits for a meal and a bed. She felt as though she had gone back in time, and she found it oddly comforting, a port in the storm. In the dark confines of the interior, she saw that the mahogany bar wrapped in a crescent around a shelf of liquor bottles reflected in a massive mirror along the back wall. Two bartenders in white shirts and black vests were serving the softly murmuring crowd. She breathed in the scene with a sigh—such strength and coziness to be drawn from the smell of liquor and a room full of strangers, maybe even a few lonely hearts like hers. She reveled in it, let it seep into her pores. She saw a single barstool available and went directly to claim it. People liked to come to bars in groups or to meet and mingle with one close friend, maybe two. Over the years, Julie had learned how to be invisible in plain sight—inserting herself, a single white female, in the middle of one of these groups, a perfectly positioned slot where she would be least noticed and most able to drown herself without interruption. Sure, sometimes she got hit on. Sometimes she allowed a little company, a little pass, a little flirtation, but it was not her style to seek it, and in general when it happened unsolicited, she swiftly rebuked it, only entertaining the handful who had the stamina and determination to be inquisitive without being intrusive. Those, though, she had learned through the years, were a rare breed.

As soon as she sat, the sandy-haired bartender came over with a smile. "Hey. How's it going? What can I get you?"

"A glass of chardonnay would be lovely, thanks," Julie answered, quickly taking her phone out of her purse to scroll through her social media. A moment later, she was happily sipping her wine, decompressing, in a state of perfect contentment, letting all that nastiness with Marie wash away.

Sometime later, halfway through her third chardonnay, she noticed the crowd had thinned and there were now a few barstools open. She figured it was a sign that she should be calling it a night and heading up to her room. She had a healthy, wonderful, intoxicated blurry fog going on, and she knew if she went upstairs and started flipping the channels of the TV in her room, she'd fall into a peaceful, mind-numbing slumber. Just as she lifted her hand to flag the bartender for the bill, a man plopped down next to her despite the fact that there were plenty of other open spots farther down the bar. Why the stool next to her? And he accidentally rubbed her arm when he shimmied himself and his stool closer. So awkward. She conspicuously leaned the other way. She didn't even bother to glance at him and simply chose to let her body language send a message. A moment later, she finally got the bartender's attention and asked for her bill.

The invasion-of-personal-space man said, "How 'bout one more?"

"Excuse me?" Julie scoffed. The gall of the man! But it was then that she actually *looked* at him and noticed he was handsome—actually, *very* handsome—like a just-stepped-off-the-red-carpet tall version of Ryan Seacrest, with a warm, open smile, thick brown hair, and large, dazzling hazel eyes framed by long, dark lashes.

She was momentarily stunned into silence, and she found her heart skipping a beat as he grinned and clarified, "I'm sorry. I meant, can I buy you a drink?"

Julie tore her eyes away from his gorgeous presence and answered quickly, "I was just leaving." The bartender placed the bill in front of her, and she fished her credit card out of her purse, handing it over.

Unfazed, Mr. Ryan Seacrest said, "I gathered that. But I thought since we're obviously twins separated at birth, we might like to get to know each other better."

"Huh?" she replied, thinking she heard wrong, and turned to stare, again struck by the effect he had on her now thundering heart.

She was standing beside her stool, pulling her purse over her shoulder, ready to flee the scene when he stood up beside her and held up both hands, palms in the air, as if to say, "See? I swear—check it out" while illustrating the fact that they were both wearing white V-neck T-shirts tucked into dark blue jeans with chocolate brown belts.

She couldn't help herself: she laughed.

They stood there for a second, grinning at each other, until she exhaled and sat back down. "All right. Why not?"

"Good," he said, taking the stool beside her again. The bartender came over with her bill, which she signed, and her twin ordered her another wine as she tucked her credit card back in her purse.

She noticed he ordered himself a club soda with lime, and she felt a little foolish then, wondering why he didn't drink with her. Instead of focusing on that, she teased, "I'm just glad we weren't wearing the same shoes." She held up a foot encased in a cream-colored strappy wedge. "Then I might have asked for a DNA sample."

He smiled and popped out a leg, saying, "Nope. Sorry to disappoint. Guess we're not related after all. Those are some kicks you have, but I'm more of a docksiders kind of guy."

"I see that. Well, not everyone can pull off a strappy sandal, so I forgive you."

He asked, his full attention and hazel eyes upon her, "What's your name?"

"Julie. Yours?"

"Mark."

No last names. Good. They shook hands. Julie said, "Nice to meet you. You live around here?"

"Yep, a few miles down the road. You?"

"Nope," Julie said, shaking her head. "Chicago."

His eyes got big. "Whoa, Chi-town, eh? My goodness, what on earth are you doing here at the Cranberry?"

Julie waited for the bartender to deliver her wine and then, taking a sip to quiet the rush of nerves that bubbled up with that loaded question, finally said, "Um, yeah, I had to attend to some business." She paused, making sure to keep her wits about her with this stranger whose hazel eyes were not only warm and inviting, but also somehow probing, like a camera lens that captures a person's essence without them knowing it. She added with feigned lightness, "But that's all done now, and here I am, just enjoying myself with…you."

He smiled a strange smile, a knowing smile, as if he could see right through her facade. He let it slide, though, and said, "Right. Here you are. And here I am. Cheers."

He clicked his club soda to her wine and let her sip, his eyes following her mouth as she did so.

She quickly put the glass down, a little unsettled, and asked, "You come here a lot?"

"I wouldn't say a lot, but yes, on occasion. It's convenient."

"No kidding," Julie said, thinking he's probably been married for thirty years, with three kids, probably one in college, two in high school, a boy and two girls. Using the tavern to get out of the house for an hour or two. "Did you walk?"

He chuckled, and Julie felt the thrum of it strike her in the chest like the twang of a tuning fork. "Nope, drove. You?"

"Did I walk from Chicago? Um, no," she countered with her own smirk. "Flew into Hartford and drove here. I did, however, make it safely down the external stairwell from the back of the hotel. This place is so funny, isn't it? Very quaint."

He followed her glance around the tavern and the wooden grill by the door and noted, "Yeah, I think they installed this back entrance to the basement bar during Prohibition. There's a whole history. It's quite famous. They have haunted tours in the fall, a winter solstice festival in December, and various events in the spring and summer. They just held their midsummer night's dream fete. The whole town was here."

"Wow, they certainly know how to bring history to life," she acknowledged, then added with meaning, looking right at him, "Your kids must have loved that."

His eyes never left her face, but the crinkles that appeared around them filled her belly with butterflies. He knew what she was doing and didn't care.

He answered openly, "Nah. My daughter's twenty-five and lives in New York now. Plus, she always hated these small-town gatherings—called them the bane of her existence. She was a little overly dramatic, which is probably why the moment she graduated from high school, she headed to the big city to pursue her dream of becoming an actress."

Julie breathed. One kid. Grown. "New York? No kidding. Good for her. How's that going?"

"She shares a studio apartment with three girlfriends and has two waitressing gigs. So yeah, about as you would expect." He smiled mildly.

"Ah, I see." Julie smiled. "And what does your wife think of that?"

He looked away for a moment—she couldn't tell why, but something was beneath that look, something ugly. Coming back to her face with pinched lips, he shook his head slightly and said, "No wife."

Not wanting to probe whatever that flicker implied, she instead asked, "What do you do?"

"I work in finance. Stocks, bonds, annuities. I manage people's money. Not very exciting, but it pays the bills."

"Oh, I don't know. Someone has to do it, right? It must be fun when the market goes up."

"Yes, it is, although, my clients are mostly older, low-risk investors, so I don't rely too heavily on the swings. I'm more of a steady, conservative manager."

Julie nodded. "Certainly makes it easier on the constitution. I bet you stay busy." She recalled the rows and rows of perfectly manicured yards on the drive in, not to mention the beautifully restored and maintained historic homes, plus Hartford, the nearest city, always seemed to be thriving, with new blocks of condos and high-rises going up every year. She imagined it would be quite the cash cow for a financial manager.

"I do. And you? How's your bread buttered?"

"Flight attendant for United. Twenty-four years."

"Wow, now *that* would be an exciting job. You travel all over?"

"Yep. It's wonderful and I love the adventure, but I'm often away for days, so that can get tedious. But it pays the bills, as you say."

They both stared into their drinks for a moment, then he asked, "And for fun? Hobbies? Sports? Crosswords? Sudoku? Quilting? Husband? Kids?"

She grinned up at him. There it was. They were both fishing. He grinned back as she answered, "Divorced. Forty-eight years old. No kids. I like bike riding along Lake Michigan in the summer and getting lost in a new destination from time to time, as my schedule permits—checking into an Airbnb so I can live like the natives, and I take two weeks in the spring every year to go to Hawaii and hike the volcanoes, read books on the beach, and surf a little. Is that enough intel for you?"

"By yourself?" he asked, an eyebrow raised.

"Mostly," she answered vaguely.

He liked that. After a pause, he said, "That all sounds amazing and interesting. So, where's the fly in the ointment?"

"Must there be one?" she asked, still smiling.

"There always is," he replied, more serious now, and for the first time she noticed the depth welling up in his hazel eyes, as if there was a sadness living there, a stream that ran slower and more fathomless than expected.

She frowned for a second and answered (somewhat out of character) with complete honesty, "Well, there *is* always something that can't be avoided. Can't be replaced. Can't be covered up. Can't be forgotten. But must be. In order to move on. In order to breathe. In order to *live*. Isn't there?" she challenged, her chin up.

"Yes, there is," he answered quickly, soberly.

They sat staring at each other, a wall down, a gaping crevasse opened up between them that was suddenly and frighteningly ripe for exploration.

Chapter XIV

PAIGE'S AND ABBY'S EYES GOT EVEN WIDER when they noticed the out-of-place black Cadillac Escalade in the rodeo parking lot that apparently was their means of transportation to the "little place down the way."

Paige whispered quickly to Abby, "Where are we going? Ma told me not to be out too late."

Abby let go of Kyle's hand and turned to Paige with a short giggle, saying (as if Paige was crazy to even ask), *"Who cares?"* Then she added with a wave of her hand, "It's Kyle's cousin. We'll be fine."

As if that answered anything. Paige nodded briefly.

Then Abby sidled up to her and said in her ear, "And did you see the way *that* one looked at you?" She nodded toward Ben and fake-fanned her face, placing the back of her hand against her forehead and tilting like a swooning Southern lady.

Paige nibbled on a finger and answered, "You saw it too? I'm not crazy. By the way, who is he anyway?"

Abby rolled her eyes as if Paige was a complete moron. "Oh my God, Paige, you don't know?"

"No, should I?" Paige answered hurriedly, feeling as though she was missing some critical link, but she couldn't think of what.

"Yes, you should! And I'm not gonna tell you either. I'll let you figure it out on your own." Abby crossed her arms with a grin and said, "This ought to be fun."

"Come on, Abby—you *can't* do that to me! Just tell me quickly, before we get in the car."

Shaking her head firmly, Abby said, "Naw, nope, no. Why not ask him?

Besides, Kyle thought this was a setup for you and *Mike*, so Kyle's probably completely oblivious just like you. No worries—we can play it cool and lay low. Follow my lead—we'll be observers. We'll let the guys have their fun and sit back and watch."

Paige wasn't satisfied but didn't have the time to push the matter, despite her growing frustration with the mystery of the cowboy and the unknown location and just about everything else about this night, which was all completely out of her comfort zone.

They piled into the Escalade, holding their hats in their hands. Paige tried not to look too closely at Ben in the rearview mirror as she caught him grinning at her several times while driving away from Gardiner. He was chatting with Mike and Kyle about the rodeo. There were a lot of loud guffaws and ribbing, and it felt so foreign to Paige (having grown up an only child in a quiet household) that she simply sat back and listened and watched and marveled. Sometimes Abby looked at her and shook her head at the outrageous things coming out of the guys' mouths. Paige couldn't help but laugh, wondering at the difference between men and women. The guys' interactions were so much more feral, crude, and base than Paige's and her girlfriends. The only time she remembered her friends getting loud about anything was when they were laughing hysterically or sobbing. With the guys, it was as if they had to one-up each other with their slaps, punches, and voices in order to feel their own significance.

After twenty minutes, Ben turned down a long gravel road that went up and over a ridge, finally ending on a paved circular driveway with the profile of a huge log cabin in the background, the Yellowstone River rushing behind it, a slash of movement behind a massive monolith. He pulled into one of the bays of the four-car garage, cut the engine, turned in his seat, and said, "Welcome to my home away from home."

He jumped out of the car and opened the back door for Paige before she had a chance to get it herself. Right out of some Renaissance fair, he said with a funny accent, "Welcome, Milady," with a wave of his hand. Paige mumbled "thanks" as she stared at his crooked smile and felt herself drawn back into the mystery of this man. So, he didn't live here, but he had a house here, and an expensive one at that. And he wore makeup and looked like a cowboy. It made no sense—Paige thought she knew most of the families in the area, including the owners of the large ranches, which was where the money in the valley came from, but she'd never seen this place before. It wasn't visible from the road, but still, it was strange that she didn't know who owned it. Plus, with Abby's veiled hints, Paige knew he must be someone important. Maybe he was somehow associated with Sage Lodge—one of the managers there? An owner? An event planner?

Paige had an even bigger question: Why was he paying her so much attention? Was it her encounter with the steer? So ridiculous. He probably thought her a silly girl. But the way he was watching her was with the eyes of a man on a woman, not a girl.

Ben led them up the stairs from the garage into the main living area, and they found themselves under a colossal cathedral ceiling supported by barn beams the size of tree trunks, a fireplace right out of *Citizen Kane*, and a Western-themed rug that spanned the wide-board hickory floors like a basketball court in the middle of an arena. One entire wall was made of glass and overlooked the mighty Yellowstone and a mountain reflected against the beginnings of a dusky starry sky.

Kyle's next words voiced the thoughts and opinions of all: "*Dude.* What is this place?"

So much for a *little* place down the way. Who *was* this guy?

Ben looked back at him with a chuckle and an earnestness that showed his own enthusiasm and admiration. He said, "Yeah, that's what I said when I first saw it. It's pretty cool, isn't it? We've been here two months already this season, and looks like we'll be here at least another two. We're behind schedule."

Kyle asked, "Who's 'we'?"

Ben answered airily, "The cast and crew. This place is owned by one of the executive producers. He's letting us stay here while we shoot. But the whole lot of them flew back to LA this morning because we're on a four-day hiatus while they scout a new location for next week's shoot. Sooo…tonight we have the place to ourselves. Can I get y'all a drink?"

If Ben had turned around from his saunter into the kitchen during this soliloquy, he would have laughed at Paige's Mack-truck-of-a-gaping mouth. She felt as though she had landed on the moon. She was having an out-of-body experience. She realized with a start and a snapping shut of her jaw that this man—this cowboy—this Ben guy—was *that* Ben, *that* hot actor on *that* hot TV show that everyone was watching and talking about. The modern-day Western. Okay, so maybe he wasn't a cowboy after all, but he certainly knew how to play one. OMG, he *really* knew how to play one.

Paige, being too busy with life and work and family—and more importantly, not a big TV watcher—hadn't seen a single episode, but she didn't live under a rock. She knew about the show, and more importantly, she knew about *him*. Every female under the age of fifty probably knew. There were memes and GIFs galore with him—swinging his long legs off a saddle, ripping a wet shirt off his back, nodding his head down at a beautiful actress's face with a tip of his cowboy hat and saying, "Babe, if that's what you want from me, I'll do that for you." Even Paige, who rarely paid attention to these things, now remembered several renderings sliding into her DMs over the past few years by drooling friends and by Abby herself, who was a total shithead for not giving Paige the big reveal at the rodeo. Paige turned to her now and scowled, to which Abby simply shrugged innocently with a toothy grin.

The show was one of those phenomena that come along rarely in the over-saturated world of streaming services, cluttered networks, and ad nauseam series. Apparently the show drew buzz and chatter like flies to a summer picnic. Literally everywhere. It was well written, well acted, and filled with violence and sex, the two magical elements that made a show stand out. Granted, it wasn't just the worldwide sensation that made Paige stand there gaping, but also the fact that the series was being filmed right outside her doorstep. Although most of the people involved set up shop in Bozeman, it was hard to miss when non-tourist newcomers were seen around town for more than a week at a time. Just as in any other small town, people talked. Who were these people? Where did they come from? They were dressed differently and acted differently from the locals. They had accents, fancy clothes and cars, and pretentious airs. They spent money like water in the local restaurants and shops, so no one was necessarily complaining, but still, it wasn't like your typical tourist or hiker or fisherman, and there were definitely a lot of rumors and questions, with few concrete answers. These Hollywood types were putting down stakes, and they were as strange to the people of Emigrant as their massive filming equipment, tractor trailers, and private jets.

Once their mission was clear, everyone could see their logic. After all, this valley wasn't called Paradise for nothing. You couldn't miss the majestic thousand-acre vistas that dotted the landscape. And Paige was certain of one thing: filming in the middle of nowhere Montana had to be cheaper and more realistic than on a studio lot in Hollywood. There would certainly be no way to recreate the splendor that was Paige's everyday backyard with smoke and mirrors. Where she lived, where Paige called home, was the real deal and could not be faked or reimagined, even with all of Hollywood's millions and powers of imagination.

But until this very second, Paige honestly hadn't taken heed of any of it. Sure, she'd heard the customers, waitstaff, and chefs at Chico, not to mention her friends, chatting about the movie industry coming to Montana, but she'd brushed it off as inconsequential to her daily life in Emigrant. So what if a bunch of random fancy people used this beautiful slice of land to create their art and amass their millions—what did that have to do with her?

Now she was thinking to herself how she should have paid more attention.

Also, the funny thing was that Paige actually *knew* someone who worked on the show. Shae, who was dating the bartender at Chico, was a costume designer on the set. Paige had never once thought to ask her (much to her regret now!), "Hey, do you enjoy working with those actors? Do you get to meet and hang out with them at all? What are they like? Are they cocky? Snobby? Stupid? Funny? Full of themselves?" And more importantly, "What about that one actor—what's his name—Ben? What's *he* like?"

Even now, she was kicking herself. She couldn't even think of his last name. Ben—? Something or other. Richmond? Richards? Richter?

Thankfully, as these racing thoughts were ping-ponging like fireworks in Paige's mind, Ben was distracted in the kitchen, pulling Bozone beers out of the fridge, so she quickly whipped out her phone and typed "Ben actor western show" and up came a dazzling photo of him with the name "Ben Richfield" underneath the caption.

Ben Richfield!

Oh. My. God. Ben. Richfield. In the flesh. Gulp.

He came back into the living room, handing each of them a beer, and took note of Paige swiftly and furtively hiding her phone in her pocket while her face revealed an inner turmoil akin to a swirling tidal wave. She sat down on an enormous recliner, placing the beer unopened on the end table with the intimidating three-foot-high wrought iron cowboy lamp. Kyle and Mike cracked their cans open immediately and settled into a brown leather couch as Abby snuggled up to Kyle's side. She gave Paige a look like a rooster settling into a warm henhouse for the night, which Paige ignored, and then asked Ben with feigned innocence, "So, you act?"

Paige gritted her teeth and rolled her eyes. Ben brought a barstool in from under the granite countertop and perched on it with one cowboy boot slung casually on the bottom rung while the other rested on the floor. He laughed a soft, easy chuckle and said, "Well, I try, anyway."

"Oh, would I know anything you've been in?" Abby went on, that snake in the grass, trying to earn her own Oscar for acting. Paige knew she was just messing with him to see how he would respond—for Paige's sake, she presumed, but also probably because she wanted to recite every word he said verbatim to their friend group later. Was he a bragger? Humble? Smooth? Charming?

Thankfully, he didn't take the bait and simply said, "Well, I don't know… we've been filming season four of this show—you might have heard of it—it's called *The Wright Side of Paradise.* Outside of that, I've been in a few plays, one Nickelodeon show, and several really bad commercials. So yeah, I doubt you'd remember those." He smiled sheepishly. Paige watched him closely and thought, self-deprecating—that was good, definitely not a bragger. Then he deftly turned the attention away from himself. "But anyway, where do y'all work? How'd you meet? Did you grow up here in Montana? And more importantly, what do ya do for fun around here?"

Mike spoke first, with false innocence, as if he didn't already know Ben, "Well, Ben, so glad you asked. I work for the rodeo. I've been on the circuit for six years. I like long walks on the beach and a good book before bed."

Ben rolled his eyes as Kyle pointed at Mike and Ben, and asked, "Yeah, how'd you two meet anyway?"

Ben answered, "Several years ago, we filmed a scene at the Livingston Roundup Rodeo for season one, and they had real rodeo folks there as extras. I thought it was absolutely freakin' insane watching Mike ride that bull! Keep in mind, I'm a city kid. Grew up in LA and never rode a horse in my life until I started this show, so watching a rodeo, I was floored. I walked right up to Mike afterward—"

At this, Mike cut in, "You would *not* believe what this guy comes up to me and asks. He says, 'Dude, how do you do that and not break your balls?!' Now how could I not be charmed by that?" They all laughed. "We went out that night and had like, um, shit, *way* too many shots, and after that, he started stalking me, and I haven't been able to shake him since."

Ben nodded in agreement. "That's exactly how it went down, except he left off the part where he gave me about a hundred hours of unpaid lessons on riding and roping and steering. He trained me so well that even the stunt doubles say I've just about written them out of a job. He taught me how to be a great horseman, or at least how to *look* like one."

Paige, drawn into his luminescent brown eyes, said, "Wait. You never rode a horse before you got the show?"

He shook his head, giving the full force of his attention to Paige's open face. "Nope. I had just finished college and this crazy, intense two-month-immersion acting class, and my agent set me up on a whole ton of cold-call auditions, so I figured I had about a one-in-a-million chance of landing anything. Meanwhile, I was paying the bills with a few commercials here and there, not really anything substantial, when boom, out of the blue I get a callback. I was astonished. Of course, they asked if I could ride and I answered, 'like the wind' because that's what you do, but afterward I was shitting bricks."

"You owe me big-time, dude," Mike noted.

"I do," Ben agreed readily. "You saved me. There's nothing worse than humiliating yourself on national TV, let me tell you, so I'm glad you agreed to help. I don't know what I would have done otherwise."

"Probably lived for months with a sore ass and a bruised ego," Mike answered quickly with a laugh.

"No doubt," Ben agreed, then with a tiny smile curling his lips, said to Abby and Paige, "But again, I want to know more about you. Are you all from around here?"

Abby said, "Uh-huh. Born and bred."

Ben nodded politely, drinking his beer, his eyes upon Paige. She gulped, not bothering to correct Abby on the technicality that she, Paige, *hadn't* been born in Emigrant.

Then Abby added (very nonchalantly, as if talking about the weather), "Oh, and fun fact: Paige is a miracle."

"Abby!" Paige hissed. She could have strangled her as Mike's and Kyle's heads both abruptly snapped to Paige. She wasn't a blusher, but she still felt heat rise up the back of her neck and into her hairline. She wanted to crawl under the oversized coffee table with its massive coffee table book about Grand Teton. She wanted to faint, vomit, cry, scream, run out of the room. But instead, she squirmed in her seat and stared into Ben's bright liquid eyes that were just now narrowing into a sliver of curiosity.

Ben's slow, intrigued smile sent a shiver up Paige's spine as he said, "Is that so?"

CHAPTER XV

MARIE DROVE HOME IN A RAGE. As if Julie could just apologize and make up for what happened, for what she did. It was infuriating! And Marie didn't even care one iota about Julie giving up the supposed "fight" against the lap baby rules. Marie had known that was a colossal waste of time from the get-go, and Marie prided herself on not being stupid enough to jump on sinking ships. What was the point anyway? The rules would never change. It was based on money. And no one ever really changed anything for the "greater good" if money was a factor. They lived in a capitalist society. What had Julie expected? It was a numbers game—the value of one life compared to what? The inconvenience and cost of millions of passengers flying on thousands of flights every year? Marie didn't have to have an MBA to know that some pissant actuary sitting in some minuscule office somewhere already did the math and determined that the cost of saving a single lap baby's life was not worth one red cent in the grand scheme of things.

And besides, it wouldn't bring back Matthew.

Come to think of it, why had Julie set up these meetings with Marie in the first place, for years? Certainly not to make Marie feel any better. It was all selfishness to appease her own guilt, not to mention her ego. Julie had to make it all about her. Narcissist. Look at me, look at me, I'm trying to make the world a better place! Marie knew one thing—that it had absolutely *nothing* to do with Marie or Matthew. It never had. Marie was only thankful (God, was she ever thankful!) that this would be their last visit and that Marie could finally wash her hands of the woman.

When she got inside her house, she hollered up the stairs to see if anyone was home. Not hearing any response, she poured herself a glass of wine, went out to the back patio, and sat down on one of the Adirondack chairs. She sighed, letting the tension and anger of the meeting drain out of her. She watched the horses wandering around the paddock, swishing their tails to shoo the flies away as the sun set in the distance, creating dabbled specks of light on the tall grass.

Looking at this scene of beauty and splendor, Marie began to wonder why she had such a deep feeling of discontent. Dissatisfaction. With her life. Not that she thought for a second that *she* was the cause of her wanting. She knew with absolute certainty that she had figured out a way to take on life's challenges in meaningful and manageable chunks and assimilate them better than anyone she knew. In fact, it was almost *because* of this acknowledged superiority that she was perplexed.

My goodness, she thought, look at my life—*I have it all.* A beautiful home, a beautiful family. She never had to worry about money, not even for a moment, her entire life. Growing up, she lived on a thriving cattle ranch, one that had been passed down from one generation to the next for over a century. The work was hard, but her parents were still running it well and intended to leave it to Marie's brother and his family, who lived on the property and assisted her dad with the day-to-day operations. During college, Marie met and fell in love with Kent, who became a successful architect. They moved into this house, where they made sure all of their dreams came true. As an added bonus, Kent's parents lived right down the road, in their own farmhouse, and played an active role in their lives but were also respectful of her family's independence, offering support but not horning in, which Marie appreciated. She had a well-organized household and a daily routine that was shipshape. She was safe, healthy, secure. She didn't want for anything.

But, somehow, despite all that, she did. Want. For something.

She was never quite sure what. She couldn't put her finger on it. She just knew that underneath, she was not very happy. In fact, she rarely even allowed herself to think about the word *happy* because it felt so odd to her, like those tribes in Africa that don't have a word for snow because they've never seen it.

Never seen it. Never experienced it. Didn't feel the loss of it because it was never encountered in the first place, and certainly wouldn't know if it slapped them in the face.

This was what being happy meant to Marie. At least for these past twenty years.

She reached for it every day with her utmost striving, goal setting, achievements, accolades, admiration, and accomplishments. And yet, it wasn't there. A nebulous blob floating just outside her reach. Why? She couldn't attribute it to anything in particular. She just knew she didn't have it, couldn't figure out how to get it, and was often wondering what it was all about and how and why (for all of her worthiness and success in life) others (much less worthy, in her mind) seemed to have it (so easily), to bask and revel in it (without a second thought), and she didn't (why not?).

Just as these ponderings were swirling in her mind without answers—with no pop-up revelations to feed that strange, lingering want and hunger—Kent walked across the field from his studio, his easy, casual stride showing his handsome form. He took a seat beside her.

"Hi," she said. "You want a glass? Let me get you one…"

She went to stand, but he said, "No, Marie, that's fine. Sit. Please."

She rested back into her chair, staring at the horses. They sat in silence for a while, and she could hear him breathing.

Finally, he asked, "How was the meeting?"

She shrugged. "I don't want to talk about it."

He didn't say anything, and when she looked at him, he nodded briefly with pursed lips and looked away.

She frowned and asked, "Where are the kids?"

"Mom came and got them. Said she was going to treat them to her homemade lasagna. And I presume ice cream at Meteor's later."

"Aww, that was nice of her. And your dad?"

He chuckled. "Do you really think Dad would miss out on a chance at ice cream?"

She smiled. "Right."

A few minutes went by. The cicadas and birds were chirping and the horses chuffing, their tails swishing back and forth. There was enough of a breeze to keep it pleasant despite the hot summer sun setting in the crimson sky. They hadn't had rain in a few weeks, so the mosquitos weren't too bad, buzzing around languidly but not striking. Marie thought, it's a perfect night. After all, with a night like this, who cared if she was happy anyway? Life wasn't always about happiness. Maybe it could simply be about security and family and nights like tonight where everything felt as though it was suspended in time and space, and there wasn't a need for anything more in this moment than to be here and find her bearings, stay still and absorb the atmosphere. Maybe that's all there was to life anyway.

Right as she had this thought, Kent cleared his throat. She glanced over at him and noticed with a strange, sinking feeling that he wasn't looking at her or at the scenery but was regarding his hands, which were twisting uncharacteristically in his lap. He was usually so cool, calm, and collected. She waited as he cleared his throat again and said, "Marie. Um, actually, I asked Mom to take the kids tonight so we—you and I—could talk."

"Oh?" she said, trying not to let the sinking feeling show in her voice.

"Yeah, um, I—I'm not sure where to begin."

"Kent. Begin? What do you mean? You're starting to scare me. What is it? Something with the kids?"

He looked at her then and said, "No, no, they're fine. I wanted to talk about…us."

"Us?" she asked, completely confused. "What about us?"

He searched her eyes and sighed. He said, "Marie, I'm afraid if you don't know, this is going to be even more difficult than I thought."

She waited patiently, still having no insight—what on earth was he talking about? Her brow furrowed as she drank her wine. Finally, she asked, "What do you mean?"

At that, he became slightly more animated, almost annoyed. So unlike him. "What I mean, Marie, and I hope you hear me when I say this because I haven't exactly noticed you listening to me or noticing me at all for months, if not years, but please, I'm begging you, *hear me now*—" He paused as if for effect, and she felt heat rise in her face. He said flatly, "In my humble opinion, I really don't think there *is* an 'us.'"

She reeled as if she'd been slapped.

He glanced out at the field, his jaw set, not waiting for or watching her reaction, and slowly went on, "First, let me say that I pride myself on being a man who doesn't require a lot in general—least of all attention. My parents, as you know, raised me to think of others before myself, and I've strived to live up to that creed. But, I suppose, just like anyone else, underneath I *am* human and require, on occasion, a modicum of…well, *some*thing…in return, and dare I say it?" His gaze turned back to her face, searching. "Maybe even love."

"Love?" Marie scoffed, confused and scrambling. "My goodness, dear, what *are* you talking about?"

The frustrated, exhausted, release of air that escaped his lips before replying caused her to stop and take stock, sitting up straighter in her chair. He continued, anger flooding his voice, "Yes, *love*. Do you remember the last time you said that word to me, Marie?"

Marie stared indignantly. She stuttered, "*Please*. Really? I say it *all* the time—"

"*No!*" he bit out. "You don't. Nor do you ever say, 'How was your day?' or 'How are you doing?' or just about *anything* to me directly anymore, ever."

"Well, I'm busy with the kids and their activities and my volunteer work and the country club—"

"*Stop*," Kent said forcefully, holding up a hand. "Please stop. I know your excuses. I've heard them all before. And believe it or not, I've quietly counted them all, helped your cause, taken them on as *my* burden, giving you a pass. I've allowed those excuses to roll around in my mind and fill in the spaces where there should have been a *relationship*." He paused, breathing hard, his accusing eyes piercing her heart. She stared back, the color draining from her face. "I've said to myself all these years, she needs to keep busy, to toil away at things, to sort through the complexities of life in order to simplify them and make them understandable, manageable, readily attainable. This is her way to cope, her way to get from one day to the next, her way to avoid thinking too much, about the past, about *anything* too deeply, really…this is her way to survive. And who am I to take that from her? Who am I to ask her to break her routine to attend to me? This is who she is and how she came to be, and I must fit myself into the mold we've established in whatever capacity I can. She is the hard edge in our relationship, and I must be the soft, yielding cushion. And above all else, I must learn to be self-sustaining, like she is. I must learn to be *alone*."

Good Lord, the intensity of his eyes at this last sentence! Like he was trying to drill something into her brain, an auger twisting into a hard piece of wood. And in a way, he was. She was flying somewhere in between denial and indignation, and was awakening as if from a bad dream in which someone was attempting to pull her out of a dark closet and bring her into the bright summer light of day, but instead of the sun being a welcome greeting, it was scorching her flesh and searing its heat into her bosom. She sat transfixed, not saying a word, her eyes wide, her hand shaking on the stem of her wineglass.

He continued, "But then, many months ago, or maybe it was a year ago, I honestly don't remember," he laughed a bitter, ugly laugh, "I thought, I'll try a little experiment. I'll simply stop talking to her, stop our daily conversations—other than the kids—stop everything, and see if she notices."

"Oh Kent…," Marie finally spoke up with a creeping sense of dread coursing through her veins.

His face set, he said softly, "No, no, I'm not done, Marie. I'm. Not. Done." He took two deep breaths and continued, "I foolishly thought, certainly she'll see, catch on, notice that things have changed. Like how the little notes I used to leave her on the bathroom mirror are gone or how I no longer tuck her in at night or admire a new outfit or hairdo or lipstick, or that I no longer race up from the studio when she calls me in for dinner so I can wrap my arms around her and plant a big kiss on her cheek as she finishes setting the table and laying out the food." He paused, and her heart was in her stomach. She couldn't breathe and was afraid to say a word. He said, "*Surely* she'll notice. And then, over time, even if it takes her a while, even if it will *break my heart* in the meantime, surely, she'll come back to me, and all will be well again."

She opened her mouth to speak then, but his hand was up again as he stabbed the knife deeper into her chest, "You'll laugh, won't you? At my naivete, my optimism back then, thinking this little experiment will be a waste of time because she'll come to me within a day or two, or maybe at most a week, and say, 'Kent, what's wrong? You're acting so strangely. Why don't we sit and talk and figure out what's going on here.' Or, I thought, maybe at the very least, a few weeks in, she'll say something like, 'Hey, listen, I know I've been busy and preoccupied lately, but I see a light at the end of the tunnel, and I want to set some time aside when we can get together and talk or hang out or go on a date. Just let me get through this rush, and then I'll be there for you.' Be. There. For you. This is what I so stupidly thought." Another pause. His eyes never once leaving her face, as if to hold her captive, he tore into her soul, "But I was wrong. I was so wrong. There was no pleading for a meeting, no recognition or acknowledgment that anything was even different, let alone *off*. Nothing. Nada. Zip. And you know what? Bridget noticed. Darby noticed. Even Ryan asked me the other day, and I quote, 'What's the deal with you and Mom?' That was the most observant I'd seen him since he became a teenager. And yet, you—not even a blip on the radar. Not even a *blip*." He shook his head, his mouth a thin, crisp line.

Marie's free hand had since drifted up and was covering her throat in abject horror, the light that had blinded and burned her now coming out of that dark closet and piercing her with a searing stab of awakening, a halo of pain-filled guilt, a raging terror. For maybe the first time in her life (or at least in the past twenty years), she didn't know what to do, didn't know the right next step to take, didn't know how to react.

What—what was happening? How? *How?* Not to *her*. She always had everything in perfect control, everything in order, everything *right* in the world. This was not possible. Simply *not*.

Her mind suddenly flashed like a movie reel to that snow-covered runway when she awoke to the realization that something was missing, and that something was her *son*, Matthew.

Now it was happening again.

How could that be?! Something was unraveling without her having realized it, right in front of her eyes, and (OH MY GOD) *it may not be fixable*.

Before she could speak or process or plead with him, he stood up and walked into the house without another word, letting the screen door slam behind him.

Chapter XVI

Julie broke eye contact with Mark, downed her wine, and flagged the bartender over. If she was going to unburden her soul, something she never did, she was going to need another drink. She glanced at Mark's barely touched club soda and asked, "You—don't…?"

"Nope," he answered flatly. "Seventeen years now."

"Um, okay, I see," she said, nodding slowly. "Well, do you mind if I…?"

"Of course not."

She waved to the bartender. "So…," she began, procrastinating, drinking from her new wine. "How did you…I mean, that must have been hard."

"It was," he said simply. Then, not releasing her eyes from his gaze, he said, "But I don't want to talk about that now. I want to talk about you."

She laughed nervously, followed by a cursory glance around the tavern, which was starting to clear out in places with only a handful of tables full and no one seated at the bar near them anymore. "What do you want to know?" she finally prompted, coming back to his face.

"Anything you want to tell me, but chiefly what happened tonight."

"Well, I'm sure that wouldn't interest you…I mean, it's a long story."

Not hesitating, he said, "Try me. I have all night."

She looked away, thinking, this is crazy—who tells a complete stranger their most intimate secrets right after meeting them? Nobody. Certainly not her, Julie Geiger, a woman who prided herself, above all else, on being discrete and practical. Heck, she couldn't remember the last time she'd been open and honest with her own mother, with whom she had weekly phone calls. Julie had trained herself to be pleasing and pleasant on the outside with everyone—her coworkers, her friends, her mother, her sisters, the passengers, the crew, the pilots, the airport workers, *every*one in her sphere. And this had worked well for her—she found if she was gracious, giving, kind, courteous, and considerate with others, focusing her attention on them, they rarely took the time or effort to notice her, let alone find out how she was really doing. Everyone wanted to be seen, heard, acknowledged, thought of (if only for a moment) as the most important, most fascinating thing in world. And because she was good at what she did, and because, for the most part, she *was* a selfless person, they assumed she was happy, healthy, and whole. Meanwhile, she was wound up tighter than a drum. No one in the longest time—maybe ever—had tried to break into that vault.

They assumed, and Julie let them assume, that she was fine. Sometimes on the rare occasions when she allowed herself a quiet a moment to herself, she thought about the duplicity, the raging storm that lived under the surface, a waterspout swirling out in the ocean, waiting to jump onshore and destroy everything in its wake. But she drank it down every night in the hope that it would remain contained so she could get from one day to the next, so she could function, so she could *survive*.

And yet, she was being asked by this man with the kind, inviting eyes to talk about herself—her *real* self—and she was scared, like a little girl who finds herself lost in an unfamiliar location, not knowing how to begin, where to turn, or how to find her way.

Trying to rid the tremor from her voice, she deflected with her own question first. "Have you ever gotten to a point in your life where you can't seem to find your bearings? You don't know what's next or how to proceed or even, really, how you got here in the first place? I mean, maybe you know, logistically, *how* you got here, but you don't know *why* the past led you to this place where you are now? Have you ever wondered *what now* and realized you have no answer—not a single thought or inkling of how to respond to that question?"

Mark tilted his head, like a curious dog might, and said in all seriousness, "Yes, I have. That's what I call a *crossroads*. I've certainly had a few in my time. They aren't easy. You can choose to stay safe, navigating the same path you've always taken, knowing the old adage is true: if you always do what you've always done, you'll always get what you've always got."

Julie nodded with a frown. "Right. Exactly."

He smiled a little and said, "Or you can make a change. It doesn't have to be all at once—it doesn't even have to be too clear-cut. You don't have to know right now *what* the change is. It can be one step in a new direction, not knowing what awaits on the other side."

"Hmm," she mumbled. "I guess. The problem is, I don't even know what the step looks like."

"Maybe I can help. I'm no shrink, but I've had one hell of a lot of first steps in my life."

She smiled and began, "Okay, be careful what you wish for—I have quite the tale."

"Hit me," he said with a grin.

"Okay, vital statistics. Brace yourself." She exhaled shakily and paused.

He encouraged, "Listen, there's nothing you can say that will shock me or make me run from this bar screaming. Alright?"

She nodded with a small smile, believing him. "Okay, here goes…I don't have many, or any, close relationships in my life anymore. I have difficulty… trusting. And committing. It just seems easier not to." She paused, waiting for a reaction, but not finding one in his patient eyes, she went on, "And sometimes I have trouble sleeping. That's because of this recurring nightmare I have. It's not every night, but even the fear of the nightmare keeps me from sleeping. The insomnia affects my job, not that anyone would notice—even on a bad day, I try to stay as sharp as a tack—but still, *I* notice when I'm off, and I hate that feeling. On those days, it's like hell pulling myself together and going to work. I use my absolute and unwavering sense of order, routine, and commitment to muddle through." She stared into the depths of his warm hazel eyes and said, "And the other thing I use is alcohol."

He nodded. No judgment in his eyes. Just comprehension. "And the nightmare?"

"Yeah, um, I—I," deep breath, deep, deep breath, "I was in a plane crash twenty years ago. Over a hundred people died. Only four of us survived."

His eyes got big, and he said through his teeth with something close to a whistle, "Wow, I stand corrected."

"About running from the bar screaming?" she tried to joke.

He snorted a little, serious, and said, "No, the shock. Wow, just *wow.* I can see why the insomnia. Were you injured? Knocked out? I mean, I realize it's probably hard to talk about…"

"I *don't* talk about it. Not really. Haven't, actually. Ever."

"Never?" he asked, more shock on his face.

"Nope. Well, not that I don't talk about having been in a crash. I actually talk about *that* quite often, and have, in front of hundreds, maybe thousands, of people. But the crash itself, not even once with anyone."

"Why is that?" His brow furrowed.

"I'm not sure," she answered truthfully, her own brow puckering because it was one of the many things she struggled with. "People have asked me about it over the years, of course, but I've always just said it's too difficult to talk about."

"Right—makes sense." He paused for a second and said, "Did you get counseling?"

"Yes, mandatory—they wouldn't let me fly again until they cleared me. But in those sessions, I spoke about my 'recovery'—about how I was getting by, focusing on my work. Not about that day. I refused."

He nodded. "And is the nightmare—is it from that day?"

"Yes," she said softly, looking away, trying not to invite those images into her mind, trying not to let them bleed like water into her field of vision and remove all sense of time and space and reality as they had done at the most inopportune times over the years, enough for her to fear them, to feel unable to know what the future might hold, to drink away the fears, numbing her body and mind with alcohol until the fears became fuzzy, manageable bites.

He broke into her thoughts, thankfully bringing her back from the abyss, "You were—conscious?"

"Yes. I had injuries—a broken collarbone and forearm, a deep gash on my leg, cuts and bruises everywhere, but I was awake through the whole thing. I remember *everything*."

She must have revealed something in her face because he reached over and took her free hand in his and said, "Julie, I'm so sorry. That must be awful."

The fact that he used present tense was not lost on her. Suddenly choked up, she only nodded, without a word, feeling the comfort of his strong hand and calm, caring eyes.

He waited. Then, "So, the issue with trust...?"

She swallowed and quickly wiped a tear from her cheek. She thought a moment before replying, "It's not that I don't trust people for who they are—in fact, I really love people. It's one of the reasons I wanted to be a flight attendant. It's more the difficulty I have letting people in, becoming close with anyone. Sharing with them. After the crash, I was a different person. I was in a state of shock. I was going through the motions of life but not really living them. It's partly why I got divorced. My ex, Rob, kept trying to get through to me, trying to get me to open up about my feelings, about my experience, but I don't know…I guess I wasn't ready. I shut down. After a while, he saw that all the connectedness we used to feel for each other, all the joy, well, it was gone from me and from our relationship, and when that happened, there was only so much longer he could remain for what came next. Eventually I told him to leave. It was the right thing to do." She paused, the sadness overtaking her.

Mark said, "Hmmm, I see. Well, I don't know about that…"

"I do," she answered with a sniff and a stiff upper lip. "I was pulling him down with me, and he was too good for that."

He frowned without saying a word.

She gently let go of his hand and used a cocktail napkin to wipe her eyes and nose, adding, "And then I got busy. Went back to work right away. I knew if I waited, I'd never set foot on a plane again."

"Wow, I can imagine. How was that first flight?"

"Horrible. Scary. I remember every moment. I had flashbacks, and it took everything I had to keep calm and keep moving. I purposely took a flight with a crew I didn't know and who didn't know me or my story. I wanted to be *forced* to perform my duties with no excuses. To go through the motions that were muscle memory, ingrained in my being from years of doing them. I wanted to be a robot, as detached as I could be, but I'll admit it was the hardest thing I'd ever done. After that, I kept making myself do it again, over and over. In the months after the crash, I took on extra flights, stayed up in the air as much as possible, and consequently stayed away from home. That didn't bode well for my marriage either, or any of my personal relationships."

She paused, took a gulp of wine, and forced the next words out of her mouth, looking right into Mark's eyes, "The other thing I did after the crash was go to *war*. A war that I've waged for over twenty years. In retrospect, it was a foolish war—quixotic, in fact—and I guess I should have known I'd never win. But I tried. I *really* tried. Gave it everything I had. And now it's done. And no one, literally *no one*, won."

He was perplexed, staring at her with concern. "A war?"

The dam broke loose, the blinders off, the alcohol fueling her fire, Julie told him everything about her battle to change the lap baby rules. He listened intently, diving deep with her into this strange, unknown world and coming up for air and finding none, just like her. He tried to empathize and comfort her, but mostly he sat and listened, which was enough because she realized as she spoke that it was more than she had allowed herself to reveal to anyone in years. Or ever. And maybe it was about time.

Chapter XVII

"No, no—that's *not*—that's not true—she's just kidding—*Abby!*" Paige implored.

Nonplussed, Abby sipped her beer silently with a Cheshire grin on her face.

Ben's brow furrowed.

Mike spoke up, "A miracle? Wow. It's not every day you get to meet a *miracle*. How does someone become a miracle?"

Paige vehemently shook her head and said, "I'm not a miracle—"

Ben cut her off as his face lit up like a light bulb, "Wait! I have an idea. Hold that thought." He stood up and they all got quiet looking at him—Paige especially, wondering whether he was deliberately trying to rescue her from her obvious discomfort by stifling the conversation or if he was going to ask her something more detailed that would cause this rather promising evening to sink into an unmitigated disaster. She held her breath.

He said, "I'm gonna order a couple of pizzas, and we're gonna play a game. An icebreaker. What do you think?"

They all waited to see if he would say more, but he didn't, standing there, holding his hands up in question, his eyes bright and expectant.

Finally, Mike said, "Um, sure, I'm in. Why not? I've got nothing better going on."

Kyle said sarcastically, "Gee thanks, cuz. A raving endorsement. I didn't know we were keeping you from your busy social calendar." Then he turned to Ben and asked, "What is it?"

Ben didn't wait for a response from Abby and Paige, and instead said, "Yes. Okay, awesome. Cool. One sec—let me order first." He took out his phone and ordered pizza, moving into the kitchen for a bit as Paige glared at Abby and Abby tried to ignore her. Mike ran to the bathroom, and a few minutes later they were all seated again in the living room. Ben took the recliner beside Paige, with the cowboy lamp end table separating them. Paige sat in anxious anticipation, hoping the whole "miracle" thing was somehow miraculously forgotten.

"Okay, here's how it works," Ben began. "It's called Two Truths and a Lie. We each go around and say two things that are true about ourselves and one thing that's a lie. Then everyone has to figure out which one is the lie."

Mike said with a laugh, "Dude, this is so not fair. You're an actor—how are we going to know when you're lying? You lie for a living!"

"True," Ben assented with a smile, "but the point is that only *one* is a lie. I'll begin and we'll see how it goes. Um, alright, let's see…by the way, you can make the stories as long or as short as you want. Embellish. Add color. No holds barred." He paused and scraped his finger along his chin. "Okay, here goes—my three: I nearly drowned when I was nine, I once did a commercial for zit cream, and I have five brothers."

Abby pulled her phone out of her pocket surreptitiously, and Ben pointed at her accusingly, "No cheating!" She frowned guiltily and set it down on the table with a pout.

Then they stared at him, weighing his truths and lie. At the same time, Paige was wondering in the back of her mind if she would be called on next and realized with a bit of dread that she had no idea what her three things would be. She stared at Ben and tried to concentrate.

He asked, "Paige, which is the lie?"

"Oh! Um, let's see—nearly drowned, um, something else, and five brothers…?" she said, stalling, "What was the middle one?"

"Zit cream commercial," Mike answered for him with a cheeky smirk.

Ben rolled his eyes and turned his attention back to Paige.

She said slowly, "Um, the brothers?"

"Kyle?" Ben prompted.

He replied, "The zit cream?"

Abby jumped in definitively, "No, the drowning thing."

"Mike?"

"I'm going to bow out because I know the answer."

"Come on, no you don't," Ben said at first, then reneged with, "well, shit, maybe you do. Okay." They all looked at Ben in anxious anticipation. He paused for effect and pointed at Paige with a big grin. "Paige was right. I don't have five brothers—I have one sister."

Abby cried, "No! Dang, I got it wrong."

Ben said, "Paige wins this round. So, yeah, unfortunately, I did a zit cream commercial, which by the way, is all a bit of witchery because I didn't have any acne, so they had to paint on my zits and then wash them off. All smoke and mirrors. And yes, I did nearly drown when I was nine. My dad and I took a day trip on his sailboat to Catalina Island, and we were hit by an unexpected storm and capsized. We held onto the hull for three hours until the Coast Guard arrived."

"Wow, were you okay?" Abby asked.

"Yep, for the most part—a few injuries, nothing major. My dad gave up sailing after that. Well, rather, Mom *made* him give up sailing. Anyway," he looked at Paige, "your turn."

Paige gulped. She asked, "Wait, what do I win?"

He laughed and said with a shrug, "Another beer?"

She held up her full, unopened can.

"Hmpf. Well then…let's wait until we've all had a chance to go. I'm not sure if there'll be prizes. Okay, go ahead."

Paige paused, then asked, "What's your sister's name?"

Ben answered, "Rhone."

"What does she do?"

"Um—"

Abby inserted with a growl, "Would you stop procrastinating? Come on, I have mine all figured out."

"Then *you* go!" Paige said with a stare.

"No, you're next. Just go!"

"Fine," Paige consented with a frown.

Ben gave her some time with "Who needs a refill?" Mike and Kyle held up their nearly empty beers, and Ben retrieved two more from the fridge.

Paige smiled gratefully when he came back in the room. She tried to come up with three totally innocuous things, but then she thought maybe it was better to reveal the "miracle" and be done with it. So…she needed to throw them off the scent…come up with some others that were just as outrageous or at least equally implausible. She took a deep breath and spit out, "When I was born, I only weighed three pounds, two ounces. I survived a plane crash. I can keep a Hula Hoop going for hours."

In a completely unexpected turn of events, Ben coughed out his beer and continued coughing until Mike got up and hit him on the back a few times. Then Ben apologized, and no one, least of all Paige, could figure out what had thrown him into a fit in the first place. Had she said something shocking? Well, yeah, the plane crash, she supposed. And possibly the Hula Hoop thing was silly and not very interesting…? But she couldn't think of anything else on such short notice, especially with Ben's probing eyes on her the entire time.

Once Ben was settled, waving his hand and confirming that he was not, in fact, needing the Heimlich maneuver, Abby opened her mouth to take her guess, but Paige pointed at her in warning, "Shush! No fair cheating. You can't play this round."

Abby turned to Ben with a plea, but Paige cut her off. "She knows everything about me."

Ben agreed, "Right. Makes sense. Sorry, you're out."

"Argh!" Abby cried. She lay back on the couch with her arms crossed over her chest.

Mike asked Paige, "When you say 'hours,' what are we talking—one, five, ten?"

Paige shrugged. "I don't know…three? I've never timed it."

Ben scolded Mike, "No fair asking qualifying questions."

"Seems like for an icebreaker, this game has a lot of rules," Mike complained with a grin, then said, "Okay, my guess is the Hula Hoop. Not because I don't believe it, but because I wanna see you prove it." He followed that with raised eyebrows and "I'm googling Guinness Book of World Records right now."

Paige smiled and shook her head…great, *that* would be interesting. She turned to Kyle.

"I guess the premature thing. I always wondered why you were so tiny."

"Hey!" Paige protested, "I'm five three—that's not *that* tiny."

"Compact?" he tried again with a grin.

"Mighty," she said, flexing her right bicep. She'd been waitressing since she was fourteen, so her arms were quite toned. She got a few appreciative murmurs from around the room.

All eyes were suddenly on Ben as he rubbed his chin in thought. He took a minute to answer, as if he was afraid to say which. "I'm gonna guess the plane crash. That's not true, is it?" His voice had an odd, expectant quality—as if he were willing something into being, or in this case, willing something *not* into being.

Paige stared at him, not sure what to make of it or of him.

Before she could speak, Abby screamed, "Yes! That's it! Paige was in a plane crash. There were only four survivors! They found her in an overhead bin!"

Ben blinked a few times, breathing out with a big whoosh, his eyes flashing to Abby, then to Paige, then staring down intently at his cowboy boots.

Paige felt something in her stomach plummet. She spoke up quickly, staring meaningfully at Abby, "No, that's *not* it! You're supposed to guess the *lie*. And you're not supposed to be playing this round anyway."

Kyle, ignoring that, said in a rapid-fire staccato, "Shit, Paige! I didn't know that! I mean, I knew you were adopted, but I didn't know you were in a *plane crash*. An overhead bin? How does *that* happen? How old were you? *How* did you survive? Where was the crash? What exactly—? I'm so confused. How did I not know this?" He looked accusingly at Abby and Paige.

With all eyes on Paige, she felt the familiar bubble of light-headedness that appeared like stars in her vision when people learned about the crash for the first time. She wanted to escape the room but instead sat still, mute, trying to focus and calm her breathing.

Ben's head was still tilted down, shaking slowly. After a minute, he looked up with a long stare at Paige—confusion, judgment, disbelief, perplexity—what *was* that look? She couldn't put her finger on it. She stared back, her brow just as furrowed as his.

Then began the usual wave of emotions—the uncomfortable pressure of people staring at her and judging her, the feeling that her blood was coursing toward her temples, the knowledge that others envisioned a fast-moving bullet falling out of the sky and crashing to the ground in a ball of fire. Like the stock footage of the Hindenburg disaster—oh the humanity!

These assertions, these assumptions made about her, were *not* hers. When she thought about the crash, her mind was only a void, a nothingness, a vague lack of memory tucked away behind a shield of darkness, a yearning to remember or to feel *something*. And, as in the past occurrences of her telling her story, people would instantly assume she had thoughts and feelings that had nothing to do with her, like Abby's miracle comment. For instance, they would wonder if she had survived for a reason—how and why—and all that heavy word *reason* implied.

In fact, she realized with sudden sadness, that was probably what Ben's look was about. She braced herself, trying to keep herself in check as she looked away from Ben's prying eyes and down at her hands.

Sometimes she got angry. After all, when someone survived cancer or a heart attack, the first response wasn't "You must have been spared for a reason." The weight of being "spared" and the "reason" behind the lack of death were too much to put on a twenty-month-old. Why did there have to be a reason? Why did any given person survive any given day versus any other day? Sometimes people lived. Sometimes people died. Paige didn't have a formula, not even a theory, to explain why. She didn't know how to unpack that for people—in relation to herself or anyone else. There were car accidents and construction fatalities and aneurisms and surgical malpractice and old age and lightning and volcanoes and earthquakes and about a thousand other ways to die in this crazy, unpredictable, unrelenting world. Why did she bear the burden of having *lived*? Couldn't she simply *be*, and not have to justify the why?

This stupid icebreaker suddenly felt rotten.

She stood up and stuttered, "Um—excuse me—I need to use the restroom."

Ben's eyes went from far away and distracted to worried as he regarded Paige's drawn face. He pointed mutely down the hall.

Paige fairly ran, finding and shutting herself in the bathroom. She bent over the toilet, feeling as though she might be sick, but she wasn't. She went to the sink, washing her hands and splashing some water on her face. She stared at herself in the mirror. She was so stupid! Why had she used that example? She could have chosen about fifty others! Abby had goaded her into it with that damned miracle comment, but still, Paige could have said just about anything else. Now when she came back out of the bathroom, they would all stare, including an actual real-life bull rider and a bona fide actor, and think *she* was something special. And then there would be an awkward silence followed by so many questions she didn't want to answer.

Had she just ruined the entire night?

Chapter XVIII

Marie felt her heart beating out of her chest and thrumming against her palm as she gripped her throat. She stared, horrified, at the loud slap of the screen door. As if from far away, the snow from her vision on the runway faded into the summer heat and translucent splashes of sunlight streaming through the trees from the rapidly setting sun. She saw the horses in the pasture, as if nothing had happened, and yet Marie felt as though a canyon had opened and swallowed her whole.

She didn't know what to do.

She sat there stunned.

Stunted. Stalled.

She couldn't move.

Minutes passed.

Finally, somewhere in the dark, foggy recesses of her mind, she knew she must.

Move.

This was what she did, after all.

She moved.

She took action.

She fixed things.

She analyzed complexities, parsed the intricate, deeply woven pieces into manageable, tightly packed chunks so they could be tackled, simplified, mastered, conquered.

She would do that now.

Right.

Now.

She stood up and followed Kent into the house. He was in the kitchen doing the dishes. God, he was such a good husband. He even did the dishes. How had she been so blind, so oblivious, so selfish? She saw it so clearly suddenly—as if a giant mirror had been handed to her and there was a monster staring back. A monster that had been lurking there for years, consuming her body and soul, and she hadn't noticed. It inhabited her, a willing host with a welcome parasite that kept her conscience, care, and empathy safely at a distance. Where had the real Marie gone? Did she know who the real Marie was anymore? It had been so long since she had stopped to notice or see herself, really see, let alone others.

She went to stand beside the dishwasher as Kent rinsed the dishes at the sink and placed each one separately, distinctly, coolly into the racks. Marie watched him for a moment. He barely acknowledged her presence. She was huffing and puffing, her breathing coming in shallow pants, feeling her world imploding.

Before she thought through her words, she spat out (with more challenge than she intended, immediately wanting to reel the words back in), "How are you so calm?"

The withering look he gave her then—she shrunk from it as if she'd been struck. He stopped, slamming a plate down on top of the heap in the sink. She jumped from the shock of it shattering.

His eyes on fire, his jaw set, he said, "I am not calm. Nothing about this makes me calm, Marie."

She blinked, completely at a loss as to what to do or how to react. After a pregnant pause, the water running from the faucet onto the broken pieces of china, her eyes locked on his, she said with a shaky voice, "Ca—can we—can we just talk? Please, um, can you come away from—the sink—and we can go—go sit down and talk?"

"Fine," he answered evenly, with exasperation, as if he was just going to indulge her for a moment in order to be done with it. To be done with *her*. It sent a shiver down her spine. He turned the faucet off, wiped his hands, and followed her into the living room, where he sat on one couch and she on the other, staring at each other.

"Talk," he commanded with no budge in his voice. She wanted to run away, pick up her purse, jump in the minivan, and drive to Mexico, somewhere, anywhere, and avoid—Every. Single. Thing. In. Her. Life.

And yet, it was so unlike her. She usually loved a challenge. But in affairs of the heart, she lacked strategy, direction; she was clueless, and she knew it.

She took a deep breath. She wasn't going to cry. No matter how hard her heart was pounding and her palms were sweating. That was not her style. She was going to try to do something she was equally abysmal at and unfamiliar with—she was going to put herself in someone else's shoes.

She began, "Kent. First let me say, I know you don't want excuses—"

"No, I don't," he interjected, hard, cold, done.

"I know. But—"

"No buts," he cut her off again.

She closed her mouth. Jesus, he wasn't even letting her speak!

She waited one beat, two. She tried again, really having to think before she spoke, another thing she was not accustomed to doing. "Okay. Let me start over. I'm sorry. There are no excuses for my behavior. I guess—I guess I didn't notice how bad things had gotten."

"No, you didn't," he agreed, as if she needed to hear it again!

"I can't even imagine how that must have made you feel. I was—I was taking advantage of you and your good nature, and I didn't even realize it." She stopped, breathing hard—God, she was awful at this. Apologies made her feel as though her skin was crawling with stinging ants. She forced herself to go on. "I was—was being selfish. I wasn't thinking about you, or about anything or anyone. But myself, I suppose. And what's crazy is that I don't even think I was thinking about myself—actually—I was—" The look he gave her then—she stopped mid-sentence.

He sat still, his face immobile, his arms crossed defiantly across his chest. Clearly, this tactic wasn't working. She stared away, out the window, gathering herself to regroup. She licked her lips.

Then she came back to his face and continued, "I think with the kids being so busy and our social activities, I got distracted. I lost track of time, forgot to stop for a second and pay attention to the world around me, to the people around me, forgot to smell the roses, as they say," she shrugged a little, nervously. "I get like that sometimes. I want you to know, though, that I *will* try to be better, I promise, in the future. I'll try to make it a priority."

Kent's eyes narrowed. She waited. He finally said, "What is *it*?"

"Huh?" She wasn't following.

"*What* will you make a priority, Marie?"

"Oh!" she said, still confused and flustered. "Um, you know…"

"No, I think in this particular situation, I *don't* know. I'm going to need you to fill in the blanks. Because, you see, Marie, I'm done doing that for you."

She wracked her brain. What was he fishing for? She was usually so astute—reading everyone's thoughts and wants and needs before they even knew they had them. Like a master event planner, she could host a buffet of fulfillment for everyone in her life and barely expend an ounce of energy doing so, always an overachiever, always praised for her excellent work. Why was this like pea soup that she couldn't see through, couldn't grasp, couldn't ladle out, couldn't contain, couldn't serve?

"I mean, you know, *things*…I'll try to pay more attention to things, try to be more present, try not to let things slide."

He shook his head—so angry, so exasperated, so many feelings flashing across his face. He said, "You really don't get it, do you?"

"Get *what*?" Marie was starting to get mad. Was this like a game of chess where she had to figure out the next move? She was horrible at games. She liked everything straightforward, direct, to the point. He knew that about her. *Why was he doing this to her?* Making her suffer through whatever this stumbling block was? She let out an infuriated sigh and said, "Listen, you know I hate puzzles. And drama. Can't you just tell me what it is you want from me? I'm happy to accommodate anything you ask for."

His jaw tightened and he spoke through his teeth, which Marie noted absently was *so* not like him. She'd never seen him this restrained, with *this* level of anger that required *this* level of restraint. "Good God, Marie, I'm not asking you to book a hotel for me—or—or to buy me a new pair of shoes." He stopped, fuming, unfolding his hands and gripping his knees, willing her to understand. "I can't believe I have to spell it out for you. I honestly feel sick to my stomach. It's insane, truly. The fact that I *have* to explain this to you…! What I'm asking is not that you *do* things for me. What I'm asking is for you to *feel* things for me. I'm not a piece of wood. Or a committee. Or a project. I'm a human. I'm your husband."

He waited to see if it was sinking in, which it finally was, a little, in the only way that Marie could let it sink in—slow, muddled, obtuse, but yes, there—like when you woke up in the morning and the blurry aftermath of sleep still lingered as you noticed the morning sunshine coming into focus through the window. She could now acknowledge that her husband was being vulnerable and asking for her to be emotional with him, not as his caretaker or organizer, but as his friend, partner, wife, lover. When that dawning came, though, a flood of abject fear raced into her core at the same time.

Before she could respond, he added, "And what I want more than anything is something deeper. I want to talk about Matthew."

At this, she gasped, her eyes wide.

How dare he!

He blew past her expression with "Yes, I said his name. Matthew. *Our son.* I want to talk about him, I want to remember him, I want to go through photos, I want our kids to know him and to think of him as their brother, not as a phantom shadow they're never allowed to mention or acknowledge, let alone love. I want us to feel like a complete family *with* Matthew. I want to honor his time with us, to remember him in our hearts. Even though the kids never met him, I want to feel that they know him, know how much he meant to us, how much he's still with us, in spirit, which I believe he is." He waited, watching Marie closely as she stared, transfixed—he was speaking sacrilege, taking Matthew's name in vain. He added, "But how can we do that if *you* refuse to breathe his name? Or let anyone else. You tell me, *how?*"

"No—no—no," Marie was muttering, looking away now, not letting herself hear his words, not letting herself go *there*. She put her hands over her ears, shaking her head.

Kent got louder. "Yes, Marie, *yes!*" he pressed. "You know, Matthew's death didn't just happen to *you*. It happened to me too. I loved that boy with all my heart, from the second you told me you were pregnant. Do you remember? We *both* cried over that damned pee stick like it was the holy grail. We *both* cried when he kicked in your womb for the first time, when he had the hiccups or moved around in there like a wave. On the day he was born, we *both* held him in our arms and worshipped the ground he walked on—we *both* swaddled him, bathed him, held his tiny hand, cooed him to sleep. We *both* spent every waking moment fawning over him for every meal, every diaper change, every nap time, every moment. We *both*—"

"STOP!" she screamed, unable to hear another word. Then, like a snake coiling, she hissed at him, low and throaty, "I said *stop*. Not another word out of your damn mouth!" She pointed at his mouth as if it were a dirty piece of filth.

She ran out of the room and up the stairs to the bedroom. As she slammed the door shut, she tried with the fierce will of her entire conscious mind to shut him and his words out.

CHAPTER XIX

WHEN JULIE WAS DONE TALKING, and all of the words, not to mention all of the spark and fight left in her, were gone, she paused and stared into the bottomless hazel eyes of this kind stranger and said quietly, "Yeah, so, that's my story. Thank you for listening." She wiped her eyes and downed the rest of her wine, waving the bartender over for her bill. "I suppose you'll be wanting to get out of here, get back to your life, and forget you ever met the crazy lady who talked your ear off at the local pub." She laughed a little self-consciously, looking down at her purse, unzipping it with concentration to retrieve her credit card, but really trying hard not to cry anymore and not let this man see how much her confession and revelation had cost her, how much she *did* have to thank him for allowing her to unburden her overwrought soul. She may have been buzzed, maybe even drunk, but she wasn't stupid. She knew this was just a chance encounter and that this man was overly kind and possibly paying penance for something (she couldn't imagine what), and that was why he had listened so intently and with such empathy. It couldn't be anything more than that. Even so, she was grateful, *so* grateful.

But then…he put his hand on hers, the one that was unzipping, to stop it from moving. It was a warm, soft hand, and firm, and Julie lifted her head quickly, not sure what to make of it. His voice, like butter, just as soft as his hand, said with feeling, "No, actually. I won't."

She felt her scalp tingle, as if she had walked into an electrical storm. She stared, not sure she understood the meaning of the sparks, nor what he said.

He went on, calmly, like a soothing balm, "It's late. And yes, I am going to head home. But would you be open to breakfast tomorrow morning? I can come here. Would eight o'clock work?"

She shook her head. Was he pitying her? Indulging her? She began to say, "You—you don't have to—I mean, thank you, but—I'm sure you—"

"Julie," he stopped her. "I want to see you again." He squeezed the top of her hand and then gently rubbed her knuckles.

She looked down and smiled. It felt…nice. She said, "Okay," and nodded.

They both paid their bills. She liked it that he didn't try to pay hers (despite his earlier offer) and she didn't try to pay his. They simply paid, stood up, and walked out the door, his hand lightly resting on her lower back as they went past the tavern's grill and up the back steps leading to the hotel entrance and the parking lot. Outside, he threw a thumb toward his car, faced her, and said, "Tomorrow then?"

"Yes," she answered, and he leaned in for a hug, which she readily gave, melting into his neck with a sigh that was probably inappropriate but which she could not seem to contain. Apparently he didn't mind, as he pulled her closer, letting all their smells and body heat intermingle in a lovely summer sweetness. When she finally pulled away, he looked in her eyes, and she wanted more than anything for him to kiss her, but he didn't. He smiled and said, "Goodbye, Julie. See you in the morning."

He walked toward his car as she stared after him, reminded of the fact that life, in the span of a few hours, could turn on a dime, and yet this was the first time in a long time she could remember it going from something horrible to something wonderful. It had almost always been the opposite, and what did it mean that now, after so much pain and heartache, and after the absolute annihilation of her cause, her purpose, her reason (she thought) for being, she was standing in a darkened parking lot, waving at an aberration (maybe a guardian angel in the form of a man), filled with an overwhelming sense of—what? What was it? She was struggling to put her finger on it, but she thought after a moment, yes, it was definitely something close to…*hope*.

The next morning, Saturday, she woke up with a spring in her step. She got ready and packed her carry-on suitcase as neatly and proficiently as always, but at the same time she let her mind wander into a few daydreams. She tried to remember the last time she had dated anyone…maybe five years ago? Maybe ten. She struggled to remember the last time she had even slept with someone. There was Keith in Hawaii two years ago, a ten-day fling with a surfer—so apropos. Very chill, very distracting, very refreshing, and very short. But that was two years ago...hmmm, maybe not the best track record for her. She wondered how often Mark dated. He was divorced, so he understood, just as she did, the sting of dating—the tightrope you walked with a new person—wanting to capture and siphon that nebulous feeling of first love that you felt at one time with the ex, but knowing in the back of your mind that, just like your marriage, it could turn ugly at any moment, and the person you loved with your entire being could suddenly become an enemy who filled you with the dread of a thousand cold winters.

With Rob, he was never an enemy, but she had let all that love slip through her fingers. Her winter was the chill she felt every time she was with him and couldn't reciprocate his love. She had simply turned away. She had been unworthy, undeserving, unlovable, and no matter how hard he tried, she couldn't let him take that burden from her—she was the only one who would own it, sanction it, carry it. She needed the self-flagellation, needed to feel his love turn sour—go from love to sadness to frustration to fear to struggle to exhaustion to—finally, blessedly—capitulation and surrender. He walked away, his glorious black eyes leaving a welcome cavern in their place—one of her own making—the winter of loneliness and drinking that she felt she'd brought upon herself and deserved.

Then, years later, when she got up the nerve to tackle the barren desert that was known as dating as a thirty-year-old, then forty-year-old divorcee with no children, there was the agony of defeat—not related in any way to past love, but simply the repeated torture of incompatible people trying to find common ground in a desperate attempt to fit a square peg into a round hole. She had more first dates than she could count. It was like reliving a root canal over and over, and she eventually stopped.

But then...last night. So strange for her to reveal herself like that, to bare her soul. She hadn't ever done it before, not even with Rob. She wasn't sure what power of enticement this Mark had over her—it was rather disconcerting, but somehow, she wasn't scared, wasn't running away as she normally would. She wasn't sure why, other than that she could see in the depths of his bottomless eyes that he had been through it too—whatever *it* was—he had life experiences that were as incongruous, raging, snarling, savage, and unsettling as hers. Maybe she was reading into things, but she sensed he had walked with self-hatred and courted it and all that went with it, just as she had. He had held hands with the longing for death, faced it, been its companion, wanted nothing more than for it to take hold and carry him away.

But, for whatever reason, just like her, he was still here, fighting the good fight, living one day to the next.

The difference, though, between them—and what she wanted to unearth more than anything—was that clearly he had somehow become reconciled to it, lived through the storm, sat in the midst of it, and come out the other side. Maybe he was scarred, damaged, torn, just as she was, but he was somehow still okay, still whole. She knew it, felt it in him, and wanted to understand it, to get to that point for herself. It had always been a sort of a nebulous dream for her. To imagine a happy, fulfilled life seemed traitorous, as if she were admitting to herself that she deserved to wake up that way. To feel worthy. To feel loved. To feel complete. But instead she drank, trying not to jinx the gods by wishing for it or feeling worthy of it. It was easier to take her poison with her lumps.

As she stared in the mirror one last time before heading down to the restaurant to meet Mark, she touched her lips with her fingertips and thought, but oh, to be touched again, to be savored, to be seen, to be kissed—wouldn't that be wonderful? Wouldn't that feel like an awakening? It had been so long since she had allowed herself to feel *anything* but control—so wasted and superficial. What's more, she sensed she couldn't fool this man. Couldn't pull the wool over his eyes, as she did every day with everyone else in her orbit, and so easily too, like a master magician. What a strange and alluring idea to think that maybe, just this once, she would reveal herself and possibly even be (dare she think it, wish it?) swept away. After all, what did she have to lose? She had already lost the *battle* of her life, so what was left but her actual *life*?

With that thought in mind, she left her packed suitcase by the door, deciding to come back up and retrieve it after breakfast when it was time to check out. It was Saturday, but she didn't fly again until Monday. She had booked the room for one night, but maybe, she thought with a little smile, if she let the gods see she was trying to be open, trying to be vulnerable, maybe they wouldn't laugh, wouldn't scoff, wouldn't punish her. They might even open a new door. Or at least a window.

She went downstairs, her heart fluttering in her chest, and turned the corner into the restaurant, immediately catching Mark's eye and broad grin as she swept past the hostess, then quickly assessed and appreciated Mark's thick brown hair in the morning sunlight, not to mention the casual fit of his clothes as he stood up to greet her—a white polo and beige khaki shorts. He looked her up and down too, his mouth slightly agape, noting her long brown hair, loose and casual around her shoulders, her formfitting coral top, black shorts, and tan legs. Then he quickly looked away, his cheeks a little red. She smiled.

"Good morning," he said, clearing his throat. "I've taken the liberty of ordering you a coffee. I hope that's okay…?"

On cue, the waitress delivered the coffees, cream, and sugar, and went away again. Julie sat down and said, "Thank you. This is perfect." She realized with her own blush that she was nervous. The bright light of day was so different from a dark, bustling, subterranean tavern.

"How'd you sleep?" he asked with a smile.

"Um, fairly well—" she looked down at her coffee, taking her time stirring in cream. "I—I really should apologize though—I know I talked for *so* long about—"

"Hey," he said firmly, and she looked up at his suddenly serious face, "don't do that."

"Don't do wha—"

"Don't apologize. To me. Ever. For talking about what you're thinking and feeling."

His face was so adamant that she exhaled in relief and appreciation. She said, "Okay. But—but, really," she said with a sigh, "we really don't know each other, *obviously*, and I want you to know, I've never—well, I've never done anything like that before. I think it's because I'm at a crossroads, as you so aptly put it, and I need to vent or process or understand…apparently *out loud*… what's going on…" She stopped and stared at him sheepishly. "Anyway, I guess I won't say I'm sorry, but I will say thank you for being such a good listener." She didn't bring up the drinking. Who knew how much that had affected what she said? When she drank, sometimes things became a bit blurry around the edges, but she always tethered herself in the center to ensure that she didn't go overboard or lose control. She didn't think she had humiliated herself last night (no slurring of words or stumbling into walls), but still, her inhibitions had certainly been on hiatus, and that didn't bode well for a first meeting.

She waited, though, with a measure of trepidation. Maybe she had been wrong. But without hesitation, he smiled. "Like I said, we're fine."

There was not a stitch of regret or pity or confusion in his eyes, so she allowed herself a swift smile, a sip of coffee, and a slow opening of her chest.

"Do you have a busy day today?" she asked.

"That all depends on you," he grinned.

She frowned a little. "On me?"

"Yes. I have a boat."

"A boat?"

"Yes, a boat," he repeated, "about twenty minutes from here. I rent a slip on a little lake. I sometimes take the boat out just to get away. There's a lovely island you can pull up to, mostly deserted, with a few tables and chairs. I thought maybe we could have a picnic. If you—well, if you're available…?"

She quickly inserted, "Sure, that sounds great."

He smiled. "Good."

They both sipped their coffees and grinned at each other. The waitress came over and took their order. When she walked away, Julie said, "Tell me more about your family. Are they all local too?"

"Yep. My dad—he's eighty-five now—he still lives in our house, the one I grew up in. I was just over there yesterday helping him with some yard work. He cracks me up—I told him to stay inside because it was so hot out, but as soon as I began mowing the lawn, there he was right behind me with the blower, clearing off the porch and the driveway. He never stops, I swear."

"Wow, that's amazing. He must be in great shape."

"Yeah, he is. Your, um, was it your mom you mentioned yesterday? She still active?"

"Yes, fairly. My one sister, Elaine, lives down the road from her with her husband and kids, so they check in on her quite often—pretty much daily. And my other sister is close by as well. I have to admit, I'm considered the black sheep in the family. I'm not around a lot, and I get a lot of grief about that from both of my sisters and my mom. This battle of mine—the one I mentioned last night—it's been rather all-consuming, plus my day job, and I guess I let a lot of stuff go by the wayside."

He nodded and said, "Well, one thing I've learned in my life is that it's never too late to rectify a wrong. Sounds like you'll be more freed up in the future…"

"I suppose," she said, thinking, yeah, she might be freed up, but would she really be *free*? Much of her avoidance of relationships stemmed from her lack of wanting intimacy or closeness with *anyone* after the crash, even her family. She knew they loved her and wanted the best for her, but they also didn't understand her sudden withdrawal and coldness toward them and everyone else in her life. She thought they probably attributed it to her being proud and spiteful (a little too self-sufficient), and they resented her pulling away from their attention and care, when in reality she couldn't allow herself a moment of indulgence or else she might just completely fall apart, or worse—let them in, lean on them, be willing to accept their undeserved kindnesses and care.

Thankfully (since she felt herself sinking), he changed the subject. "You know, I googled you last night."

Her eyes got big. "Oh God."

"No, it's impressive, what you've done. Your fight. The Senate hearings. The *20/20* episode. I had no idea. I know it's little consolation, but I think you're an absolute hero. I do."

Julie looked down at her coffee and said quietly, "Please don't say that."

"Why? It's the truth."

She didn't respond.

He said softly, with that deep, kind voice, "Julie. Look at me." Her head was still down, but she glanced up at him as he said, "You are."

She shook her head.

He went on, drawing her attention and her heart, "You failed to mention last night how you walked back into that plane when *it was on fire* and saved that little girl's life. *And* you were injured so badly, *and* it was in the middle of a blizzard, *and* it was during a massive plane crash with tons of casualties…!"

"I was just doing my job," she brushed it off.

"No, it was more than that," he countered.

She shrugged and looked away. She finally said, "See, the thing is—the thing that still hurts so much, that still haunts me—I told you about the current lap baby rules—what I had to instruct those parents on that plane to do with their children, but what I didn't tell you—the reason I was here in town last night—is that one of the lap babies from that flight, Matthew, didn't make it, and—and his mother, who *did* survive, she still doesn't understand how I could have told her to put her baby on the floor between her legs while the plane was going down. She feels I was negligent, and how can I refute that? I *am* to blame. And to make matters worse, I had to tell her last night that I was giving up my fight to change the rules. How do you look someone in the eye and tell them that their child, their son, was lost for *nothing*?"

He said kindly, firmly, "Julie, you didn't kill that baby. The *plane* killed that baby. And all of the other lost souls on board. You cannot be held responsible for a—a total accident—a random tragedy—a chance encounter. It was no one's fault, least of all yours."

She shook her head and wished she could believe it, wished she could accept what he was saying.

He went on, "And those years after the crash, no one would have blamed you for walking away, for saying a crash like that is almost unheard of, statistically so rare, that it's almost impossible, and what would be the point in trying to prevent anything related to it in the future? And yet you strived to create something constructive, something positive, from the aftermath. There aren't many people who can get up, dust themselves off, and continue on after a trauma like that—believe me, I know. A lot of people find themselves at the bottom of a pit that's impossible to climb out of. You didn't let it hold you down, bury you. That's a testament to your fortitude, in and of itself, *and* your altruism. You not only survived, Julie, but you channeled the trauma into something good. Don't you see that?"

She was trying to see, trying to absorb his words, trying to become what this kind, gentle man thought of her, but it was so hard. She had years of brick walls to contend with. All of her grit and determination and well-meaning perseverance had amounted to what? She remained quiet.

"Listen to me," he encouraged as she stared into his glowing eyes, "sometimes life isn't on a linear path. Sometimes life jumps around a bit—moving up and down, zigzagging like a crazy, thickly wooded path—but each of the cuts and jogs and jagged, harrowing twists and turns may still *not* lead to a final destination. It just may not be about the outcome you expected, nor the timing or direction you predicted. Life rarely unfolds the way we suppose it will. That doesn't mean the journey isn't just as important as the destination—and all of the stops and ruts and potholes along the way."

Intellectually, she knew this—of course she knew it—but in her heart she still felt like a failure. Maybe over time, with some perspective, she would come to see it another way, but right now it was fresh and raw, and not so easily assimilated.

He asked suddenly, "What about the baby you rescued?"

Julie's face finally bloomed into a tiny smile. She said simply with a nod, "Yes, a girl. Paige. She's…amazing." Julie was thinking about her maturity, her graciousness, her sweetness, her "Paige-ishness."

"So…there's that…"

"Yes," Julie said.

She took in a deep breath. She looked directly into Mark's eyes, thinking how this man was tapping into something inside her that needed tapping, but that also felt raw, exposed, and vulnerable, and she wasn't sure she knew what to do with all the emotions that went along with the tapping. She said sincerely, "Thank you. I appreciate everything you just said."

He was scrutinizing her face, waiting for her to go on, but seeing that there was no more to be said, no more she could absorb at this time, he simply nodded.

Their food came and they ate. Mercifully, he turned the conversation to lighter topics—the weather, the town, his job, his life. She listened and enjoyed his company, finding it fascinating the way he shared stories, with colorful details, and the way a lock of hair sometimes fell over his forehead when he laughed, the deep intonation of his voice, and the way his eyes lit up when he talked about his daughter. He had an easy, casual confidence that was very appealing. She wondered what his story was—the inner demons she thought she sensed earlier. How did he end up where he was today—so calm, peaceful, reconciled? If only she could draw one-eighth of that into her own life, she would be as light and bright as this room at the Cranberry Inn.

When they finished eating, they sat back and enjoyed their coffees, taking their time, watching the birds flit about outside the antique glass windows, noting the few other restaurant patrons, who seemed to be just as leisurely and sedate as they were. She was pleasantly surprised at how she felt such a comfortable ease with someone she had just met less than twenty-four hours ago. It was so unexpected, especially after the experience with Marie. What a difference a day made!

After he paid (for both of them this time, despite her protests), they stood up to leave, and he asked if she needed to get anything out of her room. "No, I don't think so, but I—" she said a little shyly, "um—I'll need to check out and put my suitcase in the rental car if...well—if I'm planning to head home later today. *Or*, um—I could book the room for another night—if I'm going to stay. What should I do...?"

He grinned with a slightly raised eyebrow. He asked, "When do you have to be back in Chicago?"

"Monday."

He said with no hesitation, "Then you should extend your stay."

She nodded with a smile and said, "Okay, let me check with reception."

"Sounds good. I'll swing the car around."

She nodded and started to walk away just as he said over his shoulder with that deep voice, "Don't take too long," which sent an electric thrill through her body. She couldn't exactly define the whys or hows of this man's quick infiltration into her psyche, but there it was—a warming pulse coursing, tightening, expanding like a heartbeat into her very marrow.

She wondered what it would be like to get lost for a day in his eyes. Then she realized with an exhilarating rush that it was only ten o'clock, and she already had!

Chapter XX

ABBY KNOCKED ON THE BATHROOM DOOR, whispering, "Paige, let me in. You okay?"

Paige took a deep breath and opened it.

Abby came in, closing the door behind her. "What was *that* all about? You looked like you might puke."

Paige glared. "You *know* I hate talking about the crash."

Abby looked down guiltily. "I know—I'm sorry. It's been so long since I've heard you talk about it and I thought, well, it *is* a good icebreaker. But I'm sorry. I shouldn't have done that. I got excited. Please don't hate me. You want to come back out? Mike's about to do his three, and I can't *wait* to hear those," she said with a soft smile, giving Paige an encouraging side hug.

Paige shook her head slowly. "I don't know…I'm afraid. Will they ask me more questions? And didn't I kind of…kill the mood?"

"Nah, it's fine—come. They think we're in here freshening up and talking about them. You know—the egos," she said, rolling her eyes, trying to get Paige to smile. "Besides, the pizzas will be here in a minute, and you and I both know that they'll forget our existence the moment that happens. Plus, Kyle went running down to the garage, looking for a Hula Hoop. I'm afraid that's one truth you're gonna have to prove to them, and after that they won't remember their own names, let alone *what* your two others were."

Paige's lips twitched up into a tiny smile. "Ugh, I didn't think that one through either. By the way, the whole point of that game was to talk about the *lie*—not the truths."

"Yeah, of course, I know that *now*. Sorry—I'm an idiot. Will you forgive me?" Abby asked with an apologetic plea.

Paige sighed and said, "I guess...*don't* do that again, though."

"I won't. Cross my heart," Abby agreed, her forefinger swiping across her chest, followed by a quick hug to Paige. Then she opened the door, leading them both out into the hall.

Paige stumbled out behind her only to be greeted by Ben the moment they set foot in the living room, back to his happy-go-lucky self, holding out a Hula Hoop to Paige and saying flatly, "Truth."

"Ugh," she said. "Really?"

"Yes, really," he answered, grinning.

Well, it was better than talking about the crash or thinking she had spoiled the evening. She stood in front of the fireplace, weapon in hand, under the watchful eyes of the crowd in the room and the buffalo head suspended over the mantel. She slipped it around her waist and began. There was a curious silence, all eyes focused on her gyrations. If she didn't have to concentrate to keep it going, she might have been embarrassed or slightly mortified, but instead she just looked straight ahead at the flat-screen TV that was hanging on the opposite wall. She blocked out their stares and smiled like she imagined the Hawaiians did when they invented this thing. About thirty seconds in, she ventured a glance at Ben, whose mouth was agape, his eyes glowing, and felt heat rise in her face.

Trying to distract everyone from focusing on her, she asked, "Is anyone timing this?"

That did it. As if popping out of a dream, Ben pulled his phone out of his pocket and set the timer. "We'll grace you a minute."

"Gee, thanks," Paige said with a nod, then turned to Mike, "Go ahead. Your two truths and a lie. I'll just keep this going in the background, if y'all don't mind."

Mike, who was also staring quite openly, said, "No ma'am, we don't mind at all." He grinned, and she felt a small twinge of regret about the fact that she had been matched with him on this rodeo "date" night, and here she was feeling the side of her face warmed by a different (even more unlikely!) prospect.

She gave Mike a conciliatory smile as he cleared his throat and began, "Okay, um, I had to really think about these because Kyle and I, we were thick as thieves as kids, and I didn't want him to guess mine. Here goes. I have a birthmark on my ass. My favorite candy bar is a Snickers. I've had these cowboy boots for ten years." He held them up, and everyone took a gander. Paige was still concentrating and Hula-Hooping away, so she couldn't look for more than a second, but the boots did have a weatherworn look about them.

Ben jumped in, very confident, with "I think the lie is the birthmark." Paige wondered if maybe as an actor, he could tell when someone was lying.

Kyle had his say. "Dude, how did you manage to pick three I didn't know? I'd say the boots. No one can keep boots that long—certainly not around here."

Abby said, "I guess I'll say the Snickers."

They all turned to Paige, "Um, birthmark." She peeked at Ben, who raised his eyebrows.

Then, all eyes on Mike, he stood up, slowly unbuckled his belt, unbuttoned and unzipped his jeans (Abby gasped), turned around, bent over, and pulled everything down enough to reveal a large brown birthmark on the upper quadrant of his right butt cheek. They all burst out laughing. Kyle stood up quicker than a cat and smacked the birthmark as hard as he could with his hand, and Mike screamed like a little girl. Chasing Kyle around the couch, Mike's pants dropped down to his knees, causing him to fall face-first over the back of the couch toward Abby, who ducked to keep from being smashed. One of Mike's hands groped clumsily for the waist of his boxers, which had nearly slipped off, and the other snagged on a piece of Kyle's shirt. Kyle shook him off and ran hollering into the kitchen. Ben's laughing eyes were ping-ponging back and forth between them and Paige, seeing if she was catching all this in between her Hula-Hooping. She was, laughing with eyes wide.

After about five minutes of shenanigans, Mike and Kyle simmered down, and Mike revealed, "Abby was right. I hate chocolate."

"Yay! I win!" Abby cried, clapping her hands.

Ben said to Mike, "Holy shit, you've had those boots for *ten* years?"

"Uh-huh, maybe more—I honestly don't remember. I've had them resoled four or five times. They fit like a glove, and I treasure them more than my favorite horse."

Kyle said with a fake pout, "That is *so* sad."

Mike tossed a pillow at Kyle's head as Paige asked no one in particular, "Hey, can I stop now?"

Ben glanced down at the timer on his phone just as the doorbell rang and, ignoring her, jumped up to get the pizzas. Paige rolled her eyes and kept going. She said to Abby, "I feel like one of those hula bobbleheads you put on the dashboard of your car."

"I think you look great," Abby replied, and Paige glared back with an exasperated sigh.

Ben went into the kitchen, telling everyone to "come 'n get it." He asked Paige, "What toppings do you like? We have sausage, pepperoni, veggie, and cheese..."

Trying her utmost to keep the concentration on her frenetic, whirling rotation and feeling thankful for the circle of personal space that was the Hula Hoop, she found herself diving into his deep, beautiful eyes that were just now boring into hers as if he could pull another truth out of her, or maybe *all* of her hidden truths. She smiled and faltered, wondering if he was planning to feed her a slice, feeling the hoop wobble in an unsteady rhythm around her waist. Her eyes got big as she tried to get it back on center, but then it tottered and spilled down off her hips and around her ankles in a clatter on the hard fieldstone hearth.

The others cried from the kitchen, "Awww, bummer, noooo!"

Meanwhile Ben's face was all innocence, saying, "Oh, I'm sorry—did I do that?" Paige flapped her hands to her sides and bit her lip. It was impossible to even pretend to be mad with those shiny eyes and crooked grin on her. He said, "Let's see, you still managed, hmmm, twenty-three minutes. Not bad. But...not hours—"

"Now, wait a minute!" Paige protested, "Y'all didn't have to prove your truths—why did I have to prove mine?"

Mike, with a mouth full of pizza, came into the room and screamed, "Hey, I just showed you my bony ass, didn't I?! By the way, Guinness Book—*one hundred* hours." Then he slapped his hand on Ben's shoulder, swallowed and said directly to Paige, "But, yes, you're right. Proof may be in order. I think it's time to google that zit cream commercial—don't *you* think so, Ben?"

Slightly vindicated, Paige smiled into Ben's suddenly scared face.

"Oh no—no no no no, you don't!" Ben snapped around and grabbed Mike's phone from his hand, and they both ran down the hallway, tag-teaming each other. Paige let them wrestle it out, glad she was off the hot seat, and went into the kitchen to grab food, wondering how else the night would unfold and how her heart would fare at the end of it.

Paige was starting to acclimate to the testosterone-filled antics, and the night progressed much the same for another hour or two, including at least ten minutes where Mike cast the zit cream commercial onto the eighty-five-inch flat-screen TV, playing it over and over again until Ben seized the remote and turned off the TV.

Abby and Kyle did their two truths and a lie, which were innocuous references to "braces" and "broken wrists" and, in the case of Abby, something about "painting her face with her mom's lipstick at the age of five." Paige knew Abby's answers, so she abstained, but the others guessed easily. Eventually, the icebreaker was over, and apparently the rules stated that no one really won and that it was all just an elaborate exercise to get to know one another, which of course worked. They settled into a slightly beer-buzzed state of comfort around the coffee table, telling tall tales of high school, the rodeo, and meeting movie stars. Coincidentally, they had all separately met or seen at least one celebrity in person (Ben's present company excluded). Paige had once served dinner to Matt Damon and his wife at Chico, Abby waited on James Spader at Sage, Kyle saw Kourtney Kardashian on the ski slopes at Big Sky, Mike met Kevin Costner at a coffee shop in Bozeman, and, of course, Ben rattled off a list of bigwigs he cavorted with on a regular basis, causing Mike to claim that Ben was living the easy life with the Kens and Barbies of Hollywood and how he was probably getting soft and needing Botox to fill in his laugh lines and a tummy tuck to maintain his girlish figure.

Ben chuckled—a low, throaty rumble—and turned to Mike with a sputter and a suddenly serious scoff. "*Please* don't lump me in with that lot. I like my face and figure exactly how they are, thank you very much, and I wouldn't change a thing."

He smiled boldly at Paige, and she sat still, feeling a wave of liquid fire dive into her chest.

Mike said, "So, that's your real nose and your real face and your real everything? No joke?"

"Yes," Ben said, rolling his eyes at Mike, then with one hand up, a pledge of truth, he repeated, "Yes, all real, genuine, one hundred percent authentic Ben."

Abby chimed in, "Thank God! I'm so over those actresses with the wind-tunnel faces and puffed-up lips," she gestured with her hand pulling away from her mouth like a slide whistle.

"You have no idea...," Ben said, sounding almost exhausted by the topic.

Good, Paige thought. He wasn't into all that superficial, fake plastic surgery crap that seemed to run rampant in California. Even in Montana, she saw people coming into town (especially with the filming these past few years) who looked as though they were right out of a shop of horrors—their faces blown back, their boobs hiked up to their chins, their skin like polished porcelain, their makeup caked on like plaster. Paige hated the whole thing, almost felt affronted by it, thinking, if she had learned to be okay with the way she looked (which was, to say the least, untraditional), why did these people feel the need to change every physical attribute about themselves? It made no sense, and when she wasn't irritated by it—about the fact that little girls were watching them and trying to emulate them—she actually felt sorry for them. What level of insecurity and culture of insipidness, narcissism, and triviality had caused this fissure in the world, where up was down and down was up? Where appearances meant more than the mind, more than unconditional love, more than the soul and heart of a person, maybe more than the person themselves? It was ridiculous, absurd, self-serving, even negligent, and more than anything, *sad.*

Ben tore his eyes away from Paige (possibly reading her thoughts—she wasn't sure) and regaled Mike with "Oh, by the way, if you want to see how 'soft' I am, my friend, I'll take a truth or dare right now."

"Oh, we're playing *that* game now, are we?" Mike challenged, his face lighting up. "Dare?"

"Dare," Ben agreed quickly.

"Let's see...race you around the house and barn. Whoever wins has to clean and polish the boots of the other."

"You're on!" Ben exclaimed.

As they went toward the front door, Paige whispered to Abby, "It's getting late."

Abby looked at her as though she was insane and said, *"And...?"*

Paige answered, "My parents might worry."

"Then call them."

Paige was too afraid of waking them, so she texted her pa and said she was staying out another hour or two. Thankfully he replied right away (at least she hadn't woken him), "Where are you?"

"At a friend of Kyle's." It wasn't exactly untrue.

"Okay, sweetie. Call me if you need anything. Be safe. Love you."

"Okay, love you too," she wrote back, then to Abby, "I'm good."

"Cool."

They were outside now. Kyle started the race with a gunshot sound clip from his phone, and they were off. Abby and Paige clapped and screamed and then fell into a puddle of giggles because it was all a total sham—Ben was ahead by a mile from the start with his long, lean legs, and Mike lagged yards behind with his bowlegs like a bike with two flat tires. The race was over in under a minute, and Ben promptly took his boots off and shoved them directly under Mike's nose, and they all went back inside, the two breathing hard, Mike whining about his defeat as Ben grabbed the shoe polish and brush from under the sink and handed them to Mike with a grin.

When they settled back down again, Abby promptly suggested, "Who's next for truth or dare?"

Kyle added, "You mean, dare or dare. We already did the truth."

Abby grinned, "Good point—dare or dare then. Paige?"

"Me?" Paige protested. "I just did a Hula Hoop for twenty-three min-utes—*you* go!"

"Fine. Dare."

"Okay," Paige said, thinking, "Hmmm, I dare you to…piggyback Kyle around the house and post it to your social media."

"I'm in!" Kyle cried, his face beaming as he stood up, dragging Abby with him as she turned around and groaned.

"I'm too little for this—he's a cow!" she protested, but Kyle proceeded to pile on, causing her to bow over like an old lady with a large, lumpy turtle shell on her back.

Paige started the video on her phone and said, "Giddyup, lassie!"

Abby was cheesing it up then, laughing and galloping around the living room as Kyle smacked her with his invisible horse whip.

Mike polished away at the boots, pouting a bit, but finally laughing along with the rest of them.

When the shenanigans were over, Paige sent the video to Abby, and she promptly posted it to all her accounts with the caption, "Truth or dare, beware!"

A second later, Abby, panting on the couch, said, "Okay, Paige, your turn."

"Ugh," Paige replied reluctantly, her laughter suddenly dead on her lips.

Abby continued with glee, "Paige, I dare you to go into a bedroom and kiss Ben Richfield on the lips for at least ten minutes. I'm setting my timer... and...*go!*"

Paige felt all the air drain out of her body, staring back and forth between Abby and Ben as if stuck in a tug-of-war. She sat stark still, frozen. But before she had a chance to think or object, Ben grabbed her hand and led her down the hall into the nearest bedroom, closing the door behind them. Once they were alone in the darkened room, with just a dim light from outside shining through the window, he whispered, very close to her face, "Yes?"

She felt her heart in her chest pounding like an African drum. She nodded and he leaned in tentatively at first, brushing his lips against hers. None of their body parts were touching. He smelled like grass and sweat and like a *man*—something she wasn't used to. He pulled back and stared, his eyes glowing embers in the half light. His mouth formed into that light-hearted crooked grin, and she licked her lips and smiled back. *She couldn't believe this was happening.* How did she go from sitting in a random living room ten seconds ago to standing in a darkened room with the hottest, most famous, most *desired* man in America? Unknown, obscure Paige Montgomery, an only child who worked at Chico Springs and lived in Emigrant, Montana, the tiniest town in the middle of nowhere.

His arms were by his sides, but she felt his physical presence like a magnet drawing her in, so before she lost her nerve, she took two shaky breaths and reached up slowly, draping her arms lightly around his shoulders, marveling at the feel of them under her hands. She turned her face up to his, and he willingly and eagerly fell to her mouth. It was an explosion, his lips on hers, like nothing she'd ever felt before. At first, he danced along the surface, clearly knowing how to tempt and draw her out, a magical, combustible energy beginning to spark and rumble in her belly, then his lips went deeper, more potent, and he parted her mouth with his tongue. She complied, offering her mouth to him fully, feeling the spark ignite and spread through her entire body like a raging fire.

He wrapped his arms around her back, pulling her to him, so their chests were pulsing against each other. He groaned, and she felt something kinetic and electric dance up her spine as his throat reverberated like a bass guitar into her core. She was pressed to him, the entire length of their bodies suctioned together, her hands gripping his shoulders, and she felt her knees wobble as he lifted her up on her tiptoes. He had a hold of her but broke the kiss for a moment to check her. She laughed breathlessly and he went back in, rubbing his hands along the length of her spine and then cupping her bottom to him as she felt the front of his jeans grow against her.

She gasped, and he murmured, "Paige…my favorite steer whisperer!" He said it seriously, like a gravelly hum, but when she drew back, he was grinning, and she threw her head back and laughed. He added, "And she can Hula-Hoop for twenty-three minutes." She giggled as he placed a stream of kisses along her jawline and down her neck. She shivered with the sensation of it. She felt such an instant liquid warmth in her body—like a river flowing down her chest and stomach and in between her legs. She laced her fingers through his hair and arched her back as his hands traced the sides of her waist, finding the soft spot of skin that was exposed under her top and grabbing onto it, his hot touch sending her into oblivion.

Then, like an unwelcome visit from the FBI, there was a pounding on the door, not a foot from where they were standing, and Abby's voice shouting through the wood, "Ten minutes are up, lovebirds! You can come out now."

Ben and Paige broke apart as if they'd been tased. They stared at each other, their breathing ragged, their chests pumping hard. Paige touched her lips, which felt plump and raw, and Ben (coming to his senses), gently wove his fingers through hers, leaned down, and said, "That was *some* dare!"

"Yes!" was her raspy reply.

He laughed a wonderful, carefree laugh. Then they both quickly smoothed themselves, Paige pulling her shirt down and running her hands through her hair as Ben reached into his pants to make an adjustment and then promptly nodded at Paige. She nodded back, and he opened the door. As she stepped through and he followed, Paige wondered if Abby could detect the essence of unrequited sex on their bodies as they walked past her without a word and arrived in the living room. In the lamplight of the room, Paige quickly glanced at Ben and saw that his cheeks were red, his feathered hair sticking up in back. She grinned and he grinned back, his eyes fixed on her.

Kyle and Mike stared knowingly between them, and Mike let out a low whistle and a "Whoa, boom-chick-a-boom-boom."

Ben and Paige didn't say a word and sat down.

Kyle's dare was up then, so Mike had him drink a small shot of hot sauce. He drank it down quickly, then jumped around the kitchen like a hyena caught in a snare, quickly dashing outside and running around in circles, screaming and hooting, and finally coming back in and chugging a quart of milk directly from the jug.

After that, things started to wind down. Paige was lost in the memory of Ben's mouth on hers, like a trace drawing that kept the impression of the original. She couldn't speak or think clearly with the heat still coursing through her body. She kept gazing over at Ben and, more times than not, he was staring right back with his inviting smile and smoldering eyes.

Abby noticed, and perhaps not sure what that meant for Paige and for all of them, finally said, "Hey y'all, we should get going."

Ben said, "Sure—I'm ready whenever you are." They piled into the Escalade, and Ben returned them to their cars in the rodeo parking lot with a promise that they could hang out again soon. Ben asked for everyone's contact information, and before he pulled away from the parking lot, he sent them a group text that said, "Thanks for a great night. Remember: Good skin is the hallmark of a good life." The quote from the zit cream commercial caused Abby and Paige to fall into a fit of giggles as Kyle waved at Mike's retreating pickup truck and then drove them home.

Abby marveled that they had just spent an entire (insanely awesome!) evening with *the* Ben Richfield! Paige spent the next few minutes in the back seat looking through online images of Ben, showing a few to Abby and garnering a plethora of "ohs!" and "holy shits!" and "no ways!" in response.

Thankfully, Abby didn't ask too many details in front of Kyle about what exactly had happened in the bedroom. Paige didn't think she could put it into words, even if Abby had asked. It was almost otherworldly.

Dropped off, Paige quietly opened the front door and saw her pa asleep on the recliner in front of the TV. She touched his shoulder lightly and said, "Go to bed, Pa—I'm home now." He jerked awake, then smiled and nodded without a word, heading upstairs. Paige grabbed some water from the kitchen and followed. In her bathroom, she brushed her teeth and stared in the mirror with a grin, touching her lips, which were still red and plump from Ben's indelible imprint. A few minutes later, settled into her bed, she shut off the lights and snuggled under the covers just as a text came through, causing her heart to jump into her throat.

"Paige, did you make it home okay? Text me and let me know. I really enjoyed meeting you. I'd love to take you to dinner tomorrow night if you're available."

Paige wrote back, "I'm home. I enjoyed meeting you too." The understatement of the year. Then she frowned, adding, "But I have to work tomorrow night."

"Oh. That's too bad."

She waited. No response. Tick. Tock.

Paige's screen went blank.

She thought, oh well, that was probably that. As amazing as the kissing was, Paige wasn't so naive as to think Ben Richfield hadn't had many other kisses with many other girls in his lifetime (who knew how many?!). And not *just* kisses either. When Paige had scrolled through the images online, there were photos (so many photos!) of him with his arm draped over the shoulders or around the waists of one beautiful woman after another. Granted, it was hard to say whether these were staged publicity shots or legitimate relationships. Who knew in this age of paparazzi, reality TV, and Twitter? But Paige wasn't stupid. He could have his pick of famous, stunningly rich and gorgeous actresses and models from Hollywood. Paige didn't want to even think about that. He was probably just bored, being all alone in that big house for the weekend. She really didn't want to be a flash in his pan or a feather in his cap. She didn't want to be anything except herself, Paige Montgomery, who was, in her own mind and in the minds of her friends and family, a great catch. She didn't want to be compared to anyone, let alone the Hollywood contingent.

Oh well. She sighed, laid her phone face down beside her pillow, not wanting to think any more about Ben Richfield. She closed her eyes and dozed off.

A chirp. Clear as a bell. Her eyes flew open. She picked up her phone. It had been eleven minutes. What the—?

"Paige?"

"Yes."

"I'm sorry, but it can't end like that."

She smiled. "Um, okay, so…?" she typed back.

"I have to see you again. I can't sleep."

She felt a slow smile in every part of her body, including her curling toes. Maybe those eleven minutes meant he *was* thinking about her.

"What about tomorrow morning?"

"Morning?" she wrote, confused.

His reply, "Now?"

She giggled. She typed about five different responses, swiftly deleting them all before finally writing, "What do you have in mind?"

"Do you hike?"

"Yes."

"I know a trail with a waterfall. Pick you up at 10?"

"Okay."

"Perfect. Text me your address."

"Okay."

"Can't wait. Night, Paige."

"Night, Ben."

Just like that, Paige's heart was exploding.

God, she thought, that kiss *was* the be-all and end-all, wasn't it? Who was she kidding, thinking she could wipe that from her memory? Her body still trembled with the heat of it, sending that same liquid feeling into her belly and groin. Maybe, just maybe, *he felt it too.* Maybe he wanted more from her than another notch on his belt. Maybe he wasn't what all those online photos seemed to imply. Maybe all the antics of the evening were just a cover for something more interesting, more meaningful. And maybe, just maybe, *she* was ready to try something new and different in her own life. The thought filled her with equal parts fear and excitement. One thing was for sure: it would be thrilling to find out.

She was going to give him the benefit of the doubt.

And herself.

CHAPTER XXI

MARIE WAS SO MAD, SHE COULDN'T SEE STRAIGHT, couldn't breathe, couldn't think. She went in the bathroom and stared at herself in the mirror, holding onto the vanity. She was red in the face, sweating, eyes wild.

All she could think was, *"How dare he!"*

She growled and repeated out loud, "How dare he!"

Then she paced back and forth between the bathroom and the bedroom, muttering, "How dare he say that we're having the *same* feelings about Matthew, as if he has *any* idea what I went through, what I've gone through every day since. As if he could possibly feel the same way I do about losing him. As if he could understand holding my baby in my arms one moment and then not the next. He has no idea what that feels like, what kind of pain that is. He has *no* idea."

Her breath was coming in jagged gasps now. She sat down on the bed for a second, then got up again, her mind in a swirl, nervous energy fueling her anger. He wanted her to talk about Matthew, to bring him up to the kids? How could she do that? Didn't he realize *(how did he not realize?!)* that every thought about Matthew, every image of him in her mind, every mention of his name shot a dagger of ice into her veins, brought her right back to that day—to the cocoon of safety in which she had secured him (in her arms) until that woman ripped him away and put him on the floor of an airplane that was hurtling like a lead arrow toward the ground. Then the horrific memories of the thunderous roar, the detonation on the ground, the snowy tarmac, the burning fuselage (both sections), her shattered feet and legs, that same woman handing her a baby *that was not Matthew!*

She put her hands to her templates, feeling an unfamiliar swell of pressure, knowing something massive was coming, like a flood that had been held off for years by a dam that was no longer able to hold. Suddenly, in a swift beat, the dam was obliterated. The gush came, a bloodcurdling scream escaped her lips, the sobs wracked her chest, and she heaved and gasped for air. She let it take over—a slave to its force—jumping up on the bed and shoving her face into a pillow, screaming and wailing, pulling her knees up under her, rocking back and forth in the fetal position.

She stayed like that a long time—maybe half an hour, maybe an hour, maybe more—completely feral, an animal trapped in a cage with no hope for release—about to gnaw her own foot off. She shrieked, cried, yelled, howled, cursed, tore at her hair. It was a time bomb exploding, a complete annihilation, an earthquake cracking her in half, all the way to the deep well of her innermost being, the part of her that was never touched, never even glanced at, never felt.

She was suspended, unable to stop, rocking back and forth, in this strange parallel universe of pain that held no time, no connection to the real world, no meaning to her daily life, to herself—Marie—wife, mother, caretaker, person.

Finally, after what felt like an eternity of torment, the screams came out as croaks, her mouth dry as a bone, her tears no longer able to flow, her head pounding. That was when she came back into her body.

She felt a dip in the bed behind her and someone's arms draw her near.

Kent.

He pulled her into his embrace and as she clung to him, burying herself in his lap, feeling his shoulders shake with hers. He was a wreck, just as she was. For some reason, this brought her comfort. The anger and agony dissipated. She was spent, exhausted. Minutes went by—ten, fifteen, twenty—until they were both quiet, still clinging to each other. Eventually, she sat up and looked at him. He rubbed his eyes with the pads of his thumbs and stared back soberly.

She said haltingly, "I—I don't know if—if I *can*." It was too hard to find the words, to make them form from this place of guttural instinct, primal emotion, this unknown otherworldly plane of torment. "I just don't know— *how*. I can't." These words had never left her mouth before. *I can't* was simply *not* in her vocabulary.

Kent's wide eyes acknowledged that as he replied, "Okay." He waited a beat, then added, "You could start by letting me in, you know."

She looked away. It was so hard. To admit she needed someone's help. To acknowledge that she had *failed* and then, worse, to let someone in to hear *how*. It seemed utterly impossible. It was not in her nature. She recoiled from all weakness, from all signs of vulnerability, from hypocrisy, from *need*. She shook her head, resistant.

Then she sighed, her shoulders slumping forward, collapsing against his chest.

She paused.

Tired. Oh, *so* tired.

She willed the smallest shred of bravery to weave back into her blood. She mumbled a whisper into his collarbone. "I'm afraid."

He laid his cheek against her head, rubbing her back, and said softly, "Of what?"

She drew back to see his face, and her eyes dove into his, an abyss waiting to devour her. "Of feeling helpless," she said, her voice cracking. He waited. She went on, "Of facing my life. Of you and the kids. Of not being able to control the things I can't change. Of the what if's. Of myself. Of *everything*."

His eyes went back and forth between her own, acknowledging this admission with quiet hesitation.

Then she added with an embarrassed groan, "Of having to apologize. It's beyond humiliating."

His lips pursed a little, and his hold on her became more lax.

Feeling her misstep, knowing she was deep into uncharted territory and unsure how to navigate, she quickly clarified, "Of losing everything I've spent my whole life building. Of losing you. Of losing the kids. Of losing what we have together."

His eyes were guarded now, trying to decipher her intent, her authenticity, her heart. He wasn't totally convinced.

She looked down at her hands and stammered, "When—when *Matthew* died," his name a scant whisper, unfamiliar and rough on her tongue, "something inside me died too. I became—a different person. I was angry, resentful, confused—wondering how this could have happened to me, what I had done to deserve such horror, such heartbreak, such agony. I guess I didn't know how to handle that, so I shut down. Maybe…maybe I'm *still* shut down. I don't know…" She shook her head, lost. She went on, "How did something that was so easy before—happiness, fulfillment, gratitude— become so hard, so *impossible*? Oh, Kent!" she cried, wrapping her arms around his shoulders and burying her face in his neck. "I'm a wreck. I know I am! I'm sorry. I recognize it! I guess the plane crash and losing Matthew messed me up. How can I blame you for telling me so, right to my face? Maybe I needed a wake-up call. Even if I don't know what to do about it." She pulled away, paused, and said pitifully, "Maybe you *should* leave me."

He was still, regarding her with some caution, but his mouth had softened a bit, taking the edge off, not agreeing or denying her words, just listening.

She continued, "I thought if I kept at it, kept plugging away from one triumph to another, with the kids, with my activities, I would eventually plug all the holes that were left in me. But you know what? It didn't change a thing. In the end, none of that mattered. I was still…vacant." She put her hands to her cheeks, letting a fresh tear slide down. In a jagged, sobbing voice, she said, "I couldn't stop his death, couldn't bring him back, couldn't fix what was broken. I can't fix what *is* broken. I don't know how anymore. I don't know *how*—I don't know what else is to be done. Oh, Kent, it's *so* hard to acknowledge it! I don't know how to be *alive* anymore—how to *feel* anymore—how to love anymore—how to be like others—how to be what is expected of me. When *he* isn't here! It all seems so pointless—like reaching for a star or some nebulous, unattainable orb that I can't grasp or understand or accept. How do I move on from that? *How?!*"

He opened his mouth to speak, but she cut him off, "And I'm still *so angry*. That things couldn't have been different, that I couldn't protect him, that I was forced to do something I *knew*—in the bottom of my mother's heart—I shouldn't do. Why did I listen to that woman? Why didn't I listen to my inner voice, my *own* gut instinct? Why? Kent, why?" Her sobs turned to growls. She shook her head and stared at him, saying quietly, "You must *hate* me."

"No—" he began, but she interrupted again, "It's okay, you can say it— I know you must. I hate myself. And I would hate you, if the roles were reversed. I wouldn't be able to forgive you. I wouldn't be able to understand. I want to know if you *do* blame me. If so, I'd understand." She knew her words were blunt, unfiltered, evil, but she couldn't help but say them—they were the truth.

His jaw was set as she wiped her tears and sucked in her breath.

His mouth opened, but this time he waited. She didn't say another word, so he took both of her hands in his and said, "Marie, I do *not* blame you. I've never blamed you. Or anyone. It was a plane crash in a snowstorm. That's all. You did what you had to do, in a moment of complete chaos, following instructions you'd been given, based on precedent and protocol, not based on anything else or any*one* else. *Not* based on you or Julie. Based on circumstance."

He moved closer to her, looking her in the eye. He said, "You survived. Only three other people did, and you know what? I'm grateful that *you* survived. Am I sad—every single day—that Matthew isn't here with us? Of course! I miss him terribly. But I also think about how thankful and lucky I am—that I have you, that I have our other kids, that I have an amazing life, that we were—*are*—so lucky to have known Matthew for that short time —that I felt his love in my heart—that he was our first child and he'll *always* be our first, the first manifestation of our love for each other in the form of a baby, our souls connected in a perfect little human. I'll always think of him that way. I choose to remember and savor those amazing days and weeks and months spent in his presence, watching his little personality and heart develop and grow. And you know what? I choose to think about him *still*, living on, in our hearts, in our minds, in our everyday lives—here," he took their joined hands and placed them on his heart, "forever."

She nodded, unable to speak, the anger gone, leaving only sadness, defeat, exhaustion.

He waited a few minutes, squeezing her hands to him, letting her sink into his shoulder for a while. When she finally quieted, he waited even longer, feeling the silence envelop them for a time. Then he gently extricated himself and stood up next to the bed. He sighed, facing her, and said softly, "Sweetie, I'm glad we talked about this. I know it's been a long time coming, and I know it's difficult, but I also need you to acknowledge that *this* can't be it. There must be more. Do you—do you...know what I mean?"

She frowned. She didn't, not really. He wanted to talk about Matthew, and she had. Well, he had done most of the talking, but wasn't that enough? He saw how it devastated her. What more could he want?

He clarified, "You said you felt vacant. Frustrated, angry. These are emotions that I can empathize with, for sure, but that I, quite frankly, in my humble husband role, can't fix." Kent tucked a few strands of hair behind her ear. He said, "Honey, more than anything, what I want for you is to become what and who you're *supposed* to be—all you're capable of being—not just what the kids and I need from you. It's like that expression: not seeing the forest for the trees. We're all guilty of missing the forest sometimes, but perhaps what's happened with you is that Matthew's death got you off course, threw you into a perpetual state of seeing to our physical and practical needs. Then your own overachieving has allowed you to stay busy and drown out the painful memories and feelings. I think you may have been missing the obvious object of those needs and activities—the heart of yourself, the heart of me, the heart of your kids. We want you to tap into that, to sort through those feelings. Yes, it will be scary. Yes, it will be hard, at least in the beginning. Yes, it will feel uncomfortable and awkward and strange, but in the end, you'll see—I *promise*—you'll see that life can be fulfilling instead of empty."

She was still staring at him with a frown, processing. It all seemed impossible to her, which she recognized was ridiculous. This was her family—she should know how to make them happy, and herself. But she didn't. Maybe she *had* been blocking everything all these years—her emotions, her feelings, her pain—all of it wrapped up in a past that she masked with an exhausting flutter of day-to-day *stuff*. And for what? To *not* feel? Was that what was happening?

He gave her an encouraging smile, acknowledging her mute perplexity. He said, "Things are going to have to change. I'm not exactly sure how—you'll need to figure that out for yourself," he added, touching her cheek, "but I'll be here to help. For instance, first of all, why don't you start by asking me how I am. Wouldn't that be a nice change of pace?"

As he grinned, she gave him a small smile back. An hour ago, she thought her world was coming to an end, and she had no idea how to face that, how to stop the flood, how to repair the crack that had formed in her perfect veneer, underneath the ground she stood on that used to bear all her weight, all her cares, all her earthly thoughts. Now she was discombobulated, scared, walking on eggshells, unsure of everything and herself. She said tentatively, "How are you doing, Kent?"

His grin turned into a fake pout. He said, "I'm rather pissed, actually."

"You are?" she gasped, her eyes getting big.

"Yes."

"Why?"

"Because what normally follows a fight and an apology from a spouse… is, well…?"

His eyes narrowed, but she was so dense, she asked, "What?"

He tilted his head and gave her an expectant look.

She cried out with a laugh, "Sex? Are you talking about sex?"

His eyes got wide, and his face broke into a broad grin.

He didn't hesitate, nuzzling her neck and breathing her in. She felt chills all over her body as she pressed her cheek into his hair. He pulled back and planted a kiss on her lips, and she felt something inside that had long been dead, barren, shriveled and was now (so unexpectedly!) warming into something pliable, subtle, open. A slight gasp escaped her lips, and he came back for a deeper kiss then, his intent suddenly nothing short of ravenous. He leaned into her, groaning.

Feeling her concrete walls shatter in a million pieces, she groaned back, scooting up the bed, pulling him on top of her, reveling in the sudden need that came out of nowhere and gripped them both like a tight, white-hot clamp. She ground her hips into his and pressed her breasts against him. His hands were everywhere, urgent, pleading, pleasing. Their clothes came off in a frenzy, their mouths finding each other as their hands explored every exposed, inviting expanse of skin and flesh like an oasis in the desert. They savored, growled, moaned, ached for each other. At some point, Marie felt she might die from the overwhelming feeling of letting herself go—so rare for her—abandoning herself to his touch, his mouth, his fingers like she hadn't done in years—maybe ever. It was almost embarrassing—the way he was affecting her, but she didn't—couldn't—stop because it felt like…*pure ecstasy*. When he had fulfilled and sated her every need, her every desire, he was inside her in an instant, exploding like a cannon and finally collapsing on top of her in a heap.

Many moments later, she lay down beside him, her arm splayed across his chest as he hugged her, rubbing her shoulder blades with soft circles as they breathed hard in unison.

He said, "Wow—I'd forgotten."

"Mmmm," she murmured, not yet able to form words.

He answered, as if she had asked a question, "About us. The way it used to be."

She grunted in agreement.

He kissed her temple. A second later, he added with a smile, "By the way, not that I'm complaining, like really, I'm *so* not complaining, but when I said what was expected from a spouse after a fight and an apology, I was actually looking for an 'I love you.'"

She laughed out loud, leaning up to peer into his shining face.

He added, "But let's just say I'm okay with your guess too."

She slapped his chest playfully and said, "Um—whoops, sorry-not-sorry."

She kissed him, only drawing away long enough so she could look into his eyes as the most lighthearted feeling washed over her—as though the dam was truly obliterated and she couldn't be any happier about that—and said, "I'm sorry, Kent. And I love you."

He kissed her and echoed, "I love you too, Marie. Always have. Always will. Now let's try to make things better."

She nodded, breathing in this new feeling. Was it that elusive word she had been imagining? The word for snow that those tribes in Africa had never experienced before and thought they never would. Was she feeling... *happiness?*

Happiness. Period.

She sunk her head onto Kent's chest, listening to his gloriously strong, gentle, and forgiving beating heart.

And smiled.

CHAPTER XXII

As Julie slipped into the passenger seat of Mark's Lexus, she felt that strange magnetic heat get into the car with them like an additional passenger. She looked over at him with a smile, and his eyes danced, which is how she knew he felt it too. And also because, just then, he grabbed her hand and squeezed. How could something with someone she barely knew feel so right so quickly? Outside of Rob, it had never happened to her before. She tried to breathe through the jitters that ran through her body at his touch and said with as much composure as she could, "Tell me more about yourself."

"Sure. What would you like to know?"

"Hobbies? Politics? Religion? Age? Social Security number?"

He laughed. "Okay, okay, slow down there. I'm gonna hit you up like you did last night, so get ready. I'm fifty-two. Divorced with one grown daughter, but you already knew that. My parents are both, thankfully, healthy and wonderful parents. I have two brothers, younger, married, two kids each. They're locals too, although my youngest brother travels a lot for work, so I don't see him very often, but I check in on his wife and kids quite a bit because they live right around the corner from me. The other brother lives about ten miles away. I like to boat, fish, run, listen to audiobooks, and, on occasion, travel."

She nodded. "Where've you been?"

"I love hiking the national parks. I just got back from Arches, Bryce, and Zion last month."

"Wow, I haven't done those yet. How were they?"

"Amazing! I'll show you my photos sometime. Like nothing I'd ever seen before."

"Sometimes I begin to think about booking a trip to Europe or Iceland or Asia, but then I think about all of the great places here in the States, and I figure, why would I go so far away when I can catch a quick flight—for free!—and be in one of the most beautiful places on Earth? Such a hassle with jet lag and customs and passports and all of that, you know? It's one of the reasons I decided to be a domestic flight attendant. That, and I suck at foreign languages." She held her hands up with a sheepish grin.

He said, "I hear ya—all English for me too. And I totally agree that there's plenty to see here in the States."

"Have you tried mountain climbing?"

"You mean with the crampons and gear? I'm a little afraid of heights, so no, not my thing."

"Me either. I'm envious of those people who do it, but I can't get myself to try it."

"I used to be a big risk-taker when I was younger, but that all went by the wayside…"

She nodded with a smile, wondering what was behind that 'wayside' comment. When he didn't go on, she redirected, "So, you run too?"

"Uh-huh, a few times a week, just five or six miles at a time. That's about all my knees can handle. I used to run marathons, and I finished a few triathlons back in the day, but I've slowed down these past few years."

The running explained his fit, lean body. She really loved the look of his forearms and hands—tan and strong. She asked, "So, the audiobooks…?"

"Right. While I run. Takes my mind off the pain." He grinned. "And before you ask, mostly boring finance books, you know, *Mad Money* and all that. I'm not much of a fiction guy. Every once in a while, I download a biography, but mostly I stick with nonfiction informational content. What about you? You read? Run?"

"No, actually, I've never been much of a runner or a reader. I love to bike, and I try to make it to the gym as often as I can, given my erratic schedule. Sometimes all I can manage is forty-five minutes in a hotel fitness center at four or five in the morning or nine at night. But summer is my favorite time of year because when I'm home, I try to make a point of riding on the bike path along the lake. It goes for miles, and it's really lovely this time of year."

"I bet," he said.

"Have you been to Chicago?" she asked.

"Yes, years ago for a work conference, but it was the dead of winter. I must admit, it didn't make the most welcoming impression on me."

She sighed. "Yeah, sorry about that. Chicago can be a fickle friend, I'm afraid. But if you come back in the summer, that's when you'll see the real magic of the city."

He turned and winked. "Is that an invite?"

"*Maaaybe*," she answered with a grin. "Let's get through today first. After all, we just met." She added sarcastically, "Um, Mark—by the way, what's your last name?"

He laughed out loud and said, "Denton."

She laughed with him and said, "Two strangers meeting in a bar—such a cliché. And I guess you already know mine."

He nodded and held out his hand for a shake. "Yep—thank you, Google. Julie Geiger, I presume." He smiled.

She squeezed his hand back. A few seconds later, she reflected, "It's kind of crazy…I feel like I've known you forever. I've never had that happen before."

He stared at her for a long moment with an appreciative glance and said seriously, "Me either." He let go of her hand and picked up his phone from the console, unlocked it, and handed it to her, "Would you mind—? Put your contact info in and then call yourself so we have each other's info. A bike ride in Chicago sounds perfect. We need to set that up."

She did as she was told, smiling with a warm glow the whole time. "I will."

They drove along in happy silence for a while, both of them ruminating on what they just said. Julie admired the pretty countryside, and Mark commented on some of the history of the area. When they parked the car at the marina, she saw how beautiful the lake was—not overly populated, the water green and clear, a great blue heron fishing beside the launch pad.

She helped him gather the picnic basket and cooler, and they walked over to the slip. When he stopped at a sleek, good-sized white-and-blue motorboat, she said, "Very nice!"

"Thanks," he said, stepping into it and taking her hand to help her on board. "I bought it on a whim a few years ago. One of my clients had a stroke and couldn't use it anymore. His wife gave me such a good deal that I couldn't refuse."

"How often do you take it out?" she asked, taking the cushy seat next to his captain's chair as he untied the boat, revved the engine, and backed out smoothly into the water.

"Not as often as I'd like—maybe once or twice a week. I like to fish, but mostly I just drive around the lake and anchor somewhere, lay back, get some sun, swim, watch the world go by."

"Sounds wonderful," she said, looking up at the blue sky and open water, thinking, not a bad life, but then also wondering in the back of her mind with a strange queasiness if he brought a lot of women here, just as he was doing with her now. She asked as casually as she could, "How many people do you normally fit on a boat this size?"

As usual, he saw right through her and laughed. His sideways smile set her to grinning. He answered, "Mostly just one—*me*. And sometimes my nieces and nephews, and their friends, so five or six rowdy kids. The nephews are old enough now that they like to wakeboard, so I spend a lot of weekends whirling them around until they're sufficiently banged up and waterlogged. My sister-in-law loves it when I take them for the day—she gets a break, and in the end I deliver them home exhausted and happy. And my little nieces just like to sit on my lap and quote 'drive the boat.'"

She laughed, picturing it. She could see him being great with kids, and that made her smile.

The boat glided easily through the tranquil water, hugging the coast as he navigated away from the shallow buoy markers. He pointed to a house that was under construction. "See over there? Mostly this lake doesn't allow residences because it's one of the reservoirs for the city, and the county's pretty strict about limiting building permits. Just having a few older cottages sprinkled around keeps the traffic down—I mean, it's kind of amazing that there are days like today, midweek, when we're the only ones out here."

She took a deep breath, sitting back in her seat and looking around at the spectacular three-hundred-sixty-five-degree views of the rolling hills and thickly wooded forests surrounding the clear, sparkling water. "Yes, it is. Simply beautiful," she sighed.

He nodded, looking around as well, drinking in the perfect weather and scenery.

They idled along as Mark shared more of the history of the lake and how he knew the owner of the marina from high school, and that was how he ended up selecting this lake to moor his boat. That led him into a story about his childhood and how he almost got arrested and expelled during the last week of his senior year of high school.

"How is that possible? What did you do?" she asked.

"Well, Tom, the owner of the marina—we were good buddies and rather the rebellious, wild kids back then. For weeks, we'd been pulling the most atrocious senior pranks on all our friends—you know, stuffing lockers with dead fish and stealing underwear from gym classes and tacking it up on the bulletin board—that kind of thing."

"I'm afraid to hear more…," she said with a laugh.

"Yeah, well, there's more," he gave her a smirk and she grimaced. She'd grown up with sisters, and she'd never quite understood the practical jokester mindset.

He went on, "Yeah, so one night we're driving home from a party at our buddy's house, which was about a mile from the school. And, well, as you might imagine, there may have been some alcohol involved. And maybe more too. There's this street sign that's fallen over along the side of the road that says 'Rough Break Ahead'—right near a hairpin turn—and Tom pulls over and says, 'Dude, we should take that and put it up the flagpole.' I couldn't even imagine what he meant, but when I realized he was talking about the flagpole at the front entrance of school, I was like, "No way," but he was adamant. When Tom got an idea in his head, especially a prank, he followed through, no matter what. So, it's pitch black out, and we're heaving this sign *and* the post it's attached to out of the ground and into the flatbed of his truck. We head to his house, which happens to be right across the street from the school, and proceed to remove the sign from the post, spray-paint a bunch of obscene things on it, changing some of the words—I'll spare you the details, but use your imagination—and we jog over to the school, pull down the flagpole rope, attach the sign to the same clip as the flag, and start running the thing back up, and it's about three-quarters of the way to the top when we hear the sirens."

"No!" Julie said, her hand to her mouth.

"Oh yes, indeed. There was a cop in the parking lot of the school that night, just hanging out—we hadn't even noticed—and that whole time he'd been watching us—saw us spray-painting the sign in Tom's front yard, saw us sneak over and try to get it up the flagpole. He just waited to see what we were up to, then boom! He beamed the bright spotlight in our faces, sirens blasting, gun pulled, telling us to put our hands up. Right out of a movie. I thought Tom would soil his pants. Stood there like a bunch of dolts with our hands in the air."

At this point, he was laughing as he told the story, so Julie laughed as well, thinking he must not have gone to jail because he wouldn't be laughing about that, even after all these years. She asked, "Well, what happened?"

"We got lucky, so lucky. The cop—Tom *knew* him—it was one of his brother's friends, so as soon as he recognized Tom, he put his gun down and said, 'Fucking hell, Tom Davenport, you little shit, what are you doing?' Tom blew out a breath—the first gasp of air he'd taken for a few beats—and said all nonchalant, 'Hey, Dewie, how's it going?' Well, Dewie clearly wanted to strangle Tom, but instead he turned the sirens off, came over and berated us, all about the consequences of stealing state property, vandalizing school grounds, desecrating the American flag—and like an idiot, Tom interrupted, 'We weren't gonna hurt the flag' and Dewie just replied, 'Shut up, you imbecile.' He went on to say we were the luckiest sons of bitches in the state of Connecticut because if we promised to chuck the sign into the forest or somewhere it could never be found and put the flag back where it belonged, he would look the other way and not arrest us or tell our parents or the principal of the school. I tell ya what, I nearly hugged the guy after that."

"I bet. Wow. Dodged a bullet."

"Totally." After a moment, he glanced over at Julie with a little grin and added, "Yeah, so if you happen to see an obscene sign pop up out of the water anytime today, don't be alarmed."

She burst out laughing. *"Here?"*

He nodded. "We tied it to a cinder block and tossed it into the lake the next day. I swear that's why Tom bought the marina when it came up for sale a few years ago. It had sentimental value to him—a reminder of the stupidest *and* luckiest night of his life."

"No doubt." She smiled over at him. He was a good storyteller, and she enjoyed learning more about his youth and the place where he grew up— so different from her childhood in a huge suburb of Chicago, where she was mostly an overachiever with few friends and even fewer ties today. In contrast, Mark seemed so grounded and connected to the people in his small-town world, both then and now.

After a while, the sun getting high in the sky, the heat coming down on them, she asked if he had any sunscreen, and he handed it over from the console of the boat. Then he offered her a drink from the cooler. There was only water, soda, and flavored seltzers—no beer or wine or other alcoholic beverages. She had a momentary burst of panic, but then steeled herself against it, feeling for the first time in a long time that she wanted to feel and remember this day, no matter what happened, with crystal clarity, like the resplendent water they were drifting over. She didn't want to numb herself like she usually did. She could be fully aware (or at least she was going to try). She wasn't sure what caused the shift in her thinking—she just knew she felt comfortable with this man with his understanding eyes, calm demeanor, and compassionate words. She wanted so much to see *how* he was so understanding. So far, he had talked about his early years and about his current life, but not much about what happened in the middle, and she had a feeling that was where the rub came in—not from the grace of years living a sterile and virtuous life, but something else. She hoped he would reveal that side of himself in time.

She declined the drink offer. After a few moments, they came to an inlet that led deeper into a long, wide finger of the lake. He pointed to a beautiful crop of land just ahead filled with thick trees, surrounded by a perimeter of sand, with a path cut through it, a welcoming invitation into the center of what appeared to be a tiny oasis. He said, "That's the island. I'm going to cut the engine so we can drift into the shallows."

A few minutes later, like a duck coming in for a soft landing, they glided slowly into the sand. He jumped off the front into the water, grabbing the rope to pull the boat closer to shore, then coming back to grab the picnic basket and cooler. Finally he helped her off, his hands reaching around both sides of her waist. For a moment their chests met, and Julie noted the flicker of light in his eyes as he smiled down at her. She smiled back, feeling a spark running through her arms as they lay upon his shoulders.

They both quickly let go and walked together up the path with their gear in tow. She commented on how amazing and secluded the island was.

"Isn't it beautiful? It was some sort of ancient Native American settlement, and you can see why—so close to everything you need for hunting and fishing. A lot of arrowheads and other artifacts have been found along the shoreline here." He looked back at her and added, "But honestly, I love it because not many people are aware of its existence."

When they got to the clearing, there was a weatherworn picnic table in the middle, two Adirondack chairs underneath a tree off to one side, and a bunch of cut tree stumps set up around a bonfire pit dug into the sand near a hollow. It was quite rustic and cozy looking, especially for something set out in the open like this, and she breathed in the scent of leftover woodsmoke, evergreen needles, and a hint of fishiness, feeling as though she had been transported into another world, and a magical one at that.

She thought, this is the perfect place to get to know someone better.

And be known.

And wouldn't that be a change for her.

CHAPTER XXIII

PAIGE WAS SHOWERED AND DRESSED by nine forty-five, tapping her hiking boot impatiently on the front stoop, with a light backpack over her shoulders, thinking she might have a heart attack from the way her pulse was throbbing in her veins.

Ben pulled in two minutes later, his Escalade taking up the width of their gravel driveway. He got out with a sheepish grin and promptly said, "Sorry I'm early. I couldn't wait."

She smiled, standing up and wiping off her shorts. "It's okay. Me either."

He approached her and fixed her with the warmest stare, taking in every inch of her and setting her aglow. She was wearing two layered tank tops, one white and one sky blue, along with short beige shorts and white puffy socks bunched up above her green hiking boots, which showed off her toned legs. He tucked his hands into the pockets of his shorts as if to keep them from touching her. He stood there, so close she could smell his crisp, clean bodywash.

He said simply, "You look good."

"You too," she echoed as she noticed just a hint of chest hair peeking out from the unbuttoned cream Henley stretched across his toned chest. She made a motion to head toward his car, but he stopped and said haltingly, "Do you—do you mind if I meet your parents?"

Her eyes got big.

He went on, "It's just, well…I'm sure they're a little nervous about you going out in the woods with some guy you met a few hours ago. I would be. I'd like to introduce myself and set them at ease."

It was crazy because of course he had hit the nail on the head. Paige had just finished a huge discussion-slash-argument with her ma and pa about it.

They had advised her to decline or at least take Abby and Kyle with them, saying, "What kind of signal are you sending this man to go out alone with him so soon? Plus, there may not be another living soul on that trail with you. How will you protect yourself if he…well, if his intentions aren't good?"

Paige had scoffed and said, "Listen, even though I don't know him very well, he's like the nicest guy. No serial killer or rapist vibes at all, I swear. Plus, he's a world-famous actor—that kind of limits the possibility that he'd try anything."

The eye roll from Pa said it all. He thought she was being naive. She sighed and conceded as an appeasement, "I know you're just looking out for me, but I'm not a child anymore. I can handle myself." Then with a grin, "Plus, I always carry bear spray when I hike, and it works just as well on a man as it does on a bear."

Pa liked that. He gave a soft chuckle and said, "That's my girl."

Ma smiled too, but her lips were still pressed together as she assented, "Okay, you can go, but remember to make your intentions known if he tries anything."

Paige said, "I will," thinking quietly with a tiny grin, what—that I want him to kiss me until my lips fall off?

She had fled outside, hoping they wouldn't change their minds in the time it took for Ben to arrive. And here he was—asking to meet her parents and looking nervous about it!

"Okay," she said, then added with a grin, "Quickly."

He nodded, taking a deep breath as she led him into the house. Her parents were at the kitchen table, drinking their coffees. She cleared her throat as they both looked up with surprise. "Ma, Pa, this is Ben Richfield. Ben, these are my parents, Roger and Sue Montgomery." She realized at that exact moment that he probably didn't know her last name, but he took it all in stride, the charm exuding from him like a second skin despite his nerves.

He shook Pa's hand first, firmly, as Pa stayed sitting, peering up from above his reading glasses at Ben's significant height, then Ben turned to Ma with a warm smile, taking her hand in both of his for the briefest moment, softly, saying, "So nice to meet you, ma'am." He added, looking around, "You have a lovely home."

"Why, thank you," Ma replied, her hand released and reflexively reaching up with delight to the neck-hugging collar of her nightgown.

Pa stared at his wife with a frown and turned to Ben, saying stoically, "Have a seat."

"Yes, sir," Ben said compliantly.

Paige yanked her backpack off her shoulders, setting it on her lap, and took the fourth chair at the tiny circular kitchen table. She glanced at Ben, who was swallowing and still had a smile frozen on his face. She inserted, "So, Ben, what trail are we going on?"

He looked at Paige for a moment, grabbing her cue, and answered, "I thought we'd head over to Aspen Creek. It's a beautiful trail—just four miles round trip—with a nicely marked path and a spectacular waterfall. My buddy, Craig, and I hiked it two weeks ago." As an afterthought, looking at Pa, he added, "Not too rugged."

Pa gave a brief nod, still frowning, assessing Ben like a lion with its prey.

"Sounds great!" Paige exclaimed, trying to ease the tension. She willed a smile into Pa with "I've hiked it before, Pa, with Keegan, and it's perfect. Not too steep or anything. Really pretty."

Ma said sweetly, "Lovely, honey. The weather looks like it'll hold up for you."

They all glanced out the kitchen window at the blue sky and puffy white clouds.

Pa took his time saying anything else, drinking his coffee as an uncomfortable silence filled the room. Then he asked abruptly, "You some kind of movie man?"

Ben replied smoothly, "Yes, sir. Well, TV, technically, but yes, I'm an actor."

"And you've been doing that a while?"

"Yes, sir. Since I was six years old."

"Six!" Pa harrumphed.

"Yes, sir."

"And how old are you now?"

"Twenty-six, sir."

"You ever do any other kind of job?"

"Um, well, I…worked at a grocery store when I was a teenager, stocking shelves at night."

Pa nodded curtly. "And you drive one of those fancy cars?"

Ben cleared his throat. This was beginning to feel like an interrogation. "Um, well, sir, I have a shared production vehicle while I'm here in Montana," he gestured toward the front door, "but back in California, I drive a Dodge Ram pickup truck."

Pa snorted a little. Paige couldn't tell if it was a good or bad snort.

Paige butted in, "Pa, we need to get going...my shift starts at three."

Ma said, "Did you pack everything you'll need?"

"Yes, Ma." Paige pointed at the pack on her lap.

Ben gave the full force of his smile to Ma. "I've got bottled water, snacks, and just in case, extra layers, including two rain ponchos."

Pa asked flatly, "And a gun?"

"Well, um, no sir. I—I have a rifle in the SUV, but on the trail, I usually stick with bear spray."

Paige answered for Pa, "Me too. That's fine. Come on, let's go."

Paige stood up, and Ben rose too. Ben looked thoughtfully at Ma, then Pa, and said, "It was nice to meet you both. I promise to have Paige back safe and sound in a few hours."

Pa finally smiled, just a little, and said, "You better. Take care, son." He put more meaning into the word *care* than just a casual goodbye, and the fact that he used the word *son* made Paige bubble up with a flashing grin toward Ben.

Ben pretended not to notice, to his credit, and kept a serious expression on his face. He replied with a nod, "Yes, sir, I will."

Paige gave Pa's arm a quick squeeze and said, "Thanks, Pa. See ya later."

Ma stood and gave her a brief hug. "Have fun, darling. We're both working the night shift with you, so we'll see you at three." Paige nodded as Ma walked them to the door. Pa went back to reading his paper.

They nearly fled to the Escalade. Ben pulled out of the driveway, looking over at Paige with a brush of his hand across his brow. "Phew! Glad that's over."

"Yes," Paige agreed. "You did great," she added.

He smiled, and when they hit the main road, he grabbed her hand and kissed it. It was so unexpected and sweet that Paige actually gasped. A moment later, she laid her head back on the seat and looked over at him.

"Your parents work at Chico Springs too?"

"Uh-huh," she murmured, not wanting to talk or think about anything other than the way she was feeling at this very moment with his hand in hers.

He smiled at her with his glowing eyes and asked with fake menace, "Now tell me who this Keegan person is."

Paige laughed. "Oh, he's a friend from high school. We hike together sometimes. He lives on his family's ranch down the road—his dad, Randy, is Pa's best friend. We go over there a lot to horseback ride and hang out in their barn. They're a really nice family."

He nodded politely, then asked, "So, you never dated him?"

"Nope," she said. She guessed he was trying to feel her out. He didn't sound jealous or possessive or weird, just curious. Paige changed the subject, asking incredulously, "You've been working since you were *six*?"

"Yep."

"You were a child actor? That must have been rough."

He cringed a little. "Yeah, it was, at times. My mom was an actress until she married my dad. She mostly did theater in New York, and she was on a soap opera for a while. In fact, that was how they met—he was gofer for a few years. Anyway, once they married and moved to LA, the roles sort of dried up. She had us, my sister and me, and insisted we take acting classes and do summer theater workshops. She said it would teach us life skills, like how to speak in public, how to enunciate words, how to memorize, be confident, interact with others…that kind of thing."

"And did it?"

"Yes, it was good for that," he said with a glance at her, his brow furrowed, "but maybe not good for everything else."

She wondered what he meant and tried hard to concentrate on what was behind the words, but a lot of her thoughts were tied up in the feeling of being in his presence. She had never felt this way before. He was seemingly oblivious, completely comfortable, almost as if holding hands was an afterthought, like something he did every day. Then Paige had a twist in her gut, thinking, *did* he do that every day? And if so, with whom?

He continued, "I loved the acting part, took to it like a fish to water. Before I realized what was happening, Mom scored me a manager and an agent and whoosh, I was off and running."

"How did you manage it with school and everything?"

"I did the acting after school and on weekends. Mostly small bits on TV shows and a lot of commercials. Then my senior year I got a regular gig on this Nickelodeon show, so after I graduated, I worked solely on that for a while."

"Nickelodeon, eh?"

"Yep, kids' stuff, I guess."

"So, is your sister an actress?"

"She was," he began quietly, "a really good one too. She got a role in a movie on her third audition, and man, *that* role—she was extraordinary. Everyone thought she'd go on to conquer the world."

"Did she?"

He was watching the road, and the air in the car seemed to get heavier. She could see him struggling with how to say more without saying too much. Paige waited mutely, watching his jaw tighten. He finally said in a tense, low tone, "No, she got...chewed up and spit out."

Paige didn't know how to react or what to say to that. What did he mean? She whispered softly, "How?"

He said bitterly, "You know, being in this industry, you gotta have thick skin. Like rhinoceros hide. Seriously. Because the auditions are brutal. They'll say, right to your face, things like, 'He's got an okay nose and hair, but his mouth is too big' or 'His voice is too high' or 'He's too tall, too short, too fat, too thin, too dark, too light' or whatever. Literally, they pick you apart, inch by inch, like vultures feasting on a rotting carcass on the side of the road. Some of it's just physical appearance, but they also say a lot about your acting, which is essentially tapping into who you are, your ability to intuit, to be an empath, to read people. They tell you you're fake, inauthentic, reaching, stupid, spoiled, worthless, a waste of their time. The agents aren't much better, and neither are the casting directors. As a teenager, you're already going through strange growth spurts and ugly puberty, and you're not yet comfortable with your body or your hormones or your*self*, and then you have people telling you every single day that you're not good enough—that no matter what you do or how good you are at your job or how much effort you put into something, you'll *never* be good enough.

"And, you know, some people...some sensitive people, like my sister, they just can't survive that." He was breathing hard now, especially as he added, "And what's crazy—what's the most awful, fucked-up, ironic thing—is that the best, the absolute fucking *best* actors are the ones who *are* sensitive and feel things deeply because they can tap into that inner pool of resources, that delicate, complex part of another person's psyche to embody the essence of that person, *become* that person, leave everything of themselves behind in order to portray someone else wholly, selflessly. My sister was like that, and they just—they just fucking killed that amazing part of her. They *killed* it."

Paige turned her body in the passenger seat. He had let go of her hand and was gripping the steering wheel with white knuckles. She was afraid to say a word, so she sat there, feeling his pain and wondering about his sister, but also about him. How had *he* survived that environment?

He stared at the road as though it was a punching bag. He continued, still breathing shallowly, "Yeah, so, um, she did a few more movies after that, but they weren't as well received. My mom kept pushing her and pushing her to keep at it, despite the failures, for years and years, so Rhone did whatever was asked of her, getting smaller roles, lesser parts, but eventually she couldn't take it anymore, and one night—she had just turned eighteen the week before—she ran away. And she didn't come back."

Paige's eyes got big. "Ever?" she asked quietly.

"Not for a long time. Years. We weren't really sure where she was living, or *how* she was living, but we knew she was into some pretty bad stuff. She would pop up, unexpected, sometimes at our house, and my parents would stick her in rehab or send her away on a retreat, thinking that would cure her, but you know, nothing really worked. She'd get out and be fine for a few weeks or maybe a couple of months, then be gone again. This last time, my parents sent her to Arizona for six weeks, and she did well—she loved it out there, so she stayed for a while after her release, met some guy, and they bought a house together. We thought everything was finally going well for her. Then she came home one night at three in the morning. They had broken up. She was a mess—suicidal. My parents took her to the ER, but they released her after only one night. She disappeared the next day, and we haven't seen her since. That was six months ago."

Wow, Paige thought, she couldn't even imagine what kind of horror his family had been through. She also wondered what the true story was behind his mom pushing them so much into a career that seemed so harsh at such a young age. Was she trying to make up for something *she* had wanted for herself and felt as though she'd missed out on?

They were both silent for the rest of the car ride, lost in their own thoughts. When he pulled into the gravel parking lot next to the trailhead and turned the car off, she was still turned toward him in her seat, her leg up and bent at the knee, pointed his way. He took off his seat belt and laid his hand loosely on her knee, saying, "Yeah, so when I got this gig up here in Montana, I figured it would be good for me—to get out of LA for a while, get away from all that."

He smiled a sad, wistful half-smile. He didn't say whether he meant he wanted to get away from the drama with his sister or the whole judgmental acting/LA environment. He looked out the window at the great expanse of prairie grasses across the road, the mountains in the distance, the wildflower-encircled pond glimmering off to the right, the wooded forest behind the trailhead sign, and said, "See—*this*—this place is the real deal. This place reminds me of what *matters*. It's about staying connected to the world, appreciating every pulse, every sunrise, every sunset, every scent, grand view, birdsong. It's about feeling—deeply—those senses in the heart of who you are, why you're here—why every moment on God's green Earth is a *gift*."

He turned back to her, squeezing her knee gently. Paige nodded, loving how his luminescent eyes glowed with the passion of his words.

She blinked, took off her seat belt, and said in a raw whisper, "I know exactly what you mean. I feel closest to God when I'm out here. This is my temple, my church, my religion."

"Totally," he agreed.

He leaned toward her then, touched her chin lightly with his hand, and drew her lips to his, kissing her softly, subtly, with a slow, lingering movement, running his mouth back and forth on hers before finishing with a light suction that she felt in her toes.

Then, an inch away from her face, he said teasingly, "You ready to hike, hula girl?"

"Mm-hmm," she murmured, locking on his eyes, afraid to speak and break the spell.

"Come on," he said, opening his door and coming around to help her out.

Out in the bright sunshine of the spectacular morning effervescence, they quickly made sure they had everything in their backpacks and started on the trail. For the first few minutes, they walked up a straight pine-tree-lined path in silence. Paige liked to watch his strong legs ahead of hers—confident, sure-footed, unwavering. She marveled at the fact that, much like his legs, *he* never seemed out of place in any surroundings—at a rodeo, standing inside the cathedral-ceilinged living room of that huge house where he was staying, in the tiny kitchen at her house that morning, or here in the great woods of the Absaroka Beartooth mountain range.

At some point, he glanced at her and asked, "You want to play a game?"

She laughed. "What is it with you and games anyway?"

"Well, I like to win," he answered with a laugh. "But this isn't like last night. I was thinking," he grinned over his shoulder at her, "twenty questions."

"Twenty? For me? About what?"

"Whatever. To get to know you. And you can do the same. To get to know me."

"Okay," she said, feeling a slight flutter in her belly.

"I'll start. How often do you hike?"

"Hmm, maybe every other weekend, and sometimes during the week. Depends on what shifts I'm working, and the weather, which is about as predictable around here as fishing in the river—sometimes perfect, sometimes ugly."

He snorted a laugh. "I bet. What's your favorite trail?"

"Hey, is that a new question or a sub-question of the same question?" she asked with a raised eyebrow.

"Sub-questions are allowed and don't cost toward the twenty."

"Are we making up the rules as we go?"

"Pretty much," he said with a grin.

"Hmm, speaking of fish, sounds a little fishy to me," she said with fake suspicion, then, "I'll allow it. So, in answer, I love them all, but um, let's see…Gallatin has a bunch of good ones, and there's a nice Pine Creek trail about five miles from here that has spectacular views."

"Maybe we'll do that one next time," he said casually, as if it was a given that there would *be* a next time. She felt a slight uptick in her heartbeat. He added, "Okay, your turn."

She hesitated for a moment. She had about a thousand questions, all of them too much, too forward, too scary, but she was itching. Seeing her struggle, he said, "Paige. Go for it. Anything."

"Anything?"

"Anything."

She released the first question in a quick breath of air, like a shotgun, "How many girls have you kissed?"

He smiled, not fazed in the least. "A few. You?"

"Girls? None."

"Funny. Guys?"

"Three. Four, if you count, well, you."

"Oh?" he said, surprised. Then, "*Oh.*" A little frown.

She went on, "How many is a *few?*"

"Is that your second question?" he teased, the smile back on his face again.

"Sub-questions don't count," Paige reminded him.

"Then why only three?"

Paige had to think about that. Not about the number—of course she knew the exact number—it was emblazoned on her mind like a stain. Twenty-one years old and had only been kissed three, now four, times. Most girls her age had hit that number by the time they were thirteen. She glanced at him for a second, trying to gauge how much to reveal. "Well, yeah, I'm not exactly sure."

His brow creased.

She went on, "I mean, first of all, living in Emigrant, there aren't a ton of options. It's a small town. And most of the people I meet are tourists, in and out in a week or two, not the ideal candidates. Anyway, so yeah, when guys do decide to date or hook up…well, it isn't usually with me, and I guess that's because…"

Paige paused, regarding him closely, thinking how it was almost amazing to her that he didn't see anything different or unusual about her. He assumed she had grown up completely accepted and supported for exactly who she was, when in reality, in every single place she went and with every encounter, her face triggered a double-take, a whisper, a moment of question or confusion.

She let her voice drift off, shrugging. He stopped on the trail, and so did she.

He looked at her. "Because…?"

She pointed at the white spots on her face, her arms, her legs, and said, "Well, because of the—the vitiligo."

"The viti—huh?" he asked, the crease in his brow deepening.

"Vitiligo. My skin. It's an autoimmune disease. The white blotches and spots where I'm missing pigment. They've been there a long time, and I get new ones every year. So yeah, I guess some people are—put off by it."

"Oh!" he said, as if he'd just noticed it, which was completely and utterly ridiculous. He said, "Yeah, I thought it might just be scars or leftover sunburn or something. I wasn't sure."

He turned and kept walking, but she stayed still, her mouth agape. He didn't mind? How was that possible? She rushed to catch up, asking, "You don't care?"

He looked back lightly. "Care? I *care*, Paige. Don't say I don't care." A quick smile. "I'm sorry you have to deal with that. But do you mean that I might feel any differently about you because your skin is pale in certain spots? Stop a sec and look at this," he said, lifting up his sleeve. He pointed to a jagged pink scar about four inches long on the back of his arm. "Do you feel any differently about me because of this scar?"

She couldn't help but tilt her head at his silliness. "No, of course not."

"Yeah, but you might not want to kiss me again because of it, right?"

She laughed. "Definitely *not* right."

"Well, good. Because I'm going to kiss you. *Right* here, *right* now."

He pulled his sleeve down and cupped her face in his hands and kissed her long and deep, and she felt it in every part of her body. Then, as if it was perfectly natural to move on from the topic and the kiss, he let go of her face, pulled her into a hug and said, "Okay, let's see—my turn. What number are we on? Do all the 'rights' and 'huhs' and 'you don't cares' count as questions or sub-questions? If so, I think we only have about seven left."

She was breathless, thinking she wanted to ditch the hike entirely and just stay here in this pocket of peace, tucked into this accepting, nonjudgmental embrace, and kiss him for the next twenty hours. But then, just as casually, he turned and began walking again, grabbing her hand, leading her along the trail.

He said, "So, on a scale of one to four, who was your favorite kiss?"

She grinned. "That's not fair."

"Why?"

"You never told me what 'a few' meant."

He sighed. "Okay, okay, but you're not gonna like the answer." She couldn't tell if he was teasing. She waited, her breath stopped short. He added, "And this doesn't get you off the hook either."

She nodded mutely.

He couched his words with a sheepish expression. "Well, you have to understand, part of what I do for a living is pretend to be in love with complete strangers, and sometimes that entails kissing."

She swallowed. Crap, she hadn't thought of that! Her stomach turned over.

He said, "Yeah, so 'a few' is maybe like fifty, sixty, a hundred? I'm honestly not sure." He glanced back over his shoulder curiously and exclaimed, "Please don't look at me that way, Paige!"

She dropped his hand with a low whistle, "A hundred?!" She instantly thought of a hundred sets of puffed-up actresses' lips suctioned to his perfectly kissable mouth like honeybees drinking nectar from cherry blossoms. How could she compete with that?

Seeing her distress, he took her by the shoulders, squeezed softly, rubbed his hands down her arms, bending down to look into her wide eyes, and said, "Paige. Listen to me. Kissing in the acting world is almost like shaking hands in the real world. It's as innocuous as running lines. You're putting on a mask—you're trying to be someone else—so you become that other person, and if you're doing it right, what matters most about the person *you* are—the part of your heart and soul that is *you*—is that you keep it safely tucked away, protected and separate, so when you're acting or kissing or doing anything related to your role, *you're* not feeling anything other than how to make it *look* authentic."

Paige tore her eyes away from his reaching gaze. She had always thought of a kiss on the lips as so intimate, as if you were giving a piece of yourself to that person. Maybe that was another reason she hadn't attempted it more often. She was trying to imagine what it would be like to give and receive a kiss that meant *nothing*…?

She stared back at him. His fingers were still pressed against her arms. She asked, "Then how do you kiss as yourself? *Not* for a role?"

"Oh, that's easy," he said with a playful smile. "Like this."

He leaned down and pressed his lips to hers. She stood still, feeling the unfettered wetness and heat…and thinking, thinking, thinking—was it real? Was he simply feeling the pressure of their lips together and nothing else? Was there anything more? A spark? For him? For her? All of the sudden, *she* couldn't feel anything. She was too caught up in the analysis of the kiss. He sensed it and pulled away.

Frowning down at her, he prompted, "Paige?"

Her lips felt so strange, like two big slabs of meat. She didn't answer him.

Suddenly, like a cool shower of rain on a hot day, he burst out laughing, tilting his head back, pulling her in for a hug, crushing her against his chest. He kissed the top of her head, and when he could speak, he held her away from himself and said, "Paige, you poor thing. I spooked you, didn't I?"

She couldn't help but smile—he had seen right through her, like a piece of clear glass. She was flummoxed.

He ventured, "Come on, we'll try again later. When you aren't all messed up in the head about it."

He grabbed her hand again, and they kept walking. He was still laughing, and she noted with a flutter in her belly that his laugh had an infectious, endearing quality about it—a low, throaty secret encased in a splash of whimsy. It made her feel warm all over.

He added, like an afterthought, a grin on his face as he glanced over at her, "By the way, if you're wondering where you rank in the hundred—top three for sure, maybe higher."

Paige said quietly, almost not realizing it was out loud, "No."

"Yes," he retorted. "It's those lips. They're absolutely perfect, kissable, *luscious* lips." He narrowed his eyes at her mouth, and if she'd had enough pigment in her cheeks, she would have blushed, but instead she just stared, absently tracing the contours of her lips with her finger.

He brushed her finger aside and kissed her again, then added with a grin, "God, I love how *real* you are too. It's not just the lips—it's *you*. I knew it the moment I saw you stick your tongue out at that steer." Oh my God, he remembered that! "I mean, what kind of woman tries to reason with a steer? That was when I knew I had to meet you. Thank goodness for Kyle and Mike. To think you might have slipped away...I'm just glad you stuck around with us last night. I know we were rather...rough. But all I kept thinking about the whole time was how I wanted to get to know you better."

He paused, looking away to gather his thoughts, suddenly serious. "In my line of work, you never know what you'll get with people. Everyone's putting up a front, faking their way—with their appearance, with their acting, with their relationships. It can be frustrating—you often don't know where you really stand with anyone. But with you, you're just going about your life, doing what you do, being you. In that one amazing, hysterical moment when you were staring down the steer and not caring who was watching, you showed me a piece of you—the piece that was cute, funny, sweet, sassy, not afraid to be yourself, not afraid to look ridiculous, not afraid of anything. That's what I wanted to get to know better. I know we just met, but the more I'm around you, the more I can tell that you're not like the posers, the brownnosers, the fakers. You're not here to butter me up or *get* something from me. You know, people usually are. You don't need to be someone else for me—you don't need *anything* from me. And you don't expect me to be anyone but who I am—you don't expect me to be the characters I play, as if we are one and the same, as if they're real, as if they're me. You're just *you*. And I'm just *me*. We've been ourselves around each other. And you've let me ask you questions, let me get to know you. Heck, you introduced me to your parents—and let me slip into your world for a bit. You have no idea how much I appreciate that."

She was caught off-guard. Such nice things to say! She hadn't been trying, didn't even exactly understand. How could people be other than who they were? Fakers? Posers? It was so unfamiliar to her, to the way she had been raised.

She was sassy? And her lips were kissable? She never knew.

Maybe there were a lot of things she never knew about herself because no one had ever thought to tell her, to probe that soft, vulnerable side of her, to look beyond her spots and see what was inside. And maybe it was because she had never given them the chance. Wasn't it easier to have an invisible wall up? Maybe all this time she had been closed off, warding away any judgment or pity. It wasn't like she didn't know her own self-worth—she had always faced her challenges head-on with confidence and self-assurance, knowing (maybe because of her challenges) that there wasn't anything she couldn't tackle, couldn't face, even if she wasn't exactly a risk-taker. But still, it was nice to hear someone besides her parents and friends say they really saw her and liked her. Just as she was.

And she was learning, on this very revealing day, that maybe it was time for a change.

Maybe it was time for the wall to come down.

Chapter XXIV

MARIE AND KENT DOZED FOR A WHILE, then made love again, this time slower, more deeply, savoring each other's bodies like they hadn't in years, looking into each other's eyes, seeking and touching places that had been dormant and were ripe for exploration and release. Marie repeated, "I'm sorry" between the "I love you's" and "I've missed you's" and "Will you forgive me's?" trying to make up for her wretchedness, her guilt, her abject devastation at the acknowledgment that she had turned into such a shrew and hadn't even realized it.

She knew she would struggle with it, not being used to apologizing to Kent or anyone else. She had always made excuses for her behavior, her rudeness, her unflinching perfection. She had always redirected, displaced the blame to the victim of her unfeeling rules and exactitude, to their own idiocy, foibles, lack of standards. She had rationalized that there were lesser beings out there needing her direction, needing a leader, needing to be told what to do and how to do it, so why shouldn't she be the one? They were followers. She was a leader.

But now, to turn inward, to acknowledge that not everyone had asked for nor wanted her direction, her standards, or that they hadn't necessarily benefitted from them—that was going to be…difficult, maybe even impossible. Oh my God, Marie thought, how would she do it?

After all, she *was* right most of the time.

She chuckled in Kent's arms, thinking about it, and he leaned up to look at her. She just shook her head and squeezed him more tightly.

Knowing not all puzzles were solved in a day, she eventually asked Kent, "Want something to eat?"

He kissed her on the lips for the hundredth time that night and said, "God, yes. I'm starving."

They got up and dressed. She prepared a quick batch of pasta and sauce along with a salad, and the entire time (while he sipped his wine and watched her with a new radiance in his eyes), she thought, maybe I'll start right now, with Kent, in this safe space—try to tackle my demons. Because after all, what was the alternative? She hadn't misread Kent's meaning, his intentions, on the back patio. He had been at a breaking point. She wondered absently how long he'd been thinking about confronting her. Then she wondered in the pit of her stomach if he'd been thinking about the D word—or the S word, at least. Neither of them had ever, not even once, mentioned divorce or separation during the entire course of their marriage. And they'd been to hell and back more than once in their many years together. But it was one of their agreements, before they were even engaged, when they were first dating, their freshman year in college, that if they were going to be together, it would be for *life*. To be there for each other, forever, period, no matter what, end of story.

She realized with horror how close they'd come, regardless of their pledge, to the end of their story, and not in the till-death-do-us-part way, but through her own lack of self-awareness. She still wasn't sure of everything she did wrong, she thought with embarrassment. She would have to—gulp—ask.

Cutting some veggies in a neat layer on top of their salad, she inquired tentatively, "Um, hey, so yeah—I know you've been thinking about this a lot longer than I have, and once again, I'm sorry about that, but could you—possibly give me a few hints, or an inkling of how I should go about making things better?"

"Well, earlier, upstairs, was a good start," he said with a laugh.

"Kent," she stated flatly, rolling her eyes as her lips hitched up in a grin. "I'm serious."

"I know—so am I," he said. Then, clearing his throat, his face sobering, he repeated, "I know. Okay, number one on the list—exactly what we're doing right here, right now—a date night, once a week, just you and me. The kids are older now—they can fend for themselves, or we can ship them off to my parents' if we need to."

"Done," she agreed readily, looking over her shoulder at him as he sat on a barstool on the other side of the island.

"Okay, number two, I'd really like to take a family trip. Maybe next month, before school starts. Get away, just the five of us, to some beach or park or cabin or something...I don't know—I envision s'mores around a campfire, long walks in the woods, eating our meals together, no technology—we'll force the kids on a digital detox for part or maybe even all of it. A trip where we can really talk and laugh with each other, get to know one another more deeply, and not just as family, but as friends."

"That sounds wonderful, Kent," she said softly, turning to place the salad bowl on the counter in front of him. As she turned back to stir the pasta and sauce, the germ of panic that seemed to always fill her waking hours began to creep in. She couldn't keep it out of her voice as she said with an edge, "But what about the horses? And Darby has that dressage show in mid-July in New Jersey, Ryan starts soccer tryouts right after that, and Bridget said she wanted to apply for that job at the library. I'm hosting a charity walk for the Humane Society on the twenty-first, plus Dominick wanted your help on the Takeda proposal. How will—"

Her sauce stirring becoming more manic by the second before she felt Kent's comforting arms wrap around her waist. He kissed her neck and whispered in her ear, "Shhhhh."

She laid down the spoon and turned to face him, her heart beating, her eyes growing large, "But, truly, Kent, how—"

He gently took her face in his hands and said, "We'll figure it out."

"But—but—"

"Rule number three, Marie, no buts. *We* will figure it out. Together. I don't have all the details worked out, and I don't have our family calendar pulled up, and I don't have a magic wand either, but you know what I *do* have?"

Her heartbeat was settling slightly, so she asked with a sort of wondrous skepticism, "What?"

"I have faith. In you. In me. In our kids. In your ability to make something happen, even when it's difficult, even when it's complicated and messy and seemingly impossible. Isn't that what you do, after all? Make magic happen?" He smiled, grabbing another kiss. "And without a wand, I might add."

"Flattery will get you nowhere," she whispered, trying to frown but not succeeding.

"It seems to be working tonight, though."

"Yes," she agreed, pushing him lightly away so she could drain the pasta in the sink. She ladled the sauce over the pasta, grated the cheese on top, and poured more wine. After he helped her bring everything to the table, they sat down to eat.

He became rather serious as they ate in silence for a few minutes. Then he put down his fork and said, "Number four, because I *do* have so much faith in you, Marie—I was thinking you should maybe...," he paused, and she regarded his handsome, humble face and wondered why it looked slightly scared, "get some counseling."

She nearly choked on her food. "No," she said quickly, resolutely.

"Please. Hear me out," he pressed, and she only shook her head more fervently. "You went through something terrifying twenty years ago, something traumatic, something I can't possibly understand fully, something that almost *no one* can understand fully. I'm not a trained professional. Sure, I can offer encouragement and love and forgiveness..." she tensed at that last word, but he took her hand and added, "Not forgiveness of *you*, my dear. It was never about that, but about the—circumstances, our fate with little Matthew. Forgiveness of God or life's cruel injustices. I forgive that it happened to us because, well, because I don't have a choice, and I'd rather live my life in peace than wallow in endless anger. But having said that, having accepted that, and the fact that I'll give my *all* to love you and the kids and to care for you, I acknowledge that *my* all may not be enough. Only *you* can heal your heart. Only *you* can process what happened, and frankly, forgive yourself, if in fact that's what needed to make you feel whole again. That's what I want, more than anything, for you. For you to *feel* again. To feel the good in our lives. To feel the bad, even. But to feel everything and still be able to embrace life, for all it's worth, for every good, bad, and indifferent thing. That's what I wish for you."

She was hearing him but was *so* resistant to the idea, so skeptical, so uncomfortable.

He went on, stroking her hand, their pasta steaming in front of them, "And because I don't know how to make that happen, because I'm just an inept husband wishing the best for his wife, for his family, but without the tools or wherewithal to do so, I'm asking you, begging you, to get outside help. Now maybe that isn't a counselor, maybe that isn't even talking or confessing or whatever is involved in therapy, and maybe it's something entirely different, like whatever it is they do in those Native American retreats. A sweat. Yeah, maybe it's a three-day sweat or something…shamanism, clairvoyance, exorcism," he laughed a little, out of his element and not afraid to admit it. "I'm being facetious, but you get the idea." She found herself starting to smile. Despite his flippancy, he was so earnest. "Quite honestly, I have no idea, and it's probably not a one-size-fits-all kind of thing, nor is it likely to produce overnight results, so I'm going to leave it up to you to figure it out, but one thing I do know: there needs to be a change. This life you've boxed yourself into is no life at all, sweetie—for you, for me, or for the kids. A box of meticulously organized activities that fill up every waking hour may seem safe, but it's still a *box*."

He was right, of course. On a purely surface level, anyone who didn't know about Matthew might think that her life was everything anyone could ever hope for, and yet she had just been thinking earlier that evening how unhappy she was, and now she knew without a shadow of a doubt—or a shadow of unacknowledged avoidance of the trauma—that she'd been in denial—that her husband and kids were just as unhappy as she was. Maybe not every moment of every day, and maybe not directly related to anything she did or anything she was, but still…probably related to something she'd been through and hadn't yet faced. She could see that the facade was just that—a mirage—and the real world she was living in, the *inside* world, was in shambles. Her selfless, kind, caring husband was neglected, and her well-fed, well-tended-to, well-organized children were doing what kids do—moving through life easily and unconsciously, and yet even they sensed the tension between their parents, sensed that their mother wasn't quite *whole*. Didn't kids emulate what they saw, what they felt in their own homes? What would they copy when they chose a mate later on in life? A relationship built on shared purpose, activities, and drive? Is that what she wanted for her kids? Before the plane crash, hadn't she wanted a life filled with overwhelming love, emotional support, friends, family—a warm, cozy, inviting, happy *home*?

She had all the appearance of it, and yet none of the heart of it. How had that happened without her even realizing it?

She sat there so crushed by the weight of it all. Kent was still rubbing her hand, and he said, "Listen, sweetie, you don't have to figure this out tonight. All I'm asking is that you think about it. Think about what you want from this life, with me, with us, and most importantly, with yourself. And then take some steps to make that connection, that transformation, happen. It's not about the movement forward—it's about the movement within."

She nodded.

They ate quietly, staring at each other, wondering how it would work, *if* it would work.

She would need time.
And strength.
And courage.
And resilience.

Or maybe not.
Maybe this time she would need something *soft*.
Something malleable.
Something to break down her walls.
A heart.
A soul.
To make her *feel*.
Even if feelings equaled fear.
Even if feelings equaled flee.

This time they would need to equal healing, hope, home.

Heaven help her.

CHAPTER XXV

MARK PLACED THEIR THINGS ON THE PICNIC TABLE and offered Julie a drink out of a large thermos he had stowed in the picnic basket.

"What is it?" Julie asked.

"Homemade Bloody Marys—my own recipe—virgin of course, if that's alright." He said it as a statement, not a question, perhaps a little nervous about disappointing her but not about to apologize either.

She said, "That sounds wonderful." And, as much as she normally loved a good bit of vodka in her Bloody Marys, she was pleasantly surprised that he had gone to so much trouble, maybe even thinking about the fact that the drink was normally served with alcohol and showing her that it could be just as good without it. She glanced away, taking a seat on one of the Adirondack chairs and taking in a deep breath as he poured their drinks in two cups, complete with celery stalks, and joined her.

She said, "It's so beautiful and tranquil here."

"Yes, it is. I brought these chairs here a few years ago. They've aged fairly well, all things considered, being exposed to the elements and all. I like to think about how many wayfarers have taken solace and enjoyed solitude in them."

"Just like us!" she said with a smile. "This is delicious," she raved, sipping her drink and taking a bite out of the celery. "The perfect amount of kick."

"Oh good. I know not everyone likes the spice."

They drank in silence for a few minutes, taking in their surroundings. Then she said, "So, tell me more about yourself. Do you mind if I ask why you don't drink?"

"Ah," he said with a grin. "I was wondering when we'd get around to that."

"Rip the bandage off, I suppose." She shrugged.

"Right. Okay. How to begin…?" he wondered, taking a sip and then setting the cup down on the arm of the chair. He regarded her for a moment, assessing how much to reveal. "Well, like I mentioned last night, I've been sober for seventeen years. When I was younger, I sort of fiddled around on the fringes of trouble most of the time. Oh, nothing egregiously bad—I wasn't jailed or anything—thanks to Dewey, and probably just dumb luck, but I definitely liked to hang with the wild crowd, you know, the drinkers, weed smokers, rebels without a cause, or a clue," he laughed sheepishly. "Anyway, it was all just fun and games back then—lots of drinking, women, drugs, rock 'n' roll—you get the idea. For the most part, I was blessed despite my antics. I graduated from college, got a job working at an accounting firm in Hartford, bought a house, got married, had a kid. I was living my best life—you know, doing the nine-to-five thing during the week and partying hard on weeknights and weekends."

He paused for a moment, and she asked softly, "How did you meet your ex-wife?"

He took a breath. "Best friend's sister. We all grew up together, and I always thought she was cute, but off-limits because of Bill. Plus, I didn't have the balls to ask her out. Then I saw her at Bill's wedding, right after I graduated from college. She was dressed in one of those hideous bridesmaid's outfits, some neon green number, and I teased her and she gave me crap about my cummerbund being the same color, and the next thing I knew we were bonking in the bushes behind the country club terrace."

He shrugged and grinned. Julie just smiled.

He went on, "Eventually Bill got over the fact that we were dating, and the next summer we were married at the same country club, which, by the way, Bill made sure to mention during his best man's speech—something to the effect of 'Katie and Mark owe me a debt of gratitude because if it hadn't been for the well-manicured bushes on the back side of this building, he might not have gotten a good look at my *sister's* backside, and we wouldn't be sitting here with you fine folks today.' Katie and I both wanted to crawl under the table—our parents were sitting at the table right across from us! I could have slugged him."

He laughed and she did too, but then a cloud passed over his face.

"Kaylie was born five years later, and we were living the good life. Katie was running a salon, but she took a year off to care for Kaylie, and life moved quickly. Once Katie was back to work, we got into a routine where we allowed ourselves a babysitter once a week, and we'd go out with the whole gang and get trashed just like in the good ole days. We were trying to hold on to our youth, I guess, even though we were all grown up, with kids and houses and bills. We mostly stayed within our local group of friends, but then Bill and I both decided we were going to treat ourselves to a new hobby—motorcycles—Harleys. We found this motorcycle group that did long road trips every Sunday, so we hooked up with them, met and became friends with a whole new crowd. They were from all over New England—Rhode Island, Delaware, Vermont, you name it. We even had people from New York, Long Island, Philly. It was awesome. Out on the open road, we thought we were immune to life's burdens. We ruled—didn't have a care in the world and left our family obligations behind, if only for a day."

His eyes were no longer on her but far away, looking back in his mind's eye. She was almost afraid to breathe, feeling his angst build like a palpable thing hovering in the air between them.

"I was still drinking and smoking pot, pretty much every day. It calmed my nerves when work was stressful or when Katie and I were fighting, which was quite often back then. She really didn't like it that I was gone so much with my buddies on weeknights and with Bill and the bikers on weekends. Plus, she wanted more kids, and I didn't. Her salon was thriving, but that took her away from home a lot, and I kept explaining that having more kids would just put even more pressure on us both. I didn't want to give up anything I thought I deserved, like my free time—not when I was working so hard and thought everything was about me. And she was harping on me more and more about never giving her a break and how Kaylie was suffering from my lack of parenting. I didn't see it that way—she was gone more nights than I was—and it was my parents who were pitching in when neither of us were available—didn't that count for something? Anyway, you get the idea... things were starting to get tense between us. Honestly, though, thank God, despite us, Kaylie was a great kid—very responsible and a high achiever—and that maturity really saved us for many years. Even if we stunk at parenting, she somehow pulled us through the bad times.

"In the middle of it all, Bill and I planned a weekend road trip to Maine with our motorcycle group. We packed our gear, booked hotel rooms, identified special destination stops along the way. It was early October, and we left on a Friday morning. It was the middle of the tourist season up there, and even the back roads were packed with cars. It was slow going. We were with a fairly large group too—around twenty cycles, some couples, some single—and we had to stop quite frequently in order to stick together. By Friday night, we'd barely made it to Providence, Rhode Island, checked into the hotel, and went out for a long dinner at a local restaurant. Everyone else called it a night around nine thirty, but Bill and I stayed up, drinking at the bar, shutting the place down. We had to be up just a few short hours later, and when I woke up Saturday morning at the crack of dawn, I felt so lousy that I figured we'd do a little hair of the dog, so I went across the street and bought a six-pack, which Bill and I proceeded to chug down, three beers each in like twenty minutes. The rest of the group was waiting on us when we finally came out of our hotel room. We were too busy smoking a big joint in between the beers to notice the time. Then we were on our way. For the first forty-five minutes we were fine, rolling along with the group, heading north toward Boston, and then it started to rain and the traffic backed up. The whole lot of us pulled off at a gas station, and everyone said we should wait out the rain, but after a half-hour twiddling our thumbs, Bill and I were getting antsy. We went into the restroom and smoked another joint.

"One of the main guys—the leader, Butch—was yammering on about safety protocols, telling everyone once we got back on the road to stay together and go slow and watch for slick spots and tight turns. We'd booked a reservation at some lobster-roll luncheon place overlooking the harbor in Boston, but Bill and I were giggling in the back, saying how we'd ditch them and make a run for Vermont instead. The last thing we wanted to do was ride two miles an hour through Boston's one-way streets in the rain and then sit under some awning watching the gray waters of the harbor through a stream of cold, windy rain. Most of these guys were older than us, and it was our cockiness, our bravado talking—we figured we were better riders than them, younger, smarter, more carefree and fun. In our haze, we didn't have the patience or brains to understand what an asinine idea we'd hatched. These guys had way more experience on their bikes—some had been riding for ten or twenty years, and we'd only just begun the year before—and they knew how important sticking together was, especially in bad weather. There was strength and safety in numbers on a motorcycle, where cars and trucks struggle to see you in the rain and where you might need backup if you got into trouble, like a flat tire or running out of gas. But we didn't care—we were drunk, high, and arrogant, not to mention young and irresponsible.

"The rain slowed just a little, and Butch gave the signal—we were on our way, two by two for the next ten or fifteen miles, and then Bill and I rode up to Butch in the front and indicated with our hands that we were going to skip Boston and go ahead to Vermont. Butch shook his helmeted head and tried to get us to stop, tried to warn us that it was a bad idea, but we rode away anyway, raising our hand in a wave as we sped off in the other direction."

Mark's eyes, still black and brooding, staring away at the line of trees across from the island, suddenly turned to Julie as he said with obvious wretchedness, "We were fools. We didn't know how to ride in that weather. Not well enough anyway. Not on those hills." He paused and took a deep breath before he began again. "The rain picked up, teeming, just soaking us. Our tires were skidding, sliding around in certain spots. I never realized how twisty and treacherous those mountainous roads in Vermont were. It felt like we were navigating one big, long, wet, slippery, coiled snake. My arms and hands were getting sore from holding on so tightly to the handlebars and brakes, and my brain was going to mush trying to stay focused through my waning buzz. I knew Bill wasn't doing much better because he had stopped looking over his shoulder to check on me. I lagged behind, trying to keep a straight line of sight on his dark figure up ahead, but sometimes it was gone, sometimes it was there again. I wasn't even sure if we were going in the right direction. I was solely relying on him to lead the way, and it was become increasingly difficult to keep up with him.

"About an hour into the ride, there was a steep downgrade, a mountain with a hairpin turn at the bottom. I slowed way down. I'd caught up with Bill enough to see him ahead. I was starting to get concerned, though, because it almost looked like he wasn't laying on the brakes like he should be as we approached the turn. In fact, it looked like he sped up—letting the gravity of the mountain overtake his bike. I couldn't figure out what he was doing—why he wasn't downshifting, braking—but then maybe he didn't think it was that bad. Then, as if in slow motion, I saw him slide, trying to catch the turn too fast, the bike slipping out from underneath him like a flying wet tray, off the back side of the mountain, and his body slamming hard against the pavement, skipping like a stone, and launching in a wide arc over the edge. As I witnessed it, I was in such a state of shock and horror—I couldn't believe what I'd just seen—that I also crashed, my cycle flipping on top of me as I landed on my side.

Mark looked away again, maybe because Julie's eyes had first filled with intense listening, then fear, then a mirror of his own inexorable desolation and pain. Everything he said made her think about the plane crash and brought her back to that gut-wrenching feeling of helplessness and annihilation. It was as if she could feel his trauma in her chest, like a jagged knife vicariously stabbing her and dragging her back down into its void of isolation and death by proximity.

He continued, his voice hard and emotionless, "I felt the adrenaline surge through my suddenly sober veins as I spent the next few minutes trying desperately to get my six-hundred-pound bike off me. My ankle was shattered. I could feel bone shards sliding around as I skated out from under the bike and crawled over to the edge of the road, peering down the cliff to see Bill's inert, immobile form contorted at an odd angle about a hundred yards below. His bike was nowhere to be seen—just parts and pieces scattered on the rocks. His helmet was cracked in half like an egg several feet away from him, and that's when I noticed his head was bleeding—a lot—with a gouge the size of a softball dug into his skull, a battered piece of meat. That's when I realized I was too late. He was gone."

He stopped talking, his teeth clenched, not seeing her, not seeing at all.

She waited, not breathing, not knowing what to say. She knew from firsthand experience that there weren't sufficient words.

A minute, maybe two or three, later, she softly touched his hand, laying her fingertips on top of his. He blinked and came out of his trance, turning his hand over so he could interlace their fingers.

They sat like that, quiet for a long time, neither one looking at the other. Julie finally said sincerely, gently, "I'm so sorry, Mark."

His face changed a hair, like waking up from a dream and realizing where he was, and said, "So am I." He stared down at their intertwined hands, rubbing his thumb along the base of hers, and added, "But it doesn't change a thing, does it?"

She shook her head slowly, watching his eyes study hers, thinking they had crossed paths for a reason, locking on the depth of two souls acknowledging life's unexpected and unwelcome heartaches.

He laid his head against the back of the chair, so she did too, and they both closed their eyes and sat there, not speaking for a while, listening to the distant lake water lapping against the shore of the island and the birds chirping in the trees.

Without opening his eyes, he said, "I haven't had a drop since or indulged in anything else."

She turned her head to study his profile, so strong and soft at the same time, like the curves of a wooden sculpture formed with a lathe, ingrained with the lines of age, whole worlds, intense thoughts, and deep meaning. An experience and a past that would be relived for all the rest of his days. She felt it. She knew it. Like the back of her own hand. Like that spot he was still rubbing with comforting circles.

He peeked an eye open and tilted his head her way, feeling her stare on him. He didn't smile, didn't move a muscle. The sun bespeckled a kaleidoscope on his face, into his beautiful, warm eyes, and she couldn't look away.

She finally whispered, "How?"

He answered flatly, "It's easy. I don't deserve it, so I don't."

Her brow furrowed. She didn't understand.

"That *behavior*," he said, like it was a scathing curse word, "even before the accident, it was a cop-out, an avoidance. Of myself, of my responsibilities, of who I was—what I am—my inadequacies, my vulnerability, my humanity, of what I was put here on Earth to do, to be. That's heavy stuff, and I was allowing myself to skate around it, to purposefully numb it. What did I wish to gain? Wisdom in that unhealthy, self-indulgent haze? Fool! I was nothing. I was nothing then, and after the accident I was even less. I didn't deserve to *allow* myself numbing, avoidance. I was going to *feel* every bit of that guilt, stupidity, arrogance, and the pain...the pain more than anything. I was going to make myself feel for the first time in a long time—maybe in my whole life—so I did."

Julie was listening, taking it in, hearing the words and thinking how brave he was, how unbelievably strong. Even amid his self-criticism, she couldn't feel anything but admiration for him as he bared his soul without reserve, without hesitation, without the veil that most of the world's required decorum placed on people. He was the most genuine person she had ever met.

Of course, she was also thinking about his philosophy, his strategy for coping and how it had to be undeniably excruciating. Could she do something as severe and irrevocable herself? *Would* she? The thought put the fear of God in her belly. She actually shivered in the heat of the afternoon sun raining down on them.

"Did it fix anything?" she asked, wondering for herself more than him, but also wanting the answer because she was still in the quotient mode of thinking, reparation and atonement, risk versus reward. Was it worth it?

He saw to the heart of her and answered quickly, "Certainly not. It didn't fix me either. Not right away anyway. But the self-flagellation, the denial of the pleasure, the avoidance—it eventually made me realize, if nothing else, that I was more than the worst of myself, that I was more than the baser elements of my personality, and even if I was the one who lived and not Bill, I owed it to him and to myself to explore that, to find a way to be a better human."

She paused for a second, then said, "You know, ironically, I think I've always thought of the drinking in the opposite way from what you said—that I *deserve* it. When I've had a hard day, I deserve a drink. A difficult flight or two, I deserve a drink. A tough time with my family, I deserve a drink. I'm feeling sad, or angry, or glad, or whatever, I deserve a drink."

He nodded. "For me, before, maybe it wasn't that intentional, but I agree—it was a luxury that I kept close, an indulgence, so I understand."

She went on, "And because I was—am—so good, so exquisitely good, at functioning, masking, enabling everything, my day-to-day life remains perfectly ordered. I've always figured that the reward justified the means—no harm, no foul, so why not?"

He listened. No judgment. Not a word of anything, one way or the other.

She sat up in her chair and challenged, "Was it *really* easy?"

He huffed a bit, still lying back and watching her. Then he admitted with an ironic laugh, "Of course it wasn't! Still isn't! God, you're right. I lied like a criminal." He shrugged self-consciously, and she smiled a little, instantly forgiving him as he came clean. "Let me clarify—it was easy to make the decision to stop. To *stay* stopped is difficult. It's something I have to work on every single day. It's doable. I'm living proof. But yes, it's difficult." He added, suddenly solemn, "But what's the alternative?"

She nodded, her eyes narrowing.

He continued, as if it wasn't enough to imagine it, "I never want to feel that out of control again. I never want to feel like my actions, intentional or not, could cause that kind of heartache again—to others, to myself, to the universe. Ever. I'm not saying that life doesn't throw some curve balls at you, but when that happens, I'm trying to make sure I'm no longer using that particular crutch to deal with them."

"What do you use instead?"

"Oh, AA. And I run. Work a lot. Hang out with my nieces and nephews. Call my daughter or go visit her. Do other things to fill my tank. Sometimes I even have a club soda at the local pub and meet beautiful, fascinating strangers who like to listen to me talk."

She grinned and squeezed his hand. He stood up then, taking her up with him and hugging her to his chest. The movement was so fluid and spontaneous that she didn't have time to react before she was breathing in his delicious woodsy scent, luxuriating in his strong arms and the scruff of his jaw against her cheek, and feeling the way her insides seemed to instantly melt into a buttery liquid in reaction to his touch.

He murmured into her ear, sending a warm shiver up her spine, "You'll figure it out, Julie—I know you will. And when you do, I'd like to be around to see the results."

"I'd like that too," she whispered back.

Chapter XXVI

"Next question," Ben said.

"Wait," Paige asked, "how did you get that scar on the back of your arm?"

She was still thinking of that awkward kiss a moment ago. How did he do it? Faking a kiss, faking kisses with a *hundred* women?! Seemed like cruel and unusual punishment—turning something so wonderful into something so rehearsed and cheap. He *must* be a good actor, or else how could he do it over and over again? She didn't think she could. She felt his kisses not only on her lips but in her chest, along her fingertips, in her toes, and heavily, tantalizingly, in other unmentionable places. She would need to block his confession of a hundred women from her brain forevermore after this.

Meanwhile, hiking in front of her, Ben was saying, "…and then my dad and I were thrown from the boat, my arm caught on something as we capsized—not exactly sure what, but it tore a gash in me, and because we were out on the open ocean, trying to survive for three hours by gripping the sides of the hull to stay alive, the wound didn't get treated right away. Anyway, it created an ugly scar."

"Wow, was your dad okay? Were you?"

"Yeah, we both came out of it fine—just my scar, and he had some bumps and bruises. We were just glad we got an SOS call out to the Coast Guard before the boat went down. Otherwise, who knows what would have happened."

She nodded. She was glad for that too!

"Okay, my turn. How did you end up in Emigrant, Montana? I'm guessing you weren't born here."

"Um, yeah, well, it's kind of complicated."

"I've got all day," he said, smiling back at her.

"Well...," she cleared her throat, bracing herself. She was thinking about what he said about her being "real," as if she could be anything else. So strange. But then again, she wasn't oblivious to the oxymoron that was the online world of her generation, with their filtered photos and perfectly posed selfies and everything-is-perfect-in-my-life staging...she could see why hanging out with her was something new and different for him (much as hanging out with *the* Ben Richfield was for her!).

She wasn't sure exactly when or how, but at some point in her younger days she had decided that she wouldn't try to hide who she was—her spots, her heritage, her adoption, her character—she would put it all out there and be who she was and not worry about the consequences. Yes, she got stares—yes, she was asked questions—yes, she felt self-conscious sometimes—but then she figured if her parents loved her and her friends loved her exactly as she was, and, more importantly, if she loved herself, what did it matter what anyone else thought?

Granted, she was still grappling with the aftermath of the plane crash—that was the one topic she avoided, not that she denied it or was ashamed of it—after all, it was part of her history and her story—but that didn't mean she wanted to talk about it in detail or focus on it. Mostly because it was all so tied up in other people's assumptions, *not* in relation to her or who she was or her actual firsthand experience, which she didn't even remember because she'd been just a baby.

She sped through the words she'd repeated her whole life, more times than she could count, and felt the same awkwardness, despite their blatant truth. "When I was a baby, there was a plane crash in Bozeman and everyone died except for four people—one of the flight attendants, two other people, and me. It was all over the news. Both of my biological parents died, and I lived. My adopted parents heard about me through the local adoption agency after the crash, and they'd been waiting a long time for a child, so they were happy and grateful to get me despite the unusual circumstances. The adoption was a standard closed adoption, so my ma and pa were only given a few details about my background. My biological parents were Filipino—from the Philippines. My father was here in the States for his job, and my mother was a homemaker. But I guess no one could track down any relatives residing in the

U.S. or abroad, so I was adopted just a few weeks after the crash. To this day, I still don't know why my biological parents were on a flight to Montana or where my father worked or anything else about either of them. Once I asked my doctor if my vitiligo was hereditary because I thought, well, this might be something I can finally *know* about my biology, at least, if not about my actual biological parents, but the doc told me it only has a thirty percent genetic component, which is more related to general autoimmune disease and not specifically vitiligo. So, yeah, that's all I know."

Ben was walking silently ahead of her, his face turned away, so she couldn't read it. The trail had narrowed, so they were walking single file, no longer holding hands. Paige almost had the feeling she was talking into the wind. Had he heard? What did he think? Was he shocked? Confused? Did he care?

After a few minutes, during which Paige's stomach was starting to tighten, he finally asked, "Are you still seeking?"

"More about my origin?" she clarified, and he nodded briskly, still without looking at her. "I guess I'm not sure. Ma and Pa have been such amazing parents—I couldn't have asked for better, and I don't want to hurt their feelings—but I sometimes wonder if I have any biological cousins or aunts or uncles or anyone who looks like me, is like me, in any way—out there in the world, you know?"

"Of course. Right." He nodded, almost absently, glancing back at her briefly, still trudging forward. They were going up a steep, narrow section of the path among the pines, and both of them were breathing hard, so she figured he was concentrating on the climb as much as she was.

She confessed quietly, "Do you remember that *Sesame Street* skit with the song that goes, 'One of these things is not like the others'? That's been me— in every classroom, every sporting event, birthday party, outing with friends, school, work, life. Even at the rodeo last night. No one looks like me, no one *is* like me. Would you believe that I've had customers at Chico ask me, '*What* are you?' rather than '*Who* are you?'" She grunted in her frustration, in the words she was voicing out loud maybe for the first time. "It's as if they don't realize how rude that is. They think they're being polite, trying to figure out what my background is. I don't owe them an explanation, but when it happens, it reminds me how frustrating it is that *I* hardly know a thing about my background. Yes, I know my biological parents were from the Philippines, but I've never been there, never met another living person from there, and certainly no one else with vitiligo, so how could I possibly know who I am?"

A moment passed where she fell silent, wondering again what he was thinking. He was either a great listener or not paying attention. Or worse, bored. He had seemed so talkative, easy, outgoing last night and even earlier today, but now he was so quiet. It unsettled her. She decided to lighten the mood—maybe that would help loosen his tongue. She said, "One time, when a customer at Chico asked me *what* I was, I told him with a straight face, 'I'm a lemur.'"

That got Ben's attention. He stopped in his tracks, turned around as that wonderful, light, infectious laugh spilled out of him. "A lemur?!"

"Yeah," she grinned, "a lemur. You know, black-and-white and stripe-y—"

"And cheeky. And adorable," he finished her sentence, leaning down and kissing her unexpectedly. When he pulled away from her suddenly shining face, he added, "And funny. What did the guy say?"

She smirked, "Oh, I felt a little bad because he sort of sputtered out something like, 'I—I don't know what you mean, miss!' confused by my response. Don't think I got much of a tip."

"Totally worth it."

"Totally," she agreed, grinning.

They were walking again, still immersed in the pine trees. After a few quiet minutes, they came out of the forest at the top of a ridge that descended into a clearing laced with tall grasses. About a half mile ahead, they could see the trail's namesake—a beautiful grove of aspen trees fluttering in the wind beside a creek, the water rushing toward their unseen final destination—the waterfall. They both stopped to take a deep breath and admire the spectacular view.

"See," he said softly, "*this* is what it's all about—this is what's real, just like *you*. Salt of the earth. What brings us close to ourselves, to our purpose, to God, our connection to this ground, this forest, these mountains, each other. The world's creation, the world's treasure. This!" His hand swept the landscape.

"Yes!" Paige whispered back reverently. It was hard not to get this infectious feeling when seeing the wonder of nature in all its glory, splayed out like a master's painting before them.

He tucked her in beside him, his arm around her back. She felt his heart beating as she leaned into his chest. He brushed a kiss across her temple, and she sighed into his side, wondering if life got any better than this, despite their heavy conversation (or maybe because of it). She couldn't fully explain it, didn't know what luck or fate had brought them together—her and this man who was raised and lived a life so different from her own, yet in their short time together seemed to share so many of her thoughts and feelings about the world. She found herself cherishing every moment and wondering what the next would bring.

Their hearts were pounding, probably not just because of the elevation. He turned to face her and they kissed for a few minutes, sealing their shared rapture with their lips.

When he drew away, his face began to crack into a smile as he said, "I'm glad we broke the spell."

Paige didn't understand and frowned up at him. "Huh?"

He answered with a grin, "I was worried I may have ruined kissing for you for good."

"Oh!" she laughed. "I was worried too!"

He let go of her and started leading her down the descent into the field of tall grasses. "Let's never talk about that again."

"No, never," she agreed readily.

"In fact, let's not talk about past relationships either. What do you say?"

"Sounds like a great plan to me," Paige said, almost laughing—as if she had anything to share! She also breathed a sigh of relief as a quick reel of images flashed in her mind (memories of her online research)—Ben with a bevy of beauties standing by his side. She never wanted to think about them again, nor how many women he had kissed.

When they got to the bottom of the hill and began walking on the path that cut through the prairie grasses, Paige noted, "The grasshoppers are so loud!"

"Is that what those little buggers are? How do they make that sound anyway? Like a metal grater or a typewriter or something."

"Snapping their wings or legs together, or both, I think."

"You must love living here," Ben said, more of a statement than a question.

"Yeah, I'm pretty lucky. Of course, in the winter, it's a bit of a different story."

"I've never been here in winter. What's it like?"

"Wait, what question number is that?"

"Oh yeah," he laughed, "I kind of forgot about the game."

"We're probably already way over our twenty anyway. But, in answer to your question, it's cold, windy, snowy, quiet, pretty, and very bright."

"Bright?"

"Yeah, when the sun reflects off the snow, it's almost blinding. But beautiful too."

"I bet. I'll have to come visit."

Paige smiled, feeling the warmth of his comment in her chest. "Sure. I'll take you out snowmobiling. Backcountry."

"That would be awesome!" he exclaimed.

They walked in silence for a bit, still about a quarter mile from the aspen grove. Then, in a more serious tone, he asked, "So you work with your parents? What's that like?"

"Good. We're all a big family over at Chico. I've hung out there my whole life. It's kind of funny because the tourists swoop in and out every week, but the staff stays the same. Speaking of that," she just remembered something, "do you know Shae? She's a costume designer on the set of your show. She's dating our bartender, and she talks about the show sometimes at Chico."

He thought for a minute and answered, "Yeah, I think so—tall, dark hair, thick bangs, red lipstick?"

"Yep, that's her."

"Yeah, I've met her a few times."

"She's cool. She's really into that whole ancestry stuff—keeps trying to convince me to get online and look up my heritage. Apparently, she's traced her family tree back multiple generations, all the way to Ireland."

"You should!" he stopped to exclaim. "Do you have enough info to start a search?"

"I think so—I have my birth name and my biological parents' names. But like I said, I'm still a little scared to open up that can of worms. We'll see. What about your parents? What do they do? Do you have a rich family history?"

"Nah, I don't know much. I'm German on my dad's side, not sure on my mom's. Heck, maybe I'll do the search at the same time you do. Let me know. Swab our cheeks or spit in a tube or whatever they have you do. Might be fun to find out."

She nodded eagerly.

They walked in silence for a bit, her mind filled with the possibilities.

He was ahead of her again, his face turned away. Eventually, he started a sentence, then stopped, then started and stopped again. It was strange. He was usually so self-assured, so smooth and easy in everything he did, even in his dialogue, but it was almost as if he was struggling to bring up a topic, and she didn't know why. He finally said slowly, almost cautiously, "My mom was an actress, but she gave it up when she had us. Now she manages a boutique shop in Calabasas."

"Oh?" Paige said. That seemed rather innocuous, so Paige wasn't sure why he was somber all of a sudden. He wasn't looking her way, so she couldn't decipher his face or the mystery of his mood. He was certainly blasting hot and cold today. She wasn't sure how to take it.

The dusty path forged between the prairie flowers and bushes echoed their heavy bootsteps as they scampered around roots, rocks, and the noisy, jumping grasshoppers. Ben turned his head back to her for a second, still walking straight, as he continued, "My dad…yeah, well…my dad started off doing TV stuff—production—then movies for a bit, but then he went back and got his MBA, and now he's an executive at Google."

Paige said, "Oh wow, that's cool," Trying to lift his mood, she added, "Tell him thanks for me. I use Google every day."

Not a blip, not a hint of a smile. She was perplexed. She tried to get a glimpse of the front of his face instead of just the side of it. She thought that his suddenly serious expression was similar to last night when Abby revealed that Paige was a plane crash survivor. Paige was trying to put two and two together and coming up with zero. Once again, she was left wondering what that trepidatious, slightly scared, confused look on his face was. And how did it relate to Paige? Or did it?

Maybe she was reading too much into it. Maybe it had nothing to do with her at all. Why would it? Maybe his dad's job was in jeopardy for some reason. Or maybe the look was wrapped up in that story about his sister. He'd talked earlier about his mom living somewhat vicariously through her children on the acting front—maybe that had caused problems between his parents. Maybe his dad resented the consequences of her pushing the children into acting. Paige could see where the issues with his sister might have put a strain on the whole family. She was at a loss how to broach the subject again, though. After all, these were private family affairs, and as much as she felt an instant connection with Ben, she recognized that she was still mostly a stranger to him. She didn't want to pry. Plus, maybe it was worse—maybe one of his parents was sick or hurt or dying.

Her mind was racing. It could be anything! Or nothing. She needed to stop. She was frowning, concentrating on her feet, trying to figure out a way to break the silence that stretched out before them like a long, dark tunnel. What was going through that head of his?

Minutes went by.

Finally, glancing back at her, his feet still trudging forward, Ben spoke up, his voice so soft and tentative that she had to strain to hear it. "Listen, Paige, about my dad, yeah—um—I need to tell you something—you see—he— ouch, oh *fuck!* WATCH OUT!"

In an instant that felt like an hour, Ben flung his leg up in the air as if he'd been shot and screamed bloody murder. Paige gawked and saw an enormous rattlesnake coiled up next to a rock and heard the treacherous sound of its rattle shaking like a death knell. She ran right into Ben, crashing to the ground in a heap several feet from the snake's raised head as it now gave *her* a menacing stare. Paige screamed and jolted, scooting back. Ben quickly snatched her up as he danced around yelping and hauling them both in the opposite direction.

Ben's hands were on her shoulders, leading her away, but she didn't look at his face, her eyes fixed on the snake's triangular head. She was making a sound somewhere between a cry and a scream, her boots tripping over Ben's as she pedaled backward, trying with all her might not to lose her balance and fall forward toward that ominous sound.

Finally, amid a swirl of dust and chaos, they were far enough away that she saw the snake (thankfully) uncoil and retreat behind the rock. Paige stole a glance at Ben and saw something there that turned her blood cold. He was grimacing, his face a mask of pain as he reached down to the outside of his right leg where the meaty muscle of his calf met his sock and hiking boot. Paige's dilated eyes focused on the skin for the span of a half second—two distinctive holes, oozing a pinkish liquid. Ben fell to the ground, cursing, taking Paige down with him.

"Oh my God, BEN!"

She was on her knees hovering over him as he lay on his back and winced, his legs up in the air like a turtle flipped on its shell. He said through clenched teeth and deep, gulping breaths, "Paige—go get help—*right*—*now*."

She began to cry, feeling the panic rising like poison in her throat. She stuttered, "I can't—*won't* leave you, Ben."

"Just go!" he snarled.

But she didn't. She was shaking badly and beginning to sob. She had trouble focusing, but she fumbled for her phone and searched for a signal. Nothing. Not a single bar. She shoved it back in her pocket with a frustrated growl.

Meanwhile, Ben was writhing in pain, rolling around and cursing.

Paige said quickly, "Ben, the more you move, the more the venom will spread. Stay still as much as you can." She realized in a horror-stricken second that Ben could die. Death by rattlesnake was uncommon but not unheard of. *Holy shit.*

What she needed to do more than anything to prevent that from happening was to stay calm. She said out loud to herself, "Paige, stay calm." Oddly, the moment she said it, a warm blanket of stillness descended upon her like a gift from the heavens. She took a long, deep breath, wiped her eyes, and cupped Ben's sweaty red cheeks in her palms. She was trying to draw his attention away from the pain. He grabbed her wrists, agony written all over his face.

With his eyes piercing hers, she forced him to focus as she said sternly, with authority, "Ben. Listen to me. We need to get you to the hospital right away. You need antivenom. I don't have a phone signal out here, and we would be wasting time if I tried to get you help and came back, so we need to get you to the car ASAP. I'll drive you to the hospital. Bozeman's Deaconess is less than thirty miles from here. We just need to walk back through the forest. Do you think you can do that? You can lean on me with your good leg."

His eyes pinched together like clams but then snapped open, roving back and forth over her face like a scared animal. He finally gave her a curt nod, biting down on his lip. She helped him to his feet. He was unsteady as a foal, but he threw his weight onto her, one arm flung over her free shoulder, and she withstood it, thinking to herself that she'd never been more appreciative of her years working at Chico—she was used to lugging trays of heavy plates and dinnerware for hours. If she could do that, she could do this.

They made their way slowly but steadily through the prairie grass and up the hill into the forest, all the while Ben's groans causing Paige to whisper over and over again, "It's okay, you're okay, we're gonna be okay, stay with me." She began to think she was saying it more to convince herself than him, as he was using all his concentration and purpose to keep moving. At one point, she glanced down the length of him and saw that his leg was turning blue. He was sweating profusely, his shirt completely saturated. When he told her he was feeling lightheaded, Paige pushed him along even faster, wishing there was a way to magically transport them to the car. He was practically like a dead weight against her, and she had never felt such an aching in her back, arms, and legs, even with her years at Chico. She wanted to let go, drop to the ground, give up. Not an option, she kept telling herself. Not. An. Option. Keep going. Must. Keep. Going. At one point, she even thought with a short, sick, twisted laugh that she finally had a boyfriend (or something close to it) and by golly, there was no way she was going to let him die.

When it seemed as though he might just slump to the ground, Paige bolstered him up, positioning him with even more of his weight on her. She said, "Ben, stay focused. Not much farther now." Which wasn't exactly true, but she was mustering up as much encouragement (for both of them) as she could.

After what seemed like hours but was probably only twenty minutes, they were almost out of the forest, and she could see the parking lot and the Escalade like a glorious beacon in the night. She exhaled in relief, doing everything in her power not to burst into tears. Keep it together, Paige.

There were two other vehicles in the lot—pickup trucks—but she didn't see any people, and she didn't think they'd be any help since this lot led to several trailheads, all of which splayed out in different directions like bicycle spokes. She was on her own, and she was going to get Ben to the hospital no matter what.

When they finally, mercifully, reached the SUV, Paige said encouragingly, "Ben, look. We're here. Where are your keys?"

"In my right front pocket," he mumbled.

She reached her hand around and into his shorts, not even feeling a stitch of embarrassment, as if no other feelings of any kind could be squished into this intense hour of emergency. She unlocked the car, tossing both of their backpacks in the back, and helped Ben in the passenger side. She quickly hopped into the driver's seat, started the car, adjusted the seat, got her bearings, and barreled out of the parking lot in a trail of dust.

She kept both hands on the steering wheel, white-knuckled, glancing at Ben every few moments. He was pitched forward and leaning toward Paige, almost on top of the center console, perhaps missing the support of her arms around him.

A few minutes later, she detached one hand from the steering wheel to check the signal on her phone. Still none.

Paige said, "Ben, how're you doing?" She almost hated to ask and held her breath awaiting the answer.

He grunted, "Not good. It hurts like hell."

"I know, babe," Paige said, wiping away a few strands of wet hair from his face as his hollow, woeful eyes took her in before pinching shut.

He grabbed her fingers and squeezed hard. "Thank you, Paige," he said with sincerity and urgency, and she nodded, tearing her eyes away from his face to focus on the road.

She drove as fast as she could to Bozeman, all the while trying to distract Ben with innocuous, ridiculous stories from her high school, including a long, meandering tale about the first time she tried snowboarding with Abby in Big Sky.

When she looked at her phone again, she had two bars, so she did the first thing she could think of—she called her pa. "Pa," she whimpered into the phone when she heard his voice, letting go, just for a second, of the thin tether of control she had been harnessing. She sniffed and plowed through with a shaky voice, "Ben got bit by a rattlesnake. He's…he's hurting. I'm driving to Deaconess right now. We're about ten minutes out. Can you meet us there?"

Without hesitation, he answered, "On my way."

They hung up, and Paige took a long, deep breath and sat up a little straighter in her seat.

Reinforcements were on the way, and she was going to save her maybe boyfriend—the one who said he loved how real she was. He was going to be a survivor, just like she was, and she was going to make sure she did everything in her power to make that happen.

Chapter XXVII

MARIE AND KENT FINISHED EATING THEIR DINNER, mostly in silence, as Marie contemplated what road she would take to self-discovery and recovery. She really wasn't sure how to begin, but she figured a good night's sleep would be the first order of business. It had been a long day with Julie at the Cranberry Inn (which, thinking back on it, caused Marie to cringe) and the emotional meltdown followed by the lovemaking and long conversations with Kent. She hadn't remembered a day more emotionally exhausting since the plane crash. Did it portend what was to come? No wonder she was shaking in her boots.

As Kent cleared the table, she began washing the dishes. Then Kent left to go pick up the kids. It was well after eleven, and she hoped her in-laws hadn't minded having them this late. But knowing her in-laws, they'd fed the kids mountains of food and told them to go outside and start a bonfire, and loved every minute of it. They really were the best grandparents, and Marie knew how lucky she was to have them so close. With her parents on the other side of the country in Montana, the kids rarely got to spend time with them, and she sometimes regretted that, even resented the fact that Kent's parents had formed such a tight bond with her kids, whereas her parents barely knew them. Thinking about it now, though, she could hardly blame either set because it was *she* who had wanted out of her small town and had moved thousands of miles away. What did she expect would happen? She built a world here in Connecticut, and whether or not she'd intended it to happen, that meant she was separated from her Montana roots, and therefore, so were her kids.

She had a brief flash—what if the family trip Kent had suggested was to her parents' ranch? The kids had never been there. It would be an experience. Maybe they could rent an RV and drive cross-country. Lord knew she hated flying, for obvious reasons, but also, she thought, nothing could be more bonding than a week together on a cross-country road trip. Of course, it could go the opposite way—drive them all mad. Three teenagers together with their parents with no way to get away from each other. Ugh. Was she crazy? She wasn't sure. Plus, she'd have a lot of shuffling around, planning, and fixing calendars to do, but when she thought of the potential excitement in her parents' voices when she told them, it set her mind and heart racing. She'd ask Kent, see what he thought of the idea.

Meanwhile, as she scrubbed the saucepan, she chuckled, thinking Kent's dad was probably (at this exact moment) scaring the kids out of their wits with one of his drawn-out, bone-chilling ghost stories that always seemed to involve a crotchety old farmer who used a sickle to cut his crops (and apparently other things). Marie had always bristled at these stories, finding them infantile and grotesque, but her children (and her other child, she thought sarcastically—*Kent*) reveled in them, never wanting "Poppi" to stop, even though they would jump or scream half out of their wits.

By the time they came home, Marie was in bed, trying to sleep, but she heard them downstairs regaling each other about who jumped first and the unenviable victim denying vociferously that they had jumped at all. Marie smiled to herself and flipped her still damp, tear-stained pillow over, adjusting it against her head, thinking that despite her own fear of what the future would hold in this new, unknown world of her life, she was so lucky.

So, so lucky.

The next morning, Marie woke up at her usual time, five-thirty, and got the house moving, making coffee and breakfast, greeting the house cleaner at the door, feeding, packing, and moving the kids along to their various activities after they came downstairs groggy and rubbing their eyes, and kissing Kent long and hard on the lips when he stopped in the kitchen on his way to the studio.

She told him, "I'm going to tend to the horses in a few minutes and then get a few things out of the attic, so if you need me, call my cell."

"Okay," he said with a raised eyebrow. He didn't ask what she was retrieving from the attic but probably guessed and let her be.

Marie found Darby in the barn and helped her brush and feed the horses and shovel out the stalls. Marie didn't normally help, so Darby seemed pleasantly surprised to see her there and chatted away about her upcoming horse shows, which programs and events she was excelling at, and which needed improvement. Marie listened contentedly, thinking maybe she had been small-minded and jealous of Kent these past few years since he got all of Darby's attention as they traveled around to her shows on the weekends when, in reality, obviously (when it came to horses anyway) Darby was open to sharing with anyone who would listen, even her mother, who (apparently, Marie realized for the first time just this very moment) rarely had the time or inclination.

As they finished up, Darby saddled her favorite mare, leaping up on her. Marie patted Darby's boot and said, "Darby, thanks for this time together. I've really enjoyed it."

"Me too, Mom," Darby said with a warm (if not slightly shocked) smile. "Let's do it again soon."

"Let's," Marie agreed, smoothing her hand over the horse's rump as Darby clucked and kicked her heels lightly into the mare's side, leading her out of the barn.

Marie was feeling high as a kite, her mind and heart clear, which she figured was the perfect time to take on a most daunting undertaking. The manual labor and chat with Darby put her in the right headspace. Although, when she walked out of the barn toward the house, she felt her heart begin to pound in her chest, her palms begin to sweat, fear trickling through her veins. She was so uncomfortable with the lack of control over her emotions, her motivations, her destiny, herself. It was an odd feeling, and she wasn't sure what to do with it. She braced herself, remembering the encouraging words Kent had infused into her psyche the night before—about facing her feelings in order to begin to live again. Just thinking through the words didn't make the act of facing them any easier, however.

Inside the house, not wanting to allow herself the luxury of procrastination, she went directly to the attic door and opened it. She flipped on the light switch and climbed the stairs, going to the back right corner, knowing instinctively where the bulk of the unmentionable items were stashed, even though it had been over twenty years since she had seen them. She grabbed several large boxes and brought them downstairs to the living room.

One trip after another until there were seven boxes laid out in front of her. She sat down on the couch, breathing hard and thinking. She went into the kitchen for a glass of water, drinking it slowly, stalling and worrying. Then she pinched her lips together with resolve and returned to the living room.

The first box she opened contained mostly clothes—bibs, onesies, booties, tiny green-and-orange-striped socks, winter hats, and a blue snowsuit with mittens and a tiny UConn scarf. She immediately began to cry as she touched each item and then rubbed one after another against her cheek, smelling deep into the fabric, thinking about the chubby legs and arms and torso that used to live inside each of them. *Matthew*. Her Matthew. Their Matthew. The sweetest, most adorable, most wonderful baby boy.

Other boxes had stuffed animals and toys, photo albums and cards, videos and books, handmade quilts and blankets. Finally there was his baby book and two additional scrapbooks with mementos to record and document his every waking moment from the day he was born until the day he died.

Why had he been taken from them?

It wasn't fair. He was so innocent, trusting, faithful, true, pure. And then he was gone. They had boxed him away like an old coat. Discarded. Never to be brought out again. Never to be remembered or savored. Never to question, understand, process, feel the loss. It was as if they had weaned him from their hearts. Because it hurt too much. Never to be present. Until now.

God, it hurt. Like hell.

She sobbed and rocked over the contents of every box for several hours until the house cleaner came into the room cautiously, saying, "Mrs. Stanley, are you alright? Can I help in any way? I brought you these." She set a box of tissues and a cup of tea on the coffee table and stood there awkwardly.

Marie grabbed a tissue and blew her nose, muttering, "Oh Gieda, thank you so much. I'm sorry—I'm a wreck today, but I'll be fine," she lied with a small, reassuring smile.

Gieda said, "Okay ma'am, um, I'm done for today. I've left the kids' towels in the dryer if that's okay. They should be done in thirty minutes or so."

"Sure, that's fine, Gieda—you may go," Marie said, looking into Gieda's kind brown eyes, maybe for the first time ever, really looking. Marie frowned and said slowly, "Oh Gieda, by the way, thank you for everything you do. I appreciate it. I appreciate you. I don't know what I would have done without you all these years."

Gieda nearly choked, tears springing to her eyes. "Thank you, ma'am." She blinked a few times and brought her apron up to her face in slight embarrassment, but Marie kept her eyes locked on her face. Gieda added with a strained voice, "It's been a pleasure serving your family."

Gieda began to turn away, but Marie stopped her, saying, "Gieda, would you like to see a photo of our son?"

"Mr. Ryan, ma'am?" she asked, confused.

"No Gieda, our *first* son, Matthew."

Gieda's brow furrowed. "Um, okay, yes, ma'am," she answered, not understanding but curious.

Marie made room on the couch, and Gieda sat beside her and took the photo from her hand. Marie said, "This is Matthew when he was one. He had just started walking, so we took him to the park to stumble around a bit and ride the swing. He loved the swing—would squeal in delight whenever we let him go high. Look at his roly-poly legs—weren't they adorable?"

"Yes, ma'am, such a good-looking boy." Gieda stared at the photo, then at Marie, then back down again. Finally, she said tentatively, "Um, Mrs. Stanley, I didn't know you had another son. He looks a lot like you. And a little bit like Mr. Ryan. But, ma'am, wha—what happened to him?"

Marie drew in a ragged breath, letting a silent tear fall down her cheek before answering. "He died. Just a few short months after this photo was taken."

Gieda took Marie's hand, something she had never done before and probably wouldn't have ever tried, Marie realized, out of respect, caution, fear, until now, when Marie was being completely out of character—vulnerable, fragile, open. Gieda said to Marie, whose face was tear-stained, "Ma'am, I am so sorry. There is no devastation greater than losing a child. I know, ma'am. I lost my son nearly twenty-five years ago, and I still think about him every day."

"Oh!" Marie cried, shocked. She held a tissue to her mouth, thinking about how sometimes kindred spirits came in the most unusual packages and often when least expected and most needed. "I'm so sorry. How—how—old was he?"

"His name was Daniel. He was eight years old and the kindest, calmest, sweetest person I ever knew. He was born with a degenerative disease, so we cherished every second with him, not knowing if it would be our last. When he was gone, we felt blessed to have had so many happy memories of our time together. That's what got us through—knowing he led a full life, even during the hard times. We made sure of it. And knowing he is still with us today." She clutched a hand to her heart. "I'm sure you understand—we must cling to what was and what is left."

Marie's eyes were overflowing now. Unable to respond, she instead pulled Gieda into an embrace. The two women sat there like that for a few minutes, lost in their own memories and grief, until they were startled by Marie's daughter Bridget, who was standing in the doorway of the living room and said with some fear in her voice, "Um, Mom, hey, what's going on?"

Marie and Gieda broke apart as Marie wiped her eyes and said, "Bridget, hi, you're, um, you're home from the library."

Gieda stood up, cleared her throat, and said formally, "Okay, ma'am, I'll be off then." Turning to Bridget, she added, "Miss Bridget, I hand-washed your bathing suits and left them hanging on your shower rod."

"Thanks, Gieda," Bridget said, not even looking at her, instead staring pointedly at her mother, transfixed.

Gieda slipped out the door quietly, and Bridget came and took her place on the couch. She asked, "What's all this stuff, Mom?"

Marie took a deep breath and said, "This, hon, is Matthew. Your brother."

"Matthew," Bridget said softly, almost as if to feel his name on her tongue. She picked up a few of the photos and one of the scrapbooks and flipped through a few pages, saying incredulously, "Wow, I've never seen *any* of this. Where's it been?"

"Up in the attic."

Bridget leafed through the items and smiled down on her brother like a long lost friend.

Marie said shakily, "I'm sorry I've never shown you kids…I guess I was… too hurt—honestly, too *crushed* when we lost him, and well, I thought if I tucked everything about him away, I would start to feel better again."

Bridget looked up at her mom and stated, "But you didn't."

"No." Marie let out a long, drawn-out breath. "I'm starting to see that eventually you have to face even the hardest things in life or you just end up in a vicious cycle of avoidance and blame." Marie leaned back, laying her head against the back of the couch and running her fingers through Bridget's curly blond hair, saying, "You know, when you kids were younger, I figured that Matthew's soul had found a way back into our lives through your hearts. Every time one of you cried or laughed or walked or talked, I thought maybe Matthew was living on through you, almost vicariously. And I figured if I kept you kids busy and active and successful, it would take away all of the bad feelings I still had inside about losing Matthew." Bridget turned her head around to regard her mom thoughtfully as Marie continued, "But that was just me putting something on you guys that I never should have. And I'm sorry for that. Will you—can you forgive me?"

Bridget's lips hitched up into a warm smile. "Of course, Mom. We've only ever wanted you to be happy. And we've wanted to talk about Matthew—to get to know what he was like. He always seemed off-limits, and we never understood why. Dad mentioned him through the years. We just didn't know if you still thought about him because you never brought him up."

"Oh sweetie, I'm sorry you thought that," Marie said in horror. "Of course I did. I *do*. Every day. I'm sorry I never shared him with you guys. I should have. It was wrong of me." Then in a quiet plea, "I will now, though, if you like."

"Yeah, I would." Bridget leaned back to rest in her mother's arms.

Marie mumbled into her hair, "Sweetie, I was so wrong. I would never want you kids to feel pressure to be anything other than what you are—unique, independent, thoughtful, caring, wonderful children. I couldn't ask for better kids. And I include Matthew in that mix. He wasn't with us for very long, but he made a huge dent in our hearts, and I'd love to show you how much he meant to us. And how much I want to make it up to you and your brother and sister and Dad. I hope you'll let me."

"Mom, there's nothing to make up."

Marie pulled away, staring into Bridget's green eyes as she continued fiercely, "Yes, there is. And believe me, I know I've been a nightmare at times, a perfect sergeant major." Marie grimaced, which caused Bridget to laugh a little. "I'm not perfect, and I won't ever be. In fact, I'm sure I'll be a mess for a long while—bad habits die hard—but if you're willing to help me see what I can do better, I want to try."

"Okay, Mom, okay," Bridget said willingly, nodding.

Then they both turned to see Kent in the doorway, his hands in his pockets, smiling with slightly watery eyes. He cleared his throat and asked innocently, "When's lunch?"

Marie stood up, leaving Bridget to peruse the rest of the boxes.

As Marie and Kent walked into the kitchen, he took her hand and kissed it. She said somewhat guardedly, "How much of that did you hear?"

He stopped her then, taking her by the shoulders to face him. He said, "All of it," his face full of love and light and hope.

She gave him a wan smile. "Kent," she sighed. "I'm still so afraid, though. Of all the—the feelings. They're so hard. It's as if I might suffocate."

He pulled her into his chest, and she laid her head against his beating heart. "I know, honey. It's not going to be easy." He kissed the top of her head. "But I'll be here with you. And the kids. We're not going anywhere. Let's focus on what's good for right now—our fortunate, blessed lives, and how Matthew was—and is—part of our family. And when you're ready to confront the past, you can get some help to process the plane crash. You don't have to work through all the chapters of the book at once. One chapter at a time." He drew her away, looking deep into her eyes. "Okay?"

"Okay," she answered unsteadily, thinking she wasn't sure how she would be able to face it, but she would begin by focusing on Matthew and remembering how blessed she was to have been his mother.

Chapter XXVIII

MARK PULLED AWAY FROM JULIE after a long, deep squeeze and said, "Come on, let's go sit by the water." He took their Bloody Marys and set them on the picnic table, then picked up the Adirondack chairs and set them down on the shoreline a few feet from his boat. She refilled their cups from his thermos and followed. They took off their shoes and sat down, feeling the warm water lapping up on their feet and ankles.

"This is so nice," she said, leaning back and closing her eyes. "I haven't done this in years."

"What?" he asked, then with a grin, "hung out on a deserted island?"

She laughed. "Well, that either—maybe ever—but I meant taking a day to sit back, relax, and enjoy nature. I'm always running, running, running, you know? I guess it's rather difficult for me to stop and smell the roses."

"Well, it's time you started, don't you think?"

"Yes," she agreed, still not opening her eyes, letting the sound of the birds and the waves and Mark's deep voice resonate in her chest and her temples. It was nice to sit back and just be sometimes. She had almost forgotten—it had been so long.

They sat in contented silence for a while. Ten minutes turned into fifteen. Then, without a word, without a sound, Julie felt Mark's warm mouth on hers. She was startled for a second, her eyes fluttering open, then feeling his breath on her face and the smile behind it, she closed her eyes and relaxed into the kiss. He was softly pressing against her mouth as if to test its strength, willingness, subtlety. She loved the way he tasted and the pressure he was applying—it was just enough. She didn't lift her head, not even an inch, from the back of the chair, letting him do all the work as he turned slightly to get a better angle. He parted her lips, at first just to close them again with a wonderful suction, then with his tongue, and she opened to him, an invitation, which he took, greedily, his one hand suddenly in her hair, his other along her arm, rubbing and roaming around her skin with gentle squeezes. She let herself go, feeling every synapse in her body awaken to his touch, to his tongue. She was like the water flowing around her feet—fluid, loose, free. The hand that had been on her arm was now on her hip, just resting there, and she wanted more than anything to pick it up and press it against the yearning parts of her—the curve of her jawline, the cup of her breast, the space between her thighs. She felt like every part of her body was suddenly alive and throbbing, thirsting for his touch. She waited, though, not wanting to change a single thing about this moment.

Just then, he pulled away, and she opened her eyes to his smiling face.

His voice was low and gravelly as he said, "God, I've wanted to do that since I saw you wearing my outfit last night."

She laughed, breathing hard, and he sat back down, taking a long drink from his cup, never letting his eyes leave her face.

She wondered what to say, how to act. She was still in a fuzzy, tingly haze.

He had it covered, though, with an almost apology, "You looked so peaceful and beautiful just then, I couldn't resist."

"I'm glad you didn't," she murmured, and he smiled.

He sat thoughtfully for a few minutes and said, "You know that whole thing about deserving or not deserving—maybe we're looking at it the wrong way."

"Oh?"

"Yeah, I mean, maybe it's not about that, not about getting what we have coming to us, good or bad. Maybe it's about knowing what awaits us if we don't give in to it—for instance, days like this. We always think that the result of not drinking, not giving in to our baser desires, will be negative, a weight around our neck—that we'll be forced to experience all the hardships in life without a filter, without a buffer, without that high. Heck, they call it 'getting on the wagon,' as if an easy ride awaits—to tempt us, I suppose—but when you're riding in the bed of that wagon, it feels like anything but.

"Although what I've learned both on the wagon and off is that it's all a fallacy—there are no easy rides in life. But maybe with one ride, you won't even know, can't even realize, how good, how spectacular, something is—like that kiss we just shared—because you'll be in a fog, immune to its splendor, or at least will only feel it or know it fleetingly, like a quick, innocuous interlude between fixes. The surface, physical pleasure without anything deeper attached to it.

"When I'm sober, I feel everything so intensely—yes, the difficult stuff, which can be excruciating, but also the exquisite beauty in the world, ripe for the taking, that I never noticed before, never gloried in, never took into my soul and relished until I was clear enough, brave enough, to allow myself to."

Julie was drinking in every word, absorbing his heated hazel eyes like a tonic. With a shaky intake of breath, she whispered, "It scares me so..."

"I know." He took her hand in his, rubbing along the knuckles. "The power of the good in the world will do that sometimes, just as much as the bad. It's a hurdle. Not an easy one. But worth it."

"But how...?"

"That's something you'll need to think through," he said kindly.

"So—so AA, it worked for you...?" she stumbled, "Sorry, I wasn't sure if you—were okay talking about it..."

"Of course. You can ask me anything," he answered easily. "Yes, AA. It worked for me, kept me in check all these years. Especially during the dark times. My daughter, Kaylie, she really helps too. My own personal barometer." He chuckled. "Kids have no filter. If I'm acting irrationally or veering toward the edge, she'll just flat-out tell me. That's always helped. It brought us a lot closer, knowing she was there for me, no matter what, and that she would keep me honest."

"And your ex?"

"Yeah," he said, clearing his throat and glancing away toward the tree-lined woods across the lake. "Um, that didn't go so well. She was very bitter, rightfully so, after the accident. After all, it was her brother who died. Even before the accident, though, we'd been drifting apart, both working too much, not focusing on each other enough, plus, I was spending entirely too much time and attention on smoking and drinking. There was very little left for her or anything else. I was still really immature back then. And I foolishly thought that having mutual friends and her brother in common translated into us being compatible and meant for each other. At the time, I didn't think about the fact that she and I didn't have anything in common. My addictions allowed me to avoid seeing what was right in front of my face—put a barrier between what I was and what I needed from a relationship—and, of course, what she needed. It was a recipe for disaster from the beginning, really. The accident just threw everything into overdrive—it was the last straw."

Julie nodded, understanding "the last straw"—she'd confronted it too. Friends and family saying it was *their* last straw with her, and instead of bending, yielding, or giving in, she refused to change, feeling it was easier, safer, better for them if they walked away and left her. She didn't deserve any more forgiveness, graciousness, any more straws. But was she willing to change now?

She asked, "Is she—still around?"

"Oh yeah—she's local, remarried, has two more kids, they're in high school. I know her husband—he was Kaylie's soccer coach. Good guy."

"You get along?"

"Not in the beginning. She was bitter, but she came around slowly after she saw that I was sticking to my program and that she could trust me with custody of Kaylie. It was a hard road at first—I'm not gonna lie—but we ended up in a good place and with mutual respect, and that's what matters. We both always put Kaylie first." He looked at her and asked softly, "What happened with your marriage?"

"Oh, well, the love was there, and the compatibility was never an issue," she said slowly, sadly. "But after the crash, *I* wasn't ever fully there again. I wasn't ready to purge myself of the aftermath, I guess. I had to jump into action—that was my way to handle the…trauma of it, but that didn't leave room for anything or any*one* else. He tried to stick it out, but two people can only live separate lives for so long and pretend they're still married. I was the one who finally walked away. He wouldn't have ever pulled the plug—I was his ride or die—but I couldn't keep hurting him, so I set him free."

He nodded. "Do you ever see him?"

"Nah, not in years. He owns a bar in Chicago, and once in while I used to stop by just to check in and see how he was doing, but it got to be too hard. For him. For me. Then last time I was there, a few years ago, he introduced me to his new wife. Gulp. I had to get out of there. On the one hand, I felt so happy for him—he'd finally moved on and found love again—but my God, it hurt like hell. I went home and drank so much that night, I threw up for a day and a half afterward."

Mark stared gently, still rubbing her knuckles, still seeing her, accepting her words, her openness, her heart. After a few minutes, he said, "You know, you mentioned last night that you've never talked about what happened that day—the day of the crash. I don't want you to feel any pressure, but I'm here to listen if you'd like to purge yourself, as you say. It might do you good. Sometimes just telling someone—a person who hasn't been involved, doesn't know the history, can't form any judgments or associations or opinions about an experience—sometimes that's the best person to help you work through something. It's what's worked for me in AA—telling a room full of strangers my innermost thoughts, confessions, sins, feelings, fears, hopes. I don't know why, but it helps me face everything in a way I can't with close friends and family."

Julie nodded, taking a deep breath. She knew he was probably right. She had twenty years of pent-up emotions, failures, nightmares, unresolved feelings—maybe it was time to release them to the universe. Let them go. Not that they would ever truly be gone, but if she could wrench them out of her soul and crack them open, the healing might begin. She found the thought almost…hopeful. And she hadn't felt that in so long.

So she began, taking her time talking through every aspect of that day— the blizzard, the busy airports, the deicing—which in retrospect seemed too quick, too superficial for Denver—and the crash. How the pilot knew something was wrong, how she went into emergency mode, giving orders and readying the passengers as best she could, how and what she told the parents of the lap babies, how the plane fell, racing through the air before finally smashing into the ground, the sound and feeling of being nearly torn apart, how she was injured, how the plane looked split in two and on fire, how she tried to get the few survivors out, how she went back into the burning plane to find a baby alive in an overhead bin, how she reunited the baby with its mother only to find out that she wasn't the baby's mother. How many dead bodies and body parts she saw that day, scattered in the white snow like bloody red stains amid the remains of the fiery fuselage and ejected luggage.

How, even today, certain images never leave her mind and come back to her in nightmares. How sometimes when she's awake, those images are like living nightmares just behind her eyes—always. How she's tried to make amends, in so many ways, but has never felt successful, complete, reconciled. Yet. How she feels a need to keep in touch with Paige, the baby she found in the overhead bin, even though she knows Paige wishes she would go away and leave her alone.

By the end, Julie was crying, and Mark simply said, "Come here," pulling her by the hand to come sit on his lap. He held her close, letting her cry into his shoulder as he gently rubbed her back and placed his other hand comfortingly on her knee. They stayed like that for a long time until she quieted. She said, "What am I going to do, Mark? How can this ever get better?"

He kissed her forehead and said, "I know it feels like that sometimes—maybe *all* the time—but there may be a day—maybe not tomorrow or the next day or even anytime soon, but someday—when a sliver of light will shine through and lead the way for you to come toward it. And maybe every day after that you'll allow yourself the privilege of moving toward that light and not going back down the tunnel of darkness. It won't be easy—you'll have to fight the urge to wallow or berate yourself. But if you resist—if you let yourself feel the healing powers of reconciliation—you may find a place of peace. I certainly think so. After all, you're a survivor, Julie. And survivors must *live*."

She sank deeper into his arms as he wrapped her in a hug, locking his fingers together around her waist. She turned her face up to his, taking his cheeks in her hands, and said, "Thank you," sealing her appreciation with a kiss that felt like an awakening into an uncharted, frightening, and potentially exhilarating new world.

Chapter XXIX

Paige pulled into the emergency entrance of the hospital, throwing the Escalade in park, and said to Ben, "We're here. I'm gonna go get help."

She saw a few nurses standing by the registration desk and ran up to them. "Snakebike—please come quick!"

They sped into action, following her out the door.

Paige opened the passenger door, and Ben spilled out as the nurses helped him into a wheelchair. Paige followed behind as they rushed him inside, adrenaline surging in her veins.

A doctor appeared and asked Paige, "What kind of snake?"

"Rattler," she said, her voice wobbly.

"When?"

She was so focused on Ben and the swollen blue mass that was his lower leg that she nearly wretched and had difficulty following the doctor's words.

He asked again, "When?"

"Um—I—I don't know—maybe an hour—maybe more…?" she said distractedly.

"Name?"

"Me?"

"Yes, and him." he nodded his chin at Ben, who was slumped over in his wheelchair, groaning.

"Paige Montgomery. Ben Richfield."

"Are you his wife?"

Paige's eyes got big at that word. "No," she answered.

He said, "Okay, we've got him from here. We'll let you know as soon as he's stable."

Paige shook her head, not wanting to leave Ben. The doctor told one of the nurses to retrieve the antivenom and another to set up the IV. Paige touched Ben's wrist and he glanced at her, his face pale and withdrawn.

"Ben, they're gonna help you now, okay? I'll be right outside in the waiting room. My pa's coming."

He nodded. He put his hand on hers briefly and said, "Thank you, Paige." Then, quickly, as an afterthought, he pulled his phone out of his shorts pocket, screaming as his leg scraped the side of the wheelchair. He unlocked the phone, handed it to Paige and said stiltedly, through his teeth, "Call—my—dad."

"Of course," she said, taking the phone and squeezing his hand before reluctantly watching him be wheeled away, dodging the suddenly cluttered frenzy of hospital staff following him into a room.

She found "Dad" in his call log and dialed, taking a deep breath. His dad answered on the second ring, "Hey, buddy."

Paige—feeling half-sick or half-dead, suddenly shocked back into consciousness, cleared her throat and said, "Um—sir—I—um—my name is Paige, and I was hiking with your son Ben today, and we—we almost stepped on a rattlesnake that was sunning itself next to a rock on the trail, and well—sir—I don't know how to tell you this, it all happened so fast, *so* fast—sir—but Ben—he—he—got bit. We're in the ER at Deaconess Hospital in Bozeman. He's—he's in a lot of pain. They're—working on him right now. He wanted me to call you."

"Holy—! Is he going to be alright? Can you put him on the phone?"

"No, sir, we just got here a few minutes ago, and they've taken him into a room. I don't know—they have antivenom—I heard the doctor talking about it."

"Okay," he said, breathing loudly into the phone. "Let me think," he added, half to himself. "Betty, Betty," he shouted. "Get in here. Ben's been hurt." Then to Paige, "Miss—miss—I'm sorry, I've forgotten your name."

"Paige."

"Paige, right. We'll catch a flight as soon as humanly possible. Can you call me with any updates?"

"Yes, sir, of course I will."

"Okay—thank you."

"Uh-huh."

They hung up and Paige added his contact information to her phone, then fell into a chair beside a man with a gouge in his shin, a bloody cloth held to it, who barely glanced at her.

She put her head in her hands and tried to get a handle on everything that had just happened. How could your life completely shift on its axis in the blink of an eye? One moment she'd been sharing an intense and spectacular hike, kiss, and deep conversation with Ben, and the next, she was nearly dragging him through a forest and driving him eighty-five miles an hour to an emergency room for lifesaving treatment for a snakebite! How does that happen?

When she finally sat up and held her hands out in front of her, they were shaking so violently, she thought they might never go back to normal. She bundled them into fists, tucking them into her crossed arms. She wondered if Ben would live or die. Would he have permanent damage, be disfigured? How would this affect his career? Would they both be too shaken to resume what they had begun, what they had the potential to become, to each other? Would he now associate their brief time together with the most painful experience of his life? Her mind was a swirling pool—a tangled mess.

She stood and started pacing back and forth in the waiting room. A minute later, turning on her heel, she noticed through the window that the Escalade was still out front. Shit, she'd forgotten. She went and moved it, her legs a nervous bundle of energy. She returned to the waiting room and kept pacing. Thirty minutes went by, and then her pa was there, coming through the doors like a savior. Paige fell into his arms and sobbed like a five-year-old girl. He patted her head and let her cry. The release felt good after holding back the torrent of tears for so many hours.

When she pulled away, he asked, "How is he?"

"I don't know. They haven't come out to tell me."

He nodded, pursing his lips. He said, "Come on, let's find out, shall we?"

He guided her toward the registration desk. "Miss, may we get an update on the gentleman who came in with the snakebite?"

"Name?" she asked.

"Ben Richfield," Paige answered.

"Are you family?"

"No—I brought him in. I was with him when it happened..."

"Okay, let me find out. One moment."

She went to talk to a nurse and came back. "Someone will be right out to give you an update."

"Thank you," Pa said and led Paige to a chair.

Paige asked, "Did you tell Ma?"

"Yes—she's worried, wants us to call her as soon as we know anything. She told me she'd hold down the fort at Chico. She called in Gary and Samantha to take our shifts."

"Okay, good." Paige hadn't thought about work. Thank goodness her parents were so reliable and rational, even under pressure, both so good in an emergency. Paige, on the other hand, felt as though her brain and body had been scrubbed clean.

He took both of her hands in his and asked, "How are *you* doing?"

"I don't know, Pa," she shook her head, staring into his eyes, "it was crazy! I'd never seen a rattlesnake up close before. It blended in—the same color as the rock it was coiled beside—and the rattle—it was a warning. Ben jumped up and grabbed me out of the way. The whole thing happened so quickly. Then I had to help him walk back to the car, which was probably a mile away. My legs feel like Jell-O, and Pa, oh my God," she sobbed, her eyes filling with tears again, "his *leg*, Pa, it's so swollen—huge, discolored—like a rotten slab of meat, and—and he's in pain, Pa, *so* much pain." She put her hand to her mouth. He smoothed her hair as she cried.

A few minutes later, a doctor came out and they stood up. "We've already administered several vials of antivenom, and we have him on morphine for the pain. The poison is still coursing through his veins, so we've been taking blood regularly to ensure that the venom doesn't kill the blood vessels in the area or cause the blood to stop flowing, which can lead to long-term circulation problems. It's kind of a waiting game at this point. We won't know more for a while…but with these situations, there are risks." He paused and they both stared. His mouth grim, his face stone cold, he added, "There's always the possibility of needing to remove destroyed flesh as well as a chance of permanent damage—and of course, if it gets a lot worse, amputation. But we're hoping it doesn't come to that. We're hoping we caught it in time." He turned to Paige then. "It's good you got him here as quickly as you did. Every moment counts—it can mean the difference between keeping or losing a limb or, in some cases, even between life and death." Then he asked, "Have you—have they—" he pointed toward the front desk, "contacted his family?"

"Yes, I did. His parents are on their way, but they live in California, so it'll be later today before they can get here."

The doctor nodded.

Paige asked tentatively, "Can I see him?"

"Yes—he asked for you. He's rather groggy with medication, but follow me." They went into the room and stood at the foot of his bed while the doctor went away, leading the nurses out of the room.

In his hospital gown, the extent of the damage was clearly visible, and it was overwhelming. Pa took a step back as if to distance himself from the monstrosity that was Ben's leg. Paige went around to the other side of the bed, pulled up a chair next to Ben's head, and took his hand as his luminescent eyes opened and his crooked smile peeked out, just a twitch, as he said softly, "Paige."

Not knowing what to do or how to help him, Paige leaned down and kissed his hand. She thought briefly about how just a few short hours ago—and a lifetime ago—he had done the same to her during their car ride to the trail. She asked, "Does it hurt?"

"Yes," he said with clenched teeth. "But not as much as before."

He glanced up at Pa, who was hovering somewhat awkwardly. Ben said, "Sir, I guess we didn't need that bear spray after all."

Pa's light laugh warmed Paige's heart. "No you didn't, son, you sure didn't. Maybe a gun would've been handy after all…"

Ben tried to chuckle, but it came out more like a grunt with a wince. He said, "Maybe…although I didn't see it, didn't even know it was there until, well, until the damage was done."

"Right—that's how it goes sometimes."

Ben turned to Paige and asked, "What did the doctor say?"

Paige thought for a moment before answering. "Um, he said it's a waiting game but that it was good that we got you here when we did. They're going to keep administering antivenom and see what happens." She didn't mention that horrific word the doctor had used: *amputation*. When Paige thought about it and the implications for his life, his career, his role as a cowboy, his everything, she felt a pit the size of a watermelon fill her stomach.

Ben nodded. His head lolling back against the pillow, his eyes closing, he whispered, "My parents?"

She squeezed his hand, "They're coming. You just rest for now, okay?"

"Hm-mm," he seemed to agree, letting the morphine and exhaustion wash over him, his body relaxing.

Pa went and sat down on a chair in the corner of the room. Paige stepped out of the room to call Ben's dad. The phone went right to voicemail, which she figured meant they were on a plane, so she left a voicemail, relaying the doctor's words. Then she called her ma and gave her an update.

Hours went by. Paige continued her vigil at Ben's side as he drifted in and out of consciousness and the nurses came to change the antivenom and morphine drip, check his vitals and blood, and administer ultrasounds on his leg. Everything below his knee was distended and bluish gray in color. At some point, Pa asked if she had eaten anything and she shook her head, looking at the clock on the wall and realizing it was nearly six o'clock and her stomach was growling. He left the hospital to get some food for them. Five minutes later, Ben's parents were led into the room by a nurse. Paige jumped out of her chair to make room for them, his mom quickly taking Paige's vacated spot and grabbing Ben's hand.

His eyes fluttered open and glanced between his mom and dad, saying, "Hey."

"Hey," his mom repeated, then with a motherly smile, "Never a dull moment with you, Ben."

Paige wasn't sure what his mom meant, but she caught Ben's crooked grin in response and felt better. Paige sat in the corner and watched them catch up, all three looking grateful that Ben was alive and able to sit up and talk, even if he was groggy and still in a lot of pain. His mom was a petite blonde with crisp, preppy clothes, and his dad was rugged, like Ben, tall and handsome with thick salt-and-pepper hair.

A few minutes later, the doctor came in and filled them in on Ben's condition and prognosis. He explained that they wouldn't know the extent of the nerve damage for days or, more likely, weeks or even months later. Unfortunately, this was the nature of snakebites, he said. Ben's parents asked a bunch of follow-up questions as they (and Ben) read between the lines of what the doctor was saying. The potential consequences were staggering, but they were trying to simply listen—just this moment, right now, and what they could understand and control for today.

After the doctor left, Paige was quiet, trying to sink into the wall, wondering if she should leave, when Ben called to her, "Paige, come here. I want you to meet my parents."

She stood up, feeling somewhat foolish, remembering that she had only met Ben the night before. Such unusual circumstances! And almost absurd that they would have met each other's parents already. And everything that had happened in such a short span of time. What would his parents think?

They stood in turn, his mom first, shaking Paige's hand and saying, "Nice to meet you. I'm sorry it had to be—well, like this." Paige just nodded.

Then Ben, who was watching the exchange, said with a strange emphasis on last names that Paige didn't understand as she reached a hand toward his father, "Paige *Montgomery*, this is my dad, Terry *Rhinegeist*."

Paige held out her hand and he took it. Then slowly, like coming out of a movie theater into the bright light of day, Paige's eyes and brain adjusted and shifted, and then *clicked*. Paige heard Ben's words—really *heard* them. She thought, that's odd how Ben's dad's last name is different from his. Rhinegeist, not Richfield. Then a split second later, Paige thought, even odder, the name Terry Rhinegeist…there's something about that name, something *familiar*.

There was a pregnant pause during which Terry's eyes locked on hers and his hand became a tight clamp; palm to palm, connection to connection, *survivor to survivor*.

They stared, not moving a muscle.

Five seconds, ten, fifteen.

She didn't breathe, didn't speak, didn't move.

Ben broke the spell with a chuckle. He murmured, "Yeah, that's kind of how I thought this would go down." He waited, drinking in the scene. He said, "This, Paige, *this* is what I was trying to tell you on the trail," he pointed to his leg with a groan, "when *this* happened."

Paige's mind swiftly flew to Ben's face, then back to his dad. A massive tornado of thoughts spun into her brain—that strange behavior of Ben's the night before after she said she'd survived a plane crash, and then his words earlier that day, *"Listen, Paige, about my dad, yeah—um—I think I need to tell you something—you see—"*

Cut off by a rattlesnake.

She had been speculating about all kinds of things regarding his parents, his sister, his family. Drama, divorce, drugs, good Lord, but not *this!*

Terry Rhinegeist. Paige Montgomery. Julie Geiger. Marie Stanley.

The only four survivors of a plane crash that killed one hundred forty-two people twenty years ago.

Paige had never met Terry. Never knew a single thing about him besides his name. Her name as a baby—her Filipino name (before she had been adopted)—was Diwa Abalos, but Julie had kept the four of them on a shared email and text group list over the years and filled Marie and Terry in on Paige's adoption and new name. Julie had also sent them updates about her fight to get the lap baby rules changed. Terry never responded to the emails or the texts. It was as though he'd dropped off the face of the earth, and now here he was, in the flesh, gripping Paige's hand, in the least likely of places.

Where her heart had recently been stolen by none other than his *son.*

She gulped. He blinked.

They scoured each other's faces as if they could understand the impact of the words, of what they implied, of their shared tragedy, the life forces that brought them together in the most unlikely of situations.

Like a slap, Paige's pa walked through the door with a bag of food in his hands and said rather loudly, "I've got grub." He stopped in the entrance, seeing the odd exchange, the handshake still gripped, the silence in the room. He said with a small frown, "Hey! Oh, you must be Ben's parents. So nice to meet you." He moved toward Ben's mom first and shook her hand, then turned to Ben's dad. Paige let go of his hand and said to her pa significantly, "Pa, this is Ben's dad, *Terry Rhinegeist.*"

"Nice to meet you, sir, although, I wish it had been under different circumstances. Never thought in a million years, these kids—"

He stopped. His eyes shifted between Terry and Paige.

He said, "Terry *Rhinegeist?* Well, I'll be! That's gotta be some type of crazy coincidence…same name as—"

His voice drifted off and he stared at the floor for a second.

Paige said softly, "It's not a coincidence, Pa."

His forehead creased. Pa eyes snapped up again as he said to Terry, "You—"

you were on that—*no*—come on—it can't—no—United Flight 1180—the same flight—the same *plane?*"

Terry's incredulous face lit up and he said, "Yes, sir, I was."

Pa shook his head and scratched his chin. "Wow! What are the chances of that?"

"I would guess one in a million, or more, sir," Terry agreed, also shaking his head, finally with a big smile.

"Well, come here then!" Pa cried without hesitation and pulled Terry into a bear hug until Terry was laughing, hugging him back, and grinning from ear to ear.

Ben and his mom took it all in, incredulity on their faces.

Paige stood, her hand to her mouth, flabbergasted.

When the two fathers pulled back, Ben said to Paige, "Come here."

She went to the other side of the bed and took his hand. She was beginning to cry again, feeling as though everything that had happened in the past twenty-four hours was beyond her comprehension.

Ben said—rather off topic, she thought, "You know, when I got the job on the show—I'd been auditioning with no success for months, then I got a callback, and another, and before I knew it, they were testing me with the other actors, and I had this life-altering thing placed in my lap, and I felt so—" he paused, reaching for the words, "grateful, like everything was—falling into place for me. Like somehow it was all meant to be. I wasn't sure *why*, but I felt it, you know?"

She listened, seeing how much he was concentrating on what he was saying, still under the influence of the morphine drip and the lingering pain, but forcing his focus nonetheless. What was he getting at? She stared into his glowing eyes and watched his mouth, remembering how soft and hungry it was when he kissed her.

"When you mentioned the crash last night, I couldn't believe my ears—I thought I must be dreaming. Dad rarely talked about the crash, but once or twice he showed Rhone and me some clippings from the newspaper and a few articles about Julie, and when we asked who you were, he told us your name and that you lived in Montana. I thought, *wow*." He paused with a tight laugh, looking at his dad. Ben turned his head to Paige. "When we were on that trail—I was just about to tell you. I even thought maybe one day I could bring you two together, have you meet each other, somehow…through me. Of course, I didn't think it would be quite like this." He grimaced and they all shook their heads, still in shock.

Terry and Paige simply stared at each other in wonder and then back at Ben.

Paige inquired, "But—but your names—they're not the same…?"

Ben's mom answered, "Yeah, so when the kids started their acting careers, the agents thought Rhinegeist was too hard to pronounce or too German or just *too*, so they changed it to Richfield. They became Rhone and Ben Richfield."

"Ah, a stage name…," Paige said, thinking about how Ben's name had been changed just as hers had. Paige also felt foolish for a moment—all of her speculation about them having family problems was ultimately ridiculous, thank goodness. Yes, his sister *was* having issues, but that wasn't what Ben had been trying to say. That'll teach her to speculate. She should have just asked. It was all about Paige and Terry. Not at all about Paige's "miracle" status or about his family matters.

Pa broke into their thoughts. "Hey, who's hungry? I brought plenty of subs and sides and sodas. Who wants a Coke? Sprite?"

A nurse came in to check on Ben. A few minutes later, his eyes closed, his head laid back on the pillow, and he was asleep.

Pa took the food out of the bag, and the rest of them began to eat and talk at once, as if twenty years of their lives had to be unpacked, digested, and assimilated.

Strangers until five minutes ago, now old friends.

Paige's tears came and went, filled with surprise happiness now, not dread, even with Ben's unknown prognosis.

There was light even in the midst of darkness.

FOUR MONTHS LATER

CHAPTER XXX

MARIE FINISHED WRITING THE LABEL ON THE LAST TOTE and hollered out the door, "Ryan, here—this is it. Were you able to fit in Bridget's books? I know it's tight under there." Each of them was allowed one "luxury" tote with personal things they couldn't live without, and Bridget had chosen a tote full of books, of course.

Ryan rolled his eyes and said, "Puh-lease, easy."

Marie laughed, thinking the apple didn't fall far from the tree with her oldest. Ryan was just as meticulously organized as she was and loved the thrill and satisfaction of finding the best, most perfect way to get something done. He actually volunteered to pack the compartments underneath the RV that held their gear. He said it was like playing an extreme game of Tetris. He had been so helpful, it warmed Marie's heart. Over a month ago, he'd even offered to sit down with Marie to type up a list of everything they needed on the trip, right down to the marshmallow-roasting sticks, flashlights, batteries, portable camping grill, and seventy-nine other necessities.

Marie took a deep breath. They were ready. At least she thought they were. Were they forgetting anything? Just as her brow furrowed and she felt panic rise in her throat, Kent appeared like a soothing balm, wrapped his arm around her, and pulled her in for a squeeze. He kissed her temple and asked, "We good?"

She smiled with a shaky exhale and said, "I can't believe I'm saying this, but yes, I think we're good. Let's get the kids loaded and hop on the road."

It was six in the morning, and the girls were missing. Marie was going to yell up the stairwell but decided face-to-face intervention might be in order. She found Bridget sitting on her bed, writing in her diary. "Sweetie, come on, we're leaving. Do you have everything? Your pillow? Your snacks? Your purse?"

"Yep, um, hang on—I just want to finish the title to this new entry: 'The Road Less Traveled: My Adventures in an RV with My Family. Please Shoot Me Now.'"

"Lovely," Marie said wryly. "Don't make me regret taking you kids out of school. Come on, let's go. Where's Darby?"

Bridget scoffed, "Where do you think?"

"The barn," Marie said with a sigh. Pulling Darby away from her beloved horses was like pulling Winnie-the-Pooh away from his tub of honey. Marie and Kent had cajoled all summer long, finally resorting to bribery, saying they would get her a new horse after the trip if she came away with them for a month. Darby finally conceded, but only after they had agreed to pay her best horse friend, Erika, to watch her babies while they were away.

Marie grabbed Darby's pillow and backpack off her bed on the way out the door, going directly to the barn, where she found both Darby and Kent. She said, "Ready? We really need to get going to beat the traffic."

"Yep," Kent said, taking the horse brush out of Darby's hand and leading her away from her beloved mare, saying, "She'll be fine, sweetie. They'll all be fine."

They closed up the house and locked it, piled into the RV, and got settled in their seats. Marie almost couldn't believe it, but they were finally on their way. Kent was driving the first shift. Marie mentally ticked off everything on her to-do list. Had she watered the plants, turned off the water heater, unplugged the microwave and coffee machine? Had she made their beds, put the dishes away, locked the doors? Had she packed enough towels, spices, underwear, laundry detergent, soap, food, water, bug spray? Had she reminded Gieda to check the lights, thermostat, TVs, stove, wet towels? The list seemed endless, but when she felt sure she *had* covered it all, she laid her head back on the seat, sighed, and turned to watch Kent's profile as he deftly navigated the highway, gripping the sides of the RV's big steering wheel.

He turned to her then, a smile on his face. He reached for her hand and held it, saying, "All good?"

"Yep," she smiled back, thinking with wonder and joy, how did she get to this place? She turned and saw Ryan asleep on the back-seat cushions as Darby scrolled through her phone and Bridget read a book. Marie said bluntly, quietly, to Kent, "Have I ever told you how sorry I am for the last twenty years?"

He frowned. "What do you mean?"

God, he was a good husband, pretending *he* didn't know. She rolled her eyes, and he laughed as if she were speaking nonsense. "You *know* why. Please don't make me say it." Before he could respond, she let out a puff of air. "Okay, I *will* say it. Again. It bears repeating. As many times as I can, as I should. For not seeing what was right in front of my face. For how amazing you are. And the kids. And for how sorry I am for treating you like a project I was managing, for being wrong about almost everything, and for not recognizing what I had, who I was, or how grateful I should be. Will you forgive me?"

His loving brown eyes glanced at her then, and she melted a little. He said, "Hey, listen, no one said life was going to be a piece of cake or that everyone you meet—and fall in love with—is going to be perfect. I'm not perfect. The kids aren't perfect. So, maybe you lost your way for a while. I think I did too. I should have been brave enough to sit down and talk to you about everything, about *my* feelings, about Matthew, *much* sooner. I shouldn't have let it get so bad. Letting it drag on to that point—that was on *me*. It wasn't just you."

Despite herself, her eyes filled with tears. This happened so often lately— feeling like a walking leaky faucet. For twenty years, she barely cried about anything. When the kids were born and placed on her naked chest after hours and hours of labor, Kent cried like a baby while Marie simply stared at them, marveling at the cost of birthing to a woman's body and the cost to the child, who always looked squished, peeled, and uncomfortable—unreconciled with having been born almost as much as she was with the process of bringing them forth.

Now, for these past few months, she cried over everything. If one of the kids gave her an unsolicited hug (which they did quite frequently now), if she had a breakthrough in therapy (which happened almost every time she went, thanks to an insightful and patient psychologist she'd found in Hartford who had completely transformed Marie's emotional life and maybe her practical life too), if she ran into an old friend who said she looked great ("Ten years younger! What's your secret?"), if she talked to her parents about the upcoming trip and how excited she was to see them and for the kids to see the ranch (her mother had been baking and cooking up a storm—breads and cookies and biscuits and stews and soups and chilis to last a lifetime), if Kent left her a love note on her bathroom mirror or deep kisses on her lips at night when they made love as if they were in college again, their bodies becoming the new frontier in the art of pleasure as if they had only met a few months ago instead of twenty-five years ago—she was a puddle, a river, an ocean of tears now.

And if she looked at the photos of Matthew that she'd scattered in frames around the house—up the stairwell alongside her other grown babies, in the living room where Gieda dusted them among the bookshelves, saying out loud to Marie, "Such a sweet, beautiful boy. He's with us here now...I can feel him here with my Daniel." In their bedroom, on the nightstand beside Marie's side of the bed, so she could whisper "night, night" to him before turning off the light and going to sleep. In the kitchen, dining room, basement, bathroom, front hallway, and in Kent's studio, which she now visited several times a day, bringing him coffee or a treat, standing beside his drafting table and chatting about his work, his thoughts, his joys, and her activities, the household, her progress in therapy, and their children—*all* of their children.

Kent interrupted Marie's thoughts. "You nervous?"

"About the trip? Well, I think I have everything—"

"No," he corrected, "about the picnic."

"Oh," she said flatly and thought about it for a minute before responding. "Of course, I mean, a little. They'll think I have ulterior motives or that I'm having a midlife crisis," she said with a frown, "or worse, that I've come to berate them, chastise the guilty, like I used to. I understand—that's what I would think too. In fact, I'm honestly surprised they've agreed to meet. I'm not sure I would have offered them the same grace if the roles had been reversed. It's not an easy thing to take someone at their word when all of their words up until this point have been hateful, ungracious, unkind, and accusing."

Kent didn't deny it—just nodded softly. He said, "Well, I'm proud of you. No matter what happens. And I think if they can see what you've faced head-on and dealt with these past few months—what you've needed to go through to get to this point—they'll come around, come to understand you better, as you are now, *not* your past, not *their* past either."

"We shall see...," Marie said, still somewhat anxious and skeptical.

She looked out the window at the rolling green hills and forested byways and thought back to her conversation with Julie a month earlier. Marie was surprised and then immediately scared when Julie answered her phone on the first ring.

"Hello, Marie," Julie spoke flatly, like someone awaiting a diagnosis from a doctor's office.

"Hi Julie—um—hi—this is Marie," Marie said inanely, trying to form the thousand thoughts swirling in her mind into a coherent funnel so she could express them. "I was thinking…that it would be good to get together—"

Julie cut her off. "What? About…?"

"Well, that's what I was going to explain. Um, you see, as you know, it's been twenty years since the crash, and I wondered if it might be good to meet, sort of like a reunion, a get-together—with you and Terry and Paige. You may know—well, you may *not* know—but my parents live in Montana, and I'm planning to take the kids on a road trip to visit them in about a month, and I really want to host a picnic. Well, not exactly a picnic, although that's what I'm calling it—it'll be too cold in October for a picnic—but a meal, an opportunity to break bread together. My parents have a ranch with a big farm table that seats twenty." God, she was flustered and sounding like a stuttering idiot, giving too many unrelated details. She needed to spit it out. "I want you to come. I would really like you there. And—and feel free to bring a friend or your family or whomever…I'm sorry, I don't know if you have anyone…," Marie cringed, wanting to gobble back every word, realizing she knew absolutely nothing about this woman and that every other conversation she'd ever had with her up until this point had been contentious, hateful, *unforgivable*. She stopped, out of breath, her heart pounding. She was so not used to eating crow, and at this moment she felt as though she *had* literally eaten a noxious, poisoned flock of them…her stomach roiled.

Julie was silent on the other end of the line. Marie waited, wanting to sink into an invisible fissure in the ground and never be heard from again.

Julie finally let out a big, long, exasperated sigh and said, "Fine. When?"

"October twenty-fifth. I'll text you the address."

"I'll have to check my schedule. Have you already talked to the others?"

"Nope, I figured I'd—well, I'd try you first."

"Okay" was Julie's curt reply.

Marie said, "Julie, thank you. I mean it. And um, Julie…?"

"Yes?"

"I'm sorry…about everything," Marie choked on the words—they were like dirt in her mouth, and she was still getting used to saying them (something her therapist was encouraging her to do). It was like wearing a new watch that she still found heavy and unwieldy. Her therapist told her that "I'm sorry" was just as important as "I love you" and meant nearly the same thing for people who were willing to listen and, more importantly, willing to really hear the words. Marie forged ahead, "I know the last time we met, I said those were 'just words,' but I want you to know that I've—I've since learned how critical they are to the human condition, to happiness, to life itself. I never knew before, and I'm sorry for that too. I'm sorry for a lot of things. I promise to explain better when I see you, when I can show my remorse *and* appreciation in person. I hope you'll come. I need you to come. And I hope you'll be open to listening. I know I don't deserve that from you, or from anyone, but I hope you'll do it anyway."

The seconds ticked by. Finally, Julie said simply, "Yes, okay. If the others agree to come, I'll be there."

Marie felt a wave of relief wash over her. After they hung up, she cried—those stupid tears again that kept coming at her every day, making her feel the things she hadn't felt before, making her face herself in the mirror, making her want to run away some days and fight others. Making her into a new person. Or so she hoped…

The conversations with Terry and Paige had been much the same—shocked silences followed by short replies and a final acceptance of her invitation. Oddly, they'd both admitted separately that they had their own "updates" to share. Marie couldn't imagine what. They hadn't been part of Julie's fight with the airlines about the lap baby rules, and in fact, Terry had been completely out of touch as far back as Marie could remember. He never wanted to be part of their little "survivors' club" (the club that no one would wish on their worst enemy), so could she blame him? But for him to agree so readily, and that Paige would come as well—Marie couldn't be more surprised and grateful. Like she'd said to Julie, she didn't deserve it, but they were gracious enough to agree anyway. It was more than she could have wished for.

Of course, now she was on her way, on the road to her parents' place and on her way to face her demons—head-on—and the people she had wronged. It wasn't going to be easy. But rarely in life was anything both meaningful and easy, was it?

She stared at her children in the back seat—so kind, so smart, so forgiving, so unique. Despite her crimes and misguided attempts at raising them to be overscheduled and hyperproductive members of society, she must have done something right because they were amazing kids. Kent glanced over and smiled at her, watching her admire their children. He saw it in her eyes, and that was probably more alluring to him than anything else she'd shown him in her quest for improvement and growth these past few months—that she'd grown to love their children even more than she had before, more than she thought herself capable of, more than she thought humanly possible. And she would make it up to them—her deficits, her coldness, her drive for perfection in them, in herself. She would try to gain their trust and be there for them, as a mother and a friend, not as their caretaker, chauffeur, and activity director, although she would continue to be those things too, despite the fact that she'd done something entirely out of character by pulling them out of school and their daily activities to come on this trip. She'd worked it out with their teachers, coaches, trainers, tutors. She'd found a way, as she always did. They came at her kicking and screaming at first, only to be shown it was possible—anything was possible, if you put your mind to it. She wanted to model that for them, just as she wanted to model it for herself.

They would spend a week in the RV and the rest of the month hanging out with her amazing, hardworking, and loving parents. What could be better than experiencing firsthand the wild, unruly, expansive place where she grew up, which (despite the foolish, get-out-of-Dodge feelings and actions of her youth) was one of the most beautiful valleys in the world. Sometimes she even wondered why she had been so eager to flee. Of course, she was young then, right out of high school. All she could think about was expanding her horizons, seeing and living something outside of her little rural town. But then the escape and avoidance after that time were all tied up in the crash and everything that horror came to mean to her about Montana and the loss of her baby. And the letting go of her own innocence and gullibility, her assumptions that life came with some type of guarantee for happiness and fairness.

This was why her therapist had told her the progress she'd made so far (which was significant in Marie's mind, making her think about everything she said and did in a different light, not exactly a cakewalk) would only be the beginning of the really hard work and progress she'd need to make on this trip. It hadn't been easy, and it would continue to be hard. Her world—former, present, future—had cracked open like an egg. Marie had never felt things so much before—the pain and anguish of the crash, its aftermath, the loss of Matthew, and her retreat into an action-filled, controlled, and manic life. Not to mention the impact of all of that on her friends, family, and the other survivors. She almost felt at her wits' end—what more could she do, and how much more could she handle? But the therapist had told her that now was the real battle—what happened before was the prep work. Now Marie would have to live every emotion as it happened, not hiding it away, not couching it in busywork—now she would have to feel her feelings in real time, let herself surrender to them. Spending intense close-quarters time with family and then having intimate conversations with Julie, Terry, Paige, and even her parents—all of it was surely going to let something loose in her—thoughts, feelings, experiences she'd never allowed herself to fully feel or absorb before. The therapist gave her tools—ways to cope and process—but the whole thing was like the first time on a roller coaster—absolutely terrifying, with a tiny hope for something more—something exhilarating, significant, rewarding.

She took a deep breath and squeezed Kent's hand. At least she wasn't doing this on an island. She had Kent and her kids as well as herself. She could be something different. A leopard really *could* change its spots. Or at least grow new ones.

And that was exactly what she intended to do.

Chapter XXXI

JULIE PACKED LAYERS IN HER SUITCASE, not sure what the weather would be like in October in Montana. She tucked her ninety-day AA chip—her anchor—into the front pocket of her jeans, running her fingers along the ridges as she pulled her hand away, remembering the hard work, dedication, and willpower it took to earn. One day at a time, they said, but quite often she still found herself thinking, "How can I continue?" Some days, like today, it was like fingernails on a chalkboard—it grated on her, made her want to quit and give in to the temptation. She'd done that in the beginning, the first few weeks—given in—started off strong in the morning, with resolve, then crumbled by the end of the day. After all, wouldn't it be easier to just have one glass of wine or a few shots to take the edge off? Purge the thoughts of everything that made her feel yucky inside, made her feel unworthy, unwanted, unknown?

But now, instead, she did what she should—she texted her sponsor. If nothing else, Julie was a rule follower, to a fault, and that had been her saving grace. If she had a rule book to follow, a set of instructions, like the one she'd always obeyed and perfected in her job as a flight attendant, she could be just as efficient and compliant as an AA member. Thank goodness. Because she knew if it had come down to her emotional fortitude, she would have been dead in the water before she even started.

Mark helped too. More than helped. He'd been her rock. When she faltered during those early days, he never judged—he simply said, "If not now, when?"

She'd always screamed into the phone, "Later!" then broke down crying, and he let her, understanding.

He would say calmly, "It's not easy doing something for yourself when you've devoted a lifetime to helping others, to thinking about their needs before yours. Now it's time to focus on you. It'll feel uncomfortable, unnatural at first, like you're wearing a shirt two sizes too small, but the important thing to remember is, how can you help others if you're not present, not working on your healing, not trying to become a more complete person?" Of course, he was right—he was always right—but did that make it any easier?

God, no.

But she had lasted a solid ninety days, and she was proud of herself. For sticking with it, for allowing herself to explore that innermost version of herself—even the ugly parts—and for staying around afterward.

For her, being vigilant was the key. That, and thinking about how much better she already felt—healthier, cleaner, clearer, calmer, more in control and more aware of everything, as if a door had opened up her senses to the world around her. She loved her new self, and she intended to keep it.

So, on this momentous October day, she did what she must—she texted back and forth with her sponsor—and then she called Mark. It was a Friday at ten in the morning, but she'd found that no matter when she called, day or night, he always answered.

"Hey, sweet cheeks, how's it shakin'?" he answered lightly.

She smiled despite her distress. She said, "Hey. Feeling a little overwhelmed at the moment, actually."

"Why?" There were some voices and rustling in the background. "Hang on, let me get to a place where I can talk." She heard him excuse himself from someone.

This is what he did for her, and it warmed her heart more than she could say—he took her call even though he was obviously busy. "K—go ahead. What's up?"

"Sorry about interrupting. It's just—well, I was thinking," she said with a touch of sarcasm mixed with unfiltered honesty, "wouldn't it make more sense for me to just stay here in Chicago? I could draw a bath, have Chinese delivered for lunch, binge-watch *The Bachelor* or *The Real Housewives* or some such mindless drivel. You know, stew a bit, vegetate, chill."

"And what—pour a big glass of chardonnay to go with that 'stew' you've concocted for yourself? Come on, running away is *not* the answer—or staying, as the case may be."

"Yeah, I know. But do you have to always tell me?" She sighed with a short laugh, sitting down on the edge of the bed and rubbing her forehead. She sputtered, "It's just…well, I'm freaking out a bit. I don't know what Marie's going to say or why she's decided this is the moment we should all get together, and the last time I saw her she berated me, and in my current fragile state of mind, if she tries that shit again, well, I don't know how I'll react. And then that bizarre phone call where she apologized so awkwardly—it all seems completely implausible, as if hell has frozen over or the stars have aligned—I'm not sure which—and the whole thing makes me want to puke. I don't trust her. And I don't trust myself. And to make matters worse, whenever I see Paige, it sends me down a spiral, you know?" She was breathing hard, rattling off these tick marks—the way she always did when she was wanting a drink so badly she could taste it.

Mark had talked her down more times than she could count, and he was still willing, mercifully, yet again today. "Listen, you're going to be fine. We talked about this—go into every situation, even this one, with the assumption that everything will work out, everything will be positive, and that you—a strong, smart, amazing woman with all the tools you need at your disposal—will handle this situation just fine. You're the captain of your ship, of your life, of your destiny, and that's all that matters. You can't control who speaks or what they say—you can only control how you react. And you've been doing beautifully at that so far. Don't let this one weekend ruin what you've already built. You can do it. I have confidence in you. And besides, don't forget, I'll be there—and I'll give you a very large spanking if you get out of line."

She let out a puff of air, then a laugh. He always brought her around—with his candor, his wisdom, and, most unexpected and appreciated, his humor. "You're right. I can do this. And I'm grateful you'll be with me for support. Okay, are you all set with your flight?"

"Yep. Gets in at two your time. I'll be leaving here shortly."

"Okay, I'll meet you at your gate." He was flying into Chicago for his layover so they could fly the last leg to Bozeman together.

"Perfect."

"I can't wait to see you."

His voice dropped an octave, "Me either. Although, the twin beds might just be enough to drive *me* to drink."

"Stop it," she smiled. "It won't be easy for me either."

"I keep repeating my mantra: the wait will be worth the reward."

She chuckled. "For more reasons than one."

"God, yes. I want you stone-cold sober and ready to feel *every single thing* I do to you."

"*Mark*," Julie purred a weak admonishment, blushing alone in her bedroom.

He cleared his throat. "Okay, um, I better go…I have a client in the restaurant, and I don't think it would be appropriate to walk back in, well, standing at attention, if you know what I mean."

She laughed. "No, it wouldn't. Go. I'll see you soon."

"With bells on!"

He hung up, and Julie zipped up her suitcase, brought it downstairs, and decided to spend some time journaling, a habit she began her first week at AA. She sat at her kitchen table and started. The writing kept her hands busy and allowed her to get her feelings down (and out of her system). At first, she wrote about her current struggles, her fears about seeing all of the survivors from the crash together for the first time since that day, and about seeing Marie, wondering whether her motives for the meeting were sincere. Then Julie wrote about her latest attempts at making amends with her friends and family members, including a rather heated discussion she'd had with her two sisters over the weekend about Julie's "lack of self-awareness" over the years and how she hadn't ever "chipped in" with their mom the way she should and how that had been "hateful and hurtful" to her whole family. It had felt like a punch in the gut. So, she wrote a few pages about that. She hadn't even begun to imagine what her conversation with Rob would be like and if he would even be willing to meet with her. Add it to the list. A long list. All she could do was take it one day at a time, one hurdle at a time. Otherwise, it was too overwhelming.

For today, she was going to make herself focus on the positive. Maybe this trip to Montana would be cathartic. Maybe she'd be glad she faced the survivors sober. After all, it might be nice to know they were doing well, and they might appreciate see her doing well too—maybe for the first time since she had known them.

And then there was the fact that she would be seeing Mark. She stopped her journaling for a few minutes to ruminate on the two nights of unbridled passion she'd shared with Mark at the Cranberry Inn all those months ago. Starting with that Saturday, the day after they met, which she would think back on as the perfect day. He'd spent hours listening to her and cuddling her and being so present with her on that deserted island, and when they got back to the Inn, she led him up the stairs without a word. They'd been like two caged animals let loose in that bedroom covered in ivy, their intermingled sweat and hot yearnings clenched and fulfilled enough to soothe her troubled heart and mind and body.

Sunday had been much the same—a whirlwind of heat and passion that sent her to the moon and back. Had she been sober through the whole thing? Of course not! They'd spent equal parts in bed and down in the tavern, Mark with his club soda and Julie with her wine or martini or mixed drink. But at the end of the night, they had ended up back upstairs, and she'd never felt anything so powerful—being with him, basking in his newness, his calm spirit, his kind eyes, his attention. She hadn't been savored and cherished like this since, well, maybe ever. It was as if she were a goddess and he had come to worship at her altar. It would have been disconcerting, she thought at times, if it hadn't felt *so damned good.*

At some point, when the time was drawing short and Julie started feeling dread pouring into her veins while she lay cushioned safely against his chest, his arms wrapped around her in a cocoon, he kissed her temple and said the words she knew were coming but that were like jagged pieces of flint ready to shred her heart, her mind, her soul. She actually cowered a little, shrinking underneath the warmth of his embrace, sitting up and covering her breasts with the sheet.

"Julie, darling, as heartbreaking as the truth is—for both of us—after this, we can't be together."

"What do you mean?" she asked, already knowing the answer but making him do the dirty work—selfish, unfeeling brat that she was. She wanted to keep him, hold him, ward off the bolted door that stood between them and everything else—the next day, the unknown and frightening future, the inevitable. She knew she couldn't do it—couldn't say goodbye as she knew they must. She just *couldn't.*

So she made him.

His hazel eyes, the ones that had wooed her, held her, coaxed her, were filled with a gleaming sadness mixed with empathic pity, stabbing her right through the solar plexus. He said, "Julie, I'm an alcoholic. I can't be with someone who drinks. As much as I want to—as much as you make me feel alive again in ways I thought were long dead. As much as I wish I could turn the world upside down just to make it work. But I can't—I'm just not strong enough. And more importantly, I haven't pressed this because it's entirely up to you. If you're thinking about sobriety, which I hope you are—God, I hope and pray you are because I want to be with you more than anything I've ever wanted in my entire life—but there's a consequence to wanting. For this to work," he pointed between them, "we must be put on the back burner. I'm not telling you how to go about achieving what you strive for—if, in fact, that's what you want—but no matter, it'll be for you to decide and to conquer. I can't do it for you. Regardless of the method, though, sobriety is a viciously singular activity. Your entire focus must center on that one thing. At least at first. It requires support, for sure, and I'm here for you anytime, as a *friend*, but it must be you and you alone who wields the weapon to crush it. You have to do it yourself, for *you*. Not for me. Not for us. I'm sorry."

She leaned her head back against the pillow in defeat. Before she had even begun, it felt overwhelming and impossible. Grasping at straws, she said feebly, "What if I cut down? I've already had a lot less since I've been here."

His eyes like pools of compassion, his lips brushing hers like the wings of a bird, he said, "Oh, sweetheart, I wish it worked that way."

She let a tear slip down her face, and he wiped it away with a soft knuckle, kissing her cheek and saying, "You see, it's partially my own weakness too. I don't want to put all this on you. I just know my limits—one of the great things about AA is that you quickly learn what sets you off, brings you to the edge, and stops you on the brink before you jump—and having a relationship with someone who is still addicted is my limit. I don't know why exactly—I just know it's true. I think for me, what may start as fun and acceptable would eventually turn to envy and resentment and then who knows? Growing lax, lying, lowering my guard, giving in? How would that turn out—for either of us? How would we continue after that? How would we look each other in the eye? How could we be the best version of ourselves for each other?"

She nodded, the tears flowing now, her lips buckling. It had been so long since she'd felt this way about a man and about her life—the absolute, inexorable, overwhelmingly bittersweet potential of it all. To walk away when it was just beginning seemed like the cruelest of fates, as if she had clipped the newly formed bud of a perfect spring flower. How would it ever bloom again if she walked away now with no prospect, no set date, no way to lock anything in for a future?

He saw everything in her face, in her eyes. He brushed her hair back behind her ears. "I know you're scared and sad and probably a little angry. I get that. But I can promise that it's worth it—it will *all* be worth it. Someday. Do the work. Face the truth. Feel the feelings. Then, maybe someday, come back to me, my lovely, lovely Julie—come back to me. I'll be here. Waiting."

She didn't nod, didn't confirm, didn't say anything, and instead slipped back into his arms, wanting to feel his comfort, strength, and confidence one last time.

Back in her apartment in Chicago, reflecting gratefully on the past four months, she closed her journal, feeling a tempered happy, hopeful warmth in her chest. She was thinking about how she had come so far and would keep going, even when it was hard, even when she didn't know how she could continue another day. She would. Not for Mark—for herself. And when it stuck—*when*, not *if*—she would be waiting too. She tucked her journal in her suitcase, grabbed her purse and jacket, and headed out the door to the airport.

CHAPTER XXXII

PAIGE WAS SITTING ON THE EDGE OF BEN'S BED, looking down at her feet.

"Why the sourpuss face?"

He was sitting up, leaning back against the headboard with his hands woven together in his lap, looking every inch the casual, confident Hollywood actor in his green Henley and his low-slung blue jeans, which fit him just so. He still caused a hitch in her breath every time she looked at him. She almost felt like Pavlov's dog—salivating at the mere sight of him. The good news was that she sensed it was the same for him. Well, she didn't only sense it—he told her often enough—and she had grown to believe it, to know it, to love it.

It was Friday night, and he'd just finished shooting for the week, so his housemates were gone, catching flights back to LA, and much like that first weekend when they'd met, he had the big house to himself. Paige had turned twenty-two a few days ago, but he'd been working, so they were planning to celebrate tonight—just the two of them. She'd gotten up the nerve to tell her parents that she wouldn't be home later, that she'd be staying over at Ben's. Her pa had frowned and opened his mouth to protest, but her ma had given him a tiny shake of her head. He'd clamped his mouth shut and gone back to polishing his boots, a deep wrinkle appearing in his forehead. Ma had simply said to Paige, "Okay, hon—that's fine, be careful, let us know if you need anything, and don't forget to be back by ten tomorrow morning. We're still going to the picnic together, right?"

Paige had said, "Yep, I'm riding with you, and Ben's picking up his parents at the airport and going directly there."

After her ma had said, "Okay, perfect—have a nice time," Paige had scooted out of the house as fast as she could, thinking it was probably ridiculous at her age to worry what her parents thought about her love life. But four months in, certain things were still new to her, and every step along the way had been a revelation, an awakening, a confused swirl, and a revolution. She'd begun by navigating the steps like a baby walking for the first time, and now, although she was fully running, skipping, and jumping, she still had moments of pause when she really had to think about the next step when it appeared in front of her, sometimes like a stumbling block, sometimes like a scooter wheeling her ahead in a rush.

Paige stared at Ben. "I'm nervous," she said.

"Why? About tomorrow?"

She nodded mutely.

"Come here," he said, opening his arms wide as she snuggled into his lap. He kissed her forehead. "This is going to be the coolest day ever. What's to be nervous about?"

She glanced at him as if he was dense.

"Don't give me that look, missy. Listen, pretend like you're meeting up with old friends you haven't seen in a while. Or like a family reunion, but even better because you don't have to deal with Uncle Buck farting in the corner and Aunt Hazel pinching everyone's cheeks until they bleed." Paige rolled her eyes, trying to smile but not quite managing it. "Plus, we have our big surprise reveal—that'll be fun, right? And we'll get to hear Marie's spiel, which ought to be interesting, to say the least. And I'll be there, and your pa and ma will be there, and *my* dad and mom. We'll surround you like a cocoon if that's what you want. Anything you want, babe—I'm here."

After receiving an appreciative kiss, he said softly into her hair, "I really don't think this visit will be about the crash, you know? I think it'll be about where everyone is *today*. How life has played out since then and moved on, become something real and present and good, for all of us in the here and now."

"I suppose," she agreed. "I hope, anyway." After a pause, she said, "I think they were amazed your dad agreed to come. This will be the first time they've seen him since that day."

"I know, and they're gonna freak when they find out their little lap baby survivor stole his son's heart after she sicked a deadly rattlesnake on him."

"Hey!" she cried, elbowing him in the stomach. "There are about ten things wrong with that sentence."

"What?" he asked with faux ignorance.

She didn't bother gracing him with a reply, just pulled back far enough to narrow her eyes at his crooked grin.

He said, "Okay, so maybe the son stole the survivor's heart...and maybe the son was too distracted by the lap baby's luscious lips to see the deadly rattlesnake rearing its nasty head at him."

The smile crept back on her face. She said, "Let's take a look at the leg." She slid off his lap and lifted up the right cuff of his jeans, taking off his sock and inspecting the area. From shin to ankle, the skin was still slightly swollen and reddish, but it was a thousand times better than it had been that first month when it had looked like a bloated hotdog or fresh roadkill. Ultimately, he had spent five days in the hospital and required nineteen vials of antivenom. When they discharged him, he was still in pain in spots and numb in others. His ankle, feet, and toes were discolored and quite swollen. But he hadn't needed surgery, so that was a blessing. Eventually, the feeling started to come back, like pins and needles, he said—renewed blood flow setting off tiny grenades of sensation. He was a work in progress. It wasn't something that could be fixed with physical therapy or exercise—he simply had to let the body heal, which was slow and excruciating, especially for an active, brawny man like Ben.

Thankfully, instead of putting Ben on hiatus, the TV show had altered the storyline to accommodate his injury, taking a cue from real life—his character had his own encounter with a rattlesnake. Ben said filming the scene was like reliving a nightmare over and over again. But then there he was, filming with a real live rattlesnake, then in a fake hospital bed, at the ranch with his leg propped up, walking around on crutches, radiating frustration over not being able to get back on a horse or rustle up some trouble with the other cowboys. He said the "life imitating art" thing was just about enough to make him crazy.

Paige leaned over the leg and kissed it several times before saying, "It's about the same today."

"Eh. Yeah, honestly, I can't tell that much of a difference from one day to the next."

"Maybe we should compare. I need a better view, though." She looked up from his leg with a raised eyebrow, and he gave her his most dashing, wide-eyed smile in return.

She straddled him, unbuckling his belt and jeans as he lifted himself up so she could pull them off, along with his shirt, leaving only his boxer briefs. He went to touch a strand of her hair just as she slipped away with a smile, standing at the foot of the bed to stare down the length of him. She couldn't help but admire his physique, still taut and perfect, even after the snakebite and having to alter his daily workout routine. She'd been taking her time connecting with him on every level, including the physical, and he had done the same.

Everything about their relationship had been intense and extraordinary. She felt as if she'd been shipped off to a foreign country and learned the language through a slow immersion. Ben created a safe space where her self-consciousness about her body, her vitiligo patches, and her inexperience slowly slipped away. He built her up, then gently dismantled her walls, seeking her touchpoints, her pleasure, helping her find her power. Always patient, always sweet, always selfless, always striving to seek what felt right for her first, then him. She drank everything in like a sponge until she found herself, over time, surprisingly and wonderfully proficient. She hadn't known that a relationship could be this mutually satisfying, supportive, *right*—hadn't thought it possible—in fact, couldn't have conjured it up in her wildest dreams or imagination.

"Definitely more symmetrical than it was last week," she said, comparing his two legs as she began to rub his feet, then his ankles, and upward from there, slowly focusing on the injured leg, softly kneading so as not to hurt him.

He laid his head back against the headboard and sighed, "That feels amazing."

After a few minutes, she got up on the bed, her fingers dancing up to massage his thighs, working her way from the outside in. When she looked up to his face again, his eyes were open now, dilated, lids hooded. She asked coyly, "How does this feel?"

"Like trouble," he growled.

"Oh?" she said innocently, her thumbs working dangerously close to the spot that was pitching up and taunting her. Minutes passed where they didn't speak as she continued to knead and tease, finally getting up on all fours to kiss a trail up his stomach and chest. His hands wove into her hair, moving it away from her face so he could see what her mouth was doing. As she leaned over him, she pressed her soft, sweatered breasts on top of his boxer briefs. He groaned, suddenly taking charge, sliding underneath her and bringing his mouth to her in a burst of desperation and hunger.

She giggled at his frenzy and lay full-length atop him. His hands began pawing urgently at her top, pulling it over her head. She ground her lower body into his groin, and he pulled his tongue out of her mouth to say menacingly, "Oh no you don't."

"Oh yes I do," she replied firmly.

"You know it's my turn," he argued, taking a nip of her neck, then reaching inside her bra to cup a breast in his hand, pinching the nipple gently until it grew hard beneath his touch.

She ignored that with a smile. Then, feeling reckless, she sat up in her straddle, moving her thighs back and forth along his full, hard length, watching him grin, then scowl. It was as if he couldn't decide if he would scold or screw her. She was hoping for both. His hands drifted down to squeeze either side of her ass, a happy curse escaping his lips, then like a cunning cheetah, in one deft movement, he grabbed her by the hips, sprung up, flipped her over, twisting and wrestling her softly onto the bed below him.

"No!" she cried with a desperate scream and laugh. She was no match for him—he had six inches of height and about a hundred pounds of muscle on her.

Lately this was always their battle. Her favorite was on top. His favorite was on top. So they took turns. Or they called a truce and he bent her over something.

But there would be no truce tonight.

He held her down, grinning the whole time, his hands locking her wrists to her sides so he could use his mouth to raise her nipples through the thin fabric of her bra. When he trusted she'd given up her struggle, he let go and began tracing a trail of kisses down her waist and around her navel. He murmured a millimeter above her yoga pants, "You snooze, you lose, darlin'."

She muttered unconvincingly, "I didn't snooze. It's not fair. You're faster and stronger than me."

"Paige," he slurred between muffled kisses, now circling the V between her legs, beginning to yank her pants and underwear down.

"Hmm?" she barely acknowledged.

He came up for air, leaning his chin on his hand, which was resting against her pubic bone, causing her to twitch. "It's time for connect the dots," he said with a raspy voice filled with wicked intent.

"What? NO, Ben. No."

"We'll see," he grinned, getting the rest of her clothes off in three swift movements while she watched and giggled. He slid his body down to her feet, flinging himself half off the edge of the bed in the process.

She put up a half-hearted plea, "Ben, come on, it takes too long, and it drives me to…to…" she tried to think…it was always so blurry in her mind afterward.

"To—to—what, my dear?" he asked, raising a curious eyebrow while grabbing her ankles as she, completely naked, tried unsuccessfully to inch away from him.

He began to kiss the white spots and patches on her feet, and she tried to wriggle her toes away from him, but his persistent mouth and hands held them in place.

"To—*you know…*"

"No, I don't—I'm going to need you to articulate it for me, Paige. To… what? Beg? Sigh? Whimper? Plead? Cry? Scream? Ache? Yearn? Run? Fall? *Cum?* What exactly?" His mouth moved to the spots around her knees.

"All of the above," she answered weakly, trying not to give in to his self-satisfied grin. She added, "Everything's just a game to you, isn't it?"

"A game I take very seriously," he said, all business now as he lifted her knees and spread them apart for easier access to her inner thighs, which he used as a landing strip for his tongue.

Her eyes and head rolled back on the pillow as she quivered under the heat of his mouth so close to tender places. Damn him with his connect the dots! It always sent her over the edge, to the place where she lost all control and reason.

Meanwhile, for each touch of his lips, he recited, "And this one…and this one…" as she melted a little more with each wet sensation.

"At the end, you never tell me what you see," she said, trying to maintain her loose grip on sanity.

"What I see?" he asked, confused.

"Once you've connected the dots."

"Oh!" he said. He used his hands to slowly flip her over, kissing every area along the way as she turned compliantly.

On her stomach, completely at his mercy now, he took time away from kissing spots on her back to press his hardness between her butt cheeks. Still safely encased in his briefs, he glided his erection north and south for several swipes, groaning and kissing the back of her neck as she shivered, goose-bumps popping up on the surface of her skin. He took this as a sign and reached around to cup her breasts, tweaking the erect nipples while he laid his entire body flush against hers.

He said, "I see heaven."

She laughed and felt everything in between her legs throb, both outside and in. She pressed her face into the pillow and moaned. He kissed along her jawline until she turned herself and opened her mouth to his, their tongues reaching for each other in a race for connection.

Suddenly, she was seeing stars and wanting release very badly as she ground her hips into the bed, her body still half-twisted around to reach his mouth, but it was just at this point, frustrating lover that he was, that he pulled away and began kissing her spots again, recited his mantra over and over. She screamed into the pillow and heard his low, throaty chuckle in response.

"This is exactly what I was talking about, Ben!" she scolded, a mumbled shout from the pillow.

Ignoring that, he continued his relentless trail of kisses.

Then she flipped over, her erect nipples pointing at him accusingly, her legs splayed out and shaking in anticipation. Readiness filled her, knowing she was close to getting what she wanted, so she egged him on, "You should call this game target practice instead."

His wicked, lust-filled laugh sent her groin into overdrive. "I'm close to my bull's-eye now," he replied, hovering above her and staring boldly at every vulnerable part of her.

He placed himself down on the inviting part of her then, reaching under her haunches and letting his mouth suck her in, never breaking eye contact. He liked to watch her watch him to gauge her reaction. He kissed all the white spots first, and there were a lot—in fact, she remembered that this (of all places) was the first location where her vitiligo appeared when she was a child, before she knew or understood what those parts of her body were. He was amid the patches now, worshipping and fawning over them as though she were a rare, speckled desert flower that only bloomed for him. That im-age of a flower flew into her mind, then vanished an instant later when his tongue swept along her layers, causing her to lose their staring contest. He didn't seem to notice as his focus was pulled elsewhere, his fingers separating and searching for deeper places inside her, allowing his tongue to explore the rest. His other hand came out from underneath her bottom to settle contentedly on her right breast.

The flicker of his tongue was causing everything to stir and liquefy beyond a level she could abide for much longer, so she wove her fingers into his hair, pressed his face against her (even more than it already was), and, between clenched teeth, barely above a whisper, gave a command: "Stop moving." Without hesitation, he obeyed, and she felt her orgasm spin inside her, ricocheting against every ounce of her tender flesh as Ben rode the wave, his mouth and tongue never leaving her, savoring every motion. Finally, coming back from that other place in her mind and body, she slowed, then stopped. Still quivering, still tightening, but needing him to fill that suddenly gaping void, she growled at him, "You. Now."

He drew away, a smile dancing on his lips, showing his approval of her command as he planted light kisses along her thighs and navel, on each breast, before swiftly removing his briefs while she watched, licking her lips, her arms flung over her head, her chest heaving. He stared at her boldly, every inch of her, then reached into the nightstand for a condom, rolling it down upon himself before inserting his tip into her.

His voice was guttural, gravelly, as he said, "I told you it was my turn."

She murmured, "You showed me."

He smiled and pushed inside a little deeper, then more, inch by throbbing inch. Then when he was as deep as he could go, he drew away, hovering nearly outside of her only to thrust again. Their mouths were instantly tangled together, needing each other so badly and wanting it to be known in every part of them. He ran his tongue along her nipples, a finger gently rubbing her clit until she arched her back and climbed the summit again, the tightening undoing her. Then right as her movements slowed, he whispered into her neck, "Paige, you feel so fucking good" as, with one massive stroke, he reached his own climax, a powerful grunt escaping his lips followed by several low groans, finally laying his head against her chest, his heart galloping, his breath ragged, his cheek sweaty and warm.

They were still and quiet for a time. She unbent her knees and pressed her lips against his hair, breathing him in, loving the weight of him on her.

A long while went by, then he whispered, "Paige?"

"Yes, Ben?"

"I have a surprise for you."

"You do?" she said, sitting up in excitement.

"Uh-huh, birthday girl. Come on."

They cleaned up and put on their pajamas, walking into the kitchen together. He turned the oven on and opened a bottle of wine. They sat down at the island and clinked their glasses with "Cheers."

"What's going in the oven?" she asked.

"I made a batch of chicken strata," he answered with an eyebrow wiggle, proud of himself.

"Mmm, yummy," she said, rubbing her hands together in glee. She loved the fact that he cooked and often whipped up favorite family recipes for her. It kept them from having to go out and be gaped at, or worse, having people disturb their meals with autograph requests. Plus, Paige loved this side of him, the salt-of-the-earth, homebody side, which made her feel so safe and protected. She was the same way, and it was yet another thing they'd discovered they had in common.

On a different note, Paige said with a pout, "I still can't believe Abby and Kyle. I'm so ticked at them."

"Yeah, they should have run it by you first," he agreed, "but if I'm being honest, I'm kind of glad it didn't work out."

She stared at him, appalled. "Why? You're supposed to be on my side."

"I know, I know, and I am." He gave her a peck on the cheek. "But think about it—how would that have panned out anyway? You three buy that beat-up house down by the river, carry a hefty mortgage, take a year or two—maybe more—fixing it up, then *they* get married, start popping out kids, and you're what? Third wheel? Babysitter? Nanny? Sister wife?"

She slugged his shoulder. "Sister wife! Hardy-har-har. You're a real gas."

He laughed, rubbing his fake bruise. "Look, all I'm saying is that Kyle and Abby get a free house from his parents, and you're simply *free*, Paige. Is that such a bad thing?"

Paige stuck out her lower lip. "We've been planning it for years, though."

"I know. But plans change," he said.

"I suppose," Paige admitted reluctantly. "Now what do I do?" Paige was still reeling after Abby casually mentioned that Kyle's parents decided to retire to

Arizona and leave him their family house in Emigrant. Abby was moving in with him in November, and Paige was left in the lurch. Sure, they said Paige could move in with them, but Paige could just picture it—relegated to one tiny bedroom, one tiny shelf in the fridge, one tiny spare bathroom, not allowed to contribute to the décor or renovations or anything personal. She would feel as though she was invading their new sacred space, and that had never been the intention when they'd planned a shared house project all those years ago.

"Wellll," he said, stretching out the word mysteriously as he put the casserole in the oven. "Let's go in the living room while that's cooking." He set the timer, took her hand, and plopped her down on the couch with a quick kiss. Then he built a fire in the fireplace, lighting it and filling the room with a warm glow. He went back to retrieve their wineglasses from the kitchen and set them on the coffee table. They lay lengthwise on the couch facing the fireplace, her body between his legs, her back pressed against his chest, her head leaning into the curve of his neck.

He continued, "I have a thought. First of all, as you know, we're just about done filming this season, and I'll be heading back to LA soon."

Her gut instantly tightened. She had been blocking it out—the inevitable separation and what that might mean for them. They hadn't even talked about it, were living day-to-day, not wanting to face what was to come.

He wrapped his arms around her, squeezing and saying with a brush of his lips against her temple, "I know. I'm dreading it too."

She sighed and leaned back into him even more, relieved he had the same thought.

He went on, "For right now, the show's doing well, and in theory we may keep it going—at least one more season, maybe more—and I thought it might be nice to get out from under the cast and crew in this big ole house and instead find something more permanent for myself. Even during the past off-seasons, I missed this wild, open, big sky country…and now I'll be missing *other things*." He nuzzled his face into her hair. When he pulled away, he said, "LA's like one big traffic jam with a haze of pollution—too claustrophobic for my taste. When I spend too much time there, I get cranky."

He was trying to be a little funny, a little glib, but she didn't take the bait, sitting even more quietly, thinking about the loss of his arms around her… wishing it would never come to pass. And wondering what he was getting at.

"I've been thinking about it for a while, even before I met you. I don't really like the LA vibe—never have. My apartment there is super modern, small, and cold. My lease is up at the end of the year, and I figure I'll let it go. When I need to be back in LA, I'll just stay at my parents' house." He paused for a minute and finally said, "I've been saving my earnings, and I have quite a bit built up. Enough for a house. I saw a place for sale the other day just this side of Livingston, and I'm gonna buy it."

She lifted off his chest in a flash, turning to face him, her eyes wide. "You're what?"

He laughed and said, "Paige, now hang on. Let me explain. I see the wheels turning inside that gorgeous head of yours. I know you're wondering what this means—for me, for you, for us." He paused, sighing a bit before continuing. "For right now anyway, this is something for *me* only. But that doesn't mean it couldn't be something more—later or whenever it feels right—*if* it feels right—in the future—for both of us. But there's absolutely no pressure for either of us right now. None."

She nodded slightly, still processing. After a minute, she said firmly, "I don't want you to buy me anything. Or to buy anything for yourself because of me."

"I know that, and that's *not* what this is. Hey, listen, if we stay together and things are going well, then we'll reassess, figure out how this is gonna work. Maybe I'll buy the house and sell it a year later. Maybe you'll buy a place in the meantime. Maybe we'll move in together, move into one place or the other. Or neither. Heck, with the way real estate is right now, maybe we'll both buy and sell a house by the time we want to live together. All I know is that none of this—none of the logistics behind where we live or don't live—will change the way I feel about you. Over the next few months I'll be in LA much of the time, and I want you to come visit as much as you can, and I'll come back here as well, maybe take up semipermanent residence at Chico. We'll talk on the phone every day. We'll do whatever it takes to make it work. My mom and dad have requested your presence about fifty times already, so we should get that booked right away, maybe in November. Don't be surprised if they ask you to nail down a date tomorrow at the picnic. And with Rhone being back in town, you'll finally get to meet her too."

"That would be great," she said softly. She was still pondering his decision to buy a house. What would that mean? He said there was no pressure, but it still made her question so much about her future and what that might look like. Outside of the house plans with Kyle and Abby that fell through, Paige hadn't allowed herself the luxury of speculating further. Ben had been recuperating, and Paige had lived in an amazing bubble with him for four months. She still wasn't sure if perhaps that bubble would burst one day, but at least with this decision, it was clear that his intent wasn't to test the bubble or their future. She truly hoped he meant it when he said it was to make himself happy. She couldn't ask for more, didn't want the burden of a commitment, even if her heart screamed for it, yearned for it because of their bond and their remarkable time together. There was still so much to learn, to live, to be…Paige had her own future to figure out first. So, instead of delving into the house topic more, she asked, "How's Rhone doing anyway?"

He thought about it for a minute. "Um, good, I think. My parents are really hoping this trip to rehab will stick. So far, so good. Being pregnant seems to be a big motivator. She's never had to worry about harming anyone but herself before."

"Hmm. How far along is she?"

"I'm not sure…I think maybe six months."

"I hope it works this time, for her sake and the baby's."

"Yeah, me too."

They sipped their wine for a few minutes and talked about their work-weeks. Ben wanted to know all about her birthday, which had been filled with balloons and cupcakes from the people at work, a new bike from her parents, and a night on the town with Abby, which entailed pizza at the Outpost and drinks at the Saloon. Then Paige talked about plans to go snowmobiling with Ben when he came back this winter and how she was going to teach him snowboarding at Big Sky, assuming his leg was fully healed by then. Weeks ago, they had set up these abstract dates for the future without ever acknowledging how the future came into play for them. This time, though, he pulled out his phone and sent her calendar invites for specific weekends, working it around his and her schedules, saying he was going to book airfare later that night, after they finished dinner.

Then he lifted her gently off himself and said, "Well, I'm sorry I missed the day of your birthday. Maybe I can make it up to you. One sec—I'll be right back."

She watched him walk to the bedroom as she stared at the fire and thought about the fact that her life had spun a one-eighty. She'd had such a routine life before—all the same things from one day to the next—and now somehow, by this crazy miracle of unpredictability, she was living in a way she couldn't have seen coming in a million years. On top of her relationship with Ben, she'd been meeting with Shae once a week to get help with her online ancestry profile. Paige had begun to build a biological family tree she never knew existed. It was like a window into a new world. She'd been corresponding with Filipino relatives scattered all over the globe, including several first cousins in the United States and Canada. She even had an aunt who lived in San Francisco whom she was planning to visit in December. It had all come out of the blue—as if all the days of her life before were waiting for her to find this time, this period of discovery and reinvention. She was thriving on it. And her ma and pa, still amazingly protective and sweet, had encouraged her to pursue her search for her biological family and also to pursue her relationship with Ben, telling Paige to continue to "find herself" and assuring her they would be there, supporting her and loving her through it all.

She was twenty-two years old. She didn't have anything figured out yet, but she had new dreams now. About meeting people who looked like her—had the same genes as her and maybe the same fingers and toes and mouth—and maybe even similar thoughts, feelings, tastes, opinions, and outlook on life. And maybe they didn't. Either way, she was going to find out. Maybe one day she would tell her story—about the crash, her parents, her life—maybe write a blog post or an article for a magazine. Maybe someday she would simply tell her story to a girl at the restaurant, another girl who was adopted and happened to mention it when Paige was waiting on her. Who knew? Life was like that—you never knew who was watching, who was capturing everything you said and did in their thoughts and applying it to themselves in some way, incorporating it into their life's journey.

Adding to it all, Paige and Ben's unexpected mutual connection through his dad cemented their bond as well as Paige's life's meaning in ways she never could have predicted. While Ben was in the hospital, the two sets of parents got to know each other better. Ma invited them over for dinner several times during those few days, and since then, Ben's mom called Paige's ma on the phone every week or so, both to check in and to thank her for "watching out for and feeding my boy." Whenever Ben had a free day, he could be found hanging out at the bar at Chico, talking to Paige's pa or Shae's boyfriend, or hanging out with Paige in the restaurant. He ate Sunday suppers with the Montgomerys at their tiny ranch house. Even pa had warmed to him, allowing him into his precious barn, showing him how to operate the lathe and circular saw. Ben hadn't been joking when he'd told Paige he loved how real she was—it was as if he was made for Montana life, this simple life free of pretense. Despite the fact that he was hugely famous and grew up in LA, he somehow fit perfectly here in their little paradise tucked in the mountains. It warmed Paige's heart every time she witnessed it.

The buzzer went off in the kitchen, and Ben pulled the casserole out of the oven, saying it needed ten minutes to cool down. He came back into the living room with an uncharacteristically shy smile on his face, his hands behind his back. He knelt down in front her, leaning into her, placing his head on her stomach for a moment. Then he lifted up, looked directly into her eyes, placed a small, wrapped box into her hands, and said, "I got you something."

"You did?" She smiled.

She started to tear off the wrapping paper, but he steadied her hands, saying, "Hang on." His voice was suddenly serious, and she felt a slight flutter in her chest. He said, "Paige, I know we haven't known each other very long and that this is our first shared birthday, but I wanted to do something special for you. I thought about getting you an obvious gift—you know, jewelry, chocolates, clothes—but instead I got you something to show you how much you mean to me. I hope you like it."

Her curiosity piqued, she frowned a bit, then unwrapped the gift. When she looked inside the box, her hand flew to her mouth as tears sprang to her eyes. A small laugh escaped her lips. It was so sweet. So simple. Not at all what she imagined he might do, but then seeing it in front of her, it made perfect sense and—as she'd just been thinking not five minutes ago—it fit him (and her) like a glove.

Inside the box was a piece of pink construction paper cut into the shape of a heart, as a kindergartener would do. Written in the center were the words "Paige Montgomery, I love you, Ben."

When she looked up again at him, she was astonished to see his smiling eyes filling too. She swallowed and said with a weepy grin, "You do?"

"Yes, I do," he said. He laughed then too, saying, "Don't sound so surprised."

"I'm not—I'm just—I'm just—I don't know…*happy*." She jumped into
his arms. A tear slid down her cheek as she managed to say, "I love you too,
Ben."

He pulled away long enough to cup her face in his hands, and said, "Good."

His sweet, wonderful lips were on hers then, expanding her heart like ten-
drils reaching into her soul.

❧ EPILOGUE ❧

ONCE YOU HEAR MY STORY, you'll never fly on a plane again without thinking about me. I was a lap baby on United Flight 1180. My name is Matthew Stanley. I haven't flown on a plane since then—only that one time, back when I was a toddler. In fact, I haven't done anything since then except watch over my family and the girl who survived when I didn't. Paige Montgomery.

She doesn't know it, but we're friends.

More than friends, actually.

I love her. And she loves me.

It wasn't always so. It was a long road. Twenty years.

In the beginning, I was fuzzier, more lost, more like background noise.

Then, over the years, I came into focus, or rather, I learned to focus—to find my purpose.

When the survivors' club (as I Iike to call them) got together recently, I was there with them, right in their midst. They didn't know it. Didn't sense me at first, except maybe my mother, who always feels me, even when she's busy, even when she thinks she's masking the pain of losing me by not remembering me. She still always knows.

I watched as Paige showed up with her ma and pa in her new rhinestone-encrusted cowboy boots, apparently another birthday present from her boyfriend, Ben, who thought the pink heart wasn't enough. If he only knew that no material gifts would ever mean as much to Paige as that construction paper heart. She will cherish it for the rest of her days, safely tucked away in a wooden keepsake box beside their bed.

But she appreciated the boots too.

Ben was there with Paige, but also with his parents. His dad, Terry, survived the crash too. Everyone at the picnic was amazed to hear the story of how Ben and Paige met and the subsequent story of how Paige and Terry met. The rodeo, the snakebite, the hospital.

By the way, I did that. Brought them together. All of them. It seemed only fitting. After all, I was gone, and they were still there. I thought they might need to find each other and to stick together. Life is hard without connections—even the out-of-the-blue kind—which may not be as arbitrary as you think and might just lead to something more.

Mom, Dad, and my brother and sisters were there too. They came to Montana all the way from Connecticut. My grandparents hosted the picnic at their cattle ranch, where Mom grew up, and it was a sight to behold with spectacular views of the mountains in the distance and a stretch of rugged land dotted with big barns, hay bales, pine trees, and meandering paths carved into the landscape by richly stocked streams and creeks.

I watched with a smile on my celestial face as they ate bowl after bowl of beef stew with hard, crusty bread spread with salty, creamy butter. It almost made me wish I still had taste buds. Mom got up and spoke about the fact that she'd been wrong for twenty years. She'd lost a child, and all her anger, sense of betrayal, and lack of recourse had led her to displace pent-up feelings into hateful, blame-filled rants directed falsely and injudiciously at the very people at that table whom she now owed a debt of gratitude and remorse. She admitted readily that the crash was an accident.

I helped her see the error of her ways. It didn't come easy. Or quick. But it did come.

She was blunt and brave and bold, and I was so proud of her when she said she was seeking counseling for her issues and that she hoped this picnic would be a reunion, a reconciliation—no more reproaches—and that they would all be able to heal from the events of the crash. She said she was a work in progress, but she hoped they would give her grace and accept her apology. She was looking directly at Julie, the flight attendant, as she said this, and Julie had to wipe her eyes a few times with her napkin. Then Mom took out a photo album and passed it around the table. It had pictures—so many wonderful pictures—of me, whom she called "her adorable baby boy Matthew."

Many a tear was shed, but not in frustration, not in anger, instead in remembrance, in joy for the life that had been, for the new children who came after me, sitting happily at the table, enjoying the company and the warm, delicious food.

And for the generations still to come.

Paige felt a particular, keen sense of connection with me when she looked at my photos, acknowledging silently and reverently to herself that she would strive to live a full and happy life as a tribute to me since I wasn't able to. In turn, I sent her off on a journey to reconnect with her biological family, a meandering and wondrous endeavor that seeded and grew new fruit and meaning in her life for years to come.

Later that day, I overheard Julie (who looked fabulous, by the way) as she stood next to her friend Mark (friend or boyfriend...?) speaking with Mom and Terry, saying how one of her flight attendant friends, Jeana, was going to pick up the baton of the emergency lap baby rules. Julie told Mom the timing was right for someone else to take on the mantle and champion new ideas for the next generation. Maybe nothing would change—maybe Jeana wouldn't have any more luck than Julie had—but then, you never know what the future holds.

Hours later, when I saw the four survivors seated together outside, watching the sun set into the shadow of the distant mountain, basking in the warm glow of the patio's twinkle lights, the giant bonfire's embers, and the company of friends and family, I thought about how life was so strange.

You never knew who would become a hero. Did you?

THE END

Acknowledgments

At least ten years ago, I saw a brief segment of a TV show about a flight attendant who survived a plane crash. I don't know why, but I was so moved by her firsthand account that I felt as though her story was mentally burned into my brain. Fast-forward to October 23, 2021, when I wrote this in my diary: "I was walking down the beach today and saw a man with two blades for legs (a double amputee) out running, and I thought how amazing he was, and for whatever reason, he made me think back to the TV show about the inspirational flight attendant who was trying to change the lap baby rules. Wouldn't that be a great book idea? To explore how a tragedy like that impacts survivors?"

That was it—the kernel of the idea for this book. Of course, I know nothing about the real-life flight attendant other than what I saw on that TV show all those years ago. *Lap Baby* is truly a work of fiction. Until I completed the manuscript, I purposely didn't allow myself to look up the real-life flight attendant or to find out anything about her because I didn't want my fictional account to be in any way influenced by the real person or the actual facts of what happened. If you're interested, I have since found this article about her:

https://www.abc.net.au/news/2019-12-17/infants-in-laps-in-planes-debate-over-safety-rules/11795870

I've dedicated this book to her because I think she is a hero. It's rare to find people in this world willing to advocate on behalf of others, even in the face of tragedy and adversity. No matter the outcome, she tried to make something good out of something bad, and I admire and appreciate her for it.

Another aspect of this story that you may find interesting is Paige's vitiligo. I also have this skin condition. I didn't get it until later in life, so I'm somewhat blessed in that my spots and patches have not yet spread to my face, which apparently is what causes the most stares and judgmental double takes. Just in the past year, though, I've found new areas on my hands, wrists, underarms, thighs, and elbows. The doctors tell me it is inevitable that it will eventually spread everywhere. Compared to many other autoimmune diseases, vitiligo is relatively "trivial" in that it doesn't hurt, isn't contagious or debilitating, and causes no long-term damage to the rest of the body. But from the standpoint that it is somewhat unknown, shocking, and off-putting, it can lead to self-consciousness, anxiety, and even depression. I wanted to write a story about a woman who has had to face the unwanted stares and stigma since she was a little girl and has still managed to be bold and fearless, and to live a full and satisfying life, including finding love. I hope you'll find Paige's story inspiring and that you if you ever meet someone with vitiligo, you'll recognize it for what it is—a nonthreatening skin condition that doesn't in any way define the person who has it.

I would like to thank my readers—your support has been invaluable to me and keeps me tapping away every day!

I would also like to thank the following people:

Kira Freed, my amazing editor extraordinaire. She pushes me to be a better writer while wearing kid gloves. I couldn't ask for anything more.

My alpha readers, Julie Nichols and Mrs. Nancy Roselli. I love that you both say yes when I text you out of the blue and ask you to read a book in under a week and that you still manage to find the typos and contextual errors I miss, even after I've read the thing like 10,000 times. You're the best!

My "ride or dies"—Cindy (Carroll) Nolan, Amy (Rupp) Callahan, and Terry (Schafer) Monsees. Thank you for being there for me!

The lake gang, duckers and all—thank you for the PH and the 5:00 p.m. happy hour. I appreciate your support!

To Amandah, my real-life "Rue"—you've put a song in my heart. Thank you.

To Sarah—GSP introduced us, and my life hasn't been the same since. Thank you for our deeper discussions and for knowing the power of words.

To my family—I know this is a wild journey that you didn't sign up for, so thank you for sticking with me anyway. To my nieces—I'll meet you at the 8:00 p.m. dance party.

To my husband, kids, and grandkids, I love you all. Thank you.

Thank you for reading Amy Q. Barker's imaginings set to words. If you've enjoyed this book, please consider leaving an honest review on Amazon or Goodreads.

To connect with Amy, check out her Instagram @amyqbarker_author.

Made in United States
North Haven, CT
29 September 2022